ROMAN LETTERS

ROMAN

HISTORY FROM A

WIPF & STOCK · Eugene, Oregon

LETTERS

PERSONAL POINT OF VIEW

FINLEY HOOPER
MATTHEW SCHWARTZ

Wipf and Stock Publishers
199 W 8th Ave, Suite 3
Eugene, OR 97401

Roman Letters
History from a Personal Point of View
By Schwartz, Matthew B and Hooper, Finley

ISBN 13: 978-1-5326-4912-7
Publication date 1/29/2018
Previously published by Wayne State University Press, 1991

To my uncle
C. Kingsley Allison
and to my aunt
Ruth Allison Sheppard
F.H.

To my parents
William and Pauline Schwartz
M.S.

This book was published with the
assistance of a fund established at
Wayne State University Press
in memory of
HARRIETTE LIEBERMAN SIMONS

CONTENTS

CONTENTS

ILLUSTRATIONS AND MAPS

Illustrations

Maps

PREFACE

The well-tended garden and the well-written letter are familiar touchstones of civility. Both gardens and letters date back to the ancient cradles of civilization in Mesopotamia and Egypt. It was in the time of the earliest villages that the invention of writing took place. When and where the first letter appeared we will never know but likely it was on a clay tablet written in cuneiform and dictated by a ruler among the Sumerians, the people who first established the civilized customs of Mesopotamia. Samuel Kramer, in his *History Begins at Sumer*, says this probably happened because the ruler had so much to say the herald could not remember it all.

Far removed from clay tablet days, the Romans used pen and ink and wrote on papyrus, a form of paper imported from Egypt, which was rolled up, tied, and sealed. Or, for short messages, a wax tablet could be sent, which being erased was handy for a quick reply. In the fourth century A.D., St. Augustine mentions using parchment.

In whatever manner letters were written, they have always played a major role in the study of history, for the simple reason that people saved them. It is also true, however, that being well stored they may be forgotten. News about the many letters of the ancient Romans, long since translated, published, and taken for granted, might even come as something of a surprise. Mention the Romans and most likely what comes to mind is a sturdy soldier holding a spear or a muscular gladiator poised for action. Not a letter writer in sight. But there were Romans, less physical to be sure, who took pride in their letters. Reading the correspondence covering a period of seven centuries, from Cicero in the first century B.C. to Cassiodorus in the sixth century A.D., we have been amazed, occasionally amused, but always impressed by the insights on Roman life.

"I can't stand the queen." So wrote Cicero in 44 B.C. concerning Cleopatra, who had for a time lived in Rome. His outburst about the insolence of the queen of Egypt, who was also Julius Caesar's mistress, came in a letter to his friend Atticus. There are many blunt observations in the following chapters, which include the letters of orators, teachers, and a voluble emperor, along with those of bishops, saints, and a determined pope. Chapter IV is primarily about the letters of lesser-known persons during the Roman period. Archaeologists have found many letters by chance in the sands of Egypt, the caves of Judaea, and amid the ruins of a fort in England.

In the course of this book, a running commentary provides historical continuity, but the focus goes beyond generalities to what the Romans themselves had to say. Instead of a catch-all comment about declining morals, for instance, we have indignant remarks about the behavior of women from Seneca, the leading orator in Nero's Rome, who concludes: "Because of their vices, women have ceased to deserve the privileges of their sex, they have put off their womanly nature and are therefore condemned to suffer the diseases of men."

The simple fact is that we come to know the Romans by reading their letters. Seneca says much about the vicious treatment of slaves, but it was slaves murdering their masters that later so horrified Pliny the Younger. Ausonius considers himself a good Christian even if religion doesn't interest him very much. His old friend Paulinus thinks of nothing else. The letters of Jerome reveal his piety and his pettiness. Any kind of criticism seems to have unnerved his scholarly self. From his monastic cell in Bethlehem he wrote some sharply worded letters to Augustine, whose answers gave him much unrest. Other letters of Augustine show how sensitive he was about the use of force, but in the end he explains why wars have to be fought. Controversial issues that are still so much with us capture our attention in these ancient letters. According to Seneca we should try to live for others, but eventually we have the right to choose our own time and manner of death. Regarding abortion, a letter by the Cappadocian Basil offered a little mercy but never condoned a choice.

Letters can also give a different slant to familiar stories. Sidonius Apollinaris, the bishop of Clermont in Gaul, saw the arrival of the Burgundians and the Visigoths in the fifth century. He was a heroic defender of the land, but his enemies were not all barbarians. Many Gallo-Romans freely cooperated with the invaders, and some even spied for them. Nor was all the land lost in battle. Much of it was given to the barbarians as part of an appeasement policy which, as usual, proved disastrous. And there were other things bothering Sidonius in these later days, including the increasingly slovenly speech of those around him.

These examples are indicative of the subjects in a book that, while never intended as an exhaustive study of Roman letters, will nonetheless give fair answers to the questions, What did the letters of the Romans say? and How are they useful in understanding the ancient world? At the time they were written, these letters were the primary source of news, gossip, and advice. That was why the Romans took the time to write letters, even given the trouble and expense of having one delivered. There was no postal service such as we have today. The only organized system for delivering mail was operated by the government for government purposes. Whether using freedmen, or slaves, called *tabellarii*, or military messengers, some kind of relay system by horses was commonly provided for official mail, with personal letters perhaps at times being included surreptitiously. Private citizens had to depend on their own resources. Either they sent a servant, usually a freedman, who carried letters on a special mission, or they gave them to travelers headed in a given direction. The latter person hoped to meet someone who was going farther, and so a single letter could pass through several hands before reaching its destination.

Such a system, or lack of it, had many drawbacks. Cicero, one of the busiest of correspondents, complained that he knew of letters sent to him that he never received. In fact, the difficulty of getting a letter delivered made it necessary at times to have two persons carry identical copies of the same message. Cicero mentions having to be on the lookout for reliable carriers; centuries later, Sidonius Apollinaris was calling a person who lost a letter a "mindless blockhead."

The carriers themselves had to be wary of whom they might meet on the way. There were always highwaymen about, and in wartime special difficulties arose when both sides confiscated letters or even arrested those carrying them. Sidonius Apollinaris wrote that innocent messengers with only a letter to deliver were nevertheless suspected of carrying the real news in their heads rather than their hands and so were given rough treatment.

Such suspicions were often justified, in fact, for letter carriers did carry oral messages and, in addition, gossip of their own. In the late fourth century, the orator Symmachus frequently said that more would be learned from the messenger than told in his letter, and sometimes the letter only introduced the man who had the news in his head.

And how reliable was the news conveyed by letter? When letters were copied in a hurry for circulation among friends and relatives, "misrepresentations" could creep in, as the orator Symmachus observed. Worse, there might be forgeries sent around to deceive those who relied on Symmachus's views. "Be sure that the personal seal on my letters is not broken," he cautioned a relative. Cyprian, a bishop of Carthage in the middle of the third century and much involved in church politics, also worried about letters being tampered with en route. Three centuries earlier, Cicero had mentioned the problem of disinformation being put abroad by forged letters, even one supposedly from Julius Caesar. Furthermore, where sensitive matters were being discussed, the name of the writer might be cut off before the letter was passed on to others. Unless they could guess who wrote it, subsequent readers were often unable to evaluate the credibility of the report.

Cicero worried about his own letters that might be circulated and admitted that the letter he wrote when he knew it would be read by several people differed from a letter to be seen by only one person. Ever mindful of how damaging letters could be, he urged his friend Atticus to tear up some messages and said he would tear up certain of his in return. And there were topics it might be better not to mention at all. Writing to a friend during the time of Caesar's dominion, Cicero confessed that he would not be commenting on politics because of the dangers involved. He also remarked that he was getting different accounts of events from his correspondents and couldn't be sure what was really happening. Much that he heard he believed was rumor or only wishful thinking on the part of the writer.

With the news being so painfully slow to arrive, Romans living abroad waited in suspense for news about events at home. There was a newspaper of sorts, the

Acta Diurna, akin to what we call a newsletter, available to those interested in the day-to-day business of the Senate. It was one of Julius Caesar's innovations when he was consul in 59, and Cicero speaks of this source of news in his correspondence. Its official circulation was limited to Rome, but enterprising scribes made copies and sold them abroad. Still, a man like Cicero relied on letters from his friends in Rome for the inside story of what was happening in the capital and for the political gossip that so intrigued him.

In a book on Roman letters designed to interest a variety of readers, it is necessary to make decisions about which letters to include—and then, of course, to make exceptions. Our intention, for the most part, has been to use letters written between individuals rather than those addressed to an entire community. The epistles of St. Paul and the communications of the emperors to particular cities, such as the famous letter of Claudius to the Alexandrians, are readily available elsewhere. But some letters of a public character that are less well known have been included. For instance, excerpts are given from Emperor Julian's letter to the Athenians because it is a rare autobiographical glimpse of an unusual personality.

There are some private letters in this collection that were written with an eye to publication. The letters from Seneca in Chapter II are good examples, and, in fact, they are sometimes called letter-essays. Yet they contain personal observations and remarks about conditions of the time that, although carefully worded, offer much the same kind of news as is to be found in less formal letters. The use of letters as a literary device was well-established by Seneca's day. Gaius Lucilius (180 to ca. 102 B.C.) cast some of his satires in the form of letters to friends. Horace's *Epistulae*, like the letters of Seneca, are an outlet for personal opinion but, being written in verse, are more highly stylized. Ovid's poetic letters, *Heroides*, are the imaginative messages of legendary figures.

Several complete letters are included in this volume, but only key passages from other letters are used, to avoid the repetitiousness of certain writers—Seneca, for one, who returns to the same themes over and over again. Although there are hundreds of letters from Cicero, the reader is spared the tiresome length at which the famous orator talks about himself. Yet it must be admitted that judgments about Roman letter writers vary widely among commentators. What one finds dull, another might describe as dignified. With sufficient examples at hand, readers can arrive at their own opinions.

In the study of letters, two problems persist. First, there are debates over the genuineness of certain letters, and second, for one reason or another, the numbering systems used for a given correspondence can differ from one text to another. With few exceptions, we have included only letters that have escaped any doubts about authenticity. With one exception, our numbering is the same as in the texts of the particular translations we have used, and for each set of letters the numeration is explained in a footnote to the first citation.

ACKNOWLEDGMENTS

Most of the letters reprinted in this book were exchanged by friends, and we begin by remembering friends of ours. During the early stages of this work, Jean Owen offered encouragement and asked some unlimbering questions that served to give our plans a better focus. We are much indebted to her. As the project developed, useful suggestions came in letters from James Harper and Frank Vatai.

For their professional advice and resourcefulness, it is a pleasure to thank Don Breneau and John Prince, both of the Purdy Library at Wayne State University; Shirley Solvick, chief of fine arts, and Oksang Koh, both of the Detroit Public Library; and Douglas Zyskowski and the staff of the Southfield Public Library, particularly Kitty Allen. In our presentation of certain letters in Chapter IV, we had kind assistance from Ludwig Koenen, chairman of the Classics Department at the University of Michigan.

We are grateful to Donna Monacelli, the former secretary of the History Department at Wayne State University, for having typed so much of the manuscript; and appreciation also goes to the staff of the Word Processing Center on the Wayne State University campus for their typing assistance.

We thank Robert Mandel, former director of Wayne State University Press, Alice Nigoghosian, associate director, and Norma Goldman, general editor of the Classical Studies: Pedagogy Series, for their encouraging helpfulness. Kathryn Wildfong edited the manuscript with great care, and we have benefited from her keen eye and discerning advice.

Finally, we thank our colleague Goldwin Smith because he has been a good friend and patient listener since long times past.

I
CICERO

Private Thoughts Made Public

OCCASIONALLY, gladiators appear on television strutting into an arena in ancient Rome before a seemingly excited crowd of bloodthirsty spectators. Actually, at the time, not everybody was applauding. The orator Cicero, in one of his letters, congratulated a friend for having stayed home. Romans of a philosophical mind, the Stoics for example, strongly disapproved of such spectacles. They usually preferred to be alone with their serious thoughts and deplored the thoughtlessness of the people who enjoyed the games. Yet even those present were not totally insensitive. Cicero's letter says that the crowds felt compassion for woeful elephants lumbering into the arena to die in a pitiless slaughter.

Marcus Tullius Cicero (106 to 43 B.C.), who wrote the letters in this chapter, was better known in his own day for his speeches. The ancients greatly prized the art of public speaking, and Cicero was called the greatest of the Roman orators. He would not have denied it. He was proud, too proud perhaps, of his skill in reminding his listeners of the old Roman virtues. Yet his fifty-seven speeches, while indispensible for the history of the first century B.C., lack the candidness of his correspondence. The orations were written and edited for publication. In fact, some were never delivered, only published and read. Cicero also thought about editing a select number of his letters for publication and once wrote to his friend Atticus: "There is no collection of my letters in existence: but Tiro [Cicero's secretary] has something like seventy. Moreover, there are some to be got from you. I ought to look through and correct them. They shall not be published till I have done so" (*Ad Att.* XVI.5).[1] As it happened, he was killed before he found the time to make the corrections, and when the letters were published after his death, the shortcomings were evident for all to see. For instance, there was a duplicity of saying one thing in public and writing another in private. Surely that would have been changed had he had the chance to protect his reputation.

We know Cicero perhaps better than we know anybody else in ancient times because 774 of his letters survive, and there are another 90 extant letters written to him by friends and relatives. He wrote the letter that follows to his friend Marcus Marius in the fall of 55 B.C. after attending the elaborate shows sponsored by Pompey the Great. The passage in which he criticized the killings of men and animals is frequently quoted, but it is rarely mentioned that he also called the wild beast hunts "magnificent."

> If some bodily pain or weakness of health has prevented your coming to the games, I put it down to fortune rather than your own wisdom: but if you have made up your mind that these things which the rest of the world admires are only worthy of contempt, and, though your health would have allowed of it, you yet were unwilling to come, then I rejoice at both facts—that you were free from bodily pain, and that you had the sound sense to disdain what others causelessly admire. Only I hope that some fruit of your leisure may be forthcoming, a leisure, indeed, which you had a splendid opportunity of enjoying to the full, seeing that you were left almost alone in your lovely country. . . . On the whole, if you care to know, the games were most splendid, but not to your taste. I judge from my own. . . . Why, again, should I suppose you to care about missing the athletes, since you disdained the gladiators? in which even Pompey himself confesses that he lost his trouble and his pains. There remain the two wild-beast hunts, lasting five days, magnificent—nobody denies it—and yet, what pleasure can it be to a man of refinement, when either a weak man is torn by an extremely powerful animal, or a splendid animal is transfixed by a hunting spear? Things which, after all, if worth seeing, you have often seen before; nor did I, who was present at the games, see anything the least new. The last day was that of the elephants, on which there was a great deal of astonishment on the part of the vulgar crowd, but no pleasure whatever. Nay, there was even a certain feeling of compassion aroused by it, and a kind of belief created that that animal has something in common with mankind. (*Ad Fam.* VII.1)

That letter is Cicero as he would have the world know him—a refined gentleman who admired the simple tastes of his friends. It is a far better side than the one shown in a letter written a year earlier. Then he was anxious to have history's judgment in his favor and very openly craved the renown he thought he deserved even if his friend Lucceius, a historian, must stretch the truth to give it to him. Had he lived in our century, Cicero might have followed the common practice of modern politicians and written his memoirs, presenting himself and events in which he took part as he wanted others to see him. This is what he wrote to Lucceius.

> I have often tried to say to you personally what I am about to write, but was prevented by a kind of almost clownish bashfulness. Now that I am not in your presence I shall speak out more boldly: a letter does not blush. I am inflamed with an inconceivably ardent desire, and one, as I think, of which I have no reason to be ashamed, that in a history written by *you* my name should be conspicuous and frequently mentioned with praise. And though you have often shewn me that you meant to do so, yet I hope you will pardon my impatience. For the style of your composition, though I had always entertained the highest expectations of it, has yet surpassed my hopes, and has taken such a hold upon me, or rather has so fired my imagination, that I was eager to have my achievements as quickly as possible put on record in your history. For it is not only the thought of being spoken of by future ages that makes me snatch at what seems a hope of immortality, but it is also the desire of fully enjoying in my lifetime an authoritative expression of your judgment, or a token of your kindness for me, or the charm of your genius. . . . I am quite aware, however, what little modesty I display, first, in imposing on you so heavy a burden (for your engagements may well prevent your compliance with my request), and in the second place, in asking you to shew me off to advantage. What if those transactions are not in your judgment so very deserving of commendation? Yet, after all, a man who has once passed the border-line of modesty had better put a bold face on it and be frankly impudent. And so I again and again ask you outright, both to praise those actions of mine in warmer terms than you perhaps feel, and in that respect to neglect the laws of history. I ask you, too, in regard to the personal predilection, on which you wrote in a certain introductory chapter in the most gratifying and explicit terms—and by which you shew that you were as incapable of being diverted as Xenophon's Hercules by Pleasure—not to go against it, but to yield to your affection for me a little more than truth shall justify. But if I can induce you to undertake this, you will have, I am persuaded, matter worthy of your genius and your wealth of language. (*Ad Fam.* V.12)

Whatever Lucceius thought of Cicero's request, the flattering account never appeared. Moreover, it is unfortunate that Cicero's vanity was carried to such extremes, for the facts about his career were laudable enough. From the beginning he was a stout defender of honesty in government. In his first elected office (quaestor), 75 to 74 B.C., he had become aware of the outrageous extortion and bribery in the provinces. Four years later, in Rome, his famous orations *Against Verres* brought the corrupt governor of Sicily to account. Cicero made it a point to remind the senators on the jury that they were on trial, too. If a notorious criminal such as Verres escaped punishment, it would be obvious that corruption in Rome made the abuses overseas possible. The senators got the message, and so did Verres, who fled the city before the trial was over. Cicero deserved the credit he took for this victory, but the unsavory operations he exposed in the government were not new, nor had he cured them. They were, in part, the result of Rome's emergence as a world power, which had begun long ago.

Two centuries earlier, the Romans, having defeated Hannibal's Carthage in the memorable Punic Wars, had made themselves masters of the western Mediterranean Sea. Sicily had been their first overseas possession, to which they added others: Hither and Farther Spain, for instance, and eventually the area including Carthage itself, which became the province of Africa. The expansion of Roman power during these years gave the Romans a sense of living in exciting times. But how many knew what was really happening? A few thought they did and were worried. Among them was Cato the Elder (234 to 149 B.C.), an officer in the Second Punic War (218 to 201 B.C.), who later became a magistrate serving in the provinces of Sicily, Sardinia, and Spain. What he witnessed convinced him that many weak-willed officials and businessmen were sorely tempted by new opportunities abroad to abandon the moral standards of their ancestors. Ironically, it was the Romans' long-standing reputation for honorable practices that made it easy to cheat and steal abroad—especially in the absence of close supervision from home. New circumstances had led to a variety of financial pressures. For instance, as time passed, getting elected to office at Rome became increasingly expensive. Paying for gladiatorial contests to entertain the voters was costly. Another kind of expense was sending a son to Athens to study. Then there were the temptations of luxurious imports from eastern lands. The lifestyle of the ruling elite became lavish; to pursue the new chances for wealth, by fair means or foul, seemed to be a necessity.

New styles in living meant a widening gulf between classes at Rome. The old folksy community with its common goals and common dangers gradually broke down. In former times, epidemics affected rich and poor alike. Now, those who could afford villas in the country moved away from the unhealthy conditions of a congested city.

The historian Livy wrote about the problems that resulted from Rome's success. He concluded, as did the ancient Athenian lawgiver, Solon, that a whole society could be corrupted by selfishness. Materialism affected both rich and poor. The rich simply had more of what everybody was after. And who was to blame for this moral decline? Cato pointed a finger at the influence of foreigners, especially the Greeks. In brief, the Romans had taken over the cities the Greeks had settled in southern Italy and picked up bad habits from them in the process.

The Greek historian Polybius, who pronounced the earlier Romans superior to his kinsmen in matters of morals, also saw the danger. In his account of the conquest of Syracuse during the Second Punic War, he describes the Romans as follows: "While leading lives of the greatest simplicity themselves, as far as possible removed from the luxury and extravagance which these things imply, they yet conquered the men who had always possessed them in the greatest abundance and of the finest quality. Could there have been a greater mistake than theirs? Surely it would be an

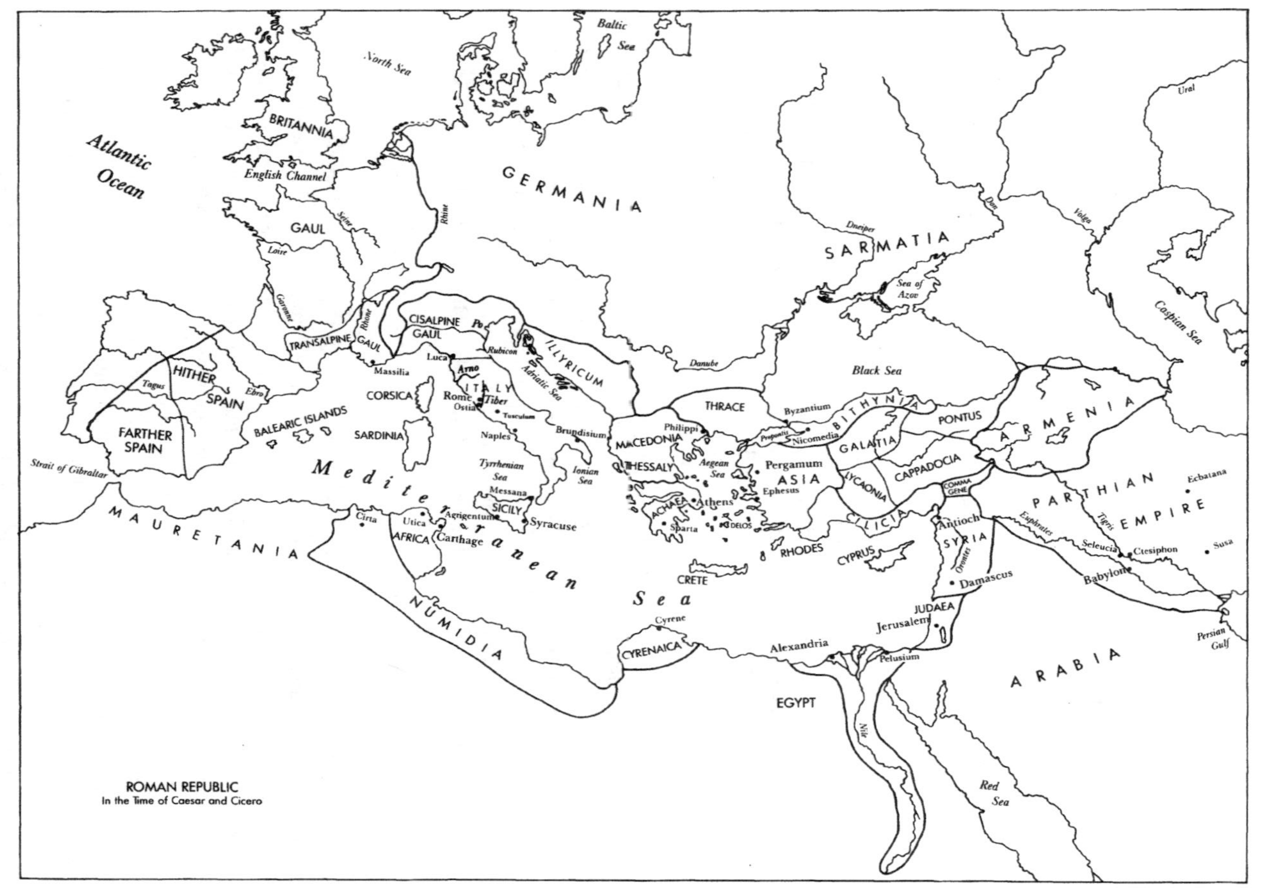

ROMAN REPUBLIC
In the Time of Caesar and Cicero

incontestable error for a people to abandon the habits of the conquerors and adopt those of the conquered; and at the same time involve itself in that jealousy which is the most dangerous concomitant of excessive prosperity."[2]

The excessive prosperity Polybius mentions was not widely shared, and by Cicero's day there existed a network of powerful families and friends with a disproportionate influence in the government. Although the offices they held were legal, it was widely suspected that the business they conducted was not.

Earlier, conflicting factions had solved pressing problems through compromise, however begrudgingly agreed upon, and the state remained united against its enemies. Now the unwillingness of some to make concessions and the impatience of others who wanted quick reforms led to chronic disorders that tore the Republic apart.

Cicero, who had made his reputation fighting corruption, was elected consul in 63 B.C. and found it his duty to defend the status quo. To do so, of course, meant that money lenders and other special interests would continue to sustain their positions and privilege. Those left out, with nothing to win or lose, tried to overthrow the government. The Conspiracy of Catiline is named after its brilliant but erratic leader. In his orations *Against Catiline*, Cicero alerted the Senate to the schemes of ruthless revolutionaries intent on setting fires in the city and amid the confusion killing the elected leaders. Those involved might be selfless idealists, bankrupt scions of prominent families, disgruntled veterans, adventurers, or the destitute with nothing at risk in an upheaval. Whatever the reasons for the plot, some of the accusations against the system were valid,[3] and Cicero knew it. Yet, entrusted to maintain public order, he stood firm. The constitution, made up of both written and unwritten laws, must be defended. With courage and some luck it was.

While Catiline rallied the discontented throughout Italy, a plot by his supporters was unmasked in the city. Five ringleaders were seized and promptly executed both for vengeance's sake and to set a stern example. Catiline died fighting the following year.

Cicero, in his letters, proudly called attention to the dedicated service he had given to the Republic in that momentous year (cf. *Ad Fam*. V.2, 7). He may indeed have saved the state from anarchy, but he had not solved its problems. The old "business as usual" under the constitution continued. Violence against the entrenched power of the ruling classes had failed. Yet within four years of Cicero's noble defense of the *status quo*, the First Triumvirate was in place and the government was given a new direction more in line with popular interests. Julius Caesar, a legally elected consul for 59 B.C., was in partnership with Crassus, who had money, and Pompey, who had loyal veterans at his call. While the First Triumvirate had no constitutional basis whatsoever, these "three unscrupulous men" (*Ad Att*. II.9), by using legal offices and much popular good will, ordered affairs in Rome to suit themselves.

Not long after the triumvirs took power, Cicero was forced into exile. He lacked powerful friends to protect him and admitted that it was his own fault. Writing from Dyrrachium in 58, he revealed that Caesar,[4] during his consulship, had made a gen-

Bust of Cicero. The Wellington Museum, London. A marble head and shoulders, dated to the first century A.D., with a third-century inscription. Purchased in 1816 by the Duke of Wellington from Cardinal Fesch, Napoleon's uncle. By courtesy of the Trustees of the Victoria and Albert Museum.

erous overture to him which he had refused. In a letter to his wife and family he realized what unhappiness that refusal had brought to all concerned.

> I have received three letters from the hands of Aristocritus, which I almost obliterated with tears. For I am thoroughly weakened with sorrow, my dear Terentia, and it is not my own miseries that torture me more than yours—and yours, my children! Moreover, I am more miserable than you in this, that whereas the disaster is shared by us both, yet the fault is all my own. It was my duty to have avoided the danger by accepting a legation,[5] or to resist it by careful management and the resources at my command, or to fall like a brave man. Nothing was more pitiful, more base, or more unworthy of myself than the line I actually took. Accordingly, it is with shame as well as grief that I am overpowered. For I am ashamed of not having exhibited courage and care to a most excellent wife and most darling children. I have, day and night, before my eyes the mourning dresses, the tears of you all, and the weakness of your own health, while the hope of recall presented to me is slender indeed. Many are hostile, nearly all jealous. To expel me had been difficult, to keep me out is easy. However, as long as you entertain any hope, I will not give way, lest all should seem lost by my fault. As to your anxiety for my personal safety, that is now the easiest thing in the world for me, for even my enemies desire me to go on living in this utter wretchedness. . . . Take care of your health, and assure yourself that nothing is or has ever been dearer to me than you are. Good-bye, my dear Terentia, whom I seem to see before my eyes, and so am dissolved in tears. Good-bye! (*Ad Fam.* XIV.3)

When Cicero wrote that "many are hostile," he was not exaggerating. At the top of a long list of enemies was the man who engineered his exile. Clodius, an aggressive politician, accused Cicero of executing the conspirators in 63 without due process. But the real reason for his hatred of Cicero was a trial for sacrilege that first gave the young Clodius notoriety. One evening in December, 62, a group of women had gathered at Caesar's house, where his wife and mother were holding a "ladies only" ceremony in honor of *Bona Dea*, the Good Goddess. Clodius, enamoured of Caesar's wife, disguised himself as a woman in order to use the occasion to be near her. When his voice betrayed him, he was driven off without his identity being certain. (Cicero said a servant girl helped Clodius in this exploit, *Ad Att.* I.12.) Later, brought to trial in 61 B.C., Clodius defended himself by saying he had been out of town. Cicero, however, testified that he had seen him in the city on the day in question. Later, Cicero sarcastically referred to Clodius as "that priest of Bona Dea" (*Ad Att.* II.4). Caesar did not take part in the trial, but he did divorce his wife, who he announced was "not above suspicion."

Passages from a letter in which Cicero tells how Clodius managed to save himself are often quoted as evidence of the unsavory operations in the courts of Rome. The following letter is one of the many Cicero wrote to his lifelong friend Titus Pomponius Atticus, whose sister had married Cicero's brother, Quintus. Atticus was noted both for his wealth and for the distance he kept from politics. But Cicero, among other prominent Romans, relied upon him heavily for advice. He was also a noted publisher employing copyists whom Cicero used and mentioned in his letters (*Ad Att.* XII.40, 44). At a time when Atticus was absent from Rome, Cicero wrote to him: "Neither my work nor rest, neither my business nor leisure, neither my affairs in the forum or at home, public or private, can any longer do without your most consolatory and affectionate counsel and conversation" (*Ad Att.* I.17). Earlier in the same year, 61 B.C., Cicero wrote a letter to Atticus that included a colorful version of the trial of Clodius.

> When the rejection of jurors had taken place, amidst loud cheers and countercheers—the accuser like a strict censor rejecting the most worthless, the defendant like a kind-hearted trainer of gladiators all the best . . . There never was a seedier lot round a table in a gambling hell. Senators under a cloud, equites out at elbows, tribunes who were not so much made of money as "collectors" of it, according to their official title. However there were a few honest men in the panel, whom he had been unable to drive off it by rejection, and they took their seats among their uncongenial comrades with gloomy looks and signs of emotion, and were keenly disgusted at having to rub elbows with such rascals. . . . good heavens, what a scandal! even favours from certain ladies, and introductions to young men of rank, were thrown in as a kind of *pourboire* to some of the jurors. . . . twenty-five jurors were yet found so courageous that, though at the risk of their lives, they preferred even death to producing universal ruin. There were thirty-one who were more influenced by famine than fame. On seeing one of these latter Catulus said to him, "Why did you ask us for a guard? Did you fear being robbed of the money?" There you have, as briefly as I could put it, the nature of the trial and the cause of the acquittal. . . . at the meeting of the senate on the 15th of May, being called on for my opinion, I spoke at considerable length on the high interests of the Republic, and brought in the following passage by a happy inspiration: "Do not, Fathers, regard yourselves as fallen utterly, do not faint, because you have received one blow. The wound is one which I cannot disguise, but which I yet feel sure should not be regarded with extreme fear; to fear would shew us to be the greatest of cowards, to ignore it the greatest of fools. Lentulus was twice acquitted, so was Catiline, a third such criminal has now been let loose by jurors upon the Republic. You are mistaken, Clodius: it is not for the city but for the prison that the jurors have reserved you, and their intention was not to retain you in the state, but to deprive you of the privilege of

exile. Wherefore, Fathers, rouse up all your courage, hold fast to your high calling. There still remains in the Republic the old unanimity of the loyalists: their feelings have been outraged, their resolution has not been weakened: no fresh mischief has been done, only what was actually existing has been discovered. In the trial of one profligate many like him have been detected." But what am I about? I have copied almost a speech into a letter. I return to the duel of words. Up gets our dandified young gentleman, . . . "You have bought a house," says he. "You would think that he said," quoth I, "you have bought a jury." "They didn't trust you on your oath," said he. "Yes," said I, "twenty-five jurors did trust me, thirty-one didn't trust you, for they took care to get their money beforehand." Here he was overpowered by a burst of applause and broke down without a word to say. (*Ad Att.* I.16)

Cicero could boast of his victory in a war of words, but that was not what mattered. Clodius was a popular tribune of the plebs, a promoter of cheap grain for the poor, and an outspoken supporter of Caesar. Lacking help from the triumvirs, Cicero was driven from the city. He never got over the disgrace, not to mention the inconvenience of having to go into exile. Time and again in later letters he mentioned how those who might have prevented it had let him down. As he traveled into exile he was so downhearted he could only manage brief notes to Atticus. From Thurii in April, 58, he wrote: "I am the most miserable man alive, and am being worn out with the most poignant sorrow" (*Ad Att.* III.5). From the seaport, Brundisium, he wrote at greater length including the following emotion-charged passage:

As to your urging me to remain alive, you carry one point—that I should not lay violent hands upon myself: the other you cannot bring to pass—that I should not regret my policy and my continuance in life. For what is there to attach me to it, especially if the hope which accompanied me on my departure is non-existent? I will not attempt to enumerate all the miseries into which I have fallen through the extreme injustice and unprincipled conduct, not so much of my enemies, as of those who were jealous of me, because I do not wish to stir up a fresh burst of grief in myself, or invite you to share the same sorrow. I say this deliberately—that no one was ever afflicted with so heavy a calamity, that no one had ever greater cause to wish for death; while I have let slip the time when I might have sought it more creditably. Henceforth death can never heal, it can only end my sorrow. (*Ad Att.* III.7)

Envy, forever envy, ensnared him. In a later letter he repeats: "It is not my enemies, but my jealous rivals, that have ruined me" (*Ad Att.* III.9). However, by the middle of June, he was obviously recovering his old confidence, and in a letter to Atticus from Thessalonica, he seems to be feeling better.

> Did anyone ever fall from such a high position, in so good a cause, with such endowments of genius, wisdom and popularity, with such powerful supports from all loyalists? Can I forget what I was, and not feel what I am? Of what honour, of what glory, of what children, of what means, of what a brother I am deprived? (*Ad Att.* III.10)

Cicero's moods never seem to have held for long. As he waited for news from Rome, his letters alternated between despair and hope. More than once he speaks of suicide, and in a letter dated 15 September 58, he says he would like to have some piece of Atticus's land in which to be buried (*Ad Att.* III.19). In another letter, a few weeks later, he is asking to have precise wording used concerning his property in a proposal for his return from exile (*Ad Att.* III.20). This is why we know Cicero so well. True to life, he thinks himself sincere in playing both roles: first, the defeated man crawling off somewhere to die; then, the busy politician attempting to arrange matters for his recall to Rome.

At home, Clodius was busy alienating old allies. With his brusque manner and speech, it was not difficult for him to offend Pompey, who finally retaliated by supporting a call for Cicero's return. There followed a dramatic homecoming in 57. Cicero declared himself vindicated, and lost no time in returning to politics. A letter to Atticus described his arrival back in the most enthusiastic terms.

> I then commenced my journey, amidst the compliments of the men of highest consideration at Brundisium, and was met at every point by legates bearing congratulations. My arrival in the neighbourhood of the city was the signal for every soul of every order known to my nomenclator[6] coming out to meet me, except those enemies who could not either dissemble or deny the fact of their being such. On my arrrival at the Porta Capena, the steps of the temples were already thronged from top to bottom by the populace; and while their congratulations were displayed by the loudest possible applause, a similar throng and similar applause accompanied me right up to the Capitol, and in the forum and on the Capitol itself there was again a wonderful crowd. (*Ad Att.* IV.1)

At the same time there was much unrest, due to an unusual shortage of grain. Cicero, full of gratitude to Pompey, threw himself into the effort to win his friend a commission to take charge of the food problem for five years. It was a popular move, but Cicero admits that his voice was not a welcome sound to everybody: "I am on the threshold, as it were, of a second life. Already certain persons who defended me in my absence begin to nurse a secret grudge at me now that I am here, and to make no secret of their jealousy" (*Ad Att.* IV.1).

Cicero's outspoken support of Pompey and his successful effort to win for him a powerful special assignment had a subtle purpose. He would, if he could, wean Pompey away from his close association with Caesar. But that was not yet possible. Caesar, engaged in his renowned conquest of Gaul, was kept informed about the politics at home, and at a conference at Luca, in the spring of 56, he renewed his pact with Pompey and Crassus. His co-triumvirs were to be the consuls in 55. He even sent soldiers home to vote for them.

In January 55, Cicero wrote to Lentulus,[7] the proconsul of Cilicia, about how he felt under the continuing power of the First Triumvirate, which for him meant further cooperation with Pompey. He put it this way:

> I conform myself to the wishes of him from whom I cannot dissent with any dignity: and this I do not do, as perhaps some may think, from insincerity; for deliberate purpose and, by heaven! affection for Pompey are so powerful with me, that whatever is to his interest, and whatever he wishes, appears to me at once to be altogether right and reasonable. Nor, as I think, would even his opponents be wrong if, seeing that they cannot possibly be his equals, they were to cease to struggle against him.

Further on, he writes:

> But to return to what more immediately affects your interests—I have ascertained that Pompey is warmly your friend, and with him as consul, to the best of my knowledge and belief, you will get whatever you wish. In this he will have me always at his elbow, and nothing which affects you shall be passed over by me. Nor, in fact, shall I be afraid of boring him, for he will be very glad for his own sake to find me grateful to him. (*Ad Fam.* I.8)

No matter what Cicero thought privately about the Triumvirate, he could not abstain from ingratiating himself with the high and mighty. It is apparent that Caesar, although rebuffed earlier, still sought Cicero's friendship. Cicero tells his brother, now serving with Caesar, how he intends to make the best of that good fortune.

> On the 2nd of June, the day of my return to Rome, I received your letter dated Placentia: then next day another dated Blandeno,[8] along with a letter from Caesar filled full of courteous, earnest, and pleasant expressions. These expressions are indeed valuable, or rather *most* valuable, as tending very powerfully to secure our reputation and exalted position in the state.

> But believe me—for you know my heart—that what I value most in all this I already possess, that is, first of all, your active contribution to our common position; and, secondly, all that warm affection of Caesar for me, which I prefer to all the honours which he desires me to expect at his hands. His letter too, despatched at the same time as your own—which begins by saying what pleasure your arrival and the renewed memory of our old affection had given him, and goes on to say that he will take care that, in the midst of my sorrow and regret at losing you, I shall have reason to be glad that you are with him of all people—gave me extraordinary delight. Wherefore you, of course, are acting in a truly brotherly spirit when you exhort me, though, by heaven, I am now indeed forward enough to do so, to concentrate all my attentions upon him alone. Yes, I will do so, indeed, with a burning zeal: and perhaps I shall manage to accomplish what is frequently the fortune of travellers when they make great haste, who, if they have got up later than they intended, have, by increasing their speed, arrived at their destination sooner than if they had waked up before daylight. Thus I, since I have long overslept myself in cultivating that great man, though you, by heaven, often tried to wake me up, will make up for my slowness with horses and (as you say he likes my poem) a poet's chariots. (*Q. Fr.* II.13)

That is only about half the length of the letter, but it was still relatively brief compared to many long-winded and repetitious messages he sent to his brother Quintus, four years younger than himself. He admitted to lecturing his brother and criticizing him, especially for his bad temper. But Cicero's own weaknesses were at times apparent. It was to his brother that he had revealed how much he felt sorry for himself at the time he had been in exile: "For there is neither wisdom nor philosophy with sufficient strength to sustain such a weight of grief" (*Q. Fr.* I.3).

In a letter to Lentulus, written in 54, Cicero exaggerated his own importance in so far as his opinions carried any weight. The triumvirs, especially Caesar, wished he would remain silent, but his words were probably more a nuisance than a threat. In any event, at this point he reaffirms his high opinion of Caesar.

> Caesar's memorable and almost superhuman kindness to myself and my brother, who thus would have deserved my support whatever he undertook; while as it is, considering his great success and his brilliant victories, he would seem, even if he had not behaved to me as he has, to claim a panegyric from me. For I would have you believe that, putting you aside, who were the authors of my recall, there is no one by whose good offices I would not only confess, but would even rejoice, to have been so much bound. (*Ad Fam.* I.9)

Still Cicero could not be happy with the support Caesar received from Clodius, whose tactics included the hiring of gangs of toughs to intimidate those who opposed him. There was rivalry with the equally unruly adherents of Milo, a strong supporter of Pompey. So, while Caesar and Pompey appeared to be on good terms, these lower level partisans carried on an unofficial war. In a riot which broke out between them on the Appian Way on 18 January, 52 B.C., Clodius was killed. At last Cicero had his revenge, and he savored it by later referring to incidents as being so many days past that particular event (*Ad Att.* V.13, VI.1).

No matter what the circumstances, win or lose, Cicero would continue to do his duty. In 51, he went out to Cilicia as governor. A letter to Atticus gives a good account of the state of affairs there.

> Though the letter-carriers of the *publicani* are starting while I am actually travelling and on the road, and though I am still engaged on my progress, yet I thought I must snatch a moment to prevent your thinking me forgetful of your charge. So I have sat down actually on the road to write you in brief what follows, which really calls for a somewhat lengthy essay. Let me tell you, then, that with the highest possible reputation I entered, on the 31st of July, into a province in a state of desolation and lasting ruin; that I stayed three days at Laodicea, three at Apamea, the same at Synnada. It was the same tale everywhere: they could not pay the poll-tax: everybody's securities were sold: groans, lamentations, from the towns: acts of savagery worthy of some wild beast, rather than of a man. In short, they are absolutely weary of their life. However, the wretched towns are somewhat relieved by my costing them nothing, nor my legates, nor quaestor, nor anyone. Let me tell you that I not only refuse to accept hay, which is customarily furnished under the Julian law, but that no one of us accepts even firewood, or anything else, except four beds and a roof to cover us; in many districts we do not accept even a roof, but remain, as a rule, under canvas. Accordingly, we are greeted by extraordinary throngs from farms, villages, houses, every sort of place. By Hercules, on my mere arrival, the justice, purity, and merciful heart of your Cicero seems to give them new life: so far has he surpassed everyone's hopes. (*Ad Att.* V.16)

In another letter to Atticus (*Ad Att.* V.21), Cicero provides a record of his administration, of which no doubt he had every right to be proud. He felt that the year in Cilicia proved him to be the dedicated public servant he said he was. His reputation was paramount. So, too, his personal attachments and obligations to friends. They were the webbing of Roman politics. Parties were mentioned, but they were not formal organizations as in democracies today. Alliances were made by marriage or friendship between persons of the same class or economic interest. A letter to his friend Lentulus in 56, written after the triumvirs had renewed their pact at Luca, offers a typical example of the preoccupation with personal relationships.

> I am, in fact, not able to bear witness to any one of the consulars shewing zeal or kindness or friendly feeling towards you. For you are aware that Pompey, who is very frequently accustomed, not on my instigation but of his own accord, to confide in me about you, did not often attend the senate during these discussions. It is true your last letter, as I could easily conceive, was very gratifying to him. To me, indeed, your reasonableness, or rather your extreme wisdom, seemed not only charming, but simply admirable. For by that letter you retained your hold on a man of lofty character, who was bound to you by the signal generosity of your conduct towards him, but who was entertaining some suspicions that, owing to the impression prevailing among certain persons as to his own ambitious desires, you were alienated from him. (*Ad Fam.* I.7)

The politics of ancient Rome were akin to those of Renaissance Italy in that decisions were made among families and friends. Here it might be well to add a note of caution about the choice of words in these translations. The words *love* and *intimate* are frequently used, and they do properly evoke the intensity of emotions freely expressed between friends in ancient times. The word *intimate*, for instance, means "confidant" and should not be interpreted as necessarily having any reference to physical relations the way the word *intimacy* is now used.

Cicero wrote a number of letters of recommendation. He was widely acquainted and considered himself a generous person willing to do a favor. Nor was he a man to forget his hometown of Arpinum, and he used his influence on its behalf (*Ad Fam.* XIII.11). Many individuals were put in his debt, and if one of them came to power Cicero was not shy about reminding him how he got there. A letter of recommendation written in 45 B.C. closes with the usual reminder that Cicero's favor should not go unnoticed: "I beg you, therefore, to understand that, whether he has or has not come to Sicily, he is one of my most intimate and closely united friends, and to treat him in such a way as to make him understand that my recommendation has been of great service to him" (*Ad Fam.* XIII.30).

In October of 50, Cicero returned from his tour of duty in Cilicia amid a tense political crisis in Rome. When Caesar's daughter Julia, who was married to Pompey, died in childbirth, the personal link between these two powerful men was broken. Cicero had referred to the marriage as part of Caesar's plan for "preparing a despotism" (*Ad Att.* II.17). Then the death of Crassus while fighting the Parthians in 53 ended the Triumvirate, and a contest of wills between Caesar and Pompey began. In a letter from Caelius,[9] Cicero was warned that a major crisis was imminent.

> As to high politics—I have often told you in my letters that I see no chance of peace lasting a year: and the nearer the struggle comes, which must come, the clearer does that danger appear. The point, on which the men in power are bound to fight, is this: Cn. Pompeius has made up his mind not to allow C. Caesar to become consul, except on condition of his first handing over his army and provinces: while Caesar is fully persuaded that he cannot be safe if he quits his army. He, however, proposes as a compromise that both should give up their armies. So that mighty love and unpopular union of theirs has not degenerated into mere secret bickering, but is breaking out into open war. . . . In this quarrel I perceive that Cn. Pompeius has on his side the senate and the *iudices*:[10] that Caesar will be joined by all whose past life gives them reason to be afraid, or their future no reason to hope: that there is no comparison between their armies. On the whole, there is time enough to weigh the forces of both, and to choose sides. . . . In a word, you want my opinion as to the future. Unless one of the other of these two goes to the Parthian war, I see that a violent quarrel is impending, which the sword and main force will decide. Both are prepared in resolution and forces. If it could only be transacted without extreme danger, fortune is preparing for you a great and enjoyable spectacle. (*Ad Fam.* VIII.14)

The underlying cause of the civil war was the astonishing success of Caesar in Gaul. Jealousy of his popularity was mixed with a genuine fear of his power. Enemies who sat in the Senate gave their support to Pompey and encouraged a simmering rivalry. As mentioned in the letter above, Caesar was determined to retain his army. The extension of his command which he requested would have protected him from prosecution until he could again under the ten-year rule, be eligible for the consulship in 48. Influential senators were equally determined to strip him of his present proconsulship and so make him liable for alleged offenses when he was serving in Spain. Pompey, overshadowed by Caesar's successes and tempted by the Senate's support, remained indecisive and so let time run out before a compromise could be reached. Caesar, convinced that a powerful senatorial faction was inventing excuses to foil him, marched his army out of Cisalpine Gaul, across the Rubicon River, and into Italy early in January 49. By doing so, the die was cast. He had committed treason. Pompey, chosen by the Senate to defend Italy, was unprepared for the swift movement of events, and fled with his army to Greece.

Cicero's letters to Atticus, written almost daily, ask over and over again whether he should support Pompey or reconcile himself to Caesar. But his constant pleading for advice strikes a false note. It would seem that his tiresome pleas stem not so much from helplessness as from anxiety lest he make an unprofitable choice. Cicero's style in both his speeches and his letters is built on self-dramatization, with no small measure of self-pity. The more letters read the more this is evident.

In many letters, Cicero, seeking to allay the suspicion that he was less than a true friend, was anxious to prove his loyalty. One soon concludes that he was not widely trusted and that he sensed he was generally felt to be insincere (Cf. *Ad Fam.* III.10).

To be fair, it must be added that the tedium of Cicero's letters is occasionally relieved by a flash of wit. For instance, in a letter to a young man, Trebatius, who was a protégé of his, Cicero writes: "I am glad you didn't go to Britain, because you have been saved some hard work, and I the necessity of listening to your stories about that expedition" (*Ad Fam.* VII.17). A young lawyer friend of Cicero's, on active duty with Caesar in Gaul, received the following comments: "If I had been by way of dining out, I would not have failed your friend Cn. Octavius; to whom, however, I did remark upon his repeated invitations, 'Pray who are you?' But, by Hercules, joking apart, he is a pretty fellow: I could have wished you had taken him with you!" (*Ad Fam.* VII.16).

Cicero mentions his joking manner and is sometimes found teasing his correspondents. So we read: "Pray, as you love me, don't suppose that because I write jestingly I have cast off all care for the state" (*Ad Fam.* IX.24).

There was certainly little to joke about in the present crisis. Pompey was impatient because Cicero could not make up his mind, but Caesar liked him best when he was undecided. On 27 February 49, Cicero wrote to Atticus: "You ask me what Caesar said in his letter to me. The usual thing: he was much obliged by my having remained neutral, and begged me to continue to do so" (*Ad Att.* VIII.11).

Cicero's vacillation was long standing and his letters during this time no doubt reflect the agony of many prominent citizens caught between the ambitions of two powerful men. Prior to the final break, Cicero tells of his meetings with Pompey and Caesar, the letters he has received from them, his regard for their abilities, and how much he distrusts them both. One letter to Atticus, written a month before hostilities began, questions Caesar's sincerity regarding the constitution.

> It is for their own supremacy that these men are now contending, but it is at the risk of the constitution. For if it is the constitution that is being now defended by Caesar, why was it not defended in his own consulship? Why was I, in whose cause the safety of the constitution was involved, not defended in the next year? (*Ad Att.* VII.3)

Two days later, Cicero told Atticus about a two-hour interview with Pompey. The story offers the reminder that seemingly unimportant events may have great political significance.

> I saw Pompey on the 10th of December: we were together perhaps two hours. . . . On the political situation . . . the tone of his remarks assumed the existence of downright war. He held out no hope of maintaining peace:

> he had felt before that Caesar was alienated from him, he had recently become quite sure of it. Hirtius, Caesar's most intimate friend, had been in the neighborhood, but had not called on him. . . . This seemed to him to be a clear "symptom" of alienation. In short, nothing else consoles me but the opinion that the man, to whom even his enemies have assigned a second consulship, and fortune has given supreme power, will not be so mad as to put these advantages in danger. But if he once begins to run amuck, I verily have many fears which I do not venture to put into writing. However, as the matter stands at present, I think of approaching the city on the 3rd of January [Cicero's birthday]. (*Ad Att.* VII.4)

Any uncertainty of course gave an advantage to a man like Caesar who was, by nature, uncommonly decisive. A letter (*Ad Att.* VII.5) written from Formiae on 17 December 50, reveals Cicero's willingness to give in to Caesar rather than fight—at least at the hour he was writing. On the same day, in another letter, what he is thinking is not what he is saying publicly.

> At the political situation I am thoroughly alarmed, and up to now I have found hardly anyone not convinced that it would be better to yield to Caesar's demand than to fight. That demand, it is true, shameless as it is, is more serious than we thought. But why begin resisting him *now*? . . . than when we voted his additional five years, or when we allowed his being a candidate in his absence: for we did not, I presume, give him arms then, that we might have a well-furnished enemy to fight with now! You will say, "What, then, will be your view?" Not the one I shall express. For my real view will be "anything rather than fight": I shall *say* exactly what Pompey does. And that I shall do from no abject cowardice: but once more it is a very serious evil to the constitution, and less allowable perhaps in my case than in that of others, that in matters of such importance I should differ from Pompey. (*Ad Att.* VII.6)

A week later, on 25 or 26 December, Cicero wrote to Atticus about a meeting with Pompey after which the chances for peace seemed remote indeed (*Ad Att.* VII.8). After the dramatic events of the forepart of January 49, when Caesar had crossed the Rubicon River and Pompey had fled from Rome, Cicero wrote to Atticus on one day of his puzzlement with Pompey and on the next day of his bitterness toward Caesar.

> As yet I have received only one letter from you dated the 19th, and in it you indicated that you had written another, which I have not received. But I beg you to write as often as possible, not only whatever you know or have been told, but also what you suspect, and above all what you think

I ought to do or not to do. You ask me to be sure to let you know what Pompey is doing: I don't think he knows himself, certainly none of us do. I saw the consul Lentulus at Formiae on the 21st; I have seen Libo. Nothing but terror and uncertainty everywhere! Pompey is on the road to Larinum; for there are some cohorts there, as also at Luceria and Teanum, and in the rest of Apulia. After that nobody knows whether he means to make a stand anywhere, or to cross the sea. If he stays in Italy, I am afraid he cannot have a dependable army: but if he goes away, where I am to go or stay, or what I am to do, I don't know. For the man, whose "Phalarism"[11] you dread, will, I think, spare no form of brutality: nor will the suspension of business, nor the departure of senate and magistrates, nor the closing of the treasury cause him to pause. But all this, as you say, we shall know before long. Meanwhile, forgive my writing to you at such length and so often. For I find some relief in it, and at the same time want to draw a letter from you, and above all some advice as to what I am to do and how to conduct myself. Shall I commit myself wholly to this side? I am not deterred by the danger, but I am bursting with vexation. Such a want of all plan! so utterly opposed in every respect to my advice! Am I to procrastinate and trim, and then join the winning side, the party in power? . . . Pray, though you say you confine yourself to the limits of your own house, do give me a sketch of the city. Is Pompey missed? Is there any appearance of a feeling against Caesar? What, too, is your opinion as to Terentia and Tullia? Should they stay at Rome, or join me, or seek some place of safety? On this, and indeed on any other point, pray write to me, or rather keep on writing. (*Ad Att.* VII.12)

You perceive the nature of the war. It is only a civil war in the sense that it has originated from the unscrupulous boldness of one unprincipled citizen, not as arising from a division of sentiment between the citizens generally. But that man is strong in the possession of any army, he commands the allegiance of many by the prospects he holds out and the promises he makes: nothing that anyone possesses is beyond the scope of his desires. To such a man as this the city has been abandoned, without any garrison to protect it, crammed with every kind of wealth. What would you not have to fear from the man who regards those temples and roofs, not as constituting his fatherland, but as objects for plunder? What his proceedings are going to be, and how they are to be put into any shape, without senate and without magistrates, I cannot tell. He will not be able to keep up even a pretence of constitutional action. For us, however—where shall we be able to raise our heads or when? How utterly incapable our general is you yourself observe, in having had no intelligence of the state of affairs even in Picenum: and how devoid of any plan of campaign, the facts are witness.

For, to say nothing of other mistakes committed during the last ten years, could any terms be worse than such a flight? Nor, indeed, have I any idea what he is contemplating at this moment, though I never cease asking again and again by letter. Everyone agrees that he is in a state of abject alarm and agitation. Accordingly, as far as I can see, there is no garrison—to organize which he was kept at the city walls—nor any place where a garrison could be posted. . . . While the time for making terms has been let slip, I do not see what is going to happen. At any rate we, or our leader, have allowed things to come to this pass, that, having left harbour without a rudder, we must let ourselves drift before the storm. (*Ad Att.* VII.13a)

On 8 February, in another letter to Atticus, Cicero again turns his anger on Pompey, whose flight has left Italy in Caesar's hands. Here is the complete letter.

About our misfortunes you hear sooner than I: for they flow from Rome. As for anything good, there is none to be expected from this quarter. I arrived at Capua for the 5th of February, in accordance with the order of the consuls. Late on that day Lentulus arrived; the other consul had absolutely not come on the 7th. For I left Capua on that day and stayed at Cales. From that town I am sending this letter, before daybreak, on the 8th. What I ascertained while at Capua was that the consuls are no good: that no levy is being held anywhere. For the recruiting officers do not venture to shew their faces, with Caesar close at hand, and our leader, on the contrary, nowhere and doing nothing; nor do recruits give in their names. It is not goodwill to the cause, but hope that is wanting. As to our leader Gnaeus—what an inconceivably miserable spectacle! What a complete breakdown! No courage, no plan, no forces, no energy! I will pass over his most discreditable flight from the city, his abject speeches in the towns, his ignorance not only of his opponent's, but even of his own resources—but what do you think of this? On the 7th of February the tribune C. Cassius came with an order from him to the consuls that they should go to Rome, remove the money from the reserve treasury, and immediately quit the town. After leaving the city they are to return! Under what guard? They are to come out of the city! Who is to give them leave to do so? The consul (Lentulus) wrote back to say that Pompey must himself first make his way into Picenum. But the fact is, that district has already been entirely lost. No one knows that except myself, who have learnt it from a letter of Dolabella's. I have no manner of doubt but that Caesar is all but actually in Apulia, and our friend Gnaeus already on board ship. What I am to do is a great "problem," though it would have been no problem to me, had not everything been most disgracefully mismanaged, and without consulting me in any way; problem, however, it is, as to what it is my duty to do. Caesar himself

> urges me to promote peace. But his letter is dated before he began his violent proceedings. Dolabella and Caelius both say that he is well satisfied with my conduct. I am on the rack of perplexity. Assist me by your advice if you can, but all the same look after your own interests to the utmost of your power. In such a total upset I have nothing to say to you. I am looking for a letter from you. (*Ad Att.* VII.21)

In the following weeks, Cicero's letters show continuing bewilderment. Rumors of peace give interludes of hope followed by utter despair. In a letter to Atticus on 16 February 49, Cicero voices another complaint about Pompey: "When we were all alarmed at Caesar, he, for his part was devoted to him: now that he has begun to be alarmed at him, he thinks that everybody ought to be his enemy." (*Ad Att.* VIII.1). But five years earlier, Cicero himself had been on such terms with Caesar as to conclude a letter to him with the following words: "Be careful of your health and continue to love me as ever" (*Ad Fam.* VII.5).

On 23 February 49, Cicero wrote to Atticus that he was less than happy about the prospect of supporting Pompey.

> As to my remark which you praise and declare to be memorable, that I preferred defeat with Pompey to victory with those others, it is quite true: I do prefer it—but it is with the Pompey as he was then, or as I thought him. But with a Pompey who flies before he knows from whom he is flying, or whither, who has betrayed our party, who has abandoned his country, and is about to abandon Italy—if I did prefer it, I have got my wish: I am defeated. For the rest, I cannot stand the sight of what I never had any fear of seeing, nor of the man on whose account I have to give up not only my friends, but my own past. (*Ad Att.* VIII.7)

By the first of March, in a letter to Atticus, Cicero is ready to admit why Caesar is so successful. Here is the entire letter.

> Take the handwriting of my secretary as a sign of my eyes being inflamed, and let the same fact excuse my brevity, though at this particular time I have nothing to write. We are hanging entirely on news from Brundisium. If Caesar has caught our friend Gnaeus, there is a dubious hope of peace; but if the latter has got across beforehand, there is a fear of a fatal war. But do you see upon what sort of man the Republic has fallen? How clear-sighted, how alert, how well prepared! By heaven, if he puts no one to death, nor despoils anyone of anything, he will be most adored by those who had feared him most. The burgesses of the country towns, and the country people also, talk a great deal to me. They don't care a farthing

for anything but their lands, their poor villas, their paltry pence. And now observe the reaction: the man in whom they once trusted they now dread: the man they dreaded they worship. What grave mistakes and vices on our side are accountable for this I cannot think of without sorrow. However, I have already written to tell you what I thought was threatening; and I am now waiting for a letter from you. (*Ad Att.* VIII.13)

In spite of his high praise of Caesar, Cicero two days later had decided that honor was on Pompey's side. He wrote to Atticus:

There is danger in the angry passions of both; and though victory, of course, is uncertain, yet now the worse side seems to me to be the better prepared. Nor am I influenced by the consuls, who are themselves more easily moved than feather or leaf. Consideration of duty tortures me, and has all this while been torturing me, with indecision. To remain is certainly the more cautious policy, to cross the sea is considered the more honourable. . . .

Your most recent letter is dated on the 1st of March, in which you express a wish that there might be a meeting between them, and say that you do not despair of peace. But at the moment of writing I am of opinion that they will not meet, and that, if they do, Pompey will not yield to any offer of terms. (*Ad Att.* VIII.15)

Although Cicero was leaning in Pompey's direction, he kept in touch with Caesar, and in a letter of 19 March 49, he asks him how he can be of help in bringing peace. He respects both men and stresses that he advocated fair treatment of Caesar.

On reading your letter, handed to me by our friend Furnius, in which you ask me to come to the city walls, I was not so much surprised at your wishing "to avail yourself of my advice and position," but what you meant by speaking of my "influence and assistance" I did ask myself. My thoughts, however, were so far dominated by my hope, that I was induced to think that you wished to consult for the tranquillity, peace, and harmony of our fellow citizens: and for a policy of that kind I regarded both my natural disposition and my public character as sufficiently well adapted. If this is the case, and if you are at all anxious to preserve our common friend Pompey, and to reconcile him to yourself and the Republic, you will assuredly find no one better calculated than myself for supporting such measures. For, as soon as opportunity offered, I pleaded for peace both to him and the senate; nor since the commencement of hostilities have I taken any part whatever in the war; and I have held the opinion that by that war you are being wronged, in that men who were hostile to and jealous of you were striving to prevent your enjoying an office granted you by the favour of the Roman people. But as at that period I was not only personally a supporter of your rights, but also advised everybody else to assist you, so at the present moment I am strongly moved by consideration for the position of Pompey. It is now a good number of years ago since I picked out you two as the special objects of my political devotion, and—as you still are—of my warm personal affection. Wherefore I ask you, or rather entreat you, and appeal to you with every form of prayer, that in the midst of your very great preoccupations you would yet spare some part of your time to reflect how by your kindness I may be enabled to do what goodness and gratitude, and, in point of fact, natural affection demand, by remembering the extreme obligation under which I stand. If these considerations only affected myself, I should yet have hoped to secure your assent; but, in my opinion, it concerns both your own honour and the public interest that I—a friend to peace and to you both—should, as far as you are concerned, be maintained in a position best calculated to promote harmony between you and among our fellow citizens. (*Ad Att.* IX.11a)

Cicero kept Atticus informed about his correspondence and on one occasion, in lieu of any news, sent along to him a pleasant letter he had received from Caesar.

Though I have nothing to write to you about, yet I send you this that I may not omit a single day. On the 27th it is announced that Caesar will stop at Sinuessa. I received a letter from him on the 26th, in which he now talks of looking forward to my "resources," not my "aid," as in his former letter. I had written to compliment him on the moderation of his conduct at Corfinium, and he answered me as follows:

Caesar Imperator to Cicero Imperator.

"You judge me quite accurately—for my character is well known to you—when you say that nothing is more remote from my disposition than cruelty. For myself, as I take great delight in this policy for its own sake, so your approval of my action gives me a triumphant feeling of gladness. Nor am I shaken by the fact that those, who were allowed to go free by me, are said to have departed with the intention of renewing the war against me: for there is nothing I like better than that I should be what I am, they what they are. I should be much obliged if you would meet me at the city, that I may, as ever, avail myself in all matters of your counsels and resources. Let me assure you that nothing gives me more pleasure than the presence of your son-in-law Dolabella. This additional favour I shall owe to him: for it will be impossible for him to act otherwise, considering his great kindness, his feeling, and his cordial goodwill towards myself." (*Ad Att.* IX.16)

Two days later, Cicero wrote to Atticus about his meeting with Caesar, whom he thought he must have annoyed by refusing to appear with him in Rome.

> I followed your advice in both particulars: for I spoke in such a manner as rather to gain his respect than his thanks, and I stuck to the resolution of not going to Rome. I found myself mistaken in one respect—in thinking that he would be easily satisfied. I never saw anything less so. He kept remarking that he was condemned by my decision, that the rest would be the slower to come, if I did not do so. I remarked that their case was unlike mine. After much discussion he said, "Come, then, and discuss the question of peace." "At my own discretion?" said I. "Am I to prescribe to you?" said he. "My motion will be this," said I, "that the senate disapproves of any going to Spain or taking armies across to Greece, and," I added, "I shall make many regretful remarks as to Gnaeus." Thereupon he said, "Of course, I don't wish such things said." "So I supposed," said I, "but I must decline being present there, because I must either speak in this sense, and say many things which I could not possibly pass over, if present, or I must not come at all." The upshot was that, by way of ending the discussion, he requested that I would think it over. I couldn't say no to that. So we parted. I feel certain, therefore, that he has no love for me. But I felt warm satisfaction with myself, which hasn't been the case for some time past. . . . He is extraordinarily vigilant, extraordinarily bold: I see no limit to the mischief. Now, at any rate, it is time for you to bring out your counsels. This is where you drew the line. Yet his closing remark in our interview, which I had almost forgotten to mention, was very offensive, that "if he was not allowed to avail himself of my counsels, he would avail himself of such as he could, and would scruple at nothing." "So you have seen with your own eyes," say you, "that the man is such as you described him to be. Did it cost you a sigh?" Yes, indeed. . . . But I wait for a letter from you. For you can't say, as in former ones, "Let us see how this turns out." The final test was to be our meeting, and in that I feel certain I have offended him. All the more prompt must be my next step. Pray send me a packet, and full of politics! I am very anxious for a letter from you. (*Ad Att.* IX.18)

Later, in April, Caelius warned Cicero that recent news about him was very displeasing to Caesar and that for his own and his family's sake he should at least remain neutral. Why not retreat to some out-of-the-way place and wait for the trouble to pass? (*Ad Fam.* VIII.16).

As late as May, Cicero mentions that his family and friends were urging him to wait for the outcome of Caesar's campaign in Spain before deciding what to do (e.g., *Ad Att.* X.9). But he seems to have been making plans to join Pompey ever since his inconclusive meeting with Caesar in March. Early in June 49, he wrote a farewell letter to his wife and daughter from aboard a ship taking him to Pompey's camp. His young son was with him (*Ad Fam*. XIV.7).

Even a year later, in May 48, a letter from his son-in-law Dolabella urged him to change his mind. Caesar by this time had triumphed in Spain (August 49) and had arrived in Greece to challenge Pompey directly. Dolabella assured Cicero that his family was safe in Rome. Caesar's kindness was mentioned, and it seemed clear that past mistakes would be forgotten if Cicero, having "satisfied the claims of duty or friendship," would now withdraw from what appeared to be the losing side. His telling Cicero "you should consult for your own interests, and at length be your own friend" sounds superfluous, but was obviously a subtle bit of flattery (*Ad Fam*. IX.9).

Cicero stayed where he was, and in a letter written to Atticus from Pompey's camp he said he had lent Pompey money, for which he expected to get both honor and profit (*Ad Att* XI.3). There was to be neither.

The struggle between Caesar and Pompey reached a climax at the battle of Pharsalus in Thessaly on 9 August 48. Pompey was decisively defeated and fled to Egypt, where he was treacherously murdered by agents of the king from whom he sought asylum. Caesar was successful everywhere. There was a close call in Egypt during the brief Alexandrian War, in which he saved his new friend Cleopatra from her enemies, but in Asia Minor he won an easy victory over Mithradates' son, Pharnaces, at the Second Battle of Zela ("I came, I saw, I conquered"). There followed sensational triumphs in North Africa, in which he overcame forces loyal to Pompey's memory. At that point, Cato the Younger, trapped in Utica, killed himself rather than accept Caesar's clemency. A hard-won victory over Pompey's sons in Spain, with the older Gnaeus captured and killed, made Caesar the master of the Roman world.

Cicero was among those who had given up any further resistance after Pharsalus. He returned to Italy and waited at the southern port of Brundisium for Caesar's eventual arrival. According to Plutarch's story, a meeting that had the prospect of being at least embarrassing for Cicero turned out to be rather pleasant after all. Caesar took Cicero by the arm and walked and talked with him alone. What was said is not recorded, but it seems likely that Caesar told Cicero he was safe so long as he remained out of politics and devoted himself to his scholarly writings. That, in any event, is what Cicero did.

With Caesar in full control, Cicero's letters took on a decidedly reflective tone amid the solitude (*Ad Att*. XII.23) which allowed him to write some of his famous books. At times he and Atticus exchanged two letters a day, but their content has mostly to do with commonplace matters. Cicero writes: "I gather from your letter, as you certainly will from mine, that we neither of us have anything to say. Yet I cannot omit writing to you day after day on the same subjects—now worn threadbare—in order to get a letter from you" (*Ad Att*. XII.27).

As Cicero grew older, the unhappiness of his public life was matched by events in private. Earlier, while in exile and during his term as governor of Cilicia, he wrote many letters to his family. He often mentioned his teenage son, who was with him, and his beloved daughter Tullia. The letters are lavishly sentimental and show Cicero to be a dedicated family man. In a letter written as he began his exile in 58 (*Ad Fam*. XIV.4), he told his wife Terentia that she was the "most faithful and best of wives" and that he wanted to die in her arms. After Caesar invaded Italy in January 49, Cicero, in a letter to "my darlings," had been greatly concerned about what his wife and daughter should do in the event that Rome was taken (*Ad Fam*. XIV.18). As it happened, they came through the Civil War without harm. Later, he changed his mind about Terentia and eventually divorced her.

It was after Cicero himself returned to Italy that his relations with his wife became decidedly cool. On 1 October 47, he wrote his last letter to Terentia. It clearly exhibits the calculated indifference of a doomed marriage.

> I think I shall arrive at my house at Tusculum either on the 7th or the day after. See that everything is ready there. For there will perhaps be several others with me, and we shall stay there a considerable time, I think. If there is no basin in the bath, have one put in: and so with everything necessary for supporting life and health. Good-bye. (*Ad Fam*. XIV.20)

They had had their differences from time to time. He had been especially annoyed by her alleged mismanagement of his affairs while he was governor in Cilicia. Her bad temper seems to have been a continuing complaint. Finally, after thirty-three years of marriage, they were divorced. Cicero then married, in some haste, a much younger woman whose wealth prompted talk about his motives. But gossip aside, the marriage was not a happy one. It failed altogether when his daughter Tullia died and his young wife, Publilia, did not share his deep grief.

For him it was a devastating loss. In his letters to Atticus, Cicero revealed how deeply saddened he was by his daughter's death and sought his friend's help in arranging the purchase of property where there could be planted gardens as a memorial to Tullia. Three letters are almost exclusively on this subject (*Ad Att.* XII.35, 36, 37). The shrine became a kind of foolish obsession with him. It was, in fact, never built.

At the time, no other topic could be said to come close to Cicero's grief over Tullia, but the subject of money did often come up. His divorce from Terentia in 46 meant her dowry had to be paid back, and Tullia's divorce, a year before she died, meant her dowry was due from Dolabella. In such matters installment payments were arranged. There were other finanical matters on Cicero's mind, including rents due him and worries that he would not receive them as they fell due. He also mentioned loans he had made to friends. Finally, he wondered how much money he should send to his son, who was studying in Athens.

Other letters discuss his writing projects. Keeping busy distracted him from his sorrow about the deceased Tullia and the living Caesar. The letters tell how he shifted around the speakers in his dialogues (cf. *Ad Att*. XIII.2). In the following letter to

Atticus he awarded a role to Varro, whom he wished to honor, and who, it might be added, had strong ties to Julius Caesar. He said he did not use living persons in his dialogues, but he made exceptions for himself and Atticus as well as Varro.

> As to Varro, I should not be influenced by the motive you mention, that is, to avoid being thought fond of great men—for my principle has always been not to include any living person among the interlocutors of my dialogues. But as you say that it is desired by Varro and that he will value it highly, I have composed the books and finished a complete review of the whole Academic philosophy in four books—how well I can't say, but with a minute care which nothing could surpass. . . . My five books *de Finibus* were so arranged as to give L. Torquatus the Epicurean arguments, Marcus Cato the Stoic, Marcus Piso the Peripatetic. I thought that could rouse no jealousy, as all those persons were dead. This new work *Academica*, as you know, I had divided between Catulus, Lucullus, and Hortensius. It was quite inappropriate to their characters: for it was more learned than anything they would appear likely to have ever dreamed of. Accordingly, I no sooner read your letter about Varro than I caught at the idea as a godsend. For there could be nothing more appropriate than Varro to that school of philosophy, in which he appears to me to take the greatest pleasure, and that my part should be such as to avoid the appearance of having arranged to give my side of the argument the superiority. (*Ad Att.* XIII.19)

During the years of the Republic, Cicero was the foremost writer on philosophy. Although not an original thinker, he introduced the Roman reading public to Greek ideas. His own preference was for the eclectic, mostly skeptical, position of the Academy in Athens. Yet he found enough to his liking in Stoicism that he often sounded like a Stoic, especially in his *Laws, On Ethics*, and his essays *On Old Age* and *On Friendship*. There is, however, a treatise on the greatest good and the greatest evil (*De Finibus Bonorum et Malorum*), mentioned in the above letter, in which he discusses the pros and cons of the foremost philosophies of the day. In this work he skillfully points out the weaknesses of Stoic doctrine, which he considered to be almost entirely borrowed from earlier thinkers. Still, in his letters, whenever for some reason or another he was out of the heady whirl of politics, the Stoic notion that virtue was the only possession worth having became especially appealing. A paragraph from a letter to A. Torquatus[12] in Athens, written from Rome in January 45, captures that mood.

> Let us then take the view, which reason and truth alike enjoin, that in this life we should not feel ourselves bound to guarantee anything except to do nothing wrong: and that, since we are free from the imputation, we should bear every misfortune incident to humanity with calmness and good

> temper. And so my discourse amounts to this, that, though all be lost, virtue should shew that she can after all support herself. (*Ad Fam.* VI.1)

Sincere as Cicero may have been in writing that passage, it remains true that philosophy was not a way of life for him. In his letters he often showed the unphilosophical side of his character. For instance, it is not pleasing to find him rejoicing over the downfall of a man toward whom he expressed great hatred (*Ad Fam.* VII.2). The practicing Stoic, as he himself said, valued virtue above all else and was unaffected by the loss of material things. But Cicero can be found complaining about one of his slaves who has stolen some books and run off. He was greatly upset about the loss and wanted to have the man returned (*Ad Fam.* XIII.77). His attitude was in sharp contrast with the sayings and the actual life of Epictetus, a Stoic saint, who a century later lived under the most meager circumstances.

Cicero's first interest was politics, and if in these letters there was any living person who came into his thoughts it was Julius Caesar. The times required Cicero to ask for favors, and Caesar had the power to confer them. In a letter to Marcus Marcellus in September 46, Cicero makes a point about the pathetic state of freedom when he writes: "You may not be able, perhaps, to say what you think: you may certainly hold your tongue. For authority of every kind has been committed to one man. He consults nobody but himself, not even his friends" (*Ad Fam.* IV.9).

Consequently, it was a matter of the greatest importance when to write to Caesar, what to write, or whether to write at all. To be on the safe side, he cleared his letters through some of Atticus's friends who were on Caesar's side. Ashamed of having to flatter Caesar, he was nonetheless reluctant to offend him. Yet on the rare occasions when they met in person, all seems to have been congenial enough. In a letter to Atticus, written about three months before Caesar was assassinated, Cicero describes a high-class dinner party which he hosted.

> Well, I have no reason after all to repent my formidable guest! For he made himself exceedingly pleasant. But on his arrival at the villa of Philippus on the evening of the second day of the Saturnalia, the villa was so choke full of soldiers that there was scarcely a dining-room left for Caesar himself to dine in. Two thousand men, if you please! I was in a great taking as to what was to happen the next day; and so Cassius Barba came to my aid and gave me guards. A camp was pitched in the open, the villa was put in a state of defence. He stayed with Philippus on the third day of the Saturnalia till one o'clock, without admitting anyone. He was engaged on his accounts, I think, with Balbus. Then he took a walk on the beach. After two he went to the bath. Then he heard about Mamurra without changing countenance.[13] He was anointed: took his place at the table. He was under a course of emetics, and so ate and drank without scruple and as suited his taste. It was a very good dinner, and well served, and not only so, but

> "Well cooked, well seasoned food, with rare discourse: A banquet in a word to cheer the heart." [Lucilius]

> Besides this, the staff were entertained in three rooms in a very liberal style. The freedmen of lower rank and the slaves had everything they could want. But the upper sort had a really *recherché* dinner. In fact, I shewed that I was somebody. However, he is not a guest to whom one would say, "Pray look me up again on your way back." Once is enough. We didn't say a word about politics. There was plenty of literary talk. In short, he was pleased and enjoyed himself. He said he should stay one day at Puteoli, another at Baiae. That's the story of the entertainment, or I might call it the billeting on me—trying to the temper, but not seriously inconvenient. I am staying on here for a short time and then go to Tusculum. When he was passing Dolabella's villa, the whole guard formed up on the right and left of his horse, and nowhere else. This I was told by Nicias. (*Ad Att.* XIII.52)

Cicero's picture of Caesar in that letter agrees with what we know about the man: urbane, self-satisfied, a man of extraordinary self-confidence, a charming mixture of aloofness and nonchalance. Uninterested in what others thought of him, he was blind to the conspiracy aborning and even dismissed his Spanish bodyguard two weeks before the fatal Ides of March. On that day, accompanied by his chief aide Mark Antony, he made his way to a theater built by his late rival Pompey. It was in the foyer of this building that the Senate planned to meet. By prearrangement, Antony was detained at the door, and Caesar, entering without him, was immediately surrounded by senators whom he assumed to be the usual petitioners. Casca stabbed him first. Then a crowd of sixty senators, daggers drawn, moved in for the kill. He went down with twenty-three wounds, dead at the foot of Pompey's statue. So ended the dictatorship of Julius Caesar. His planned reforms attest to his statesmanship, but he lived only long enough to guarantee a new calendar, which is still being used.

Those who murdered Caesar soon found their deed buried under the many honors paid him after his death. Especially galling to Caesar's enemies was the renaming of the month of Quinctilis for the Julian gens to which Caesar belonged, which of course then became our July. Cicero notes the change in a letter to Atticus (*Ad Att.* XVI.1). He later wrote that Brutus was perturbed enough to refuse to use the new name in his announcements (*Ad Att.* XVI.4).

Whether or not, as it has been said, Cicero "shrieked with joy" upon hearing that Caesar had been assassinated, there can be no doubt how he felt, for he wrote: "But come one, come all, the Ides of March console me" (*Ad Att.* XIV.4). There are similar sentiments in several other letters. They offer a sharp contrast to what Cicero wrote to his friend Servius Sulpicius nearly a year earlier.

Andrea Mantegna (1431–1506), *The Triumph of Caesar,* is one of nine panels. Hampton Court Palace, The Royal Collection, copyright reserved to Her Majesty The Queen. The panels were purchased by Charles I (reigned 1625–1649) to celebrate his personal authority.

> For myself, while I have many reasons for wishing to see you as soon as possible, there is this one especially—that we may discuss beforehand on what principles we should live through this period of entire submission to the will of one man who is at once wise and liberal, far, as I think I perceive, from being hostile to me, and very friendly to you. But though that is so, yet it is a matter for serious thought what plans, I don't say of action, but of passing a quiet life by his leave and kindness, we should adopt. Good-bye. (*Ad Fam*. IV.6)

Apparently Cicero never harbored such soft words for Caesar's mistress, who had been living in Rome. He wrote to Atticus about Cleopatra: "I can't stand the Queen. . . . The Queen's insolence . . . when she was living in Caesar's trans-Tiberine villa, I cannot recall without a pang" (*Ad Att*. XV.15).

Joy at the removal of Caesar was shortlived. After his death, the conspirators, with no plan of action of their own, allowed the reins of power to drift into the hands of Antony, a much less able man. Cicero writes: "Good God, the tyranny survives though the tyrant is dead!" (*Ad Att.* XIV.9). There was great consternation over the way Antony and others masked their own desires under the cover of the dead Caesar's unfulfilled wishes. Cicero was blunt about it: "For measures which Caesar would never have taken or sanctioned are now produced from his forged minutes" (*Ad Att.* XIV.13).

Antony, as consul, wrote to Cicero asking if he would object to the return of Sextus Clodius,[14] son of his old enemy Publius Clodius (*Ad Att.* XIV.13a). The reply by Cicero to a man he greatly distrusted is a prime example of a letter written from a position of weakness. Here are the opening sentences.

> The request you make to me by letter I have only one reason for wishing that you had made personally. For in that case you would have been able to perceive my affection for you not merely by my language, but from my "expression, eyes, and brow"—as the phrase goes. For while I have always loved you—incited thereto at first by your zeal in my service and then by your actual favours—so in these times the interests of the state have so recommended me to you, that there is no one whom I regard with warmer affection. (*Ad Att.* XIV.13b)

But the following day, Cicero wrote to Atticus that Antony was lying about Caesar's interest in the return of young Clodius: "Things which Caesar never intended to do are being done: as in the case of Clodius—in regard to which I have full assurance not only that Caesar was not likely to have it done himself, but that he would have actually forbidden it" (*Ad Att.* XIV.14). When it came to decisions that affected his friend Atticus's financial interests, Cicero was quick to stand by Caesar's intentions. Concerning property Caesar had exempted from being confiscated and given to his veterans, Cicero wrote to a praetor-elect asking him to be sure to honor the provision.

> The fact is that though many of Caesar's arrangements—as was inevitable in the multitude of his occupations—are not now thought good, I am yet accustomed to support them with the utmost vigour for the sake of peace and quietness. I think you ought by all means to do the same, though this letter is not meant to persuade but to prefer a request (*Ad Att.* XVI.16b)

In another letter to a friend of the praetor, written in a similar vein, Cicero referred to Caesar's assassination with unaccustomed subtlety: "After that, as chance would have it, he met with a sudden death" (*Ad Att.* XVI.16C). Indeed!

The mutual respect Cicero had shared with Caesar was altogether missing in his relationship with Antony. But the cordial correspondence over Clodius's son shows that for a time they did behave properly toward one another. It was not to last. More than once Cicero said he wished that Antony had been killed with Caesar. To Gaius Trebonius he wrote: "How I could wish that you had invited me to that most glorious banquet on the Ides of March! We should have had no leavings" (*Ad Fam*. X.28). In a letter to Cassius in October 44, he made an attack on Antony. Again, as in a previous letter, reference was made to Antony's contention that Cicero was the ringleader of the conspiracy to assassinate Caesar.

> He has caused "To the father for his eminent services" to be inscribed on the statue which he has placed on the rostra, so that you are now condemned not only as murderers, but as parricides. But why do I say "you"? Rather I should say "we" are condemned: for that madman asserts that I was the head and front of that most glorious deed of yours. Would that I had been! He would not have been troubling us now. (*Ad Fam*. XII.3)

Actually, Antony was outwardly conciliatory and accepted the decree of amnesty which Cicero proposed, and the Senate approved, on behalf of those who had murdered Caesar. One of the conspirators, Decimus Brutus,[15] was given the governorship of Cisalpine Gaul. Soon afterwards, however, Antony decided he needed this province for his own purposes and was determined to take it back by force. At the same time, the tide seemed to be turning against him. His uneasy truce with the Senate had come to an end because of his spendthrift ways and his unscrupulous habit of handing out favors to his friends. In addition, by the time Antony led his troops northward, late in 44, Cicero had launched his famous *Philippics*, orations in which he sought to rally the Senate, and so the people, against the threat of Antony setting himself up as a dictator. These are among Cicero's best-known speeches, delivered between 2 September 44 and 21 April 43. He named them after similar examples of invective by the Greek orator Demosthenes aimed at Philip the Great of Macedon in the fourth century B.C.

In the spring of 43, in a letter to Decimus Brutus, Cicero urged him to crush Antony immediately. He also commented on the fickleness of the Roman people when they were free to do as they pleased.

> I have received three letters from you on the same day: one a short one which you had intrusted to Volumnius Flaccus; two of greater length, one of which the letter-carrier of Titus Vibius brought, the other was forwarded to me by Lupus. To judge from your letters and from what Graeceius says, the war, so far from being extinguished, is hotter than ever. However, I feel sure that your eminent wisdom makes it clear to you that, if Antony gets any firm foothold, all those brilliant services of yours to the state will come to nothing. For the news that reached Rome, and what everybody

> believed, was that Antony had fled with a small body of men, who were without arms, panic-stricken, and utterly demoralized. But if he is in such a position, as Graeceius tells me, that he cannot be offered battle without risk, he appears to me not to have fled from Mutina, but merely to have changed the seat of war. Accordingly, there is a general revulsion of feeling. Some people even grumble at your not having pursued him: they think that he might have been crushed if expeditious measures had been taken. It is ever the way with a populace, and above all with that of Rome—they vent their freedom without restraint on the very man who secured it for them. All the same, we must take care that there is no just cause of complaint. The fact is this: that man will have finished the war, who has crushed Antony. The point of that remark I would rather leave you to grasp than express it more openly myself. (*Ad Fam.* XI.12)

Despite Cicero's speculations, it had been the arrival in Rome of the eighteen-year-old Octavian, Caesar's grandnephew and heir, that had changed everybody's plans. Cicero at first praised this "fine young fellow" and urged him to assume Caesar's popular role with the Roman people and free the state from the domination of an ambitious Antony. The Senate, under Cicero's spell, having turned against Antony's presumption of power, declared him a public enemy, and when his soldiers were defeated in northern Italy, it appeared that he was finished. Ironically, however, it was the young man from whom he felt he had the most to fear who rescued him. With Antony beaten, neither Cicero nor the Senate felt any great need for Octavian's services. So, sensing he had been used and now rejected, Octavian reversed himself and arranged a partnership with his former rival. The Second Triumvirate, which included Antony's aging ally Lepidus, was given legal status as a result of a law of 27 November 43. Ten days later, on 7 December 43, Cicero was murdered. The shrewd and careful Atticus was spared, but many others would die as the triumvirs settled old scores and rid themselves of enemies, including, if necessary, each other's friends and relatives. Octavian, later in life, spoke of Cicero's great works, but given the bargain at the time, Antony's sworn enemy had to be sacrified.

A bad bargain it turned out to be. Antony, although married to Octavian's half sister, would soon be spending his time in Alexandria with the brilliant and enchanting Cleopatra. This was not the only bad news. His campaign against the Parthians was a dismal failure. Moreover, the generous parceling out of lands to Cleopatra was a betrayal that increased fears at Rome about a wealthy queen's ambitions. Octavian and Antony had on occasion patched up their differences, but eventually that became impossible. In a naval battle at Actium in 31, Octavian's chief military aide, Agrippa, decisively defeated Antony, who then retreated to Egypt and there took his own life. Cleopatra's suicide shortly afterwards foiled a plan to march her through the streets of Rome in chains. Octavian received a spectacular welcome home without her. There was no doubt who was in full control. Lepidus, never very prominent or powerful, retained the harmless post of Pontifex Maximus, the chief priest in Rome. Octavian, surrounded by good advisers, made a series of shrewd moves, including taking over crucial offices and symbolic titles. Finally, in 27, the Senate dignified his position by proclaiming him to be Augustus, a name which acknowledged his special role within the state. His awesome power discouraged dissent. There were no ruthless purges such as had ensnared Cicero. Though never of particularly robust health, Augustus, patient, modest, and in command of all the armies, reigned for forty years as the first emperor of Rome.

The success of Augustus's long reign made the problem of the succession more difficult. Both grandsons who were possible choices died young, and he was finally forced to accept his stepson Tiberius, the son of his third wife Livia, as the heir to his power. The abuses that took place under this sinister and suspicious ruler are well described by the historian Tacitus in his *Annals*.

Tiberius was succeeded by Gaius, better known by his nickname Caligula, who gave all the proof necessary of how wrong succession by heredity could be. There was no release from the whims of such misfits except by assassination. Or suicide: Nero, the last of the Julio-Claudian line, killed himself in A.D. 68.

II
SENECA

Letters Written for Publication

IF the author of the letters in this chapter sounds sour on the human race, perhaps it is because he knew the Emperor Nero so well. Lucius Annaeus Seneca, orator, scholar, and writer of tragedies, was, in fact, Nero's tutor and later rose to prominent posts under his rule. It was in A.D. 54 that Nero, at sixteen, became one of the youngest of the Roman emperors. That regrettable event resulted from his mother, Agrippina the Younger, having married her uncle, the reigning Emperor Claudius, who then adopted Nero, her son by a previous marriage. Nero was even placed ahead of Claudius's own son, Britannicus, to be next in line for power. Later, Claudius may have had second thoughts about that decision, but he was poisoned with a dish of mushrooms before he could make up his mind about it. So Nero succeeded him, and the early years of his reign were respectable enough so long as Seneca and the chief of the palace guard, Burrus, guided his speech and actions. Tacitus said that "Burrus' strength lay in soldierly efficiency and seriousness of character."[1] But sterling qualities could not save either of these prominent aides, and both eventually fell from power. The letters included here were written after Seneca, in his late sixties, had retired from Nero's service.

Seneca was born at Corduba in southern Spain about 4 B.C. and grew up during a time when provincials were becoming increasingly prominent in Roman society. His wealthy father was a leading authority on the history and practice of rhetoric, the art of effective speaking and writing. The elder Seneca was also remembered for having lived an exceptionally long life. Born about 55 B.C., he lived over ninety-two years, until sometime after A.D. 37. By that time his second son was already well known as a writer and, before long, for his involvement in a high-level scandal. The charge of adultery with one of the sisters of the recently murdered Emperor Caligula caused Seneca's exile in A.D. 41.

Seneca returned to Rome in A.D. 49 and, in his early fifties, with the help of

Agrippina, Nero's mother, began a public career. Six years later he was one of the most powerful figures in the imperial household. Among the benefits he enjoyed while in Nero's favor was the honor of a suffect consulship[2] in 56. Through it all his writing continued. He turned out rather ponderous treatises on philosophy and natural science, but on the light side there was a lampoon on the late emperor Claudius which combined poetry and prose. The nine plays Seneca wrote are the only extant tragedies by a Roman author. There are also numerous epigrams among the variety of writings he left, in addition to the letters for which he is best known.

Nero's reign took a downhill slant as soon as the young emperor began to rely on his own unnatural instincts. Then he sought to rid himself of all restraints or opposition: his mother he ordered murdered in 59; Burrus, the palace veteran who had served three emperors, died mysteriously, possibly poisoned, in 62. The following year, Seneca's conscience at last compelled him to withdraw as best he could. Tacitus described a tense scene in which Seneca politely asked the emperor to allow him to retire. Nero pretended to regret the request of his "dearest friend." But Seneca insisted: "I am an old man, unfit even for the lightest task, and I can no longer sustain my own wealth. Take it, let it be administered by your agents, and be incorporated with your property. I am not plunging myself into poverty, but I am dazzled with all you have given me" (*Annals* XIV.54).

Seneca left Rome and rarely returned. In the remaining two years of his life, 63 to 65, he wrote many letters, of which 124[3] to his friend Lucilius have been preserved. Lucilius was a much younger man than Seneca, but there is no reason to see him as a substitute for Seneca's only son, who died in A.D. 41. Their friendship was founded on mutual interests. Lucilius had a fair amount of talent as a philosopher and poet as well as a respectable career in business and public life. He was especially to be admired for how far his abilities had taken him from his obscure beginnings. And, of course, knowing the right questions to put to an older man who is full of answers is a talent that should not go unrewarded. Seneca gave him fame. He said his name would live just as the name of Atticus was kept alive by Cicero's letters. Nero's name is never mentioned, but there is a shadow now and then, especially when Seneca is warning Lucilius about the dangers that come with worldly success. His own experience was likely on his mind when he pointed out what risks had to be taken to acquire money and fame.

It is apparent that the two men had agreed beforehand how their correspondence was to develop. Seneca mentions that it was understood that Lucilius would write the first letters. The younger man would ask the questions and so give Seneca a point from which to launch a letter-essay on some theme dear to his heart. Consequently, the letters, when published, became a series of lessons for future readers. The virtues of the simple life, the evils of luxury, the necessity to overcome the fear of death are familiar subjects, timeless and universal. But he did occasionally write about something unusual. For instance, he said it was only in his lifetime that clear glass had been put in windows. He also had seen the invention of shorthand. But when he wrote about a fire that destroyed the important Gallic city of Lyons, it was not just to comment on a sad event. He used the story to launch a discourse on the need to "fortify our minds against the evils which may possibly come."

Or those already with us. Seneca often complained about the "vices of mankind," which he acknowledged were present in all periods of history. As often happens with age, however, he idealized the past when life was less "complicated." His disgust with the ugly behavior of his own times is evident in the following excerpt, in which he makes the arresting comment that women are adopting men's vices and so beginning to suffer the same ailments.

> People say: "The old-style wisdom advised only what one should do and avoid; and yet the men of former days were better men by far. When savants have appeared, sages have become rare. For that frank, simple virtue has changed into hidden and crafty knowledge; we are taught how to debate, not how to live." Of course, as you say, the old-fashioned wisdom, especially in its beginnings, was crude; but so were the other arts, in which dexterity developed with progress. Nor indeed in those days was there yet any need for carefully-planned cures. Wickedness had not yet reached such a high point, or scattered itself so broadcast. Plain vices could be treated by plain cures; now, however, we need defences erected with all the greater care, because of the stronger powers by which we are attacked. Medicine once consisted of the knowledge of [how] to stop the flow of blood, or to heal wounds; then by degrees it reached its present stage of complicated variety. No wonder that in early days medicine had less to do! Men's bodies were still sound and strong; their food was light and not spoiled by art and luxury, whereas when they began to seek dishes not for the sake of removing, but of rousing, the appetite, and devised countless sauces to whet their gluttony—then what before was nourishment to a hungry man became a burden to the full stomach. Thence come paleness, and a trembling of winesodden muscles, and a repulsive thinness, due rather to indigestion than to hunger. Thence weak tottering steps, and a reeling gait just like that of drunkenness. Thence dropsy, spreading under the entire skin, and the belly growing to a paunch through an ill habit of taking more than it can hold. Thence yellow jaundice, discoloured countenances, and bodies rot inwardly, and fingers grow knotty when the joints stiffen, and muscles that are numbed and without power of feeling, and palpitation of the heart with its ceaseless pounding. Why need I mention dizziness? Or speak of pain in the eye and in the ear, itching and aching in the fevered brain, and internal ulcers throughout the digestive system? Besides these, there are countless kinds of fever, some acute in their malignity, others creeping upon us with subtle damage, and still others which approach us with chills and severe ague. Why should I mention the other innumerable diseases, the tortures that result from high living?

Men used to be free from such ills, because they had not yet slackened their strength by indulgence, because they had control over themselves, and supplied their own needs. They toughened their bodies by work and real toil, tiring themselves out by running or hunting or tilling the earth. They were refreshed by food in which only a hungry man could take pleasure. Hence, there was no need for all our mighty medical paraphernalia, for so many instruments and pill-boxes. For plain reasons they enjoyed plain health; it took elaborate courses to produce elaborate diseases. Mark the number of things—all to pass down a single throat—that luxury mixes together, after ravaging land and sea. So many different dishes must surely disagree; they are bolted with difficulty and are digested with difficulty, each jostling against the other. And no wonder, that diseases which result from ill-assorted food are variable and manifold; there must be an overflow when so many unnatural combinations are jumbled together. Hence there are as many ways of being ill as there are of living. The illustrious founder of the guild and profession of medicine [Hippocrates] remarked that women never lost their hair or suffered from pain in the feet; and yet nowadays they run short of hair and are afflicted with gout. This does not mean that women's physique has changed, but that it has been conquered; in rivalling male indulgences, they have also rivalled the ills to which men are heirs. They keep just as late hours, and drink just as much liquor; they challenge men in wrestling and carousing; they are no less given to vomiting from distended stomachs and to thus discharging all their wine again; nor are they behind the men in gnawing ice, as a relief to their fevered digestions. And they even match the men in their passions, although they were created to feel love passively (may the gods and goddesses confound them!). They devise the most impossible varieties of unchastity, and in the company of men they play the part of men. What wonder, then, that we can trip up the statement of the greatest and most skilled physician, when so many women are gouty and bald! Because of their vices, women have ceased to deserve the privileges of their sex; they have put off their womanly nature and are therefore condemned to suffer the diseases of men.

Gluttony and Other Vices

Physicians of old time knew nothing about prescribing frequent nourishment and propping the feeble pulse with wine; they did not understand the practice of blood-letting and of easing chronic complaints with sweat-baths; they did not understand how, by bandaging ankles and arms, to recall to the outward parts the hidden strength which had taken refuge in the center. They were not compelled to seek many varieties of relief, because the varieties of suffering were very few in number. Nowadays, however, to what a stage have the evils of ill-health advanced! This is the interest which we pay on pleasures which we have coveted beyond what is reasonable and right. You need not wonder that diseases are beyond counting: count the cooks! All intellectual interests are in abeyance; those who follow culture lecture to empty rooms, in out-of-the- way places. The halls of the professor and the philosopher are deserted; but what a crowd there is in the cafes! How many young fellows besiege the kitchens of their gluttonous friends! I shall not mention the troops of luckless boys who must put up with other shameful treatment after the banquet is over. I shall not mention the troops of catamites, rated according to nation and color, who must all have the same smooth skin, and the same amount of youthful down on their cheeks, and the same way of dressing their hair, so that no boy with straight locks may get among the curly-heads. Nor shall I mention the medley of bakers, and the numbers of waiters who at a given signal scurry to carry in the courses. Ye gods! How many men are kept busy to humor a single belly! . . . Do you judge that the corrupted dishes which a man swallows almost burning from the kitchen fire, are quenched in the digestive system without doing harm? How repulsive, then, and how unhealthy are their belchings, and how disgusted men are with themselves when they breathe forth the fumes of yesterday's debauch! You may be sure that their food is not being digested, but is rotting.

I remember once hearing gossip about a notorious dish into which everything over which epicures love to dally had been heaped together by a cookshop that was fast rushing into bankruptcy; there were two kinds of mussels, and oysters trimmed round at the line where they are edible, set off at intervals by sea-urchins; the whole was flanked by mullets cut up and served without the bones. In these days we are ashamed of separate foods; people mix many flavors into one. The dinner table does work which the stomach ought to do. I look forward next to food being served masticated! And how little we are from it already when we pick out shells and bones and the cook performs the office of the teeth!

They say: "It is too much trouble to take our luxuries one by one; let us have everything served at the same time and blended into the same flavor. Why should I help myself to a single dish? Let us have many coming to the table at once; the dainties of various courses should be combined and confounded. Those who used to declare that this was done for display and notoriety should understand that it is not done for show, but that it is an oblation to our sense of duty! Let us have at one time, drenched in the same sauce, the dishes that are usually served separately. Let there be no difference: let oysters, sea-urchins, shell-fish, and mullets be mixed together and cooked in the same dish." No vomited food could be jumbled up more helter-skelter. And as the food itself is complicated, so the resulting diseases are complex, unaccountable, manifold, variegated; medicine has begun to campaign against them in many ways and by many rules of treatment.

The Madness of War

Now I declare to you that the same statement applies to philosophy. It was once more simple because men's sins were on a smaller scale, and could be cured with but slight trouble; in the face, however, of all this moral topsy-turvy men must leave no remedy untried. And would that this pest might so at last be overcome! We are mad, not only individually, but nationally. We check manslaughter and isolated murders; but what of war and the much-vaunted crime of slaughtering whole peoples? There are no limits to our greed, none to our cruelty. And as long as such crimes are committed by stealth and by individuals, they are less harmful and less portentous; but cruelties are practised in accordance with acts of senate and popular assembly, and the public is bidden to do that which is forbidden to the individual. Deeds that would be punished by loss of life when committed in secret, are praised by us because uniformed generals have carried them out. Man, naturally the gentlest class of being, is not ashamed to revel in the blood of others, to wage war, and to entrust the waging of war to his sons, when even dumb beasts and wild beasts keep the peace with one another. Against this overmastering and widespread madness philosophy has become a matter of greater effort, and has taken on strength in proportion to the strength which is gained by the opposition forces.

It used to be easy to scold men who were slaves to drink and who sought out more luxurious food; it did not require a mighty effort to bring the spirit back to the simplicity from which it had departed only slightly. . . . Men seek pleasure from every source. No vice remains within its limits; luxury is precipitated into greed. We are overwhelmed with forgetfulness of that which is honorable. Nothing that has an attractive value is base. . . .

Amid this upset condition of morals, something stronger than usual is needed—something which will shake off these chronic ills; in order to root out a deep-seated belief in wrong ideas, conduct must be regulated by doctrines. It is only when we add precepts, consolation, and encouragement to these, that they can prevail; by themselves they are ineffective. If we would hold men firmly bound and tear them away from the ills which clutch them fast, they must learn what is evil and what is good. They must know that everything except virtue changes its name and becomes now good and now bad. Just as the soldier's primary bond of union is his oath of allegiance and his love for the flag, and a horror of desertion, and just as, after this stage, other duties can easily be demanded of him, and trusts given to him when once the oath has been administered; so it is with those whom you would bring to the happy life: the first foundations must be laid, and

> virtue worked into these men. Let them be held by a sort of superstitious worship of virtue; let them love her; let them desire to live with her, and refuse to live without her. (XCV)[4]

Seneca's denunciation of those who overindulged themselves was perhaps to be expected in view of his own fussy eating habits and, real or imagined, delicate health. His grumpiness about the intemperance of some persons was matched by his poor opinion of the population at large. He quotes the Greek philosopher Epicurus (341 to 270 B.C.): "I have never wished to cater to the crowd; for what I know they do not approve, and what they approve, I do not know" (XXIX.10). What he did know was that they were noisy. The following letter to Lucilius was likely written from an unhappy stopping place during Seneca's travels in the last years of his life.

> Here am I with a babel of noise going on all about me. I have lodgings right over a public bathhouse. Now imagine to yourself every kind of sound that can make one weary of one's years. When the strenuous types are doing their exercises, swinging weight-laden hands about, I hear the grunting as they toil away—or go through the motions of toiling away—at them, and the hissings and strident gasps every time they expel their pent up breath. When my attention turns to a less active fellow who is contenting himself with an ordinary inexpensive massage, I hear the smack of a hand pummelling his shoulders, the sound varying according as it comes down flat or cupped. But if on top of this some ball player comes along and starts shouting out the score, that's the end! Then add someone starting up a brawl, and someone else caught thieving, and the man who likes the sound of his voice in the bath, and the people who leap into the pool with a tremendous splash. Apart from those whose voices are, if nothing else, natural, think of the hair remover, continually giving vent to his shrill and penetrating cry in order to advertise his presence, never silent unless it be while he is plucking someone's armpits and making the client yell for him! Then think of the various cries of the man selling drinks, and the one selling sausages and the other selling pastries, and all the ones hawking for the catering shops, each publicizing his wares with a distinctive cry of his own. (LVI)[5]

Seneca was even more caustic than Cicero when he wrote about the popular gladiatorial shows. In the following letter, he singles out the noon-hour combats as "pure murder" for which there was not even the pretense of a contest.

> You ask me to say what you should consider it particularly important to avoid. My answer is this: a mass crowd. It is something to which you cannot entrust yourself yet without risk. I at any rate am ready to confess my own frailty in this respect. I never come back home with quite the same

moral character I went out with; something or other becomes unsettled where I had achieved internal peace, some one or other of the things I had put to flight reappears on the scene. We who are recovering from a prolonged spiritual sickness are in the same condition as invalids who have been affected to such an extent by prolonged indisposition that they cannot once be taken out of doors without ill effects. Associating with people in large numbers is actually harmful: there is not one of them that will not make some vice or other attractive to us, or leave us carrying the imprint of it or bedaubed all unawares with it. And inevitably enough, the larger the size of the crowd we mingle with, the greater the danger. But nothing is as ruinous to the character as sitting away one's time at a show—for it is then, through the medium of entertainment, that vices creep into one with more than usual ease. What do you take me to mean? That I go home more selfish, more self-seeking and more self-indulgent? Yes, and what is more, a person crueller and less humane through having been in contact with human beings. I happened to go to one of these shows at the time of the lunch-hour interlude, expecting there to be some light and witty entertainment then, some respite for the purpose of affording people's eyes a rest from human blood. Far from it. All the earlier contests were charity in comparison. The nonsense is dispensed with now: what we have now is murder pure and simple. The combatants have nothing to protect them; their whole bodies are exposed to the blows; every thrust they launch gets home. A great many spectators prefer this to the ordinary matches and even to the special, popular demand ones. And quite naturally. There are no helmets and no shields repelling the weapons. What is the point of armour? Or of skill? All that sort of thing just makes the death slower in coming. In the morning men are thrown to the lions and the bears: but it is the spectators they are thrown to in the lunch hour. The spectators insist that each on killing his man shall be thrown against another to be killed in his turn; and the eventual victor is reserved by them for some other form of butchery; the only exit for the contestants is death. Fire and steel keep the slaughter going. And all this happens while the arena is virtually empty.

"But he was a highway robber, he killed a man." And what of it? Granted that as a murderer he deserved this punishment, what have you done, you wretched fellow, to deserve to watch it? "Kill him! Flog him! Burn him! Why does he run at the other man's weapon in such a cowardly way? Why isn't he less half-hearted about killing? Why isn't he a bit more enthusastic about dying? Whip him forward to get his wounds! Make them each offer the other a bare breast and trade blow for blow on them." And when there is an interval in the show: "Let's have some throats cut in the meantime, so that there's something happening!"

. . . A single example of extravagance or greed does a lot of harm—an

> intimate who leads a pampered life gradually makes one soft and flabby; a wealthy neighbour provokes cravings in one; a companion with a malicious nature tends to rub off some of his rust even on someone of an innocent and openhearted nature—what then do you imagine the effect on a person's character is when the assault comes from the world at large? You must inevitably either hate or imitate the world. But the right thing is to shun both courses: you should neither become like the bad because they are many, nor be an enemy of the many because they are unlike you. Retire into yourself as much as you can. Associate with people who are likely to improve you. Welcome those whom you are capable of improving. The process is a mutual one: men learn as they teach. (VII)

Unlike Cicero, Seneca was a professed Stoic and often mentioned his Stoic beliefs, especially the power of reason to triumph over evil. The Stoics had many names for God, and Reason was, in fact, the one most frequently used. The spectacles of the arena did not conform with Reason and so did not come from God. They arose from human passions, as did all evils, which were therefore to be despised.

> Let us strengthen our inner defences. If the inner part be safe, man can be attacked, but never captured.
>
> Do you wish to know what this weapon of defence is? It is the ability to refrain from chafing over whatever happens to one, of knowing that the very agencies which seem to bring harm are working for the preservation of the world, and are a part of the scheme for bringing to fulfilment the order of the universe and its functions. Let man be pleased with whatever has pleased God; let him marvel at himself and his own resources for this very reason, that he cannot be overcome, that he has the very powers of evil subject to his control, and that he brings into subjection chance and pain and wrong by means of that strongest of powers—reason. Love reason! The love of reason will arm you against the greatest hardships. Wild beasts dash against the hunter's spear through love of their young, and it is their wildness and their unpremeditated onrush that keep them from being tamed; often a desire for glory has stirred the mind of youth to despise both sword and stake; the mere vision and semblance of virtue impel certain men to a self-imposed death.[6] In proportion as reason is stouter and steadier than any of these emotions, so much the more forcefully will she make her way through the midst of utter terrors and dangers. (LXXIV.19–21)

Seneca has been accused of hypocrisy because of an obvious contrast between the lofty moral tone of his writings and his self-serving behavior when he was seeking power and wealth alongside Nero. But the letters presented here were written toward the end of his life when his part in the worldly scene was over. Why should he not then, encouraged by weariness as some are, sincerely embrace the virtues he had been extolling for so long? In any event, the letters exhibited great compassion toward his fellow man. For instance, he raised a question we rarely hear asked: How did the gladiators themselves feel?—especially those who did not become popular heroes of the crowd. Seneca described the mental torture of slaves who were being trained to use their swords on each other and reported bizarre episodes in which gladiators committed suicide rather than enter the arena.

> Men of the meanest lot in life have by a mighty impulse escaped to safety, and when they were not allowed to die at their own convenience, or to suit themselves in their choice of instruments of death, they have snatched up whatever was lying ready to hand, and by sheer strength have turned objects which were by nature harmless into weapons of their own. For example, there was lately in a training-school for wild-beast gladiators a German, who was making ready for the morning exhibition; he withdrew in order to relieve himself—the only thing which he was allowed to do in secret and without the presence of a guard. While so engaged, he seized the stick of wood, tipped with a sponge, which was devoted to the vilest uses, and stuffed it, just as it was, down his throat; thus he blocked up his windpipe, and choked the breath from his body. That was truly to insult death! Yes, indeed; it was not a very elegant or becoming way to die; but what is more foolish than to be over-nice about dying? What a brave fellow! He surely deserved to be allowed to choose his fate! How bravely he would have wielded a sword! With what courage he would have hurled himself into the depths of the sea, or down a precipice! Cut off from resources on every hand, he yet found a way to furnish himself with death, and with a weapon for death. Hence you can understand that nothing but the will need postpone death. Let each man judge the deed of this most zealous fellow as he likes, provided we agree on this point—that the foulest death is preferable to the fairest slavery. . . .
>
> . . . .Lately a gladiator, who had been sent forth to the morning exhibition was being conveyed in a cart along with the other prisoners; nodding as if he were heavy with sleep, he let his head fall over so far that it was caught in the spokes; then he kept his body in position long enough to break his neck by the revolution of the wheel. So he made his escape by means of the very wagon which was carrying him to his punishment. . . .
>
> . . . During the second event in a sham sea-fight one of the barbarians sank deep into his own throat a spear which had been given him for use against his foe. "Why, oh why," he said, have I not long ago escaped from all this torture and all this mockery? Why should I be armed and yet wait for death to come?" This exhibition was all the more striking because of the lesson men learn from it that dying is more honorable than killing. (LXX.19–20, 23)

How was Seneca to find an escape from the noise and brutality of the times? Philosophy was the answer. It was his favorite subject and he intended to have his letters "cover the whole of moral philosophy," especially as it pertained to prudent behavior. In all of this there was rarely anything technical. In fact, Seneca mentioned his dislike for those philosophers "who reduce a most glorious subject to a matter of syllables" and "do their best to make philosophy seem difficult rather than great" (LXXI.6). He wanted to be down-to-earth: "I prefer that my letters should be just what my conversation would be" (LXXV.1). Even so, there was at times a literary flavor as in the charming remark that "philosophy is peaceful and minds her own business" (XIV.11).

The moral line in Seneca's writings is familiar. True happiness is achieved by the wise man who seeks a simple life. The fact that Seneca owned a country house which once belonged to Scipio Africanus, the general who defeated Hannibal three centuries earlier and so won for Rome the Second Punic War, needed some explaining. Only a few Romans in any period could have afforded such a country house, so Seneca was at pains to describe the modesty of this one, especially its rustic bath without fancy mirrors. What else to expect from a man such as Scipio, he wrote, who was known "to cultivate the soil with his own hands as the good old Romans were wont to do" (LXXXVI.5)? And how better to insult an unnamed ruler than to praise a much greater man who lived a long time ago?

As usual, the old ways were unappealing to the young looking for something new and exciting. A passage from Seneca to the young Lucilius has a familiar ring: "I warn you . . . not to act after the fashion of those who desire to be conspicuous rather than to improve, by doing things which will rouse comment as regards your dress or general way of living. Repellent attire, unkempt hair, slovenly beard, open scorn of silver dishes, a couch on the bare earth, and any other perverted forms of self-display, are to be avoided. . . . Inwardly, we ought to be different in all respects, but our exterior should conform to society" (V.1–2). How Lucilius responded to this advice is not known, for his letters did not survive.

Seneca thought that the study of philosophy should help us to happiness even if we are poor. His own life went the other way. He became enormously wealthy in Nero's service and at the same time increasingly miserable. As time passed, he seems to have worried more and more about the cruelties inflicted on the less fortunate. In the following letter, he describes the mistreatment of slaves. It should be mentioned that these people were of no particular race or color but were usually prisoners of war, or those born as descendants of captives, and so, the same as persons captured and sold by pirates, kept in servitude. Seneca, given the times, does not attack the ownership of slaves. He owned slaves himself. But the complete letter that follows gives a sorry picture of the degrading circumstances under which some slaves were forced to work in contemporary Roman society.

> I'm glad to hear, from these people who've been visiting you, that you live on friendly terms with your slaves. It is just what one expects of an enlight-

ened, cultivated person like yourself. "They're slaves," people say. No. They're human beings. "They're slaves." But they share the same roof as ourselves. "They're slaves." No, they're friends, humble friends. "They're slaves." Strictly speaking they're our fellow-slaves, if you once reflect that fortune has as much power over us as over them.

This is why I laugh at those people who think it degrading for a man to eat with his slave. Why do they think it degrading? Only because the most arrogant of conventions has decreed that the master of the house be surrounded at his dinner by a crowd of slaves, who have to stand around while he eats more than he can hold, loading an already distended belly in his monstrous greed until it proves incapable any longer of performing the function of a belly, at which point he expends more effort in vomiting everything up than he did in forcing it down. And all this time the poor slaves are forbidden to move their lips to speak, let alone to eat. The slightest murmur is checked with a stick; not even accidental sounds like a cough, or a sneeze, or a hiccup are let off a beating. All night long they go on standing about, dumb and hungry, paying grievously for any interruption.

The result is that slaves who cannot talk before his face talk about him behind his back. The slaves of former days, however, whose mouths were not sealed up like this, who were able to make conversation not only in the presence of their master but actually with him, were ready to bare their necks to the executioner for him, to divert on to themselves any danger that threatened him; they talked at dinner but under torture they kept their mouths shut. It is just this high-handed treatment which is responsible for the frequently heard saying, "You've as many enemies as you've slaves." They are not our enemies when we acquire them; we make them so.

For the moment I pass over other instances of our harsh and inhuman behaviour, the way we abuse them as if they were beasts of burden instead of human beings, the way for example, from the time we take our places on the dinner couches, one of them mops up the spittle and another stationed at the foot of the couch collects up the "leavings" of the drunken diners. Another carves the costly game birds, slicing off choice pieces from the breast and rump with the unerring strokes of a trained hand—unhappy man, to exist for the one and only purpose of carving a fat bird in the proper style—although the person who learns the technique from sheer necessity is not quite so much to be pitied as the person who gives demonstrations of it for pleasure's sake. Another, the one who serves the wine, is got up like a girl and engaged in a struggle with his years; he cannot get away from his boyhood, but is dragged back to it all the time; although he already has the figure of a soldier, he is kept free of hair by having it rubbed away or pulled out by the roots. His sleepless night is divided between his master's drunkenness and sexual pleasures, boy at the table, man in the bedroom.

> Another, who has the privilege of rating each guest's character, has to go on standing where he is, poor fellow, and watch to see whose powers of flattery and absence of restraint in appetite or speech are to secure them an invitation for the following day. Add to these the caterers with their highly developed knowledge of their master's palate, the men who know the flavours that will sharpen his appetite, know what will appeal to his eyes, what novelties can tempt his stomach when it is becoming queasy, what dishes he will push aside with the eventual coming of sheer satiety, what he will have a craving for on that particular day.
>
> These are the people with whom a master cannot tolerate the thought of taking his dinner, assuming that to sit down at the same table with one of his slaves would seriously impair his dignity. "The very idea!" he says.

The letter continues with an account of sudden shifts in fortune. Certain slaves, being sold to a more generous master, might then be granted their freedom. Seneca tells of one freedman who found favor in high places and so was able to snub his original owner. He also recalls how persons of prominence could by chance fall prey to pirates and so become slaves themselves.

> Yet have a look at the number of masters he has from the ranks of these very slaves. Take Callistus' one-time master. I saw him once actually standing waiting at Callistus' door and refused admission while others were going inside, the very master who had attached a price-ticket to the man and put him up for sale along with other rejects from his household staff. There's a slave who has paid his master back—one who was pushed into the first lot, too, the batch on which the auctioneer is merely trying out his voice! Now it was the slave's turn to strike his master off his list, to decide that *he's* not the sort of person he wants in *his* house. Callistus's master sold him, yes, and look how much it cost him!
>
> How about reflecting that the person you call your slave traces his origin back to the same stock as yourself, has the same good sky above him, breathes as you do, lives as you do, dies as you do? It is as easy for you to see in him a free-born man as for him to see a slave in you. Remember the Varus disaster: many a man of the most distinguished ancestry, who was doing his military service as the first step on the road to a seat in the Senate, was brought low by fortune, condemned by her to look after a steading [a small farm], for example, or a flock of sheep. Now think contemptuously of these people's lot in life, in whose very place, for all your contempt you could suddenly find yourself.
>
> I don't want to involve myself in an endless topic of debate by discussing the treatment of slaves, towards whom we Romans are exceptionally arrogant, harsh and insulting. But the essence of the advice I'd like to give is

this: treat your inferiors in the way in which you would like to be treated by your superiors. And whenever it strikes you how much power you have over your slave, let it also strike you that your own master has just as much power over you. "I haven't got a master," you say. You're young yet; there's always the chance that you'll have one. Have you forgotten the age at which Hecuba became a slave, or Croesus, or the mother of Darius, or Plato, or Diogenes? Be kind and courteous in your dealings with a slave; bring him into your discussions and conversations and your company generally. And if at this point all those people who have been spoilt by luxury raise an outcry protesting, as they will, "There couldn't be anything more degrading, anything more disgraceful," let me just say that these are the very persons I will catch on occasion kissing the hand of someone else's slave.

Don't you notice, too, how our ancestors took away all odium from the master's position and all that seemed insulting or degrading in the lot of the slave by calling the master "father of the household" and speaking of the slaves as "members of the household" (something which survives to this day in the mime)? They instituted, too, a holiday on which master and slave were to eat together, not as the only day this could happen, of course, but as one on which it was always to happen. And in the household they allowed the slaves to hold official positions and to exercise more jurisdiction in it; in fact they regarded the household as a miniature republic.

"Do you mean to say," comes the retort, "that I'm to have each and every one of my slaves sitting at the table with me?" Not at all, any more than you're to invite to it everybody who isn't a slave. You're quite mistaken, though, if you imagine that I'd bar from the table certain slaves on the grounds of the relatively menial or dirty nature of their work—that muleteer, for example, or that cowhand. I propose to value them according to their character, not their jobs. Each man has a character of his own choosing; it is chance or fate that decides his choice of job. Have some of them dine with you because they deserve it, others in order to make them so deserving. For if there's anything typical of the slave about them as a result of the low company they're used to living in, it will be rubbed off through association with men of better breeding.

You needn't, my dear Lucilius, look for friends only in the City or the Senate; if you keep your eyes open, you'll find them in your own home. Good material often lies idle for want of someone to make use of it; just give it a trial. A man who examines the saddle and bridle and not the animal itself when he is out to buy a horse is a fool; similarly, only an absolute fool values a man according to his clothes, or according to his social position, which after all is only something that we wear like clothing.

"He's a slave." But he may have the spirit of a free man. "He's a slave." But is that really to count against him? Show me a man who isn't a slave;

one is a slave to sex, another to money, another to ambition; all are slaves to hope or fear. I could show you a man who has been a Consul who is a slave to his "little old woman," a millionaire who is the slave of a little girl in domestic service. I could show you some highly aristocratic young men who are utter slaves to stage artistes. And there's no state of slavery more disgraceful than one which is self-imposed. So you needn't allow yourself to be deterred by the snobbish people I've been talking about from showing good humour towards your slaves instead of adopting an attitude of arrogant superiority towards them. Have them respect you rather than fear you.

Here, just because I've said they "should respect a master rather than fear him," someone will tell us that I'm now inviting slaves to proclaim their freedom and bringing about their employers' overthrow. "Are slaves to pay their 'respects' like dependent followers or early morning callers? That's what he means, I suppose." Anyone saying this forgets that what is enough for a god, in the shape of worship, cannot be too little for a master. To be really respected is to be loved; and love and fear will not mix. That's why I think you're absolutely right in not wishing to be feared by your slaves, and in confining your lashings to verbal ones; as instruments of correction, beatings are for animals only. Besides, what annoys us does not necessarily do us any harm; but we masters are apt to be robbed of our senses by mere passing fancies, to the point where our anger is called out by anything which fails to answer to our will. We assume the mental attitudes of tyrants. For they too forget their own strength and the helplessness of others and grow white-hot with fury as if they had received an injury, when all the time they are quite immune from any such danger through the sheer exaltedness of their position. Nor indeed are they unaware of this; but it does not stop them seizing an opportunity of finding fault with an inferior and maltreating him for it; they receive an injury by way of excuse to do one themselves.

But I won't keep you any longer; you don't need exhortation. It is a mark of a good way of life that, among other things, it satisfies and abides; bad behaviour, constantly changing, not for the better, simply into different forms, has none of this stability. (XLVII)

The charitableness of Seneca's attitude toward slaves endeared him to later Christian writers and even encouraged the notion that he had exchanged letters with St. Paul. But it was philosophy that taught Seneca that man should treasure his own goodness. And if proud of anything, let it be that. Who can rob him of his virtue? But if it be power and wealth he cherishes, then let him beware, for they can be lost, and humiliation and despair will follow. It is a simple message, often repeated. Seneca in his letters says it in many different ways. In the formal sense he was a Stoic, and what is commonly known about Stoicism, a philosophy brought to Rome by Greek teachers, is that it abjures emotions and has a resigned acceptance of what naturally happens to be. There are no surprises from Seneca. His advice is in strict conformity to the Stoic platform. "The question has often been raised," he writes, "whether it is better to have moderate emotions, or none at all. Philosophers of our school reject the emotions." This, he says, is because "Every emotion at the start is weak, afterwards, it rouses itself and gains strength by progress; it is more easy to forestall it than to forego it" (CXVI).

The Stoics had a formula for happiness: "To have whatsoever he wishes is in no man's power; it is in his power not to wish for what he has not, but cheerfully to employ what comes to him" (CXXIII). Here is a familiar aspect of Stoic resignation: happiness is wanting what you already have.

Today, students might accept as quaint a professor's remark that education is to learn how to live and not how to make a living. Seneca was blunt about it: "I respect no study, and deem no study good, which results in money making" (LXXXVIII.1). He would count it of little use for a man to learn how to harness the forces of nature and yet not be able to control his own temper.

In reading Seneca's advice-filled letters it is soon evident how often he repeats himself. He would have defended the repetitiousness as benefiting a good cause. We must be constantly reminded of our own high standards. He writes: "The mind often tries not to notice even that which lies before our eyes; we must therefore force upon it the knowledge of things that are perfectly well known" (XCIV.25). But at one point he decries the learning of maxims, which he calls crutches useful only for those who have not yet acquired the imagination to create sayings of their own. Nevertheless, he continues the practice of adding a maxim at the end of a letter. A good example of one of his "daily gifts," as he calls them, would be his remark, "How closely flattery resembles friendship!"

If there is anything about Seneca's letters that might dampen popular interest it is his preoccupation with death. In fact, at the end of one long discussion of the subject, he wonders if Lucilius might not hate the length of the letter more than he would dying (XXX.18). Nevertheless, he returns to the subject frequently, for as he once announced, "Death is on my trail." It was an event to be anticipated with philosophic calm—a part of nature's plan and so to be accepted without rancour or regret (cf. Cicero's *Essay on Old Age*). The fear of death is what must be conquered. This he qualifies at one point with the frank observation that "the fear of going to the underworld is equalled by the fear of going nowhere" (LXXXII.16). He voiced another familiar Stoic saying when he said that each day should be lived as though it were the last (cf. Marcus Aurelius's *Meditations*). And Seneca wants to be cheerful about it: "Before I became old I tried to live well; now that I am old, I shall try to die well; but dying well means dying gladly." The letter ends with the following words: "I have lived, my dear friend Lucilius, long enough. I have had my fill; I await death" (LXI.4).

Events hastened the day. If Seneca thought withdrawing from the sordidness of

Jacques-Louis David (1748–1845), *The Death of Seneca,* with authorization of Ville de Paris, Musée du Petit Palais, Paris; and the permission of the Artists Rights Society, Inc., New York.

Nero's court was the cure for his troubles, he was soon to discover that the cure could also be fatal. In 65, he was accused of having knowledge of a conspiracy against Nero. It was not true, but he was now out of favor, and the truth didn't count. As it happened to others among Nero's old friends, Seneca was left only with the choice of how to end his life. What he wrote about suicide in this excerpt has therefore a special interest. He was not speaking for himself alone. As mentioned earlier, the Stoics generally approved suicide under the conditions Seneca outlined.

> Frugal living can bring one to old age; and to my mind old age is not to be refused any more than it is to be craved. There is a pleasure in being in one's own company as long as possible, when a man has made himself worth enjoying. The question, therefore, on which we have to record our judgment is, whether one should shrink from extreme old age and should hasten the end artificially, instead of waiting for it to come. A man who sluggishly awaits his fate is almost a coward, just as he is immoderately given to wine who drains the jar dry and sucks up even the dregs. But we shall ask this question also: "Is the extremity of life the dregs, or is it the clearest

and purest part of all, provided only that the mind is unimpaired, and the senses, still sound, give their support to the spirit, and the body is not worn out and dead before its time? For it makes a great deal of difference whether a man is lengthening his life or his death. But if the body is useless for service, why should one not free the struggling soul? Perhaps one ought to do this a little before the debt is due, lest, when it falls due, he may be unable to perform the act. And since the danger of living in wretchedness is greater than the danger of dying soon, he is a fool who refuses to stake a little time and win a hazard of great gain.

Few have lasted through extreme old age to death without impairment, and many have lain inert, making no use of themselves. How much more cruel, then, do you suppose it really is to have lost a portion of your life, than to have lost your right to end that life? Do not hear me with reluctance, as if my statement applied directly to you, but weigh what I have to say. It is this: that I shall not abandon old age, if old age preserves me intact for myself, and intact as regards the better part of myself; but if old age begins to shatter my mind, and to pull its various faculties to pieces, if it leave me, not life, but only the breath of life, I shall rush out of a house that is crumbling and tottering. I shall not avoid illness by seeking death, as long as the illness is curable and does not impede my soul. I shall not lay violent hands upon myself just because I am in pain; for death under such circumstances is defeat. But if I find out that the pain must always be endured, I shall depart, not because of the pain, but because it will be a hindrance to me as regards all my reasons for living. He who dies just because he is in pain is a weakling, a coward; but he who lives merely to brave out this pain, is a fool.

But I am running on too long; and besides, there is matter here to fill a day. And how can a man end his life, if he cannot end a letter? So farewell. This last word you will read with greater pleasure than all my deadly talk about death. Farewell. (LVIII.32–37)

Another letter was devoted entirely to the subject of suicide, including the previously quoted passages on the deaths of gladiators. Seneca anticipated his own death with a reference to Drusus Libo, one of the Emperor Tiberius's victims who was "dead" as soon as he was accused of treason.

Scribonia, a woman of the stern old type, was an aunt of Drusus Libo. This young man was as stupid as he was well born, with higher ambitions than anyone could have been expected to entertain in that epoch, or a man like himself in any epoch at all. When Libo had been carried away ill[7] from the senate-house in his litter, though certainly with a very scanty train of followers,—for all his kinsfolk undutifully deserted him, when he was no longer a criminal but a corpse—he began to consider whether he should

> commit suicide, or await death. Scribonia said to him: "What pleasure do you find in doing another man's work?" But he did not follow her advice; he laid violent hands upon himself. And he was right, after all; for when a man is doomed to die in two or three days at his enemy's pleasure, he is really "doing another man's work" if he continues to live.
>
> No general statement can be made, therefore, with regard to the question whether, when a power beyond our control threatens us with death, we should anticipate death, or await it. For there are many arguments to pull us in either direction. If one death is accompanied by torture, and the other is simple and easy, why not snatch the latter? Just as I shall select my ship when I am about to go on a voyage, or my house when I propose to take a residence, so I shall choose my death when I am about to depart from life. Moreover, just as a long-drawn-out life does not necessarily mean a better one, so a long-drawn-out death necessarily means a worse one. . . . Every man ought to make his life acceptable to others besides himself, but his death to himself alone. . . . The best thing which eternal law ever ordained was that it allowed to us one entrance into life, but many exits. Must I await the cruelty either of disease or of man, when I can depart through the midst of torture, and shake off my troubles? This is the one reason why we cannot complain of life: it keeps no one against his will. Humanity is well situated, because no man is unhappy except by his own fault. Live, if you so desire; if not, you may return to the place whence you came. . . . If you would pierce your heart, a gaping wound is not necessary; a lancet will open the way to that great freedom, and tranquillity can be purchased at the cost of a pin-prick. (LXX.10–12, 14–16)

Seneca was with friends when he received the order from Nero that he must die. The historian Tacitus describes how a doomed man rallied those who where there: "Their tears he checked now by conversation, now by calling them urgently to the need to play the man. 'Where are all the doctrines of Stoicism?' he said; 'or where those resolutions we formulated over the years against the evils which now threaten us? Was anyone unaware of Nero's cruelty? Clearly the man who had murdered his mother and brother could not stop before he had added the death of his tutor and the instructor of his youth'" (*Annals* XV.62).

Seneca severed his veins, but his "body was old, emaciated by long abstinence, and his blood flowed slowly, so he also cut the veins in his ankles and behind his knees." Still, "death was protracted and slow. He asked his physician, Statius Annaeus, a loyal friend of long standing and a skilled doctor, for a draught of poison that had long been prepared. This was the poison (hemlock) formerly used to execute condemned criminals in Athens. It was brought and he drank it, but in vain. His limbs were cold, and his body impervious to the poison's action. Finally, he entered a bath of hot water, sprinkling a few drops on the slaves within reach and saying,

'This water is a libation to Jupiter, the giver of freedom.' Then he was carried into the vapor bath and suffocated in its steam" (*Annals* XV.63, 64). According to his wishes, the body was cremated and there was no funeral.

Nero's own ignoble end came three years later in A.D. 68 when his provincial commanders abandoned him and the Senate declared him a "public enemy." Then he killed himself, not by the order of one man, but, as it were, according to the will of the whole Roman people.

III
PLINY THE YOUNGER

Gentleman and Public Servant

MT. VESUVIUS, 24 August A.D. 79. The volcanic eruption on that date is one of the best-remembered events of Roman times. Three towns were devastated. The excavations and restorations at two of them, Pompeii and Herculaneum, are popular tourist attractions today. Sculptures and paintings from these sites are on display in the National Musuem in nearby Naples. At Pompeii, the exhibits in the local museum include plaster casts that show people and animals as they fell. The letters in this chapter were written by a survivor of the disaster, who describes what he saw and how he felt.

Pliny the Younger (ca. 61 to ca. 120) is so named to distinguish him from his mother's brother, Pliny the Elder (ca. 23 to 79), who wrote the encyclopedic *Natural History*, one of the enduring works of ancient times. On the day of the eruption, the younger Pliny, then seventeen, was with his mother visiting his uncle, the commander of the navy at Misenum, located on the Bay of Naples. It fell upon the elder Pliny to take charge of rescuing victims, but while doing so, he himself, like so many others, died of suffocation. The younger Pliny tells how he and his mother escaped. The letter was addressed to the historian Tacitus, who had written asking for firsthand information.

> For several days past there had been earth tremors which were not particularly alarming because they are frequent in Campania; but that night the shocks were so violent that everything felt as if it were not only shaken but overturned. My mother hurried into my room and found me already getting up to wake her if she were still asleep. We sat down in the forecourt of the house, between the buildings and the sea close by. I don't know whether

I should call this courage or folly on my part (I was only seventeen at the time) but I called for a volume of Livy and went on reading as if I had nothing else to do. I even went on with the extracts I had been making. Up came a friend of my uncle's who had just come from Spain to join him. When he saw us sitting there and me actually reading, he scolded us both—me for my foolhardiness and my mother for allowing it. Nevertheless, I remained absorbed in my book.

By now it was dawn, but the light was still dim and faint. The buildings round us were already tottering, and the open space we were in was too small for us not to be in real and imminent danger if the house collapsed. This finally decided us to leave the town. We were followed by a panic-striken mob of people wanting to act on someone's else's decision in preference to their own (a point in which fear looks like prudence), who hurried us on our way by pressing hard behind in a dense crowd. Once beyond the buildings we stopped, and there we had some extraordinary experiences which thoroughly alarmed us. The carriages we had ordered to be brought out began to run in different directions though the ground was quite level, and would not remain stationary even when wedged with stones. We also saw the sea sucked away and apparently forced back by the earthquake: at any rate it receded from the shore so that quantities of sea creatures were left stranded on dry sand. On the landward side a fearful black cloud was rent by forked and quivering bursts of flame, and parted to reveal great tongues of fire, like flashes of lightning magnified in size.

At this point my uncle's friend from Spain spoke up still more urgently: "If your brother, if your uncle is still alive, he will want you both to be saved; if he is dead, he would want you to survive him—why put off your escape?" We replied that we would not think of considering our own safety as long as we were uncertain of his. Without waiting any longer, our friend rushed off and hurried out of danger as fast as he could.

Soon afterwards the cloud sank down to earth and covered the sea; it had already blotted out Capri and hidden the promontory of Misenum from sight. Then my mother implored, entreated and commanded me to escape as best I could—a young man might escape, whereas she was old and slow and could die in peace as long as she had not been the cause of my death too. I refused to save myself without her, and grasping her hand forced her to quicken her pace. She gave in reluctantly, blaming herself for delaying me. Ashes were already falling, not as yet very thickly. I looked around: a dense black cloud was coming up behind us, spreading over the earth like a flood. "Let us leave the road while we can still see," I said, "or we shall be knocked down and trampled underfoot in the dark by the crowd behind." We had scarcely sat down to rest when darkness fell, not the dark of a moonless or cloudy night, but as if the lamp had been put out in a closed room. You could hear the shrieks of women, the wailing of infants, and the shouting of men; some were calling their parents, others their children or their wives, trying to recognize them by their voices. People bewailed their own fate or that of their relatives, and there were some who prayed for death in their terror of dying. Many besought the aid of the gods, but still more imagined there were no gods left, and that the universe was plunged into eternal darkness for evermore. There were people, too, who added to the real perils by inventing fictitious dangers: some reported that part of Misenum had collapsed or another part was on fire, and though their tales were false they found others to believe them. A gleam of light returned, but we took this to be a warning of the approaching flames rather than daylight. However, the flames remained some distance off; then darkness came on once more and ashes began to fall again, this time in heavy showers. We rose from time to time and shook them off, otherwise we should have been buried and crushed beneath their weight. I could boast that not a groan or cry of fear escaped me in these perils, had I not derived some poor consolation in my mortal lot from the belief that the whole world was dying with me and I with it.

At last the darkness thinned and dispersed like smoke or cloud; then there was genuine daylight, and the sun actually shone out, but yellowish as it is during an eclipse. We were terrified to see everything changed, buried deep in ashes like snowdrifts. We returned to Misenum where we attended to our physical needs as best we could, and then spent an anxious night alternating between hope and fear. Fear predominated, for the earthquakes went on, and several hysterical individuals made their own and other people's calamities seem ludicrous in comparison with their frightful predictions. But even then, in spite of the dangers we had been through and were still expecting, my mother and I had still no intention of leaving until we had news of my uncle.

Of course these details are not important enough for history, and you will read them without any idea of recording them; if they seem scarcely worth even putting in a letter, you have only yourself to blame for asking for them. (VI.20)[1]

Not long after the frightening experience at Vesuvius, Pliny lived through a different kind of danger, one akin to what Seneca had faced under Nero. Now it was the intolerant Domitian who was to be feared. He was the last of the Flavians, a dynasty that began with his father's reign in A.D. 69, the "Year of the Four Emperors" following Nero's suicide. A contest for power had produced three poor choices and one very good one. Galba, a bully, Otho, a weakling, and Vitellius, a glutton, had each had a brief reign and a sudden departure. They were followed by the shrewd Vespasian, who ruled, and ruled exceptionally well, for ten years, from 69 to 79. Vespa-

Angelica Kauffmann (1741–1807), *Pliny the Younger and His Mother at Misenum, 79 A.D.* (1785). The Art Museum, Princeton University. Museum purchase, gift of Franklin H. Kissner. Angelica Kauffmann's records reveal that she composed this scene according to Pliny's description of the event in his letter to Tacitus.

sian, tough-minded and fair, insisted the government be run by competent officials worthy of their pay. He fired the rest.

Falling asleep during one of Nero's musical performances had not endeared Vespasian to his late predecessor, who nevertheless had chosen him to command the Roman forces putting down a revolt in Judaea which began in 66. Even Nero knew that Vespasian was the kind of man to get a job done, and Vespasian was doing that when he was hailed by his troops as the leader most likely to restore order in the troubled aftermath of Nero's death. Vespasian thought so, too. He left his son Titus in charge of the siege of Jerusalem and made his successful bid for power.

Vespasian's rule restored the courts through the example of his own common sense, the treasury by the example of his stinginess, and the moral tone in society by the modest way in which he lived. His no-nonsense management of the government was a product of his experience, which included having once worked as a mule driver. He was not a man to welcome the advice of intellectuals. Bothersome critics, sitting in judgment on those dealing with everyday problems, were sent into exile. Neither his handsome and generous son, Titus, who ruled only a brief two years,

79 to 81, nor his unwholesome son Domitian, who ruled from 81 to 96, were any more receptive to criticism. Domitian was particularly severe, being a less reasonable man than his father and less personable than his brother. Some of his critics were put to death. In the following letter written to the little-known Julius Genitor, Pliny tells how he assisted a mutual friend in trouble when others were afraid to do so.

> The natural generosity of our friend Artemidorus always makes him enlarge on his friends' services, and so he is spreading an account of my merits which is not untrue, but more than I deserve. It is true that, when the philosophers were expelled from Rome, I went to see him in his house outside the city, and as I was praetor at that time the visit involved some risk for the attention it attracted. He was also in need of a considerable sum at the time to pay off his debts contracted in honourable causes; I raised the money and lent it to him without interest, when certain of his rich and influential friends hesitated to do so. More recently I acted again, when seven of my friends had been put to death or banished . . . so that I stood amidst the flames of thunderbolts dropping all round me, and there were certain clear indications to make me suppose a like end was awaiting me.
>
> However, I do not believe I deserve the exaggerated reputation in these matters which Artemidorus gives me: I have not disgraced myself, but that is all. (III.11)

Later, in the same letter, Pliny comments on the philosophers of the time and makes it plain why Artemidorus was worthy of the risk he took on his behalf: "Of all those who call themselves philosophers today, you will scarcely find one with his sincerity and integrity."

Reputation was a matter of the highest importance to Pliny, as is evident in the following reply to a dinner invitation from his prominent friend Catilius Severus.

> I will come to dinner, but only on condition that it is simple and informal, rich only in Socratic conversation, though this too must be kept within bounds; for there will be early-morning callers to think of. Cato himself could not escape reproach on meeting them, though Caesar's adverse comment is tinged with admiration. The passers-by whom Cato met when drunk, blushed when they discovered who he was, and (says Caesar) "You would have thought they had been found out by Cato, not Cato by them." What better tribute to Cato's prestige than to show him still awe-inspiring when drunk! But our dinner must have a limit, in time as well as in preparations and expense; for we are not the sort of people whom even our enemies cannot blame without a word of praise. (III.12).

Pliny took great pleasure in writing letters and eventually decided to publish 247 of them, which appeared in a series of nine books.[2] Here is a letter he used to dedicate them to his friend Septicius Clarus, whom he elsewhere calls "the most genuinely reliable, frank and trustworthy man I know" (II.9).

> You have often urged me to collect and publish any letters of mine which were composed with some care. I have now made a collection, not keeping to the original order as I was not writing history, but taking them as they came to my hand. It remains for you not to regret having made the suggestion and for me not to regret following it; for then I shall set about recovering any letters which have hitherto been put away and forgotten, and I shall not suppress any which I may write in the future. (I.1)

By A.D. 96, the Emperor Domitian had killed so many relatives and associates that those who were left decided to murder him. After he was gone, the Senate, finally given the chance, named one of their own, the aging and respectable Nerva, to take his place. But the psychological scars of the former despotism are clearly seen in the following letter, in which Pliny tells how his senatorial colleagues continued to warn him that he might be speaking too boldly. In the letter, Pliny writes about a speech he made in the Senate attacking Publicius Certus, an "atrocious criminal," during Domitian's reign. He charged him with responsibility in the death of Helvidius Priscus, son and namesake of a famous Stoic philosopher who had been executed earlier.

The letter was to Ummidius Quadratus, a young man active in the courts—too young, in fact, to have known what Pliny said.

> One of my friends amongst the consulars took me aside privately and seriously rebuked me for coming forward too rashly and recklessly, advised me to desist, and added that I had made myself a marked man in the eyes of future Emperors. "Never mind," said I, "as long as they are bad ones." Scarcely had he left me when another began: "What are you doing? Where are you heading? What about the risks you are running? Why such confidence in the present when the future is uncertain? You are challenging a man who is already a Treasury official and will soon be consul, and has besides such influence and friends to support him!"

But Pliny's speech won the day. He writes:

> Almost the entire Senate embraced me with open arms and overwhelmed me with enthusiastic congratulations for having revived the practice, long fallen into disuse, of bringing measures for the public good before the Senate at the risk of incurring personal enmities; I had in fact freed the Senate

> from the odium in which it was held amongst the other classes for showing severity to others while sparing its own members by a sort of mutual connivance. (IX.13)

Pliny was intent on having a useful life, and he could afford to make a choice, having inherited sizable land holdings. He became a skillful lawyer, an expert in finance, who did not charge fees but accepted a case simply on its merit and saw it through court as a matter of public duty. A meticulous attention to detail was matched by fastidiousness in matters of taste. In a long letter he gives many details about a villa he owned at Laurentum, near Ostia, about seventeen miles from Rome. The description was sent to a certain Clusinius Gallus, who is among those friends of Pliny known to us only by such letters. The following excerpts reflect the careful planning which Pliny brought to his endeavors.

> You may wonder why my Laurentine place (or my Laurentian, if you like that better) is such a joy to me, but once you realize the attractions of the house itself, the amenities of its situation, and its extensive seafront, you will have your answer. It is seventeen miles from Rome, so that it is possible to spend the night there after necessary business is done, without having cut short or hurried the day's work. . . .
>
> The house is large enough for my needs but not expensive to keep up. It opens into a hall, unpretentious but not without dignity, and then there are two colonnades, rounded like the letter D, which enclose a small but pleasant courtyard. This makes a splendid retreat in bad weather, being protected by windows and still more by the overhanging roof. Opposite the middle of it is a cheerful inner hall, and then a dining-room which really is rather fine: it runs out towards the shore, and whenever the sea is driven inland by the southwest wind it is lightly washed by the spray of the spent breakers. It has folding doors or windows as large as the doors all round, so that at the front and sides it seems to look out on to three seas, and at the back has a view through the inner hall, the courtyard with the two colonnades, then the entrance-hall to the woods and mountains in the distance.
>
> To the left of this and a little farther back from the sea is a large bedroom, and then another smaller one which lets in the morning sunshine with one window and holds the last rays of the evening sun with the other; from this window too is a view of the sea beneath, this time at a safe distance. . . . Round the corner is a room built round in an apse to let in the sun as it moves round and shines in each window in turn, and with one wall fitted with shelves like a library to hold the books which I read and read again. Next comes a bedroom on the other side of a passage which has a floor raised and fitted with pipes to receive hot steam and circulate it at a regu-

lated temperature. The remaining rooms on this side of the house are kept for the use of my slaves and freedmen, but most of them are quite presentable enough to receive guests. . . .

At the far end of the terrace, the arcade and the garden is a suite of rooms which are really and truly my favourites, for I had them built myself. Here is a sun-parlour facing the terrace on one side, the sea on the other, and the sun on both. There is also a bedroom which has folding doors opening on to the arcade and a window looking out on the sea. . . . When I retire to this suite I feel as if I have left my house altogether and much enjoy the sensation: especially during the Saturnalia[3] when the rest of the roof resounds with festive cries in the holiday freedom, for I am not disturbing my household's merrymaking nor they my work. (II.17)

Pliny did not have the intellect of a Thomas Jefferson, but his villa at Laurentum does bring Monticello to mind. There is the emphasis on the landscape, the careful planning of facilities—the dining rooms, the library. Jefferson and Pliny both sought to combine practicality and civility in a house of great charm. Unlike Jefferson's home, which is today intact and a magnet for tourists, there are only scant remains of Pliny's villa.

In another letter, Pliny states, perhaps too precisely for some ears, what qualities he thinks a good wife should possess. His third wife, Calpurnia, fulfills all his hopes, as is evident in this letter to her aunt, Calpurnia Hispulla.

She is highly intelligent and a careful housewife, and her devotion to me is a sure indication of her virtue. In addition, this love has given her an interest in literature: she keeps copies of my works to read again and again and even learn by heart. She is so anxious when she knows that I am going to plead in court, and so happy when all is over! (She arranges to be kept informed of the sort of reception and applause I receive, and what verdict I win in the case.) If I am giving a reading she sits behind a curtain near by and greedily drinks in every word of appreciation. She has even set my verses to music and sings them, to the accompaniment of her lyre, with no musician to teach her but the best of masters, love. (IV.19)

Pliny tells of his young wife's miscarriage in a letter to her grandfather, Calpurnius Fabatus. There is the hope of children in the future, but that was never to be.

I know how anxious you are for us to give you a great-grandchild, so you will be all the more sorry to hear that your granddaughter has had a miscarriage. Being young and inexperienced she did not realize she was pregnant, failed to take proper precautions, and did several things which

> were better left undone. She has had a severe lesson, and paid for her mistake by seriously endangering her life; so that although you must inevitably feel it hard for your old age to be robbed of a descendant already on the way, you should thank the gods for sparing your granddaughter's life even though they denied you the child for the present. (VIII.10)

Although Pliny and his wife never had any children, he was a generous contributor to the schools of his hometown of Comum. In a letter to the historian Tacitus he stressed the importance of local control of schools and on the matter of hiring teachers wrote: "People who may be careless about another person's money are sure to be careful about their own, and they will see that only a suitable recipient shall be found for my money if he is also to have their own." (IV.18)

A laudable pride in charitable work was a sign of happier times under the Good Emperors of the second century A.D. Especially important was a shift in the official policy of the government towards the poor and other unfortunates. Usually, widespread misery was taken for granted in the ancient world. Those too ill, too old, or too broken in spirit or body to care for themselves were left to the mercies of their relatives or friends, and lacking that sank out of sight, only to be replaced by nameless others. But now the government began to offer help for the destitute, especially children. Earlier, individual benefactors had created what we would call foundations to help those in need. In Nerva's day the emperor himself set the example and so encouraged others to follow his lead. He is credited with initiating a system known as the *alimenta*, which used money from the imperial treasury to make low (5 percent) interest-bearing loans to farmers. The interest earned was channeled by civil servants to those who needed government help to survive. The new imperial policy was a welcome improvement, but it was not entirely for humanitarian purposes. Assisting farmers in Italy gave them a boost in competition with other parts of the empire. Help in the care and nourishment of children would assure healthy soldiers in years to come.

Pliny's own contribution, described in a letter to his friend Caninius Rufus, is evidence of the new interest in caring for less fortunate persons in the population.

> You want my advice on what provision to make for securing now and after your death the money you have offered to our native town to pay the cost of an annual feast. It is an honour to be consulted, but difficult to give an immediate opinion. You might hand over the capital to the town, but there is a danger of its being dissipated. Or you might make a gift of land, but it would be neglected as public property always is. Personally I can think of no better plan than the one I adopted myself. I had promised a capital sum of 500,000 sesterces for the maintenance of free-born boys and girls, but instead of paying this over I transferred some of my landed property (which was worth considerably more) to the municipal agent, and

> then had it reconveyed back to me charged with an annual rent payable of 30,000 sesterces. By this means the principal is secured for the town, the interest is certain, and the property will always find a tenant to cultivate it because its value greatly exceeds the rent charged. I am well aware that I appear to have paid out more than the sum I have given, seeing that the fixed rent charge has reduced the market value of a fine property, but one ought to make personal and temporary interests give place to public and permanent advantages, and consider the security of a benefaction more than one's own gains. (VII.18)

Such generosity was a commendable gesture. At the same time, it is to be noted that Pliny's interest was caring for "free-born boys and girls." Children born into slavery were left out. What did this well-bred and well-read Roman gentleman think about slavery? Here is what he says to a certain P. Acilius, who is known to us only because of the two letters Pliny wrote to him.

> This horrible affair demands more publicity than a letter—Larcius Macedo, a senator and ex-praetor, has fallen a victim to his own slaves. Admittedly he was a cruel and overbearing master, too ready to forget that his father had been a slave, or perhaps too keenly conscious of it. He was taking a bath in his house at Formiae when suddenly he found himself surrounded; one slave seized him by the throat while the others struck his face and hit him in the chest and stomach and—shocking to say—in his private parts. When they thought he was dead they threw him on to the hot pavement, to make sure he was not still alive. Whether unconscious or feigning to be so, he lay there motionless, thus making them believe that he was quite dead. Only then was he carried out, as if he had fainted with the heat, and received by his slaves who had remained faithful, while his concubines ran up, screaming frantically. Roused by their cries and revived by the cooler air he opened his eyes and made some movement to show that he was alive, it being now safe to do so. The guilty slaves fled, but most of them have been arrested and a search is being made for the others. Macedo was brought back to life with difficulty, but only for a few days; at least he died with the satisfaction of having revenged himself, for he lived to see the same punishment meted out as for murder. There you see the dangers, outrages and insults to which we are exposed. No master can feel safe because he is kind and considerate; for it is their brutality, not their reasoning capacity, which leads slaves to murder masters. (III.14)

The harshness of life in ancient times cannot be denied. Still, the British historian Edward Gibbon made a statement, often quoted, about the period which began with Nerva's reign: "If a man were called to fix the period in the history of the world during which the condition of the human race was most happy and prosperous, he would, without hesitation, name that which elapsed from the death of Domitian to the accession of Commodus [i.e., A.D. 96 to 180]."[4] At least so it seemed to one who lived in the eighteenth century. The period Gibbon had in mind, the "Era of the Good Emperors," saw the rule of five reliable men in succession. Each one adopted as his son and successor the best available man for the job.

Earlier, Augustus's bloodline had produced the unstable Caligula. Vespasian had left Domitian in the wings. Nerva, childless late in life, made use of an old Roman custom whereby an older man could adopt another man, already perhaps middle-aged, in order to secure a son to carry on the family traditions. In this fashion, Nerva adopted Trajan, a proven military commander, to help him rule and to take over when he died. There followed Hadrian, Antoninus Pius, and Marcus Aurelius, who succeeded in a similar manner, providing the empire with nearly a century of sensible and dedicated leadership. Marcus Aurelius made the unfortunate mistake of allowing his own son Commodus to succeed him. That ended the fortuitous sequence of good emperors.

The best reason these five emperors ruled so rightly was that each of them wanted to. We know Nerva's successor, Trajan, especially well because the tenth and last volume of Pliny's correspondence consists of an exchange of letters with this emperor, who reigned from A.D. 98 to 117. Of special note is Trajan's statement that "The public interest must be our sole concern." He meant what he said and his actions proved it. That is why he was justified in putting ***Optimus Princeps*** on his coins.

Trajan had chosen Pliny to serve as his special emissary to investigate financial problems in Bithynia, a province in Asia Minor. At times the emperor seems to have grown weary of Pliny's relentless flattery, but an exchange of messages between them shows the cordial tenor of their relationship. The following letters on the employment of slaves and soldiers also typifies the emperor Trajan's close management of distant provincial matters.

Pliny to the Emperor Trajan

I pray you, Sir, to advise me on the following point. I am doubtful whether I ought to continue using the public slaves in the various towns as prison warders, as hitherto, or to put soldiers on guard-duty in the prisons. I am afraid that the public slaves are not sufficiently reliable, but on the other hand this would take up the time of quite a number of soldiers. For the moment I have put a few soldiers on guard alongside the slaves, but I can see that there is a danger of this leading to neglect of duty on both sides, when each can throw the blame on the other for a fault they may both have committed. (X.19)

The Emperor Trajan to Pliny

There is no need, my dear Pliny, for more soldiers to be transferred to guard-duty in the prisons. We should continue the custom of the province and use public slaves as warders. Their reliability depends on your watchfulness and discipline. For, as you say in your letter, if we mix soldiers with public slaves the chief danger is that both sides will become careless by relying on each other. Let us also keep to the general rule that as few soldiers as possible should be called away from active service. (X.20)

Pliny to the Emperor Trajan

Gavius Bassus, Sir, the prefect of the Pontic Coast, has called on me with due ceremony and respect, and has been here several days. As far as I could judge he is an excellent man who merits your kind interest. I told him that you had given orders that he must limit himself to ten picked soldiers, two mounted soldiers, and one centurion from the troops which you had assigned to me. He replied that this number was insufficient and that he would write to you himself; so I thought it best not to recall for the present the soldiers he has in excess of that number. (X.21)

The Emperor Trajan to Pliny

I have also heard from Gavius Bassus direct that the number of soldiers assigned him by my order was inadequate. I have ordered a copy of my answer to him to be sent with this letter for your information. It is important to distinguish between the needs of a situation and the likelihood of his wishing to extend his privileges because of it. The public interest must be our sole concern, and as far as possible we should keep to the rule that soldiers must not be withdrawn from active service. (X.22)

Marcus Aurelius, whose *Meditations* remains a major source on Stoicism, named the high principles which inspired him. But all the Good Emperors, in one way or another, seem to have been touched by a moral standard, whether Stoic or not, which Trajan saw as part of what he called the "spirit of our age." He used that phrase in a letter to Pliny about the treatment of the Christians. In the course of his duties, Pliny thought it necessary to report to Trajan that Christianity, an outlawed sect, was growing in numbers and so posing problems to local communities. He asked the emperor for guidance in the punishment of these recalcitrant citizens. Trajan, while indifferent toward individual beliefs, was insistent on obedience to Roman law, which meant worship of the state gods—a religious act, to be sure, but at the same time patriotic, for the Romans did not tolerate any separation of church and state.

Pliny to the Emperor Trajan

It is my custom to refer all my difficulties to you, Sir, for no one is better able to resolve my doubts and to inform my ignorance. . . .

For the moment this is the line I have taken with all persons brought before me on the charge of being Christians. I have asked them in person if they are Christians, and if they admit it, I repeat the question a second and third time, with a warning of the punishment awaiting them. If they persist, I order them to be led away for punishment; for, whatever the nature of their admission, I am convinced that their stubbornness and unshakeable obstinacy ought not to go unpunished. There have been others similarly fanatical who are Roman citizens. I have entered them on the list of persons to be sent to Rome for trial.

Now that I have begun to deal with this problem, as so often happens, the charges are becoming more widespread and increasing in variety. An anonymous pamphlet has been circulated which contains the names of a number of accused persons. Amongst these I considered that I should dismiss any who denied that they were or ever had been Christians when they had repeated after me a formula of invocation to the gods and had made offerings of wine and incense to your statue (which I had ordered to be brought into court for this purpose along with the images of the gods), and furthermore had reviled the name of Christ: none of which things, I understand, any genuine Christian can be induced to do.

Others, whose names were given to me by an informer, first admitted the charge and then denied it; they said that they had ceased to be Christians two or more years previously, and some of them even twenty years ago. They all did reverence to your statue and the images of the gods in the same way as the others, and reviled the name of Christ. They also declared that the sum total of their guilt or error amounted to no more than this: they had met regularly before dawn on a fixed day to chant verses alternately amongst themselves in honour of Christ as if to a god, and also to bind themselves by oath, not for any criminal purpose, but to abstain from theft, robbery, and adultery, to commit no breach of trust and not to deny a deposit when called upon to restore it. After this ceremony it had been their custom to disperse and reassemble later to take food of an ordinary, harmless kind; but they had in fact given up this practice since my edict, issued on your instructions, which banned all political societies. This made me decide it was all the more necessary to extract the truth by torture from two slave-women, whom they call deaconesses. I found nothing but a degenerate sort of cult carried to extravagant lengths.

I have therefore postponed any further examination and hastened to consult you. The question seems to me to be worthy of your consideration, especially in view of the number of persons endangered; for a great many individuals of every age and class, both men and women, are being brought to trial, and this is likely to continue. It is not only the towns, but villages and rural districts too which are infected through contact with this wretched cult. I think though that it is still possible for it to be checked and directed to better ends, for there is no doubt that people have begun to throng the temples which had been almost entirely deserted for a long time; the sacred rites which had been allowed to lapse are being performed again, and flesh of sacrificial victims is on sale everywhere, though up till recently scarcely anyone could be found to buy it. It is easy to infer from this that a great many people could be reformed if they were given an opportunity to repent. (X.96)

Trajan's answer is one of the most famous letters of ancient times.

THE EMPEROR TRAJAN TO PLINY

You have followed the right course of procedure, my dear Pliny, in your examination of the cases of persons charged with being Christians, for it is impossible to lay down a general rule to a fixed formula. These people must not be hunted out; if they are brought before you and the charge against them is proved, they must be punished, but in the case of anyone who denies that he is a Christian, and makes it clear that he is not by offering prayers to our gods, he is to be pardoned as a result of his repentance however suspect his past conduct may be. But pamphlets circulated anonymously must play no part in any accusation. They create the worst sort of precedent and are quite out of keeping with the spirit of our age. (X.97)[5]

The problem of the Christians was exceptional. Most of Pliny's questions had to do with fiscal management, and Trajan's replies had the force of law. The last time an assembly met to pass legislation was under Nerva. Over the years, the emperor's opinions became final.

PLINY TO THE EMPEROR TRAJAN

The theatre at Nicaea, Sir, is more than half built but is still unfinished, and has already cost more than ten million sesterces, or so I am told–I have not yet examined the accounts. I am afraid it may be money wasted. The building is sinking and showing immense cracks, either because the soil is damp and soft or the stone used was poor and friable. We shall certainly have to consider whether it is to be finished or abandoned, or even demolished, as the foundations and substructure intended to hold up the building may have cost a lot but look none too solid to me. There are many additions to the theatre promised by private individuals, such as a colonnade on either side and a gallery above the auditorium, but all these are now held up by the stoppage of work on the main building which must be finished first.

The citizens of Nicaea have also begun to rebuild their gymnasium (which was destroyed by fire before my arrival) on a much larger and more extensive scale than before. They have already sent a large sum, which may be to little purpose, for the buildings are badly planned and too scattered.

Moreover, an architect—admittedly a rival of the one who drew up the designs—has given the opinion that the walls cannot support the superstructure in spite of being twenty-two feet thick, as the rubble core has no facing of brick.

The people of Claudiopolis are also building, or rather excavating, an enormous public bath in a hollow at the foot of a mountain. The money for this is coming either from the admission fees already paid by the new members of the town council elected by your gracious favor, or from what they will pay at my demand. So I am afraid there is misapplication of public funds at Nicaea and abuse of your generosity at Claudiopolis, though this should be valued above any money. I am therefore compelled to ask you to send out an architect to inspect both theatre and bath and decide whether it will be more practicable, in view of what has already been spent, to keep to the original plans and finish both buildings as best we can, or to make any necessary alterations and changes of site so that we do not throw away more money in an attempt to make some use of the original outlay. (X.39)

The Emperor Trajan to Pliny

The future of the unfinished theatre at Nicaea can best be settled by you on the spot. It will be sufficient for me if you let me know your decision. But, once the main building is finished, you will have to see that private individuals carry out their promises of adding to the theatre.

These poor Greeks all love a gymnasium; so it may be that they were too ambitious in their plans at Nicaea. They will have to be content with one which suits their real needs.

As for the bath at Claudiopolis, which you say has been started in an unsuitable site, you must decide yourself what advice to give. You cannot lack architects: every province has skilled men trained for this work. It is a mistake to think they can be sent out more quickly from Rome when they usually come to us from Greece. (X.40)

Evident in the following messages is the famed Roman priority of law and order.

Pliny to the Emperor Trajan

It was a very wise move, Sir, to direct the distinguished senator Calpurnius Macer to send a legionary centurion to Byzantium. Would you now consider giving the same assistance to Juliopolis? Being such a small city it feels its burden heavy, and finds its wrongs the harder to bear as it is unable to prevent them. Any relief you grant to Juliopolis would benefit the whole province, for it is a frontier town of Bithynia with a great deal of traffic passing through it. (X.77)

The Emperor Trajan to Pliny

Byzantium is in an exceptional position, with crowds of travellers pouring into it from all sides. That is why I thought I ought to follow the practice of previous reigns and give its magistrates support in the form of a garrison under a legionary centurion. If I decide to help Juliopolis in the same way I shall burden myself with a precedent, for other cities, especially the weaker ones, will expect similar help. I rely on you, and am confident that you will be active in every way to ensure that the citizens are protected from injustice.

If people commit a breach of the peace they must be arrested at once; and, if their offences are too serious for summary punishment, in the case of soldiers you must notify their officers of what is found against them, while you may inform me by letter in the case of persons who are passing through on their way back to Rome. (X.78)

The everyday problems mentioned in these letters were somewhat overshadowed by the great wars of Trajan's regime. He alone of the Good Emperors had an aggressive foreign policy. His Dacian Wars added to the empire territory beyond the Danube, roughly modern Romania, which remained in Roman hands until 270. But annexations in the east, such as Armenia and Mesopotamia, did not long survive him. His plans were disrupted by a revolt of several Jewish communities in the empire, which coincided with renewed Parthian resistance during his eastern campaigns. These problems were part of the legacy left to his successor Hadrian. Trajan, with his health failing, was en route back to Rome when he died in Cilicia in 117. Pliny had died about four or five years earlier, probably still in the province of Bithynia.

In Pliny's letters to Trajan there is a noticeable obsequiousness. Obviously, he felt indebted to the emperor for having singled him out as a trusted aide. But in the end, it was the emperor who owed a debt to this avid letter writer, whose published correspondence fixed for all time Trajan's reputation as a just and wise ruler.

IV
LOST LETTERS FOUND BY ARCHAEOLOGISTS

Egyptian Papyri

THE letters of Cicero, Seneca, and Pliny were consciously preserved, but those written by less prominent persons, among them ordinary businessmen, housewives, farmers, or soldiers, simply disappeared. Not all of them, however, were destroyed. Most of those that have survived come from Egypt. There, the indigenous papyrus plant supplied raw material for making paper, and the dry sands provided the major means of preserving it. Some letters had been thrown away, buried in trash heaps, and were recovered during modern excavations. Other papyri were preserved by having been used for mummy wrappings of either humans or animals. It is therefore by chance that letters written by ordinary people to their friends, relatives, or, sometimes, officials, have survived. Given the circumstances, most of the letters cited here cannot be dated more specifically than to the second century A.D. or even within the second and third centuries combined. But the dating seems incidental when for the most part what they say touches on human interests that are timeless.

A letter of recommendation or a letter asking for the payment of a debt is not unusual. Nor are letters reporting on the health of a member of the family: "With the help of the gods our sister has taken a turn for the better" (136).[1] In a letter about someone less fortunate, the problem of how to bury the dead comes up, and, importantly, who will pay for it. Thus an official of a small town writes to relatives of the deceased: "And I am much surprised that you departed for no good reason without taking the body of your brother, but collected all that he possessed and so departed. And from this I see that you did not come up for the sake of the dead, but for the sake of his effects" (157). Along with the letter, he ships them the brother's body and a list of expenses.

Although not mentioned in the above letters, the hope that a dear one escapes harm by the "evil eye" is a frequent wish. But there is practical advice, too. A certain Paniscus wrote to his wife: "Bring with you your gold ornaments, but do not wear them on the boat" (155).

The best-known letter in this collection is likely the one from a "prodigal son" to his mother.

> Antonius Longus to Nilous his mother very many greetings. I pray always for your health; every day I make supplication for you before the lord Serapis. I would have you know that I did not expect that you were going up to the metropolis (Arsinoe); for that reason I did not come to the city myself. I was ashamed to come to Karanis[2] because I go about in filth. I wrote to you that I am naked. I beg you, mother, be reconciled to me. Well, I know what I have brought on myself. I have received a fitting lesson. I know that I have sinned. I heard from . . . who found you in the Arsinoite nome, and he has told you everything correctly. Do you not know that I would rather be maimed than feel that I still owe a man an obol? . . . [Addressed] To Nilous his mother from Antonius her son. (120)

There is another letter from someone else down on his luck who tells of his desire to get his clothing and jewelry out of a pawnshop (131). At the upper end of the social scale, major landowners wrote frequently, and at times threateningly, to those managing their properties. A number of such letters, even at times from the same person, have been found (142–145).

Who has not occasionally been lax in answering a letter or perhaps complained about another's shortcoming? One gentleman, Theoninus, even becomes testy about it to his friend Didymus: "For though I have often written to you and sent you papyrus for letter-writing to enable you to write to me, you have never deigned to remember me in any way; but evidently your pride in your wealth and the great abundance of your possessions makes you look down on your friends" (147).

In contrast to such neglect, the letters between soldiers and sailors and their families abound with affection. A young recruit in service in the fleet at Misenum (where Pliny was visiting when his uncle died) wrote this reassuring message to his mother:

> Apollinarius to Taesis, his mother and lady, many greetings. Before all I pray for your health. I myself am well and make supplication for you before the gods of this place. I wish you to know, mother, that I arrived in Rome in good health on the 25th of the month Pachon and was posted to Misenum, though I have not yet learned the name of my company;[3]

for I have not gone to Misenum at the time of writing this letter. I beg you then, mother, look after yourself and do not worry about me; for I have come to a fine place. Please write me a letter about your welfare and that of my brothers and of all your folk. And whenever I find a messenger I will write to you; never will I be slow to write. Many salutations to my brothers and Apollinarius and his children and Karalas and his children. I salute Ptolemaeus and Ptolemais and her children and Heraclous and her children. I pray for your health. [Addressed] Deliver at Karanis to Taesis, from her son Apollinarius of Misenum. (111)

Grain shipments to Rome from Egypt were crucial to the welfare of the city, and the subject was frequently mentioned by the high and mighty, but what a sailor was thinking about is evident in the following letter.

Irenaeus to Apollinarius his dearest brother many greetings. I pray continually for your health, and I myself am well. I wish you to know that I reached land on the 6th of the month Epeiph [early July] and we unloaded our cargo on the 18th of the same month. I went up to Rome on the 25th of the same month and the place welcomed us as the god willed, and we are daily expecting our discharge, it so being that up till today nobody in the corn fleet has been released. Many salutations to your wife and to Serenus and to all who love you, each by name. Goodbye. Mesore 9 [early August]. [Addressed] to Apollinarius from his brother Irenaeus. (113)

The families at home fretted over their men in service. Aline writes from Hermoupolis to her husband (she calls him brother) who has gone off to fight in the terrible civil war of 115 to 117. She can hardly eat or drink for worry over him.

Aline to Apollonios her brother greetings. I am terribly anxious about you because of what they say about what is happening, and because of your sudden departure. I take no pleasure in food or drink, but stay awake continually night and day with one worry, your safety. Only my father's care revives me and, as I hope to see you safe, I would have lain without food on New Year's Day, had my father not come and forced me to eat. I beg you to keep yourself safe, and not to go into danger without a guard. Do the same as the strategos here, who puts the burden on his officers . . . [The remainder of the letter is fragmentary].[4]

Bar Kokhba

It is rare to find papyri preserved away from the dry climate of Egypt, but in 1960, letters, neatly folded in a packet, were found in a cave not far from the Dead

Sea. They had been written in Judaea at the time of the Bar Kokhba revolt, 132–135. Opening these historic documents was a cautious undertaking, for some of the papyri, being brittle, broke where they had been folded.

Trajan's aggressive foreign policy in the early second century was reversed by his successor Hadrian, who sought secure frontiers rather than expansion. Where a boundary was missing he built one. Hadrian's Wall defended the Roman province in Britain. Nevertheless, there were wars to be fought inside the fixed perimeters of the empire, and the most serious one broke out in the province of Judaea.

Pompey, in 63 B.C., had made the first direct Roman intervention into Jewish affairs. His campaign in the east aimed at establishing peace everywhere. The subjugation of Syria put an end to the war-torn remnants of the Seleucid Empire. Next, he arrived in the Jewish homeland to find two brothers locked in a bitter contest to decide which of them would succeed their parents. Alexander Jannaeus had reigned as king and high priest from 103 to 76 B.C. and was succeeded by his widow, Salome Alexandra, who was queen from 76 to 69 B.C.. After a three-month siege, Pompey gained control of the temple and then decided that the elder brother, Hyrcanus, should be the high priest. He took the younger brother, Aristobulus, back to Rome where he would be a prominent prisoner in a triumphal parade.

Thus were the Jews drawn within the encircling arm of Roman protection. It was not until A.D. 6, however, that the area including Judaea, Samaria, and Idumaea formally became a Roman province under the name Judaea. Because it was a small domain, of no great strategic or economic importance to Rome, the procurators sent out to rule the land were not top career men, experienced in foreign service, but second-raters, and avaricious as well. Such officials were not likely to be sensitive to the strong religious convictions of the Jews, and that in itself was a cause for trouble.

Sporadic uprisings took place, usually fueled by a strong desire for independence by nationalist groups. In addition, as in other provinces, there were unresolved economic and social problems that produced constant turmoil. Intermittent violence foreshadowed a major revolt which evoked the wrath of the Romans and led to the destruction of Jerusalem and its temple, A.D. 66 to 70, by the future emperor Vespasian and his son Titus. The end of that story was told by the late Yigael Yadin, a famed Israeli soldier-statesman and archaeologist, in his book *Masada: Herod's Fortress and the Zealot's Last Stand*. By the time that book was published in 1966, Yadin and his colleagues had made other remarkable finds. They included the letters of Bar Kokhba, who was the leader of the second war against Rome during Hadrian's reign.

References to this event in ancient literature are difficult to assess and have provoked much controversy among modern scholars. The fullest account comes from a third-century Roman historian, Dio Cassius. He says that Hadrian made an already difficult situation worse by certain of his own acts. His decisions to build a pagan shrine on the site of the destroyed Temple and to rename Jerusalem Aelia Capitolina (his own name being Publius Aelius Hadrianus) were not designed to win friends. He also issued an edict against circumcision, which he considered to be a form of mutilation. This was another serious offense to the Jews, even if not aimed specifically at them.

Jewish bands had probably been secretly preparing for some time, and initially they gained surprising success against the Romans. Bar Kokhba was able to drive the Romans from Jerusalem, to declare Judaea independent, and even to mint his own coins, many of which have survived. However, by 135, Rome had gathered a large army, which under the command of Julius Severus, former governor of Britain and probably Hadrian's best commander, systematically devastated the towns and farms of Judaea, finally forcing Bar Kokhba into the fortress of Bethar, a few miles from Jerusalem. Bar Kokhba was killed when Bethar fell amidst great slaughter in August 135. Dio Cassius reports that hundreds of towns were destroyed in the war and hundred of thousands of people slain. Because of the heavy losses in his own army, the Emperor Hadrian omitted the customary salutation, "I and the legions are well," from his report to the Senate.

As in the first revolt, some survivors of the Romans' wrath fled to caves for refuge and there, in defiance, died, possibly of starvation in 135. It is surmised that a woman had taken with her a basket of belongings, which included letters sent to her husband. Fifteen of them were dictated by Bar Kokhba to a variety of scribes writing in Aramaic and Hebrew, some of whom named themselves. There is no letter actually signed by Bar Kokhba.

The terseness with which these despatches were written reflects the tenor of a losing cause and also apparently the manner of the man Bar Kokhba himself. In his book on Bar Kokhba Yigael Yadin says: "The letters are the most personal and direct evidence concerning Bar Kokhba and his relations with his subordinates."[5] His real name, as the letters show, was Simeon ben Kosiba. Bar Kokhba was a nickname meaning "Son of a Star."

Religious life went on despite the hardships of war. Bar Kokhba ordered the provision of palm branches, citrons (fruit greatly resembling the lemon, with a sweet smell and a tart taste), myrtles, and willow branches, all used in the ritual of the Feast of Succoth (Tabernacles). Palm branches and citrons were featured on some of Bar Kokhba's coins. The following letters seems to be from the last year of the war. There is a shortage of beasts of burden in the camp.

> Simeon to Judah ben Menashe to the town of Aravya. I have sent you two donkeys which you will send with two men to Jonathan ben Baian and to Masabalah, who will pack and send to your camp palm branches and citrons. Now you send others of your men to bring you myrtles and willows. Tithe them and send them to the camp for the troops are many. Be at peace.[6]

The letters Yadin found are similar to another cache of messages discovered in a different cave by Pere R. deVaux and published by one of his colleagues, Father

J. T. Milik.[7] These letters from Bar Kokhba had been sent to a certain Yeshua ben Galgoula, who had been in command of a nearby camp. The following brief statement speaks for an abrupt, soldierly man whose orders were blunt and often accompanied by threats of punishment.

> From Simeon ben Kosiba to Yeshua ben Galgoula and to the men of the town, Peace; I call Heaven to witness that unless you mobilize the men from Galilee who are with you, I will put you in irons as I did to ben Aflul.

During the last stages of a war he was losing, Bar Kokhba seems to exhibit a very human reaction to his frustration and disappointment by striking out at those who did not help.

> From Simeon ben Kosiba to the men of Ein Gedi, to Masabala and to Jonathan ben Baian, Peace. You are sitting in comfort, eating and drinking from the property of the house of Israel without concern for your brothers.

Britain

About A.D. 80 the Romans built a fort, Vindolanda, in northern England. Some forty years later, in need of greater security against marauders headed south, a great wall was constructed just to the north of this fort during the reign of the Emperor Hadrian. By that time at Vindolanda, many letters, written in ink on almost paper-thin wooden tablets, had been received and eventually discarded. So, as in Egypt, the residents left a rich legacy in their trash heaps and sewerage drains. With only a small area of the site as yet uncovered since excavation work began in 1973, it is likely that a great many letters remain buried. Most of those that have been found, written on alder or birch wood, are fragmented, useful largely for what they contribute to the history of Roman handwriting and to several matters of Latin language. There is, however, among the letters found in August 1988, one which runs to 45 lines. It has received considerable publicity, not only for its length, but for revealing comments on times in northern England for which there is no other documentation. As elsewhere, it is obvious that peace was the first priority of the Roman occupation. Their marvelous skill at building roads would follow. Thus the writer of this letter complains about poor roads, which prevent the prompt delivery of goods already paid for. A passage from a different letter, very fragmented, reveals that soldiers in the fort would be awaiting the arrival of daily necessities.

> I have sent [?] you . . . pairs of socks from Sattua two pairs of sandals and two pairs of underpants, two pairs of sandals . . . Greet . . . Elpis . . . Tetricus and all your messmates with whom I hope that you live in the greatest good fortune.[8]

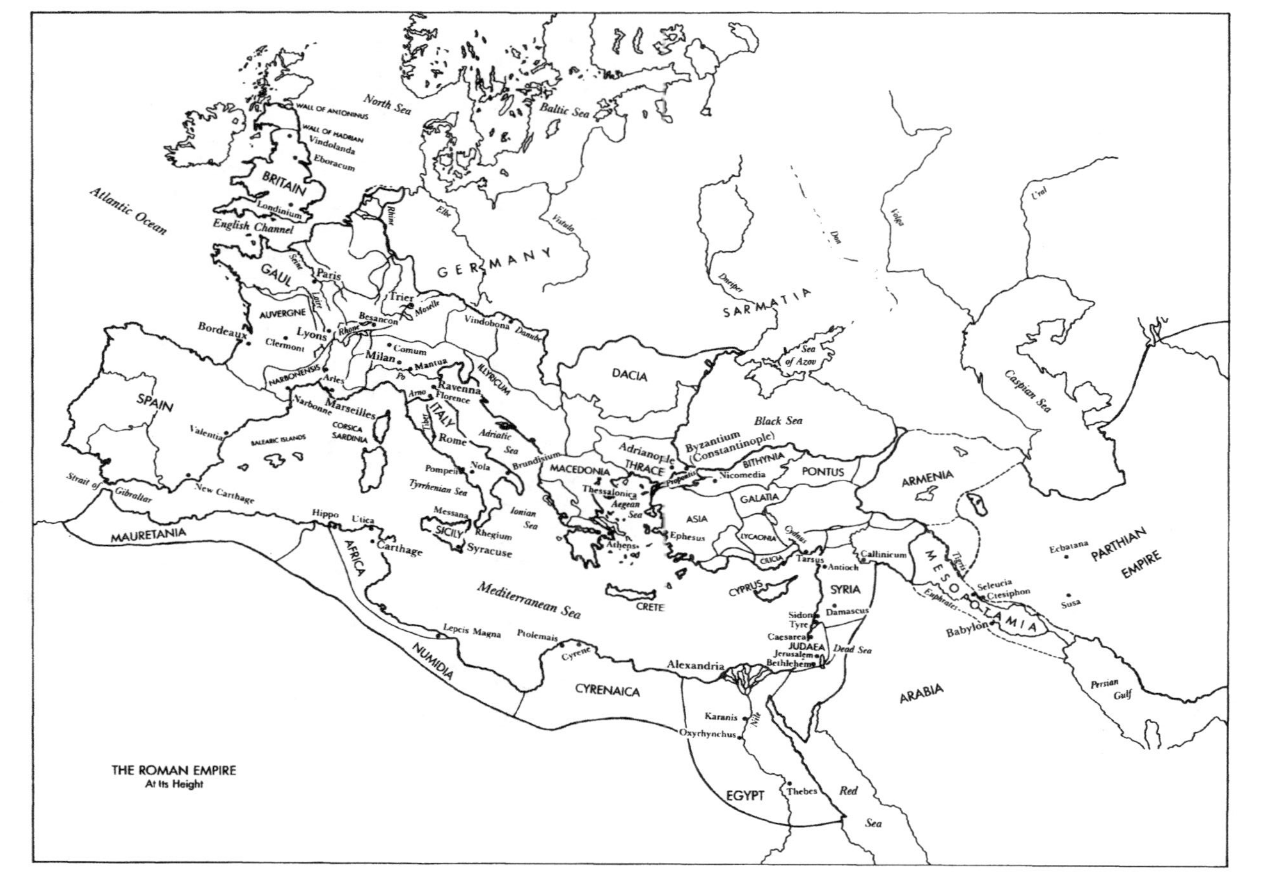

THE ROMAN EMPIRE
At Its Height

As is to be expected, many of the letters speak primarily of routine military matters and there are a number of persons named, including the Roman governor of Britain in the early second century, Lucius Neratius Marcellinus. For all of that, Vindolanda was still home to the women who lived there, and one of them, the wife of the commandant, sent a gracious letter inviting a lady friend of hers to a birthday party. Good wines were something else getting through on those bad roads. Life, then, even on the frontier, went on as elsewhere. The biggest surprise perhaps is the number of people in Britain who could read and write. This is seen in the number of different hands of varying quality in evidence on the tablets—a fact, alas, which adds to the difficulties of those who would seek to publish them.

V
FRONTO

Teacher of Emperors

IT was only incidental to Seneca's fame that he was the tutor of one of the worst of the Roman emperors. Marcus Cornelius Fronto (ca. A.D. 100 to ca. 166) would scarcely be remembered at all had he not been a teacher of one of the best. Among his letters are 143 exchanged with Marcus Aurelius, mentioned in the previous chapter as one of the Good Emperors. He was the much celebrated philosopher-king who reigned from 161 until his death in 180. As a boy, Marcus was tutored by Fronto, the leading orator of his day. In fact, most of the letters sent to Marcus were written while he was still a student, and only a few after he became emperor. Fronto was also the teacher of Marcus's half-brother Lucius and wrote to him and to a number of friends including the historian Appian.

Marcus Aurelius and Lucius Verus were the adopted sons of the Emperor Antoninus Pius, whose long reign lasted from 138 to 161. He was called Pius because of his respect, or piety, toward the Emperor Hadrian, who had previously adopted him. In gratitude, Antoninus persuaded a reluctant Senate to deify his "father," and he built a temple in Hadrian's honor. Such a show of loyalty was a sign of stability, the watchword of Antoninus's reign. Even before Hadrian died in 138, continuity was guaranteed for a second generation when Antoninus adopted Marcus, his wife's nephew, and also took as a co-heir a younger boy, Lucius Verus (A.D. 130 to 169), the son of the man whom Hadrian had first chosen to succeed him but who died shortly thereafter. Given these plans for leadership it was to be expected that the education of the young princes would be the best available. Fronto was a man careful with his own words and quick to correct the speech of others. But there was a kindly, even sentimental, gentleman inside the armor of this stout defender of the Latin language. That Marcus Aurelius and Lucius Verus greatly admired and respected him is evident in their correspondence.

In the early nineteenth century, these letters were found on palimpsests, the products of busy monks who, being short of paper, added a second text to a page by turning it upside down and writing over the previous script. By this means records of the Council of Chalcedon in A.D. 451 were written on parchment leaves that already contained copies of Fronto's letters. It is not known who preserved the originals after Fronto's death, but it is believed likely that it was his son-in-law, of whom he was fond. Worn and faded with age, Fronto's letters were first discovered in the Ambrosian Library in Milan. Later, more of them were found in the Vatican Library.

Fronto was born in the Numidian town of Cirta (modern Constantine in Algeria) early in Trajan's reign. Exactly when he moved to Rome is not known, but under Hadrian's rule his reputation was established in the capital as the foremost speaker of the day. In the fourth century, the poet Ausonius, whose letters are discussed in Chapter IX, was still praising him as a great orator. Unfortunately, Fronto's speeches did not survive, and so it is by his letters that he is now judged. Because he had a busy career as a teacher and lawyer in Rome, his instructions to the royal princes about their studies were often written to them. The following passage is a typical reply to Fronto from Marcus, who was then about nineteen or twenty.

> I need not say how pleased I was at reading those speeches of Gracchus, for you will know well enough, since it was you who, with your experienced judgment and kind thoughtfulness, recommended them for my reading. That your book might not be returned to you alone and unaccompanied, I have added this letter. Farewell, my sweetest of masters and friendliest of friends, to whom I am likely to be indebted for all the literature I shall ever know. I am not so ungrateful as not to recognize what a favour you have done me by letting me see your extracts (selections taken from famous authors), and by ceasing not to lead me daily in the right way and, as the saying goes, "to open my eyes." Deservedly do I love you. (I:79)[1]

In another letter to Fronto about the same time, around 139, Marcus exhibits a characteristic seriousness. There is also a youthful posturing which he eventually outgrew.

> I have received two letters from you at once. In one of these you scolded me and pointed out that I had written a sentence carelessly; in the other, however, you strove to encourage my efforts with praise. Yet I protest to you by my health, by my mother's and yours, that it was the former letter which gave me the greater pleasure, and that, as I read it, I cried out again and again *O happy that I am! Are you then so happy*, someone will say, *for having a teacher to show you how to write a maxim more deftly, more clearly, more tersely, more elegantly*? No, that is not my reason for calling myself happy. What, then, is it? It is that I learn from you to speak the truth. That matter—of speaking the truth—is precisely what is so hard for Gods

> and men: in fact, there is no oracle so truth-telling as not to contain within itself something ambiguous or crooked or intricate, whereby the unwary may be caught and, interpreting the answer in the light of their own wishes, realize its fallaciousness only when the time is past and the business done. But the thing is profitable, and clearly it is the custom to excuse such things merely as pious fraud and delusion. On the other hand, your fault-findings or your guiding reins, whichever they may be, show me the way at once without guile and feigned words. And so I ought to be grateful to you for this, that you teach me before all to speak the truth at the same time and to hear the truth. . . . Farewell, my good master, my best of masters. I rejoice, best of orators, that you have so become my friend. (I:15)

Fronto's relations with the royal family were always warm, but at the same time correct. He never took advantage of his standing at court. Nor, obviously, did he risk losing it. Here is a cautious note of about 148, which he addresses to Marcus as Caesar, for he had been given that title in 139.

> Please acquaint your father with my illness. Tell me if you think I also should write to him. (I:227)

There follows Marcus's polite reply.

> I will let my Lord know at once that your health necessitates this rest for you. But please write to him yourself as well. Farewell, my best and most delightful of masters. (I:227)

Fronto was not a man to forget anniversaries, and in this letter to Antoninus Pius his wishes are overflowing. Although the obsequiousness sounds like Fronto, it was not out of tenor with the times. He must certainly have been pleased by the emperor's reply.

> More dearly than with a portion of my life would I bargain to embrace you on this most happy and wished-for anniversary of your accession, a day which I count as the birthday of my own health, reputation, and safety. But severe pain in my shoulder, and much more severe in my neck, have so crippled me, that I am still scarcely able to bend, sit upright, or turn myself, so rigid must I keep my neck. But before my Lares, Penates, and household gods have I discharged and renewed my vows, and prayed that next year I might embrace you twice on this anniversary, twice kiss your neck and hands, fulfilling at once the office of the past and the present year. (I:227–229)

The emperor replied:

> As I have well ascertained the entire sincerity of your feelings towards me, so I find no difficulty, I assure you, my dearest Fronto, in believing that this day in particular, on which it was ordained for me to assume this station, is kept with true and scrupulous devotion by you above all others. And I indeed have with my mind's eye, as was right, pictured you and your vows. (I:229)

Antoninus Pius, an honest, decent family man, had a home life as tranquil as his reign. The letters his son Marcus wrote to Fronto about a happy family and its activities suggest middle-class contentment rather than majestic luxury. No doubt it was the mushy phrases found toward the end of the following letter, written when Marcus was about twenty-four, which prompted the famed classicist Sir Richard Livingstone to remark that his letters sounded "school-girlish."

> We are well. I slept somewhat late owing to my slight cold, which seems now to have subsided. So from five a.m. till nine I spent the time partly in reading some of Cato's *Agriculture* and partly in writing not quite such wretched stuff, by heavens, as yesterday. Then, after paying my respects to my father, I relieved my throat, I will not say by gargling—though the word *gargarisso* is, I believe, found in Novius and elsewhere—but by swallowing honey water as far as the gullet and ejecting it again. After easing my throat I went off to my father and attended him at a sacrifice. Then we went to a luncheon. What do you think I ate? A wee bit of bread, though I saw others devouring beans, onions and herrings full of roe. We then worked hard at grape-gathering, and had a good sweat, and were merry and, as the poet says, *still left some clusters hanging high as gleanings of the vintage*. After six o'clock we came home.
>
> I did but little work and that to no purpose. Then I had a long chat with my little mother as she sat on the bed. My talk was this: *What do you think my Fronto is now doing?* Then she: *And what do you think my Gratia is doing?* Then I: *And what do you think our little sparrow, the wee Gratia*, (Fronto's daughter) is doing? Whilst we were chattering in this way and disputing which of us two loved the one or other of you two the better, the gong sounded, an intimation that my father had gone to his bath. So we had supper after we had bathed in the oil-press room; I do not mean bathed in the oil-press room, but when we had bathed, had supper there, and we enjoyed hearing the yokels chaffing one another. After coming back, before I turn over and snore, I get my task done and give my dearest of masters an account of the day's doings, and if I could miss him more, I would not grudge wasting away a little more. Farewell, my Fronto, wherever

> you are, most honey-sweet, my love, my delight. How is it between you and me? I love you and you are away. (I:181–83)

The sweet sentimentality of Marcus's letters as a young man offers a sharp contrast to the battle-hardened self-discipline of his mature years. What turned this bookish and self-conscious youth into the courageous emperor who stood stalwart against the invaders on the northern frontier? Credit must be given to the rigorous doctrines of Stoicism. Marcus did not hear about this philosophy from the ever-ailing Fronto, but from a different teacher, Rusticus, who led him to the teachings of the famed Epictetus. The students of that Stoic saint had written down his words for posterity, and they had a powerful impact on the future emperor. Marcus eventually, as time allowed, wrote *The Meditations*, which remains a major guide to Stoic principles and behavior.

When Antoninus Pius died on 7 March 161, he was succeeded by his two adopted sons. Marcus, older and more qualified, had married Faustina the Younger, the emperor's daughter. He was obviously the senior partner in the dual kingship. Nevertheless, Marcus and Lucius ruled as brothers, and since they had been adopted from different families there was no obstacle to Lucius marrying Marcus's daughter, Lucilla, which he did in 164. Among the Romans, marriage remained a useful means of closing the inner circle.

Having two emperors at the same time was something of a blessing, for Marcus could remain in charge at Rome and send his brother to face the Parthians in the east. On his way, in 162, Verus wrote to Fronto that he was recovering from an illness serious enough for his brother to have rushed to his bedside. Here is Fronto's reply, with its reference to the accepted practice of bleeding those who were ill.

> I was so distressed in mind . . . . But on the receipt of your letter, the very fact that you had written with your own hand raised my hopes at the outset; then came your good news that after three days' fasting and a prompt and rather drastic letting of blood you have been freed from the risk of a threatened illness. So I breathed again and recovered and made my prayers at every hearth, altar, sacred grove and consecrated tree—for I was staying in the country. And now I am waiting to hear from your next letter how much the intervening days have done towards restoring your strength. For indeed, much greater care and attention are required now, that you may fill your veins gradually and not be in too great a haste to repair your lost strength. For it is a belief verified and traditional that blood when its excess must be promptly drawn off must subsequently be regained by slow degrees. . . .
>
> Greet my Lord your brother, whose health you will ensure if you are well. Farewell, most sweet Lord. (II:85)

Although Lucius was said to be incompetent and self-indulgent, and comparisons to his more resolute brother didn't help, Fronto, in this letter, even given the excessive flattery, seems to regard him well. Lucius, in his own letters, makes a better impression than he appears to have given those who knew him. A letter to Fronto, written in A.D. 163, is an elaborate apology for having appeared to neglect his aging teacher by not having written more often.

> Accept, I beseech you, the reason for so legitimate a delay. Why, then, write to others oftener than to you? To excuse myself shortly: because, in fact, did I not do so, they would be angry, you would forgive; they would give up writing, you would importune me; to them I rendered duty for duty, to you I owed love for love. Or, would you wish me to write you also letters unwillingly, grumblingly, hurriedly, from necessity rather than from choice? . . . I have been in fault, I admit it; against the last person, too, that deserved it: that, too, I admit. But you must be better than I. I have suffered enough punishment, first in the very fact that I am conscious of my fault, then because, though face to face I could have won your pardon in a moment, I must now, separated as I am from you by such wide lands, be tortured with anxiety for so many intervening months until you get my letter and I get your answer back. (II:117–19)

In the same year, another letter to Lucius Verus, longer than usual, speaks of Fronto's favorite subject, eloquence. In this letter, as might be expected, Fronto was more excited about the way Verus described to the Senate a victory in Armenia than he was in the victory itself. The letter also depicts the decline of discipline in the army, a continuing worry in the years ahead. Fronto alone seems to have given Lucius credit for having made improvements.

> From this moment, O Emperor, treat me as you please and as your feelings prompt you. Neglect me, or even despise me, in a word shew me no honour, put me, if you will, with the lowest. There is nothing you can do against me, however much in earnest you are, so harsh or unjust, that you should not be for me the source of the most abounding joys.
>
> Perhaps you think that it is your warlike qualities and your military achievements and strategy that I am now praising. True, they are most glorious for the state and Empire of the Roman people, none better or more magnificent, yet in rejoicing over them I but take my individual share of delight proportionably with others; but in the case of your eloquence, of which you have such plain evidence in your despatch to the Senate, it is I who triumph indeed.
>
> I have received, . . . and I have and hold a full return from you in like measure heaped high: I can now depart this life with a joyous heart, richly

> recompensed for my labours and leaving behind me a mighty monument to my lasting fame. That I was your master all men either know or suppose or believe from your lips: indeed, I should be shy of claiming this honour for myself did you not yourselves both proclaim it: since you do proclaim it, it is not for me to deny it. . . .
>
> The army you took over was demoralized with luxury and immorality and prolonged idleness. The soldiers at Antioch were wont to spend their time clapping actors, and were more often found in the nearest cafe-garden than in the ranks. Horses shaggy from neglect, but every hair plucked from their riders: a rare sight was a soldier with arm or leg hairy. Withal the men better clothed than armed, so much so that Pontius Laelianus, a man of character and a disciplinarian of the old school, in some cases ripped up their cuirasses with his fingertips; he found horses saddled with cushions, and by his orders the little pommels on them were slit open and the down plucked from their pillions as from geese. Few of the soldiers could vault upon their steeds, the rest scrambled clumsily up by dint of heel or knee or ham; not many could make their spears hurtle, most tossed them like toy lances without verve and vigour. Gambling was rife in camp: sleep night-long, or, if a watch was kept, it was over the wine-cups.
>
> By what disciplinary measures you were to break-in soldiers of this stamp and make them serviceable and strenuous did you not learn from the dourness of Hannibal, the stern discipline of Africanus, the exemplary methods of Metellus, of which histories are full? This very precaution of yours, a lesson drawn from long study, not to engage the enemy in a pitched battle until you had seasoned your men with skirmishes and minor successes—did you not learn it from Cato, a man equally consummate as orator and as commander? (II:129–51)

Lucius Verus wrote to Fronto asking him to prepare a history of the Parthian War that would cast him in a laudatory light. He was obviously aware that his reputation needed bolstering. The letter is reminiscent of the one Cicero wrote to his historian friend Lucceius asking him to "disregard the canons of history."

It was widely believed that Lucius's generals, particularly Avidius Cassius, deserved the credit for the Roman success against the Parthians. Nevertheless, Lucius received the title *Armeniacus* for the victory in Armenia and an old-fashioned triumph when he returned to Rome. These showy rewards were possibly something of an embarrassment to Marcus Aurelius and may have led to the later attempted coup by Avidius, who saw his own credit gone astray. As this letter from Lucius to Fronto shows, Avidius even was asked to supply evidence for Lucius's claims.

> What was done, however, after I had set out you can learn from the despatches sent me by the commanders entrusted with each business. Our

Marcus Aurelius, Antoninus Pius, Lucius Verus, Hadrian. The "Adoption Scene" from the monument built at Ephesus to commemorate Lucius Verus's victories over the Parthians. The reliefs of the monument are now in the Ephesus Museum, Vienna, and the photograph is courtesy of the Kunsthistorisches Museum, Vienna.

> friend Sallustius, now called Fulvianus, will provide you with copies of them. But that you may be able also to give the reasons for my measures, I will send you my own letters as well, in which all that had to be done is clearly set forth. But if you want some sort of pictures besides, you can get them from Fulvianus. And to bring you into closer touch with the reality, I have directed Avidius Cassius and Martius Verus to draw up some memoranda for me, which I will send you, and you will be quite able from them to gauge the character of the men and their capacity, but if you wish me also to draw up a memorandum, instruct me as to the form of it which you prefer, and I will follow your directions. I am ready to fall in with any suggestions as long as my exploits are set in a bright light by you. Of course, you will not overlook my speeches to the Senate and harangues to the army. I will send you also my parleys with the enemy. These will be of great assistance to you.
>
> One thing I wish not indeed to point out to you—the pupil to his master—but to offer for your consideration, that you should dwell at length on the causes and early stages of the war, and especially our ill success in my absence. Do not be in a hurry to come to my share. Further, I think it essential to make quite clear the great superiority of the Parthians before my arrival, that the magnitude of my achievements may be manifest. Whether, then, you should give only a sketch of all this, as Thucydides did in his *Narrarive of the Fifty Years' War* [actually, the years between the Persian Wars and the Peloponnesian War], or go a little more deeply into the subject without however expatiating upon it, as you would upon mine in the sequel, it is for you to decide.
>
> In short, my achievements, whatsoever their character, are no greater, of course, than they actually are, but they can be made to seem as great as you would have them seem. (II:195–97)

There remains the beginning of this history, effusive in its praise of Lucius. But Fronto died within a year or two, and so it was not carried far.

In his later years, Fronto continued to have requests from Marcus Aurelius, who, interestingly enough, asks to have some letters of Cicero to read. The following two letters were exchanged in 163. Marcus wrote to Fronto:

> While enjoying this health-giving country air, I felt there is one great thing lacking, the assurance that you also are in good health, my master. That you make good that defect is my prayer to the Gods. But this country holiday of mine saddled with state business is, in fact, your busy city life still. In a word I cannot go on with this very letter for a line or two owing to pressing duties, from which I enjoy a respite only for a part of the night. Farewell, my most delightful of masters.

> If you have any selected letters of Cicero, either entire or in extracts, lend me them or tell me which you think I ought particularly to read to improve my command of language. (II:157)

Fronto replied:

> This is the fifth day since I have been seized with pain in all my limbs, but especially in my neck and groin. As far as I remember I have extracted from Cicero's letters only those passages in which there was some discussion about eloquence or philosophy or politics; besides, if there seemed to be any choice expression or striking word I have extracted it. Such of these as were by me for my own use I have sent to you. You might, if you think it worth while, have the three books, two to Brutus and one to Axius, copied and return them to me, as of these particular extracts I have made no copies. All Cicero's letters, however, should, I think, be read—in my opinion, even more than his speeches. There is nothing more perfect than Cicero's letters. (II: 157–59)

When Fronto's letters were discovered, their content came as a disappointment to scholars who knew him by reputation as a famous orator to be compared even to Cicero. Now he seemed much less eminent. That assessment may not be entirely fair, since in the earlier days he was corresponding with schoolboys. Yet any judgment of the man must consider his neglect of philosophy and the amount of time he spent talking about his own health. From his letters it is soon apparent that aches and pains were much on his mind. No part of the body escaped attention. The result is a catalogue of common complaints: stomach trouble, sore throat, sore eyes, diarrhaea, a pain in one side of the groin and then the other side, sleeplessness, circulation failure, "pulse imperceptible." He once mentioned a pain in the neck that had replaced a pain which had left his foot. And if that wasn't enough, one day clumsy attendants, carrying him from the baths, slammed him against a doorway. His letters always detail a certain amount of misery.

Whether consciously soliciting sympathy or not, Fronto did receive considerable commiseration. Marcus Aurelius's letters, especially when he was young, show his deep feeling for his teacher by mentioning his own frequent illnesses, as though his being sick increased his favor. Fronto received a bonus when the young Marcus praised him for his courage: "For mercy's sake endeavor with all self-denial and all abstinence to shake off this attack which you, indeed, can endure with your usual courage, but to me it is the worst and sorest of trials" (I:83).

Fronto's physical problems limited his public service. During the sixth year of Antoninus Pius's reign, 143, he did serve as *consul suffectus*[2] for the months of July and August, but he later declined a post as proconsul in Asia because of poor health. Robinson Ellis, in a published lecture, *The Correspondence of Fronto and M. Aurelius*, wrote that Fronto "knew how to turn his pains to good purpose; they excused his attendance at court, and gave him a real plea for absenting himself from visits of ceremony which to a man so much employed as a pleader must too often have been a waste of time."[3]

Preoccupied as he was with his own pains, Fronto found nothing about the suffering in the gladiatorial arena to complain about. His letters, unlike those of Cicero, Seneca, and Pliny, show no contempt for popular amusements. On the contrary, the following brief note written in 161 to a young friend, Volumnius Quadratus, tells of his enthusiasm.

> I will gladly, my son, read your speech, which you have sent me, and correct anything that seems to require it, but by the hand of my secretary, for my own hand is useless from severe pain. In spite of the pain, however, I have been carried to the circus. For I am again seized with a passion for the games. (I:309)

As Marcus Aurelius grew older he had less to say of personal matters and more of philosophy and affairs of state. It was Socrates, the precursor of Stoicism, who had dismissed worries about the weather and personal ailments as being petty and unworthy of his time. The influence of Stoicism would mean, too, that discussion of style, especially the search for exactly the right word, so dear to a rhetorician such as Fronto, must have seemed of less importance to Marcus Aurelius as he took on the burdens of such an awesome office.

A continuing distraction of the times was the disobedience of the Christians. There is often puzzlement about the persecutions of Marcus's reign. It seems an incongruous development in view of the generous and humane sentiments of his *Meditations*. The most obvious answer is of course that he, like Trajan, considered the Christians to be disobedient citizens.

Fronto, while not directly responsible for any orders given, may have had some influence on events. His extant letters make no mention of the Christians, but in a speech attributed to him (by Minucius Felix, a writer of the early third century), he repeats the common gossip about the incestuous practices of the Christians at banquets amid "the passion of impure lust and drunkenness." Many were obviously willing to accept the outrageous stories, which slandered a people who actually prided themselves on their morality. It was, however, the austere Rusticus, Marcus's Stoic teacher, who as *praefectus urbis* actually presided over the execution of Justin Martyr and other Christians in 165.

To Marcus, there were more pressing problems than the suppression of "unpatriotic" Christians. A plague that devastated military camps was brought home by soldiers returning from the east. The resulting toll contributed to a growing manpower shortage that became acute at the very time barbarian invasions across the Danube became more serious. Marcus even allowed some Germans to settle on vacant lands in return for their helping to prevent the arrival of others. Thus, out of necessity a gradual barbarization of the Roman army had begun.

In 168, Lucius, back from the east, joined Marcus on the northern frontier, but died of a stroke the following year. Marcus, ruling alone, then faced an unexpected but serious challenge from one of his ablest generals in the eastern sector, Avidius Cassius, mentioned earlier. This unlucky warrior had decided to promote himself, but was put to death by his own aides as soon as the emperor arrived to deal with him.

Marcus returned home to face further incursions across the Danube. It was at Vindobona (modern Vienna) that he died on 17 March 180—still fighting, always Stoic, forever doing his duty.

Fronto had died before either of his famous pupils. His death in 166 or 167 was perhaps hastened by the loss of his wife and a grandchild in 165. No letter is dated after 166.

In 163, Fronto had written to Marcus Aurelius:

> Now already your full excellence has risen with dazzling disc and spread its rays on every side; and yet you call me back to that bygone measure of my dawning love for you, and bid the morning twilight shine at noonday! Hear, I pray you, how much enhanced beyond your former is your present excellence, that you may more easily understand how much larger a measure of love you deserve, while you cease to claim only as much. (II:125–27)

It was to Marcus's credit that in his later days he had become a man likely to be somewhat embarrassed by the burden of such ornate praise. But, as it happened, a more serious cause for embarrassment was a worthless son Commodus, who ruled from 180 to 192. His was a reign marked by the familiar excesses of earlier emperors: self-indulgent pastimes, neglect of duty, unsavory advisers, and summary executions of suspected critics. Perhaps the only people grateful to Commodus were tenants on the imperial estates. He curbed the illegal practice whereby these farmers were being forced to work some of the time for those who leased or supervised state properties. But it was difficult to stop this usage, which foreshadowed serfdom.

Those who knew Commodus best, his aides and ex-mistress among them, grew anxious about his erratic behavior, which included his sometimes dresssing as Hercules. He was vain about physical prowess and enjoyed having rugged companions. On New Year's Eve, 192, it was an athlete who, by arrangement, strangled him.

The planners of that event were then willing to see Pertinax, an aging trusted official under Marcus Aurelius, come to power. Pertinax wanted to put the government finances back in order, but his time was cut short. Praetorian guardsmen resented his determination to return to the old discipline. They assassinated him and hailed a foolish man and senator, Marcus Didius Julianus, who was willing to promise them large payments for the honor. That clumsy bargain lasted only a couple of months before Julianus was executed on the Senate's orders. Septimius Severus, an outstanding commander of loyal troops in Pannonia, had by this time arrived at Rome with his army.

As had happened more than a century earlier, in A.D. 69, a period of confusion in the capital gave rise to fighting among provincial commanders for the highest office. Severus had reached Rome first. After a series of deals, betrayals, and battles, he emerged victorious and strong enough to begin a line of rulers known as the Severan Dynasty, which lasted from 193 until 235. An account of this period is found in the writings of Herodian, whose extant work covers a period from the death in 180 of his hero, Marcus Aurelius, until the year 238. In his treatment of Commodus's reign, Herodian wrote about the unruly behavior of soldiers who were becoming a menace to the civilian population. Septimius Severus was able to restore order in the ranks, but at the same time gave to the soldiers a generous pay raise and the privilege of getting married while in service, which, very likely, they had been doing for some time anyway. Severus, in fact, so favored the army that the Empire became, in effect, a military state. His was certainly a military reign. After first battling with his chief competitor, Niger, for the imperial throne, he was absent from Rome on a series of campaigns. His first trouble with the Parthians resulted from their support of Niger, who was based in Syria. To punish them he marched across the Euphrates and set up a Roman presence by seizing land formerly in Parthian control. In the west, another rival, Albinus, began using forces stationed in Britain to challenge him. When Severus left to deal with that problem, the Parthians returned to claim Mesopotamia.

The defeat of Albinus cost many senators their lives. None of the letters to Albinus telling of their support have survived, but when Severus found them among Albinus's papers, their contents proved fatal to those who sent them.

After disposing of Albinus, Severus again marched to the east and there decisively defeated the Parthian king in a campaign subsequently commemorated by a grandiose triple arch in Rome, which stands on the northwest side of the Forum.

Despite his absences from Rome, the reign of Severus saw crucial changes in nonmilitary matters. He was a native of the town of Lepcis Magna in North Africa, which had been made a Roman colony by Trajan. His wife was a Syrian. Provincials were therefore given more recognition than previously, being recognized as the equal of Italians both in the army and in state offices.

A less congenial innovation under Severus can be seen as another signpost of the future. Frustration over criminal acts led to more severe punishment of the *humiliores*. As the name suggests, they were the poor and less-educated, without position or connections. For certain misdeeds they could be tortured for information, or sentenced to be ravaged by wild beasts without right of appeal. Their betters, the *honestiores*, who included the ruling classes, the bureaucracy, and soldiers, were excused from such cruel treatment. For committing the same crimes they might be sent into exile. This relationship between who you were and what you might suffer was so fixed by the Middle Ages that to many it must have seemed to have always existed.

Severus died in 211 at Eboracum (York) in Britain, where he had gone to confront rebellious Caledonians. His sons were supposed to rule jointly. However, in the following year Caracalla, who likely had plotted against his father, murdered his young brother, Geta, and then ruled alone. A memorable edict of the same year gave Roman citizenship to all free men in the empire, and so at last everybody was a Roman, subject to Roman laws, liable for Roman taxes.

Severus's elder son had the official name of Marcus Aurelius Antoninus, but history knows him as Caracalla, his nickname after a German-style coat he popularized. His own rough-and-ready manner was popular with the Germans and he used them in his bodyguard. They were unable to save him, however, from a disgruntled centurion who caught him unawares and stabbed him in the back during an eastern campaign in 217.

There soon followed a period in which women exercised more power in the state than ever before. Julia Domna, the Syrian wife of Septimius Severus and mother of his two sons, had committed suicide after Caracalla was killed. Her sister, Julia Mamaea, however, put forth the claim that each of her two daughters had given birth to a son fathered by Caracalla. These boys, the effete fourteen-year-old Elagabalus and his younger cousin, Severus Alexander, were eventually, in turn, accepted by the soldiers for their own purposes, including generous gifts of money. According to a now-monotonous scenario, they both were murdered by the soldiers, who became disgusted with the antics of Elagabalus and the weakness of Severus Alexander. During a brief time, however, the women who controlled these young emperors played a prominent role in state affairs, even addressing the Senate, although the exact degree of their influence remains a matter of some debate.

The elimination of the last of Septimius Severus's heirs in 235 brought an end to the Severan Dynasty and began yet another round of battles between military commanders eager to wear a purple cloak. This time, however, for a period of fifty years, 235 to 285, no one individual was able to stay in power long enough to bring stability. The eighteen to twenty-six claimants to power, not all of them widely accepted, are called the Barracks Room Emperors. They were hailed by their soldiers, who also kept them in power by their arms, if often only briefly. Claudius Gothicus II, who died of the plague in 270, was the only one who escaped a violent death. This period of near anarchy caused widespread insecurity. The frontier defenses were weakened, and barbarian invasions more frequent. Although the Claudius just mentioned successfully checked Gothic advances in the Balkan area, the Franks arrived to stay in Gaul, and the Saxons were on their way to Britain.

One of the short-term emperors, Aurelian, who reigned from 270 to 275, reacted to the foreboding of the times by building around Rome itself a wall of which large parts still remain. At the same time, his coins declared him to be the "Restorer of the World." In the east, he had quelled a serious revolt by the distant desert city of Palmyra, which at the height of its power claimed influence over an area from Egypt to Asia Minor. Now, as the Romans had long ago punished Carthage, Corinth, and Jerusalem, Aurelian reduced Palmyra to rubble. In the west, he recaptured a vast area, the *imperium Galliarum*, including present day Britain, France, and Spain, which had managed to break away from Rome's control. Although Aurelian fought hard to unify the empire and did succeed in that awesome task, he, too, was the victim of a plot by his own officers in 275.

It can be no surprise that literature along with everything else declined during the chaotic middle years of the third century. The foremost writer of letters in this unhappy time was not a man with a sword at all. He was a Christian bishop named Cyprian, who, along with his followers, was blamed, in part at least, for the empire's many troubles.

VI
CYPRIAN

Ruling the Church the Roman Way

TWO hundred years after Jesus was executed, the Romans were still arresting those who commemorated the event. Half-way through the third century, one of the Barracks Room Emperors, Decius, ordered, for the first time, an empire-wide persecution of the Christians; and he felt he had good reasons for doing so. Along the frontiers, barbarian tribes were threatening the existence of the empire. Maintaining internal unity against external pressures was crucial. The Romans had always been suspicious of secret societies or foreign cults with exotic rites, which might provide a cover for subversives. The Emperor Trajan even distrusted volunteer fire brigades. Christianity, which gathered in brothers and sisters from across time-honored class lines, was therefore suspect.

Decius, who reigned from 249 to 251, decided to rid the empire of a stubborn people who refused to worship the state gods or the images of the dead and deified emperors. As in the time of Trajan more than a century earlier, the Christians were officially considered to be unrepentant lawbreakers. There was no separation of church and state, and so a refusal to conform to the religious rites of the empire was a treasonous act punishable by death. Some Christians were beheaded. Others were put in jail or sent to work in salt mines, where amid harsh conditions they too might die.

Among the letters surviving from this period are eighty-one written by a remarkable, if somewhat baffling, individual named Cyprian. At the age of about forty-eight, he was chosen, in 248, to be the bishop of Carthage, only two years after his conversion and baptism as a Christian. Cyprian, a well-educated man from a well-to-do family, stood out among converts, who at the time were mostly from the lower ranks of society. He also had a strong personality, a high moral character, and the sort of control over himself that made it possible for him to control others.

At the same time, however, that he was so vigorously urging the faithful to stand firm and face death, Cyprian was himself safe in hiding. A biography by Peter Hinchliff, *Cyprian of Carthage and the Unity of the Christian Church*, suggests that Cyprian may have considered his valuable leadership so necessary for the preservation of the local church that he had to stay alive.[1] That certainly seems to be suggested in the following letter. It is also possible that he feared torture and worried that he might disgrace himself and his followers by denying Christ. The rather vague way in which Cyprian wrote, in 250, to the priests and deacons of Carthage is a good example of how he handled the question.

I had certainly hoped, my dearly beloved brothers, that the greetings I might send by letter should find the whole of our clergy safe and sound. But this hostile tempest has overwhelmed not only the majority of our people—what has caused us the greatest distress of all is that it has involved in its devastating wake even a portion of the clergy. And so we pray to the Lord that just as you now are, as we know, standing firm in faith and fortitude, so too in the future we may send our greetings to you still standing, thanks to the mercy of God.

There are, I am aware, urgent reasons why I should come to you in all haste myself. Not only is there my ardent yearning for you; this is the object of my most earnest prayers. But we would also be able, taking counsel in large numbers, together to discuss, weigh and determine questions related to the government of the Church; the well-being of our community demands answers to them. In spite of this, it has seemed better advised to continue, for the time being, quietly in my place of hiding. My decision has been made out of concern for a variety of considerations, and they involve the peace and safety of us all. Our very dear brother Tertullus will explain all this to you. He it is who counselled me on this course of action—behaviour characteristic of the earnest zeal he bestows upon the works of God; he urged that I should act with prudence and restraint, that I should not rashly commit myself to public view, more particularly in that place where I have been sought and shouted for so often.

I am relying, therefore, on your charity and devotion which I know so well. By this letter I both exhort and charge you that as your presence in Carthage causes no offence and occasions hardly any danger, you should perform in my stead those offices which are necessary for the administration of the church.

The poor, in the meantime, must be cared for to the extent that it is possible and in whatever way that it is possible, provided, that is, they remain standing with faith unshaken and have not forsaken the flock of Christ. You should take earnest care that they are provided with the means for alleviating their poverty; otherwise necessity may force them to do in their difficulties actions which faith prevented them from doing in the storm.

To the glorious confessors[2] likewise you must devote especial care. I know

> that very many of them have been supported by the devotion and charity of our brethren. Nevertheless there may be some in need of clothing or provisions; they should be supplied with whatever is necessary, as I also wrote to you previously when they were still in prison. But there must be this proviso: through you they must be informed, instructed, and taught what the discipline of the Church, based on the teaching authority of the Scriptures, requires of them. They must conduct themselves humbly, modestly, and peaceably, In this way, they may preserve the honour of their name—after uttering words of glory they may also live lives of glory. And by serving the Lord well in all things and perfecting their renown they may thereby render themselves worthy of attaining their celestial crown. (14)[3]

Because Tertullus, who is mentioned in that letter, corresponded and visited Cyprian (and possibly provided his hiding place), it has been suggested that he was a layman whose movements would have been less likely monitored than those of a member of the clergy. G. W. Clarke in his *The Letters of St. Cyprian of Carthage* also comments: "Note how Cyprian proceeds to seek some shelter behind the counsels of the eminently virtuous Tertullus. This is unusual for Cyprian, and makes it plain that he is being somewhat defensive; he is going to uncharacteristic pains to establish that his dereliction of duties is only apparent."[4]

From what little is known about Cyprian's early life, he appears to have had a great interest in miraculous happenings, especially in prophetic dreams. As he grew older, he became increasingly austere in his habits. Even before his conversion he was determined to be celibate. He also sold his fine gardens and gave the money to the poor. Thereafter, what was important to him was not to be found in the beautiful but unhappy world of the senses, but in the spiritual realm of the unmeasured and unseen. Much of the religious verbiage in his letters reflects this attitude, and it was sincere, for he did finally sacrifice himself. At the same time, the letters show Cyprian to have been a shrewd and practical leader. The Church of course could welcome both sides of such a man, particularly in the thriving metropolis of Carthage.

Four centuries before Cyprian's time, the Romans had defeated Carthage in the Third Punic War (149–146 B.C.) and then, impatient and revengeful, destroyed the city. It was claimed that they coveted the land, but if so they failed at any serious recolonizing of the area until a century later under Julius Caesar. Veterans settled there, and a prosperous city returned to its former status as a major seaport, flourishing as a trading center and capital of the Roman province of Africa. When Cyprian was born about 200 A.D., where exactly is not known, Carthage had already produced Tertullian, one of the most prominent Christian writers of the age, who taught and wrote there during the second century. Still, the Christians remained a small and beleaguered minority in the province, and few of them were found outside the city. The word pagan, from *pagus*, country district, or *paganus*, peasant, attests to the strength of religious tradition in rural areas. But in Carthage, as in other cities in the third century, the number of converts to Christianity was multiplying rapidly. The promise of a blessed eternity was especially appealing to persons who had the least to look forward to in the here and now. Cyprian, as noted, was different in that he was one of a relatively few converts from the upper ranks, possibly even a member of the senatorial class. He nevertheless had something in common with the others, for they all shared the miserable times of the mid-third century.

While the Barracks Room Emperors were fighting the barbarians and each other, the safety of ordinary citizens throughout the empire was jeopardized by roving bands of brigands, escaped prisoners, and army deserters. Because there was too much land to guard, parts of the empire became detached as separate entities, adding to the confusion and unsettledness of the times. The disruption of production and trade led to a chronic depression. Amid these troubles, the government was unable to cope with essential problems.

Given a pervasive mood of despair, increasing numbers of men and women sought security in the church, where the uncertainties of the world gave way to revealed truth and hope.

As usual, those who yearned for higher things found much to despise in the low morals of their day, whether or not conditions were, in fact, any worse than they had ever been. Ironically, the Emperor Decius could consider himself a reformer by beginning the persecution of the Christians. He wanted to firm up the practices of the old state religion. The Christians, with their vision of a new day, were clearly a stumbling block to the restoration of what was gone by.

To the especially sensitive Cyprian, haunted by fears of evil demons, the church was a needed refuge. In the unscientific and unsettled world of the third century, fear was more akin to old-fashioned terror than to modern anxiety. Hostile agents of the devil were in combat with Christ. A very real choice had to be made. Cyprian talks about his decision over and over again in his letters. Those written from his rural retreat bolstered the spirits of his frightened parishioners in the city.

News of Cyprian's safe haven reached the ears of a saddened clergy in Rome, currently mourning the loss of their own bishop, the recently executed Fabian. In a cautiously worded letter addressed to the clergy of Carthage in 250, they wonder if the flock there is not being neglected by its absent leader.

> The subdeacon Crementius has come to us from you on certain business. We have learnt from him that the blessed pope Cyprian[5] has gone into retirement and that it is maintained that he is certainly right to have done so for the special reason that he is a person of prominence.
>
> But the fact is the contest is now at hand which God has allowed to take place in the world, a combat between the adversary and his servants. It is His will that this struggle should make manifest to angels and men that the victor receives his crown but that the vanquished brings on himself as his prize the sentence which has been made manifest to us.

Now we are clearly the church leaders and it is accordingly our duty to keep watch over the flock, acting in the place of our shepherds; and so, if it is found that we are neglectful, the same words will be said to us as were spoken to our predecessors who were such neglectful leaders, namely, that "the lost we have not sought, the strayed we have not brought back, the lame we have not bound, but their milk we have eaten and with their wool we have been clothed."

Moreover, this is a lesson which the Lord Himself teaches us, fulfilling what was written in the Law and the Prophets. In His own words: *I am the good shepherd; I lay down my life for my sheep. But as for the hireling shepherd, whose own the sheep are not, when he sees the wolf coming he abandons them and flees and the wolf scatters the flock.* Furthermore He said to Simon: *Do you love me? He replied: I do. He said to him: Feed my sheep.* And we can see that these words were fulfilled by the very manner of his death, and the rest of the disciples acted likewise.

And so, dearly beloved brothers, our desire is that you are found to be not hireling but good shepherds. You are aware that there is the risk of extreme peril should you fail to exhort our brothers to stand steadfast in the faith; otherwise they may rush headlong into idolatry and be totally ruined.

And it is not by words alone that we exhort you to do this. You will be able to learn from the many travellers who come to you from us that, with the help of God, all these things we not only have done ourselves but we continue to do them with unremitting zeal in the face of worldly dangers. For we keep before our eyes fear of God and everlasting punishments, rather than fear of men and brief-lived sufferings. We do not abandon our brothers but we exhort them to stand firm in the faith and, as is their duty, to be in readiness to walk with the Lord. . . .

The brethren who are in chains send their greetings to you, likewise the presbyters and the whole Church who keeps watch herself with unresting care over all who call upon the name of the Lord. And for ourselves, we ask that you, in your turn, be mindful of us.

For your information, Bassianus has arrived. We also ask of you, zealous as you are to serve God, to send copies of this letter to as many as you can, as suitable opportunities occur, or to compose letters of your own or send a messenger, so that they may stand courageous and steadfast in the faith.

We wish that you, dearly beloved brothers, may ever fare well. (8)

The subdeacon Crementius had brought two letters to Carthage from the Roman clergy. There was the one just quoted and then a second one addressed only to Cyprian informing him of the martyrdom of Fabian, the bishop of Rome. When the other letter addressed to the Carthaginian clergy was sent to Cyprian, for a good purpose or not, he was no doubt stung by its implications, being aware of the death of Fabian. His reply under the circumstances was astute. He could not believe that letter came exactly as it was written. Someone must have tampered with it. About being in hiding while others were dying, Cyprian seems to have reached an accommodation with his own conscience and was apparently unaware that others failed to see what it was. Here is what he wrote to the clergy in Rome.

> There had been, my dearly beloved brothers, unsubstantial rumour here amongst us that my colleague, that good man, had departed this life. Whilst we still did not know what to believe, I received the letter which you sent me by the hands of the subdeacon Crementius. This informed me in the fullest detail about his glorious end, and I was overjoyed at the thought that the untarnished character of his administration had been graced with the honour and fulfilment that it merited.
>
> I congratulate you also most warmly for fostering his memory with such a distinguished and splendid testimonial. Through your good services we are consequently made aware of facts which redound to your glory through the memory of your leader and which at the same time provide us with a model of faith and virtue. There is great danger that the collapse of a leader may lead to the downfall of his followers; but, by the same token, there is great profit and aid to salvation should a bishop show his brothers by his unshakeable faith that he deserves to be imitated.
>
> I have also read a letter in which it was not specifically stated who were the persons who wrote it or who were the persons to whom it was written. And the handwriting in this same letter as well as the contents and the acutal paper have led me to suspect that something may either have been withdrawn from the genuine version or have been altered in it. And so I am returning to you the original letter; you will then be able to recognize whether it is the same letter which you gave to the subdeacon Crementius to deliver.
>
> For it is an extremely grave matter if the truth of an ecclesiastical letter has been corrupted by any falsehood or fraud.
>
> That we may know this, therefore, examine the handwriting and the concluding greetings to see whether they are yours and write back to us what is the truth of the matter.
>
> I wish that you, my dearly beloved brothers, may ever fare well. (9)

A letter written early in 250 from Cyprian to imprisoned fellow Christians makes plain what Roman officials were up against in trying to win back recalcitrant citizens. Those who were offered freedom if they would give up their faith were taught by Cyprian that their very persistence in prison brought greater rewards. "The longer your fight, the more sublime your crown!" Roman officials, still pursuing the glory and dignity of worldly office, were frustrated by the stubborn resistance of those who would deny the world altogether.

Dearest brothers, Celerinus, who has been comrade with you in your deeds of faith and valour and soldier of God in your battles of glory, has made, by his arrival here, each and every one of you present to our feelings. As he approached we saw in him all of you and as he spoke tenderly and often of your affection for me, we could hear in his words your own voices. Great indeed and profound is my joy when from you such messages are conveyed by such messengers.

There is a sense in which we, too, are there with you in prison. Being as we are thus joined to your hearts we believe that we are sharing with you the special distinctions which God in His goodness is bestowing upon you. Your undivided love binds us to your glory: the spirit does not countenance the bonds of charity to be parted. Confession immures you there, affection me. And for our part we are certainly mindful of you, day and night; not only in the prayer we offer in the company of many during the sacrifice but also in the private prayers we say in solitude, we beseech of the Lord to lend His full benison to your winning your crowns of renown.

But in fact our powers are too paltry to render you adequate return; yours is the greater gift when *you* remember us in your prayers, for your hopes are now on heaven alone, you have thoughts only for God. Indeed the heights you ascend are all the loftier the longer in fact your passion is delayed: by the protracted period of time you are not simply retarding, rather you are enhancing your glory.

A first confession—and one only—makes a man blessed. But you make your confession every time you are invited to leave the prison, and in your faith and valour you elect to stay there. Your honours are as numerous as your days in prison; as the months run their course, so your merits multiply. He conquers once who suffers at once; but the person who is constantly under torture, grappling with pain, and remains unconquered, he wins a crown every day.

Let now the magistrates parade forth, the consuls and the proconsuls; let them pride themselves in the regalia of their annual office and their twelve bundles of rods. Be assured that in your own case your heavenly office has been invested with all the brilliance of a year's honours and already, by the long continuance of its victorious glory, it has traversed beyond the full revolution of the annual cycle.

The rising sun and the waning moon gave light to the universe, but to you in your dungeon He who made the sun and the moon proved to be a brighter light. And the resplendent radiance of Christ glowing in your hearts and souls illuminated with its dazzling and eternal light the darkness

> of your place of punishment, which to others appeared so dread and so deadly. . . .
>
> Truly blessed are those from your number who have travelled along these paths of glory and have now left this world; they have reached the end of their journey of valour and faith, and they have gone to receive, to the joy of the Lord Himself, the kiss and the embrace of the Lord.
>
> And yet your glory is in no way inferior; you are still engaged in the struggle; your destiny is to follow the glorious career of your comrades; you have long been waging the fight; and steadfast with unflinching and unshakeable faith, by your acts of valor you are exhibiting each day a spectacle for God to look upon. The more prolonged is your flight, the more noble is your crown. There is but one contest, but it consists of an accumulation of numerous battles. Hunger you conquer, thirst you contemn, and by your strength and vigour you spurn the filth of your dungeon and the horrors of your cell of suffering.
>
> In your prison suffering is subjugated, cruelty is crushed. Death you do not dread, you desire it, for death is vanquished by the reward of deathlessness, so that the victor is honoured with an eternity of life. (37)

By temperament, of course, some persons are less able than others to withstand the threat of torture and death. There were Christians who lacked the will, or the strength, to share the martyrdom Cyprian praised. They were known as "the lapsed," for they returned to the pagan practices of making sacrifices and libations as ordered by the state religion. Cyprian was shocked at the ease with which so many persons left the church when the local persecutions began. On the other hand, it seems likely that among the increasing numbers joining the church in the third century were many of marginal faith.

When the pursuit of the Christians became less rigorous in one locality or another, many of those who had left to save their bodies wanted to return to the church on behalf of their souls. Should they be welcome? Fresh was the memory of the wounds and deaths of those who had stood fast. What about lapsed priests? Should they be allowed to return and even to administer sacraments? There were sharp differences of opinion. Some favored a generous amnesty which would return the lapsed to communion as quickly as possible, even without a period of penance. Others bitterly rejected those who had faltered and would shut them out entirely. This attitude of strictness was more pronounced and consistent in the African church than elsewhere.

Peter Hinchliff sees the source of this hard-line position as possibly related to the severe religious practices of the Phoenicians, a Semitic people who were the original settlers of Carthage. Today, tourists visiting the area still are shown ancient sanctuaries where sacrificed children were buried. In those early times such behavior could be explained by a belief in fearsome gods who demanded gifts even of one's own flesh and blood. Over the centuries that viciousness gave way to a concept of deity which eliminated the bloodthirstiness but remained strict in discipline. The body was still to be sacrificed, but now in holiness by giving up the sins of the flesh, countenancing them neither in oneself nor in others. A rigid austerity was pronounced in Tertullian's writings, and Cyprian's views on virginity were certainly consistent in that respect. While it might not be possible for anyone to rival St. Jerome in the praise and promotion of virgins, Cyprian came close. Although he had never known Tertullian, who had died when Cyprian was young, he was a great admirer of his works, not being himself so able a writer or theologian. Cyprian was better in dealing with practical problems of an administrative kind and in that connection wanted to temper the more severe elements of the local traditions. His position on whether to readmit those who had lapsed was a moderate one, for he did want to open the church doors to the truly penitent. In Rome, however, a group led by a priest named Novatian[6] was adamant about refusing to allow any who had once left to return.

The controversy led to a schism between those who declared themselves to be standing on the holiest ground and those who considered themselves to be more reasonable. Eventually, Cyprian refused to accept as valid the baptisms performed by priests of uncompromising inflexibility. Ironically, then, he became involved in a controversy with the bishop of Rome, Stephen, who did accept these rites. As in other matters, the practical Roman way, which was accommodating even with schismatics, proved to be more workable in the long term.

Locally, the question of the lapsed stood in the shadow of political considerations. Cyprian censured those priests who had been giving communion to the lapsed without his personal consent. As in the case of clergymen who distributed money to the poor, so, too, those who admitted numerous lapsed could count on that many more supporters amid a very human competition for position and power.

In the third century, the Christian church lacked the central authority it would come to have in later centuries. While the emperors Decius and Valerian might have wished that the Christians had one neck, even as Nero had wished to strike the mob in Rome with a single blow, it was not possible. The church in Rome was given a sentimental respect, but, as mentioned (note 5), the title *Pope* was actually accorded many bishops. Cyprian was frequently addressed that way. So the execution of Bishop Fabian did not leave the church leaderless. Authority depended more on the individual reputations and skills of certain bishops who, like Cyprian, gave freely of their advice to one another, including whoever was sitting in Peter's chair. Scholarly arguments can be posed for or against the claim that Cyprian accepted the primacy of Rome. If he did accept it, he seems to have felt the decision gave him all the more reason to hold that particular bishop in line with the truth as Cyprian saw it.

Cyprian was a strong believer in church discipline, and particularly in the authority of a bishop, a view which he states frequently in his letters. Any discussion of how a Roman hierarchical chain of command took hold on the Catholic church must include Cyprian. There is no doubt that he considered each bishop to have the last

Procession of saints and prophets in mosaic from St. Apollinare Nuovo, Ravenna. The present sixth-century Byzantine mosaic replaced an earlier Ostrogothic work which included Arian leaders. Photograph courtesy of Alinari/Art Resource, New York, N.Y.

word in his own domain. Nor did he countenance any disobedience from below. This is evident when, in 250, he went around his clergy and wrote a letter directly to the laymen seeking their support for his position.

> There is no need for me to be told, my dearest brothers, that you are pained and distressed over the downfall of our brethren. I too, like you, am pained and distressed for each one of them, and I am suffering and feeling what the blessed Apostle describes: *Who is weak and am I not weak? Who is made to stumble and do I not burn with indignation?* And again he has claimed in his epistle: *If one member suffers, the other members also share in the suffering; and if one member rejoices, the other members share in the rejoicing.*
>
> I share in the suffering, I share in the pain of our brothers; as they fell, laid low before the fury of the persecution, they tore away part of our own vitals with them, and by their wounds they inflicted a like pain on us. These are wounds which can indeed be healed by the power of our merciful God.
>
> All the same, my view is that we ought not to be hasty or do anything incautiously or hurriedly; otherwise there is the risk that if we usurp peace rashly, we may rouse God's displeasure and wrath all the more severely.
>
> The blessed martyrs have sent us a letter about certain people, asking that their requests should be examined. After the Lord has first restored peace to us all and, as soon as we have returned to the Church, these requests will be examined individually, in your presence and with the help of your judgment.
>
> In spite of this, I am told that there are certain of the presbyters who are neither mindful of the gospel nor do they heed what the martyrs have written to us: they do not preserve for their bishop the respect due to his sacred office and to his throne, but they have already begun to join in communion with the fallen, offering the sacrifice on their behalf and giving them the Eucharist, whereas they ought to go through the proper stages to reach this end. For in the case of less serious sins, not committed directly against God, a man does penance for an appropriate period; the penitent then must make public confession after his life has been examined; and nobody can be admitted to communion without first having had hands laid on him by the bishop and clergy. It follows that in the case of these most serious and grievous of sins we must comply with every observance, with all the greater reserve and restraint, in conformity with the discipline of the Lord.
>
> This is indeed the counsel which the presbyters and deacons ought to have given to our people, thereby cherishing the flock entrusted to their care and directing them, by means of the teaching of God, on to the way whereby they might beg for the recovery of their salvation. I know personally the peace-loving as well as the God-fearing disposition of our peo-

ple; I know that they would be keeping watch, making amends to God and beseeching His pardon, had they not been led astray by certain of the presbyters who wanted to win their favour.

Accordingly, you at least must guide the fallen individually and your restraining counsel must temper their attitudes to conform with God's precepts. No-one should pick sour fruit, before the proper season. No-one, when his ship has been buffeted and holed by the waves, should entrust it again to the deep, before he has had it carefully repaired. No-one should be in a hurry to take up and put on a torn tunic, before he has seen that it has been mended by a skilled craftsmen and has got it back after treatment by the fuller.

I beg them to pay patient heed to our advice: wait for our return. Then, when, through God's mercy, we have come to you and the bishops have been called together, a large number of us will be able to examine the letter of the blessed martyrs and their requests, acting in conformity with the discipline of the Lord and in the presence of the confessors, and in accordance, also, with your judgment.

On this matter I have written both to the clergy and to the martyrs and confessors, both of which letters I have instructed should be read to you.

I wish that you, my most dear and cherished brothers, may ever fare well in the Lord and be mindful of us. Farewell (1)

Then, as now, priests who went their own way, for what they considered their own good reasons, were a threat to the unity of the church. Cyprian, in a letter written in 250 to "the priests and deacons, his brethren," made plain his own displeasure with one priest over the question of the lapsed.

My dearest brothers, you have acted in conformity with propriety and discipline when you determined, upon the advice of my colleagues who were present with you, that you should cease to be in communion with Gaius Didensis, the presbyter, and his deacon. They have been admitting the lapsed into communion; they have been offering their oblations. Though they have frequently been detected in this erroneous and vicious conduct of theirs and though, as you have written to me, they have been repeatedly warned by my colleagues to desist, they have obstinately persisted in their presumptuous and defiant behavior.

They have thus deceived some of the brethren from among our laity, whereas it is our desire to look after their welfare by every profitable means: we are providing measures for their salvation not by perverted blandishments but by honest and faithful dedication, endeavouring to ensure that they appease God by genuine repentance, by sighs and profound sorrow. For it is written: *Remember whence you have fallen, and repent.* And again we are told by holy Scripture: *Thus speaks the Lord: when you have been converted and sigh, then you will be saved and you will know where you have been.*

How are they able to draw sighs and repent when their sighs and tears are being obstructed by some of the presbyters who rashly consider they should admit them to communion? They are ignorant of the words of Scripture: *Those who call you blessed cause you to err and overthrow the path whereon you walk.*

It is not to be wondered at that we are making no headway at all with our health-giving and true counsels so long as the progress of the saving truth is being blocked by pernicious allurements and flatteries. The sick and wounded souls of the fallen are suffering the same experience as often befalls also those who are sick and ailing in the flesh: health-giving food and beneficial drink they reject as bitter and loathsome whilst they crave for what seems to be sweet and pleasant at the moment. But what they are doing by their heedlessness and wilfulness is bringing upon themselves death and destruction. They will make no progress towards recovering their health by means of the genuine remedies of the specialist whilst they are still under the seducing spell of deceiving blandishments.

And so, as I have written to you, you must take action that is in conformity with faith and conducive to salvation. These are the wiser counsels; do not withdraw from them. You should read these same letters also to any of my colleagues who may be present with you or who may come later. In this way we may act in unison and harmony, adhering to the same health-giving measures for healing and curing the wounds of the fallen. Our resolve is to discuss at full length all these issues when, by the Lord's mercy, we can assemble together.

But in the meantime, if anyone—whether he be presbyter or deacon from our own or from other churches—if anyone should be possessed of such headstrong and outrageous temerity as to admit the lapsed into communion before we have come to our decision, he is to be banished from communion with us; he will have to present the case for his rash conduct in the hearing of us all when, by the Lord's leave, we have assembled together.

You have also made the request that I write back to you my judgment concerning the subdeacons Philumenus and Fortunatus and the acolyte Favorinus. They withdrew for a time and have now come back.

I do not consider that it is proper for me to give a decision on this question by myself alone; many of the clergy are absent still and have not considered it to be their duty to resume their station even at this late date. We will have to hold an examination and inquiry into each case separately and investigate them of the entire congregation as well. This is a matter which may establish a precedent for the future concerning ministers of the church; we must, therefore, exercise mature deliberation in weighing such a question and making a pronouncement upon it.

In the meantime, it would be best if they merely refrain from taking their monthly allotment. The purpose is not that they should be understood to be stripped of their ecclesiastical ministry but that their case may be deferred completely without prejudice, until we can be present.

I wish that you, dearly beloved brothers, may ever fare well. Give my greetings to all of the brethren. Farewell. (34)

A year or so later, when the aging Bishop Rogatian of Numidia wrote to Cyprian complaining of a rebellious deacon, Cyprian declared that the man should be made to do penance. Such disobedience unchecked could lead to heresy and schism.

I and those colleagues who were present were deeply shocked and disturbed to read your letter, my dearest brother, in which you complain that you have been harassed by the insolent and contemptuous conduct of your deacon who has disregarded your dignity as bishop and left unheeded the duties of his own station.

For your part, you have shown us honour and acted with your customary humility in choosing to lay before us your complaint about him, whereas you possessed the right, by the power and authority of your episcopal chair, to exact immediate punishment from him; you could have rested assured that all of us your colleagues would welcome whatever action you took by virtue of your episcopal power against this insolent deacon of yours. In fact, you have injunctions from God concerning men of this character, since, in Deuteronomy, the Lord our God says: *And whatever man acts with such arrogance that he pays no heed to the priest or the judge, whoever he may be in those days, that man shall die, and when all the people hear of it, they will be afraid and will desist, henceforth, from their wickedness.*

There is another text which demonstrates to us that these words of God were uttered with all His true and solemn majesty in order to secure honour and vindication for His priests. When three of the temple servants, Core, Dathan, and Abiron, had the arrogant presumption to lift up their heads and act in opposition to Aaron the priest and set themselves on an equal footing with that priest, their appointed leader, the earth opened up, swallowed and devoured them and they were punished forthwith for their insolence and sacrilege. And they were not alone: two hundred fifty others as well who were their companions in rebellion were consumed by the fire that burst forth by the power of the Lord, thereby proving that priests of God are vindicated by Him who makes priests.

Furthermore, when, in the Book of Kings, the Jewish people held Samuel their priest in scorn because of his age—as you now have been—the Lord cried out in anger and said: *They have not despised you, they have despised me.* And as vengeance for this, He raised up Saul to be their King to beset them with grave hardships and to tread underfoot and oppress this arrogant nation with all kinds of insult and punishment. In this way through divine retribution the priest was avenged for the scorn in which this arrogant nation had held him.

For their part, deacons should bear in mind that it was the Lord who chose Apostles, that is to say, bishops and appointed leaders, whereas it was the Apostles who, after the ascension of our Lord into heaven, established deacons to assist the Church and themselves, in their office of bishop. Are *we* really in a position to rebel in any way against God who makes us bishops? Equally is it possible for deacons to rebel against us who make them deacons?

Therefore, it is proper that the deacon of whom you write should do penance for his outrageous conduct, thereby acknowledging the reverence due to his bishop and making amends, with full humility, to the bishop, his appointed leader.

In this sort of behaviour, indeed, pleasing themselves and treating their appointed leaders with arrogant contempt and scorn, in this lie the origins of heretics, the source for the onslaughts of evil-minded schismatics. This is how men come to abandon the Church, set up an unholy altar outside that Church and rebel against the peace of Christ and the establishment and unity appointed by God.

Should he harass and provoke you further with his insolent behaviour, you should exercise against him the powers of your office, either by deposing him or by excommunicating him. The Apostle Paul, writing to Timothy, said: *Let no man despise you for your youth.* Your colleagues have, accordingly, all the more reason for saying to you: Let no man despise you for your age.

You write that there is a certain person who is in league with this same deacon of yours and a partner in his arrogance and rebellion. This man, too, and any others who prove to be like them and act in opposition to a bishop of God, you have the power to curb or to excommunicate.

But what we really urge and advise is that they rather acknowledge their offence, make amends, and thereby permit us to keep to our own intention—for our wish and desire is to overcome by kindly forebearance the insults and outrages of individual offenders in preference to exacting punishment by virtue of our episcopal powers.

I wish that you, my very dear brother, may ever fare well. (3)

Roman officials in the third century who wanted to be rid of the Christians were perhaps unaware of how bitterly the Christians quarreled among themselves and even sought to be rid of each other. Cyprian's eight years as bishop, from 250 to 258, were fraught with animosity among clergymen both at home and abroad. From the first, there was ill feeling over his election when he defeated seniors of long standing in the church. Cyprian also became involved in a quarrel over who was the rightful bishop of Rome. In 251, Cornelius, challenged by Novatian on his right to this office, received support in a series of letters from Cyprian, of which the following brief message, a covering letter for 46, is an example.

> My dearest brother, I have judged it to be an obligation upon me and my religious duty towards you all to write a brief letter to the confessors over there in Rome who have forsaken the Church, seduced through the viciousness and perversity of Novatian and Novatus. My purpose is to induce them out of fraternal affection to return to their own true mother, that is, to the Catholic Church.
>
> I have given instructions that this letter should be read to you beforehand by the subdeacon Mettius as a precaution against any false claim being made that I have written something that is not contained in my letter. I have, moreover, given instructions to this same Mettius (whom I am sending over to you) that he is to act in this matter according to your discretion: he is to deliver this letter to the confessors only if you have considered that it should be handed over to them.
>
> I wish that you, my dearest brother, may ever fare well. (47)

For several years after Emperor Decius was killed in battle in 251, the Christians were in less danger. Cyprian, after a year in hiding, returned to Carthage, where, in the following years, by the force of his personality and extraordinary self-confidence, he became a leading figure in the church. The Christian community which he headed in Carthage also grew in prominence. But, later, in Valerian's reign (253 to 260), the persecutions were revived with renewed vigor.

When the attack came in 257, the official church position was uncompromising, believing that it was better to die for one's faith than to worship idols or to offer sacrifices to the deified emperors whom the pagan world revered (at least officially) as gods. Cyprian glorified martyrdom in a letter written in 257 to fellow bishops, priests, and laymen confined in the mines at Sigua.

> Your glory, indeed, would demand, most blessed and beloved brethren, that I myself should come to see and to embrace you, if the limits of the place appointed me did not restrain me, banished as I am for the sake of the confession of the Name. But in what way I can, I bring myself into your presence; and even though it is not permitted me to come to you in body and in movement, yet in love and in spirit I come expressing my mind in my letter, in which mind I joyfully exult in those virtues and praises of yours, counting myself a partaker with you, although not in bodily suffer-

ing, yet in community of love. Could I be silent and restrain my voice in stillness, when I am made aware of so many and such glorious things concerning my dearest friends, things with which the divine condescension has honoured you, so that part of you have already gone before by the consummation of their martyrdom to receive from their Lord the crown of their deserts? Part still abide in the dungeons of the prison, or in the mines and in chains, exhibiting by the very delays of their punishments, greater examples for the strengthening and arming of the brethren, advancing by the tediousness of their tortures to more ample titles of merit, to receive as many payments in heavenly rewards, as days are now counted in their punishments. . . . Moreover, they have put fetters on your feet, and have bound your blessed limbs, and the temples of God with disgraceful chains, as if the spirit also could be bound with the body, or your gold could be stained by the contact of iron. To men who are dedicated to God, and attesting their faith with religious courage, such things are ornaments, not chains; nor do they bind the feet of the Christians for infamy, but glorify them for a crown. Oh feet blessedly bound, which are loosed, not only by the smith but by the Lord! Oh feet blessedly bound, which are guided to paradise in the way of salvation! Oh feet bound for the present time in the world, that they may be always free with the Lord! Oh feet, lingering for a while among the fetters and cross-bars, but to run quickly to Christ on a glorious road! Let cruelty, either envious or malignant, hold you here in its bonds and chains as long as it will, from this earth and from these sufferings you shall speedily come to the kingdom of heaven. The body is not cherished in the mines with couch and cushions, but it is cherished with the refreshment and solace of Christ. The frame wearied with labours lies prostrate on the ground, but it is no penalty to lie down with Christ. Your limbs unbathed, are foul and disfigured with filth and dirt; but within they are spiritually cleansed, although without the flesh is defiled. There the bread is scarce; but man liveth not by bread alone, but by the word of God. Shivering, you want clothing; but he who puts on Christ is both abundantly clothed and adorned. The hair of your half-shorn head seems repulsive; but since Christ is the head of the man, anything whatever must needs become that head which is illustrious on account of Christ's name.[7]

In a letter written in 258 to a fellow clergyman, Successus, Cyprian describes an edict of the previous year in which Valerian made it plain that he intended to eliminate the leaders of the movement.

Know that those have come whom I had sent to the City for this purpose, that they might find out and bring back to us the truth, in whatever manner it had been decreed respecting us. For many various and uncertain things

> are current in men's opinions. But the truth concerning them is as follows, that Valerian had sent a rescript to the Senate, to the effect that bishops and presbyters and deacons should immediately be punished; but that senators, and men of importance, and Roman knights, should lose their dignity, and moreover be deprived of their property; and if, when their means were taken away, they should persist in being Christians, then they should also lose their heads; but that matrons should be deprived of their property, and sent into banishment. Moreover, people of Casesar's household, whoever of them had either confessed before, or should now confess, should have their property confiscated, and should be sent in chains by assignment to Caesar's estates. The Emperor Valerian also added to this address a copy of the letters which he sent to the presidents of the provinces concerning us; which letters we are daily hoping will come, waiting according to the strength of our faith for the endurance of suffering, and expecting from the help and mercy of the Lord the crown of eternal life. But know that Xistus was martyred in the cemetery on the eighth day of the Ides of August, and with him four deacons. Moreover, the prefects in the City are daily urging on this persecution; so that, if any are presented to them, they are martyred, and their property claimed by the treasury.
>
> I beg that these things may be made known by your means to the rest of our colleagues, that everywhere, by their exhortation, the brotherhood may be strengthened and prepared for the spiritual conflict, that every one of us may think less of death than of immortality; and dedicated to the Lord, with full faith and entire courage, may rejoice rather than fear in this confession, wherein they know that the soldiers of God and Christ are not slain, but crowned. I bid you, dearest brother, ever heartily farewell in the Lord. (81)

It seems certain that Cyprian could have gone into hiding again at this time, but his mind was made up precisely the other way. He was taken before the proconsul on the charge of refusing to worship the state gods and, being high-born, was treated in a formal manner. After being formally found guilty he was beheaded, publicly in the amphitheatre at Carthage on 14 September 258. It was reported that many in the crowd treasured cloths soaked in his blood.

Much less is known of other Christian martyrs of this period who were also beheaded. One of them was the obscure Valentine on whose festive day, 14 February, there later intruded, ironically, some practices of pagan origin.

A little more than twenty-five years after the death of Cyprian, the chaotic conditions of the mid-third century came to an end. In 285, Diocletian, a seasoned Illyrian commander, gave up the pretence that there was anything constitutional about the Roman emperorship, or monarchy, and established a thoroughly autocratic government. In the past, in theory at least, a citizen obeyed orders in a more or less cooperative manner. Now he would obey because if he didn't he would be executed. Or so Diocletian said in his edict (301) which, in setting a list of maximum prices on goods for sale, stated, "fear is the most effective regulator and guide for the performance of duty."[8] This practice of using fear rather than loyalty as a means of control was now simply more pervasive than before. Commodus and Septimius Severus, for instance, had seized the children of certain provincial commanders and held them hostage for their fathers' good behavior. Under the Autocracy, all citizens were intimidated and, as in authoritarian societies everywhere, the individual was swallowed up by his protectors.

Diocletian dramatized his power by bedecking himself with golden garments and dazzling jewels. The gulf he created between himself and his subjects was further widened by requiring them to bow down before him. As the historian Edward Gibbon wrote: "It was the object of Augustus to disguise his power and of Dioclectian to display it."

More than fear was involved. Roman society had suffered a series of shocks that had sapped initiative and confidence. The "collective mentality," as the late Harvard professor William L. Langer called it, was one of despair. As when a succession of severe disappointments and losses causes an individual to feel a sense of helplessness, so in this circumstance there was a willingness, even eagerness, by great masses of people to give in to some agency which offered help and protection. In the late third century, Diocletian, calling himself the agent of Jupiter, would henceforth take care of everybody.

The Senate at Rome under the new Autocracy, although representative of the leading families throughout the empire, no longer exercised any power beyond the limits of the capital itself. Carus, one of the last of the Barracks Room Emperors, did not bother to ask the Senate for recognition, but simply announced that he was the emperor. Announcements were all the Senate would get from now on.

Under Diocletian, the empire, too large for one man's supervision, was divided into quadrants. Three colleagues joined Diocletian in a tetrarchy, each ruling one-fourth of the whole. As for economic problems, it was hoped that a rampant inflation would be curbed by the government regulations fixing prices and wages. The Edict on Maximum Prices vigorously attacked the greediness of profiteers, but they were not entirely to blame for the problem. Although some goods disappeared from the market, shortages were also due to lower production as a result of the unsettled times. Moreover, the government's own mounting costs for a lavish building program and an expensive oriental-style court were met with a debased currency, which only made matters worse.

Another instance of a solution to one problem leading to another was the practice of dividing provinces into smaller units for the purpose of efficiency, with the added hope of reducing the threat from powerful provincial commanders. The result was an increase in the number of bureaucrats. But the problem was not just a bigger payroll. No matter how strict an authoritarian Diocletian appeared to be, neither he nor his successors could halt the corruption in the imperial system. Offices were for sale and so were promotions. Inspectors sent to check on wrongdoing could be bribed. It was the same old story, made worse by the emperor's preoccupation with frontier problems.

Although Diocletian presided over the last major persecution of the Christians in 303, it should be emphasized that they did not suffer alone. In an edict of 296, Diocletian had ordered the execution of the leaders of the Manichaean movement. This cult of Persian origin was seen, as was Christianity, as a threat to the stable heritage of paganism so vital to unity in the empire.

Diocletian's plan for an orderly succession within the Tetrarchy did not survive the ambitions of those passed over or left out. His retirement in 305 was followed by civil wars which were still being fought when he died in 316. It was not until 324 that there emerged, victorious and ruling alone, Constantine, to be called the Great, whose policies continued those of Diocletian. There was an emphasis on maintaining stability by eliminating choices. Under Constantine, serfdom was legalized. Since taxes were based on both the buildings on a given piece of property, and the number of persons living there, it was advantageous to keep workers where they were. If they were not forced to stay, it could be argued that the owners of great tracts of land could not produce the crops necessary to pay their taxes. Constantine was therefore willing to see formerly free tenants become serfs, legally bound to the owner's land. Their descendants in the Middle Ages would never know the difference. Similarly, the sons of soldiers or veterans were compelled to join the army. Every new regulation meant fewer individuals who were making decisions about their own future. Nor did the middle class escape this structuring of society.

When the rich find ways of hiding their money and the poor don't have any to be taxed, those of average means are in trouble. So it was under Constantine when the *curiales*, citizens of modest income eligible to be local council members, were held responsible for the collection of taxes in their districts. They had to pay what was due whether they could collect it or not. The not unwarranted impulse to escape from this duty caused Constantine to make the obligation hereditary. That might not have been necessary if so many people had not been given exemptions. Again, as in the case of judicial punishments, the ruling classes, including senators, the bureaucrats, and eventually the Christian clergy, were excused from such a burden. As more of the ordinary taxpayers went under, there were of course fewer left to pay more, and in the long term the imperial government, with its rising costs, was headed toward bankruptcy.

Constantine's one major exception to Diocletian's direction concerned the Christians. Instead of continuing the persecutions, he first offered toleration and then accepted Christianity as a legal religion. Although Constantine retained the title of Pontifex Maximus, which meant he was the head of the state religion, he now openly courted the Christians. They had persevered and had become numerous enough and strong enough to be able to do something for him. According to Constantine's biographer, Eusebius, the Christian God had already guaranteed a victory in 312 over a rival, Maxentius, at the Milvian Bridge outside Rome. There, according to a dramatic story, Constantine had ordered a Christian symbol, the Chi-Rho, the first two letters of *Christos*, to be painted on his soldiers' shields and by this invocation, it was said, he had won the day.[9] Later, in 325, Constantine presided in glittering array over a council of 318 bishops at Nicaea. The mission of this group was to achieve an undivided church by devising a statement of faith binding all members. The result was the Nicene Creed, which proclaimed a belief in a triune God. That was expected to end the bitter struggle with the followers of Arius, an Alexandrian presbyter, who insisted that Christ the Son, though divine, was not co-equal with God the Father. There is still controversy about what exactly Constantine thought about theological matters that so convulsed the clergy and laymen of the time, or how sincere a Christian he was when baptized shortly before his death. His own personal life appears to have been circumspect enough, certainly so in sexual matters, but the execution of members of his family, including his eldest son, Crispus, sounds like business as usual.

The expectation of unity in the church was premature. The Arian belief was too strongly fixed in too many minds to be so easily overcome. In the chapters to follow it becomes evident that even on into the sixth century, Arianism continued to be of major importance, especially in the eastern half of the empire.

In the forepart of the fourth century, the focus on the Roman Empire shifted from Italy to the east. Diocletian set up his headquarters in Nicomedia, a city in the province of Bithynia, which bordered the Black Sea. Constantine founded a "New Rome" on the site of the ancient Greek colony of Byzantium located on the Bosporus: Constantinople. For over a thousand years, from it dedication in 330 until its fall in 1453, it was a city of civilization, rich in art and invention, mother city of the Greek Orthodox faith.

After Constantine's death, the most successful of his sons, Constantius II, ruled from Constantinople for twenty-four years, 337 to 361. He was succeeded by his more famous cousin, Julian the Apostate, whose letters have been preserved. Julian was born in Constantinople in 331 or 332, more likely the former year. Never in his short life of thirty-two years did he visit Rome.

VII JULIAN

Loyal to the Old Gods

A LIGHTHEARTED emperor of Rome? It hardly seems possible. Yet the letters of the much-celebrated Julian show what a glad touch he had. Here is Julian, in 362, busy as he was, writing to his friend Evagrius[1] about a small piece of property he has given him. Since grasping emperors are better known, it may be surprising to find one who was giving something away for a change.

> A small estate of four fields, in Bithynia, was given to me by my grandmother, and this I give as an offering to your affection for me. It is too small to bring a man any great benefit on the score of wealth or to make him appear opulent, but even so it is a gift that cannot wholly fail to please you, as you will see if I describe its features to you one by one. And there is no reason why I should not write in a light vein to you who are so full of the graces and amenities of culture. . . . if you walk up on to a sort of hill away from the house, you will see the sea, the Propontis and the islands, and the city [Constantinople] that bears the name of the noble Emperor; nor will you have to stand meanwhile on seaweed and brambles, or be annoyed by the filth that is always thrown out on to seabeaches and sands, which is so very unpleasant and even unmentionable; but you will stand on smilax and thyme and fragrant herbage. Very peaceful it is to lie down there and glance into some book, and then, while resting one's eyes, it is very agreeable to gaze at the ships and the sea. When I was still hardly more than a boy I thought that this was the most delightful summer place, for it has, moreover, excellent springs and a charming bath and garden and trees. When I had grown to manhood I used to long for my old manner of life there and visited it often, and our meetings there did not lack talks about literature. Moreover there is there, as a humble monument of my

> husbandry, a small vineyard that produces a fragrant, sweet wine, which does not have to wait for time to improve its flavour. . . . Well then, I now give this to you as a present, dear heart, and though it be small, as indeed it is, yet it is precious as coming from a friend to a friend, "from home, homeward bound," in the words of the wise poet Pindar. I have written this letter in haste, by lamplight, so that, if I have made any mistakes, do not criticise them severely or as one rhetorician would another. (25)[2]

Julian's jaunty style is further evident in a brief note to the pagan orator Libanius in the same year.

> Since you have forgotten your promise—at any rate three days have gone by and the philosopher Priscus [a close friend] has not come himself but has sent a letter to say that he still delays—I remind you of your debt by demanding payment. The thing you owe is, as you know, easy for you to pay and very pleasant for me to receive. So send your discourse [on Aristophanes] and your "divine counsel," and do it promptly, in the name of Hermes and the Muses, for I assure you, in these three days you have worn me out, if indeed the Sicilian poet [Theocritus] speaks the truth when he says, "Those who long grow old in a day." And if this be true, as in fact it is, you have trebled my age, my good friend. I have dictated this to you in the midst of public business. For I was not able to write myself because my hand is lazier than my tongue. Though indeed my tongue also has come to be somewhat lazy and inarticulate from lack of exercise. Farewell, brother, most dear and most beloved! (52)

For Julian to say his tongue lacked exercise may have been something of a joke. By all accounts he was high-strung, talkative, given to outbursts of unreserved laughter, fervid in action, and fiery of eye. Yet in his letters, he speaks in a measured tone and chooses his words carefully. Obviously, the letter gave him the opportunity to present himself in a philosophical stance, which was how he thought of himself, or wanted to. So it is that history may find in letters a person's own picture of himself rather than that of detractors or even of friends. Still, Ammianus Marcellinus writes: "his eyes were fine and full of fire, an indication of the acuteness of his mind."[3]

He is called Julian the Apostate because although raised as a Christian, and rather strictly so, he gave up his religion in favor of the old gods. It was politic, however, to remain quiet about it until after he became emperor. Then, the sportier side of his humor became evident when in the following letter he tells how he punished some unruly Arian Christians for their misbehavior. He was writing to a certain Hecebolius, perhaps an official in Edessa in northern Mesopotamia.

> I have behaved to all the Galilaeans [Christians] with such kindness and benevolence that none of them has suffered violence anywhere or been dragged into a temple or threatened into anything else of the sort against his own will. But the followers of the Arian church, in the insolence bred by their wealth, have attacked the followers of Valentine [founder of an obscure sect of Gnostics] and have committed in Edessa such rash acts as could never occur in a well-ordered city. Therefore, since by their most admirable law they are bidden to sell all they have and give to the poor that so they may attain more easily to the kingdom of the skies, in order to aid those persons in that effort, I have ordered that all their funds, namely, that belong to the church of the people of Edessa, are to be taken over that they may be given to the soldiers, and that its property be confiscated to my private purse. This is in order that poverty may teach them to behave properly and that they may not be deprived of that heavenly kingdom for which they still hope.(40)

It was Julian's intention to rule firmly but not in a despotic way. He had seen enough of despotism himself. As a child, he was lucky to have survived a court purge, in 337, in which his father, a half-brother of Constantine the Great, was murdered along with eight others among his relatives. Since his mother, Basilina, had died within months of his birth, he became an orphan at age five or six. During an unhappy later time, from when he was twelve until he was eighteen, he was held, he said, as a prisoner in a remote area of Asia Minor. It was from one of his tutors that he acquired a thorough training in both Greek and Latin literature. In early adulthood, Julian was allowed to go to Athens to hear the philosophers there, and throughout his life he remained devoted to scholarly habits. He wrote essays on philosophy and theology in addition to many letters, of which seventy-three are extant.[4]

G. W. Bowersock, in *Julian the Apostate*, states: "All his writings, taken together, provide an insight into character and disposition such as can be had for no other classical figure apart from Cicero."[5]

Julian's studies in Athens were interrupted in 355 when his cousin, the emperor Constantius II, appointed him to be governor of the province of Gaul. Totally inexperienced, Julian faced the challenge of a land burdened with economic problems and suffering under the barbarian incursions. On the job, he accomplished more than anyone had expected. Prosperity and morale were revived and the barbarians defeated. But, as it happens, success was dangerous. Jealous courtiers convinced the suspicious Constantius that his cousin was plotting against his power.

The last word, however, belonged to Ammianus Marcellinus. He was particularly anxious to present Julian as a man of justice, popular with the citizens of Gaul because of his interest in their welfare. Reporting on how Julian settled one case, Ammianus writes: "And when the accused defended himself by denying the charge, and could not be confuted on any point, Delphidius, a very vigorous speaker, assailing him violently and, exasperated by the lack of proofs, cried: 'Can anyone, most mighty Caesar, ever be found guilty, if it be enough to deny the charge?' And Julian was inspired at once to reply to him wisely: 'Can anyone be proved innocent, if it be enough to have accused him?' And this was one of many like instances of humanity" (XVIII.1.4).

From Paris, Julian wrote to his friend Oribasius about how he intended to expose the base behavior of one of Constantius's officials, a prefect of Gaul named Florentius.

> But with regard to my behaviour towards him [Florentius], the gods know that often, when he wronged the provincials, I kept silence, at the expense of my own honour; to some charges I would not listen, others I would not admit, others again I did not believe, while in some cases I imputed the blame to his associates. But when he thought fit to make me share in such infamy by sending to me to sign those shameful and wholly abominable reports [recommending higher taxes], what was the right thing for me to do? Was I to remain silent, or to oppose him? The former course was foolish, servile and odious to the gods, the latter was just, manly and liberal, but was not open to me on account of the affairs that engaged me. What then did I do? In the presence of many persons who I knew would report it to him I said: "Such-a-one will certainly and by all means revise his reports, for they pass the bounds of decency." When he heard this, he was so far from behaving with discretion that he did things which, by heaven, no tyrant with any moderation would have done, and that too though I was so near where he was. In such a case what was the proper conduct for a man who is a zealous student of the teachings of Plato and Aristotle? Ought I to have looked on while the wretched people were being betrayed to thieves, or to have aided them as far as I could, for they were already singing their swan-song because of the criminal artifices of men of that sort? To me, at least, it seems a disgraceful thing that, while I punish my military tribunes when they desert their post—and indeed they ought to be put to death at once, and not even granted burial—I should myself desert my post which is for the defence of such wretched people; whereas it is my duty to fight against thieves of his sort, especially when God is fighting on my side, for it was indeed he who posted me here. And if any harm to myself should result, it is no small consolation to have proceeded with a good conscience.(4)

Julian was in a precarious position in 360 when the emperor ordered him to send most of his troops to the east to garrisons on the Persian border. To obey would have seriously weakened Gaul's defences. And there was a personal danger for Julian. In the eastern sector he would become especially vulnerable to court intrigue, even to the point of arrest or murder. Julian's troops, some of them native Gauls, refused reassignment. Nor did they want to see their commander in danger. As a consequence, at Paris, they hailed him as Augustus and so proclaimed him to be co-emperor with his cousin. Convinced that this act had the approval of the gods, and in any case left with little choice, Julian accepted the honor and marched east to face Constantius. A letter to his uncle, his mother's brother, also named Julian, explained that he had not sought the conflict with Constantius, and, even while taking arms, he still hoped to reach a peaceful settlement. Again, the mild tone and reasonableness of the letter reflect qualities at odds with his reputation for excitability. Julian also refuted the suspicion, which some must have had, that he had connived at his soldiers' acclamation in Paris. Still, there was certainly no hesitation in the production of coins which proclaimed him to be an Augustus.

> The third hour of the night has just begun, and as I have no secretary to dictate to because they are all occupied, I have with difficulty made the effort to write this to you myself. I am alive, by the grace of the gods, and have been freed from the necessity of either suffering or inflicting irreparable ill. But the Sun, whom of all the gods I besought most earnestly to assist me, and sovereign Zeus also, bear me witness that never for a moment did I wish to slay Constantius, but rather I wished the contrary. Why then did I come? Because the gods expressly ordered me, and promised me safety if I obeyed them, but if I stayed, what I pray no god may do to me! Furthermore I came because, having been declared a public enemy, I meant to frighten him merely, and that our quarrel should result in intercourse on more friendly terms; but if we should have to decide the issue by battle, I meant to entrust the whole to Fortune and to the gods, and so await whatever their clemency might decide. (9)

There would be no civil war. Constantius died suddenly in 361. Julian then ruled alone. Those who had conspired against him at Constantius's court had worried that his influence would be against their machinations and immoralities. Their fears were confirmed when he came to power. He was able to bring some of the worst of the intriguers to justice, as he mentions in a letter, written late in 361, to Hermogenes, a former prefect of Egypt: "Since many accusers are rising up against them, I have appointed a court to judge them" (13).

Julian took his responsibilities seriously. Several aides and servants, working in shifts, were kept busy with his long daily chores. Even so, nothing could interfere with his sacrifices to the gods. As soon as Constantius was dead—his death obviously another gift of the gods—Julian revealed his true religious feelings, which had been kept secret for ten years. It was in 351, he admitted, that he had converted to paganism, and since that time had only posed as a Christian so long as his devout Christian cousin was a reigning emperor. Now, no matter where he was, Julian performed the old rites of worship early in the morning and again in the evening.

In a letter to his friend Libanius, he mentioned that he tried to convince some local Christian senators that they should repent and return to making sacrifices. Writing at a time when he was leading an army toward combat with the Persians, he showed his contempt for passivity and meekness. He did not admire the timidity of the Christian senators, who did not stand up to him and boldly answer his challenges to their faith. Nor, although spare in his own habits, was he a man to approve of monkish practices, so opposed to Roman vigorousness. In this respect, he seems to have set the stage for the criticism of Christianity by the historian Edward Gibbon, whose *Decline and Fall of the Roman Empire* accuses the triumphant Christians of having taken the steel out of the empire and so left it prey to bold and insensitive barbarians.

Here is part of his letter to Libanius.

> I stayed [in Beroea, modern Aleppo in northwest Syria] for a day and saw the Acropolis and sacrificed to Zeus in imperial fashion a white bull. Also I conversed briefly with the senate about the worship of the gods. But though they all applauded my arguments very few were converted by them, and these few were men who even before I spoke seemed to me to hold sound views. But they were cautious and would not strip off and lay aside their modest reserve, as though afraid of too frank speech. For it is the prevailing habit of mankind, O ye gods, to blush for their noble qualities, manliness of soul and piety, and to plume themselves, as it were, on what is most depraved, sacrilege and weakness of mind and body. (58)

It was not only the faintheartedness of certain Christians that alarmed Julian, but the gross behavior of others who had come to power. Earlier, in the third century, when the Christians were still a persecuted minority, they stressed the goodness of their lives in thought and deed. As has been shown, Cyprian's letters were overflowing with a sense of moral superiority, the invisible scaffold of martyrdom. A century later, the son of the mighty Constantine was himself a professed Christian, but Julian, in a letter to the Athenians, written as he was marching eastward, describes Constantius as having been no better than the evildoers among earlier pagan emperors. It was in this letter that Julian could finally express his long pent-up hatred of his cousin, whom he blamed for the slaughter of his family. Charging Constantius with hypocrisy was not unexpected. Julian leveled that complaint at Christians in general. It went alongside his distaste for their unseemly interest in corpses.

In his public letter to the Athenians, Julian was writing about personal matters and not just affairs of state. And he was capable of arranging the news to suit his own feelings. For instance, he mentions his half brother Gallus's cruelty, but blames it, in part, on an unfortunate childhood, which, in turn, was Constantius's fault.

Although Ammianus's history says Gallus had a "disordered mind," he also describes him as a vicious ruler who was deservedly put to death for his abuses.

Bowersock makes frequent references to the letter to the Athenians. Comparing Julian's own interpretation of recent history with other evidence, he finds the letter to have been in certain respects self-serving and proof of the calculating side of Julian's nature. For instance, he and his cousin may actually have cooperated more than Julian now wished to be known. Bowersock's treatment of Julian is generally less sympathetic than that of Robert Browning, whose book *The Emperor Julian* mentions an interest in secret societies as follows: "Starved of affection and isolated for so much of his youth, Julian had a need to be accepted and to belong to a group of some kind."[6]

Here, in part, is what Julian wrote to the Athenians justifying his attitude towards his cousin, Constantius, shortly before learning that he had died.

> Our fathers were brothers, sons of the same father. And close kinsmen as we were, how this most humane Emperor treated us! Six of my cousins and his, and my father who was his own uncle and also another uncle of both of us on the father's side, and my eldest brother, he put to death without a trial; and as for me and my other brother (Gallus), he intended to put us to death but finally inflicted exile upon us; and from that exile he released me, but him he stripped of the title of Caesar just before he murdered him . . . we had been imprisoned in a certain farm in Cappadocia; . . . How shall I describe the six years we spent there? For we lived as though on the estate of a stranger, and were watched as though we were in some Persian garrison, since no stranger came to see us and not one of our old friends was allowed to visit us; . . . For no companion of our own age ever came near us or was allowed to do so.
>
> From that place barely and by the help of the gods I was set free, and for a happier fate; but my brother was imprisoned at court and his fate was ill-starred above all men who have ever yet lived. And indeed whatever cruelty or harshness was revealed in his disposition was increased by his having been brought up among those mountains. It is therefore I think only just that the Emperor should bear the blame for this also, he who against our will allotted to us that sort of bringing-up. As for me, the gods by means of philosophy caused me to remain untouched by it and unharmed; but on my brother no one bestowed this boon. (Letter to the Athenians)

Much has been made of Julian's apostasy, but according to his own testimony, the line between Christianity and paganism was not everywhere strictly observed. A letter described the behavior of a Christian bishop who actually continued the old practices. Of course, the emperor admitted that he was testing the man, but the maintenance of the old shrines speaks for itself. It is believed that this letter was written to a pagan high priest, but that is not certain.

Julian, courtesy of the State Hermitage Museum, Leningrad.

> I should never have favoured Pegasius unhesitatingly if I had not had clear proofs even in former days, when he had the title of Bishop of the Galilaeans [Christians], he was wise enough to revere and honour the gods. . . . after rising at early dawn I came from Troas to Ilios about the middle of the morning. Pegasius came to meet me, as I wished to explore the city—this was my excuse for visiting the temples—and he was my guide and showed me all the sights. So now let me tell you what he did and said, and from it one may guess that he was not lacking in right sentiments towards the gods.
>
> Hector has a hero's shrine there and his bronze statue stands in a tiny little temple. Opposite this they have set up a figure of the great Achilles in the unroofed court. . . . Now I found that the altars were still alight, I might almost say still blazing, and that the statue of Hector had been anointed till it shone. So I looked at Pegasius and said: "What does this mean? Do the people of Ilios offer sacrifices?" This was to test him cautiously to find out his own views. He replied: "Is it not natural that they should worship a brave man who was their own citizen, just as we worship the martyrs?" Now the analogy was far from sound; but his point of view and intentions were those of a man of culture, if you consider the times in which we then lived. Observe what followed. "Let us go," said he, "to the shrine of Athene of Ilios." Thereupon with the greatest eagerness he led me there and opened the temple, and as though he were producing evidence he showed me all the statues in perfect preservation, nor did he behave at all as those impious men do usually, I mean when they make the sign on their impious foreheads, nor did he hiss to himself as they do. For these two things are the quintessence of their theology, to hiss at demons and make the sign of the cross on their foreheads. . . . This same Pegasius went with me to the temple of Achilles as well and showed me the tomb in good repair; yet I had been informed that this also had been pulled to pieces by him. But he approached it with great reverence; I saw this with my own eyes. (19)

Julian left no doubt that it was the old state cults he favored. According to his edict of 17 June 362, professed Christians henceforth were not allowed to teach the classics. The thinking behind this proclamation was that teachers should not teach material they did not personally accept. In Julian's eyes, to do so would be immoral. Also, Christian churches were no longer to receive subsidies, but government funds for the use of the official religion were available. Any temples taken from the pagans were to be returned, and the state would restore those that had been destroyed (29). Other actions could be excused by needs of the government and his suspicion about those who sought ways to avoid onerous duties. For instance, he rescinded the measures which excused the Christian clergy from serving in state offices (39).

Still, Julian could boast that he was far more tolerant of all faiths than his Christian predecessor had been. Constantius, a fanatical Arian, was harsh on orthodox

Christians. Julian offered toleration to both sides. He said he was appalled at the way the Christians fought each other. The subject comes up in a letter, dated 1 August A.D. 362, to the citizens of Bostra (under Trajan, the capital of the Roman province of Arabia). At the same time, he urged the Christians of this community to rebel against their bishop Titus, not on account of religion, but because Titus was a troublemaker. Violence toward the Christians themselves, Julian specifically forbid.

> I thought that the leaders of the Galilaeans would be more grateful to me than to my predecessor in the administration of the Empire. For in his reign it happened to the majority of them to be sent into exile, prosecuted, and cast into prison, and moreover, many whole communities of those who are called "heretics" were actually butchered, as at Samosata and Cyzicus, in Paphlagonia, Bithynia, and Galatia, among many other tribes also villages were sacked and completely devastated; whereas, during my reign, the contrary has happened.[7] For those who had been exiled have had their exile remitted, and those whose property was confiscated have, by a law of mine received permission to recover all their possessions. Yet they have reached such a pitch of raving madness and folly that they are exasperated because they are not allowed to behave like tyrants or to persist in the conduct in which they at one time indulged against one another, and afterwards carried on towards us who revered the gods. . . . but do you, the populace, live in agreement with one another, and let no man be quarrelsome or act unjustly. Neither let those of you who have strayed from the truth outrage those who worship the gods duly and justly, according to the beliefs that have been handed down to us from time immemorial; nor let those of you who worship the gods outrage or plunder the houses of those who have strayed rather from ignorance than of set purpose. It is by reason that we ought to persuade and instruct men, not by blows, or insults, or bodily violence. Wherefore, again and often I admonish those who are zealous for true religion not to injure the communities of the Galilaeans or attack or insult them. . . . (41)

Again, in 362, writing to an official in Mesopotamia named Atarbius, Julian insisted that Christians go unmolested.

> I affirm by the gods that I do not wish the Galilaeans to be either put to death or unjustly beaten, or to suffer any other injury; but nevertheless I do assert absolutely that the god-fearing must be preferred to them. For through the folly of the Galilaeans almost everything has been overturned, whereas through the grace of the gods are we all preserved. Wherefore we ought to honour the gods and the god-fearing, both men and cities. (37)

Julian's sincerity in his profession of toleration is open to debate. Bowersock strongly contends that his ultimate aim was to be rid of the Christians altogether, although he renounced force. But the great emphasis Browning gives to Julian's interest in Neoplatonism suggests that he must have truly meant to be fair, since according to that philosophy all faiths are manifestations of the one Spirit or Truth.

The founder of Neoplatonism, Plotinus, lived in the third century, and by Julian's time his teachings had undergone alterations by later followers with whose writings Julian was familiar. To be brief, they enabled Julian, on the philosophical side, to envision a single ruling principle in the world, which sounds like monotheism. At the same time, on the religious side, Julian could make sacrifices to a variety of deities who all expressed this one Spirit, although that sounds like polytheism. The advantage of this arrangement was that it could bring everybody into a state of mutual acceptance. (He would have admired modern Bahaism, which argues for the spiritual unity of mankind.) The problem was that the Christians and Jews were never going to accept the existence of any god except their own.

Julian kept an eye on the worshippers of the old gods and, in particular, instructed a high priest, Theodorus, to monitor the behavior of the pagan priests. They should behave with piety and benevolence towards the gods and men. He considered the devotion of the Jews to their God a good model to follow, but their rejection of all other gods was to Julian a "barbaric conceit."

> I have written you a more familiar sort of letter than to the others, because you, I believe, have more friendly feelings than others towards me. . . .
>
> What then is this office which I say I now entrust to you? It is the government of all the temples of Asia [meaning Rome's eastern provinces] with power to appoint the priests in every city and to assign to each what is fitting. Now the qualities that befit one in this high office are, in the first place, fairness, and next, goodness and benevolence towards those who deserve to be treated thus. For any priest who behaves unjustly to his fellow men and impiously towards the gods, or is overbearing to all, must either be admonished with plain speaking or chastised with great severity. . . . For I hold that we ought to observe the laws that we have inherited from our forefathers, since it is evident that the gods gave them to us. . . . Therefore, when I saw that there is among us great indifference about the gods and that all reverence for the heavenly powers has been driven out by impure and vulgar luxury, I always secretly lamented this state of things. For I saw that those whose minds were turned to the doctrines of the Jewish religion are so ardent in their belief that they would choose to die for it, and to endure utter want and starvation rather than taste pork or any animal that has been strangled or had the life squeezed out of it; whereas we are in such a state of apathy about religious matters that we have forgotten the customs of our forefathers, and therefore we actually do not know whether

> any such rule has ever been prescribed. But these Jews are in part god-fearing, seeing that they revere a god who is truly most powerful and most good and governs this world of sense, and, as I well know, is worshipped by us also under other names. They act as is right and seemly, in my opinion, if they do not transgress the laws; but in this one thing they err in that, while reserving their deepest devotion for their own god, they do not conciliate the other gods also; but the other gods they think have been allotted to us Gentiles only, to such a pitch of folly have they been brought by their barbaric conceit. (20)

In a letter to Arsacius, an archpriest of Galatia, in late 362 or early 363, Julian admits his admiration for Christian charity. And being a man of spare habits, he, the same as the Christians, denounced the indulgent pleasures of the theater and chariot races.

> Why . . . do we not observe that it is their benevolence to strangers, their care for the graves of the dead and the pretended holiness of their lives that have done most to increase atheism [Julian often refers to Christianity this way]? I believe that we ought really and truly to practice every one of these virtues. And it is not enough for you alone to practice them, but so must all the priests in Galatia, without exception. . . . In the second place, admonish them that no priest may enter a theatre or drink in a tavern or control any craft or trade that is base and not respectable. Honour those who obey you, but those who disobey, expel from office. In every city establish frequent hostels in order that strangers may profit by our benevolence; I do not mean for our own people only, but for others also who are in need of money. . . . For it is disgraceful that, when no Jew ever has to beg and the impious Galilaeans [Christians] support not only their own poor but ours as well, all men see that our people lack aid from us. (22)

Julian liked to present himself as a man whose temper was under control. That it wasn't always is evident in this letter of October 362 to Ecdicius, the prefect of Egypt. The obstreperous Bishop Athanasius was to be expelled from Alexandria. Athanasius was surely getting used to leaving. Between 326 and 373 he spent about twenty years away from Alexandria as a result of repeated expulsions.

> You know that, though I am slow to condemn, I am even much slower to remit when I have once condemned. *Added with his own hand*. It vexes me greatly that my orders are neglected. By all the gods there is nothing I should be so glad to see, or rather hear reported as achieved by you, as that Athanasius has been expelled beyond the frontiers of Egypt. Infamous

> man! He has had the audacity to baptize Greek women of rank during my reign! Let him be driven forth! (46)

Despite sharp personal differences with some church leaders, a letter to Basil, who later became a bishop in the province of Cappadocia, shows how cordial Julian could be to persons who "have abandoned themselves to the superstition of the Galilaeans." It also shows the strength of old school ties. They had known each other in student days in Athens.

> But we, though we refute and criticize one another with appropriate frankness, whenever it is necessary, love one another as much as the most devoted friends. . . . I have dispatched this letter to you to convince you that your presence, wise man that you are, will be serviceable to me rather than any waste of my time. Make haste then, as I said, and use the state post. And when you have stayed with me as long as you desire you shall go your way whithersoever you please, with an escort furnished by me, as is proper. (26)

As mentioned earlier, according to Bowersock, the amiability of such a letter to a leader in the Christian community, or Julian's repeated emphasis on toleration, could be misleading. He writes: "There can be no doubt that as early as spring of 362, and almost certainly well before that, Julian looked forward to the ultimate eradication of Christianity" (p. 82). If so, it might explain Julian's decision to cater to the Jews.

In an open letter to the Jewish people, called a rescript because it announced state policy publicly, Julian makes plain his intention of treating them fairly. He may have seen them as partners in opposition to Christianity. The Jews were permitted to settle again in Jerusalem, a privilege denied them for 290 years. They could also rebuild their temple. The project was in fact begun, but the foundations were destroyed, most likely by an earthquake. Nor was this considered unfortunate by all Jews, for many of their leaders suspected Julian's motives, and they certainly did not consider him to be a messiah. Plans for rebuilding the temple were left unfulfilled when Julian died.

> Since I wish that you should prosper yet more, I have admonished my brother Iulus, your most venerable patriarch, that the levy which is said to exist among you should be prohibited, and that no one is any longer to have the power to oppress the masses of your people by such exactions; so that everywhere, during my reign, you may have security of mind, and in the enjoyment of peace may offer more fervid prayers for my reign to the Most High God, the Creator, who has deigned to crown me with his own immaculate right hand. For it is natural that men who are distracted

> by any anxiety should be hampered in spirit, and should not have so much confidence in raising their hands to pray; but that those who are in all respects free from care should rejoice with their whole hearts and offer their suppliant prayers on behalf of my imperial office to Mighty God, even to him who is able to direct my reign to the noblest ends, according to my purpose. This you ought to do, in order that, when I have successfully concluded the war with Persia, I may rebuild by my own efforts the sacred city of Jerusalem, which for so many years you have longed to see inhabited, and may bring settlers there, and, together with you, may glorify the Most High God therein. (51)

In the last months of his life, in 363, Julian launched the invasion of the Persian Empire mentioned in that letter. After initial successes, the campaign ran into some difficult going and then, suddenly, Julian was struck by a spear in his groin during a skirmish. He died some hours later when renewed bleeding from his wound could not be stopped. It was never positively determined whether the mortal blow was struck by the enemy or by a soldier, possibly a Christian, in Julian's army. Libanius, the pagan orator of Antioch, who was a great friend, admirer, and correspondent of Julian, decided that a Christian plot was to blame. Ammianus Marcellinus, who was at the battle but did not witness the attack on the emperor, simply said it could not be known who threw the spear.

The question about Julian's death was widely discussed. Certainly so by the Cappadocian Fathers, Basil, and Gregory of Nazianzus, whose letters are the subject of the next chapter. They were students in Athens at the time Julian was there. Letter 26 to Basil, above, suggests that he and the emperor were good friends. But Julian did not have many friends, and after he was gone, Gregory's bitter condemnations of him were likely well received.

VIII
GREGORY OF NYSSA
BASIL
GREGORY OF NAZIANZUS

Uncommon Men with Common Interests

Gregory of Nyssa

THE names of the eastern church fathers may be only slightly familiar. It helps, therefore, to have personal letters to undercut the stereotype and give them lives of their own. Gregory of Nyssa (ca. 330 to ca. 395), for instance, overshadowed by his famous brother Basil, emerges from his letters as an engaging personality.

If there is something missing in the demeanor of the church fathers, east or west, it seems to be a sense of humor. It is all the more surprising, then, to find the monastic-minded Gregory making a joke about poverty. The amusing passage appears in a letter containing a detailed architectural description of a church under construction. Gregory was trying to persuade an official named Amphilochius to send more help, and the details were to assist in estimates of how many workmen were needed. The letter ends with the following paragraph.

> Now if my account has explained the work in detail, I hope it may be possible for your Sanctity, on perceiving what is needed, to relieve us completely from anxiety so far as the workmen are concerned. If, however, the workmen were inclined to make a bargain favourable to us, let a distinct measure of work, if possible, be fixed for the day, so that he may not pass his time doing nothing, and then, though he has no work to show for it, as having worked for us so many days, demand payment for them. I know that we shall appear to most people to be higglers, in being so particular about the contracts. But I beg you to pardon me; for that Mammon about whom

God's presence from visible symbols, one might more justly consider that He dwelt in the Cappadocian nation than in any of the spots outside it. For how many Altars there are there, on which the name of our Lord is glorified! One could hardly count so many in all the rest of the world. Again, if the Divine grace was more abundant about Jerusalem than elsewhere, sin would not be so much the fashion amongst those that live there; but as it is, there is no form of uncleanness that is not perpetrated amongst them; rascality, adultery, theft, idolatry, poisoning, quarreling, murder, are rife; and the last kind of evil is so excessively prevalent, that nowhere in the world are people so ready to kill each other as there; where kinsmen attack each other like wild beasts, and spill each other's blood, merely for the sake of lifeless plunder. Well, in a place where such things go on, what proof, I ask, have you of the abundance of Divine grace? . . . Wherefore, O ye who fear the Lord, praise Him in the places where ye now are. Change of place does not effect any drawing nearer unto God, but wherever thou mayest be, God will come to thee, if the chambers of the soul be found of such a sort that He can dwell in thee and walk in thee. But if thou keepest thine inner man full of wicked thoughts, even if thou wast on Golgotha, even if thou wast on the Mount of Olives, even if thou stoodest on the memorial-rock of the Resurrection, thou wilt be as far away from receiving Christ into thyself, as one who has not even begun to confess him. Therefore, my beloved friend, counsel the brethren to be absent from the body to go to our Lord, rather than to be absent from Cappadocia to go to Palestine; and if any one should adduce the command spoken by our Lord to His disciples that they should not quit Jerusalem, let him be made to understand its true meaning. Inasmuch as the gift and the distribution of the Holy Spirit had not yet passed upon the Apostles, our Lord commanded them to remain in the same place, until they should have been endued with power from on high. Now, if that which happened at the beginning, when the Holy Spirit was dispensing each of His gifts under the appearance of a flame, continued until now, it would be right for all to remain in that place where that dispensing took place; but if the Spirit "bloweth" where He "listeth," those, too, who have become believers here are made partakers of that gift; and that according to the proportion of their faith, not in consequence of their pilgrimage to Jerusalem. (On Pilgrimages)

Basil

Later history has focused on more prominent men than Gregory, such as Basil (ca. 330 to 379), whose rules for community living rescued many monks from solitary extremism and gave them a more regularized life. Yet there was in his own day an obscure figure named Glycerius whom some young people found more attractive.

Three of Basil's letters deal with the strange affair of this deacon in Cappadocia who became a cult figure to a group of impressionable youths. Their parents, as the following letter, written about 374, shows, were greatly perplexed. Whether Basil, who became the bishop of Caesarea in 370, wrote this letter to his brother or to his friend Gregory of Nazianzus is not certain.

> You have undertaken a kindly and charitable task in getting together the captive troop of the insolent Glycerius (at present I must so write), and, so far as in you lay, covering our common shame. It is only right that your reverence should undo this dishonour with a full knowledge of the facts about him.
>
> This grave and venerable Glycerius of yours was ordained by me deacon of the church of Venesa to serve the presbyter, and look after the work of the Church, for though the fellow is in other respects intractable, he is naturally clever at manual labour. No sooner was he appointed than he neglected his work, as though there had been absolutely nothing to do. But, of his own private power and authority, he got together some wretched virgins, some of whom came to him of their own accord (you know how young people are prone to anything of this kind), and others were unwillingly forced to accept him as leader of their company. Then he assumed the style and title of patriarch, and began all of a sudden to play the man of dignity. He had not attained to this on any reasonable or pious ground; his only object was to get a means of livelihood, just as some men start one trade and some another. He has all but upset the whole Church, scorning his own presbyter, a man venerable both by character and age; scorning his chorepiscopus, and myself, as of no account at all, continually filling the town and all the clergy with disorder and disturbance. And now, on being mildly rebuked by me and his chorepiscopus, that he may not treat us with contempt (for he was trying to stir the younger men to like insubordination), he is meditating conduct most audacious and inhuman. After robbing as many of the virgins as he could, he has made off by night. I am sure all this will have seemed very sad to you. Think of the time too. The feast was being held there, and, as was natural, large numbers of people were gathered together. He, however, on his side, brought out his own troop, who followed young men and danced round them, causing all well-disposed persons to be most distressed, while loose chatterers laughed aloud. And even this was not enough, enormous as was the scandal. I am told that even the parents of the virgins, finding their bereavement unendurable, wishful to bring home the scattered company, and falling with not unnatural sighs and tears at their daughters' feet, have been insulted and outraged by this excellent young man and his troop of bandits. I am sure your reverence will think all this intolerable. The ridicule of it attaches to

> us all alike. First of all, order him to come back with the virgins. He might find some mercy, if he were to come back with a letter from you. If you do not adopt this course, at least send the virgins back to their mother the Church. If this cannot be done, at all events do not allow any violence to be done to those that are willing to return, but get them to return to me. Otherwise I call God and man to witness that all this is ill done, and a breach of the law of the Church. The best course would be for Glycerius to come back with a letter, and in a becoming and proper frame of mind; if not, let him be deprived of his ministry. (CLXIX)[3]

That letter has a businesslike tone. Basil was a down-to-earth individual who could have given the more scholarly Jerome some sensible advice. For instance, Basil insisted that departing to the wilderness was no solution in itself, for a person took his inner faults and disorders with him. Jerome's hallucinations as a hermit were symptomatic of the problems in that lonely life. Organizing monks into groups that would live according to rules of a good Christian life was the answer. Basil became the founder of the monastery (the cenobitic as against eremitic asceticism), and his Basilian Rule provided the basis for the great Benedictine formula of the sixth century. A description of his own early days as a monk is found in a letter, written about 360, to his friend Gregory of Nazianzus, whom he urged to join him. The renunciation of worldly pleasures did not blind Basil to the beauties of nature. In his retreat, he prized tranquility of the mind, not the struggle against temptation.

> My brother Gregory writes me word that he has long been wishing to be with me, and adds that you are of the same mind; however, I could not wait, partly as being hard of belief, considering I have been so often disappointed, and partly because I find myself pulled all ways by business. I must at once make for Pontus, where, perhaps, God willing, I may make an end of wandering. After renouncing, with trouble, the idle hopes which I once had, [about you] or rather the dreams, (for it is well said that hopes are waking dreams), I departed into Pontus in quest of a place to live in. There God has opened on me a spot exactly answering to my taste, so that I actually see before my eyes what I have often pictured to my mind in idle fancy. There is a lofty mountain covered with thick woods, watered towards the north with cool and transparent streams. A plain lies beneath, enriched by the waters which are ever draining off from it; and skirted by a spontaneous profusion of trees almost thick enough to be a fence; so as even to surpass Calypso's Island, which Homer seems to have considered the most beautiful spot on the earth. . . . the chief praise of the place is, that being happily disposed for produce of every kind, it nurtures what to me is the sweetest produce of all, quietness; indeed, it is not only rid

> of the bustle of the city, but is even unfrequented by travellers, except a chance hunter. It abounds indeed in game, as well as other things, but not, I am glad to say, in bears or wolves, such as you have, but in deer, and wild goats, and hares, and the like. (XIV)

Basil's letter to a pupil named Chilo outlined the proper behavior for a monk, even one still living the life of a solitary. It has a tone of moderation, and it emphasizes the need to build gradually and carefully toward true asceticism and not try to swallow it all at once.

> Wherefore do not straightway attempt extreme discipline; above all things beware of confidence in yourself, lest you fall from a height of discipline through want of training. It is better to advance a little at a time. Withdraw then by degrees from the pleasures of life, gradually destroying all your wonted habits, lest you bring on yourself a crowd of temptations by irritating all your passions at once. When you have mastered one passion, then begin to wage war against another, and in this manner you will in good time get the better of all. Indulgence, so far as the name goes, is one, but its practical workings are diverse. First then, brother, meet every temptation with patient endurance. And by what various temptations the faithful man is proved; by worldly loss, by accusations, by lies, by opposition, by calumny, by persecution! These and the like are the tests of the faithful. (XLII)

Basil had studied classical literature and philosophy in Athens and taught rhetoric at Caesarea in Cappadocia before he entered the religious life. Although his attachment to scriptures grew, he never rejected the pagan classics. On the contrary, he insisted that much could be learned from them about the practice of virtue. There was no emotional crisis such as Jerome had over his love of pagan writings.

The contrast between this generally mild-mannered man and the rigorist Jerome should not mislead anyone into thinking that Basil was equivocal on matters of orthodoxy. A passage from a letter in which he gives a lengthy response to an inquiry on a number of points of church law shows his firmness on abortion. The letter was written to his close friend Amphilochius in 374.

> The woman who purposely destroys her unborn child is guilty of murder. With us there is no nice enquiry as to its being formed or unformed. In this case it is not only the being about to be born who is vindicated, but the woman in her attack upon herself; because in most cases women who make such attempts die. The destruction of the embryo is an additional crime, a second murder, at all events if we regard it as done with intent. The punishment, however, of these women should not be for life, but for

> the term of ten years. And let their treatment depend not on the mere lapse of time, but on the character of their repentance. (CLXXXVIII)

In contrast to the solemnity of that letter there is another one (CCCXXIV) in which Basil lightheartedly warned a physician friend, Pasinicus, about the wiles of a confidence man who pretends to be inexperienced but is actually the opposite. Basil was well aware of the way of the world. Along with advice he gave sympathy to those faced with injustices. In the following letter there is consolation for one of many government workers whose lot in the later Roman Empire was not a happy one. Public office had become an onerous duty subject to bureaucratic intrigue, special forced gifts to the treasury, and the usual routine headaches. It is not surprising to find that Basil, a pragmatic man, had something to say on the subject. In this letter he tried to cheer up an honest tax collector who had become discouraged. In keeping with the times, the best rewards were those from God.

> I was aware, before you told me, that you do not like your employment in public affairs. It is an old saying that those who are anxious to lead a pious life do not throw themselves with pleasure into office. The case of magistrates seems to me like that of physicians. They see awful sights; they meet with bad smells; they get trouble for themselves out of other people's calamities. This is at least the case with those who are real magistrates. All men who are engaged in business, look also to make a profit, and are excited about this kind of glory, count it the greatest possible advantage to acquire some power and influence by which they may be able to benefit their friends, punish their enemies, and get what they want for themselves. You are not a man of this kind. How should you be? You have voluntarily withdrawn from even high office in the State. You might have ruled the city like one single house, but you have preferred a life free from care and anxiety. You have placed a higher value on having no troubles yourself and not troubling other people, than other people do on making themselves disagreeable. But it has seemed good to the Lord that the district of Ibora should not be under the power of hucksters, not be turned into a mere slave market. It is His will that every individual in it should be enrolled, as is right. Do you therefore accept this responsibility? It is vexatious, I know, but it is one which may bring you approbation of God. Neither fawn upon the great and powerful, nor despise the poor and needy. Show to all under your rule an impartiality of mind, balanced more exactly than any scales. Thus in the sight of those who have entrusted you with these responsibilities your zeal for justice will be made evident, and they will view you with exceptional admiration. And even though you go unnoticed by them, you will not be unnoticed by our God. The prizes which He has put before us for good works are great. (CCXCIX)

In a similar vein, aware that certain government workers had decided to reward themselves, Basil asked the governor of Cappadocia to do something about officials who were stealing grain.

> I know that a first and foremost object of your excellency is in every way to support the right; and after that to benefit your friends, and to exert yourself in behalf of those who have fled to your lordship's protection. Both these pleas are combined in the matter before us. The cause is right for which we are pleading; it is dear to me who am numbered among your friends; it is due to those who are invoking the aid of your constancy in their sufferings. The corn, which was all my very dear brother Dorotheus had for the necessaries of life, has been carried off by some of the authorities at Berisi, entrusted with the management of affairs, driven to this violence of their own accord or by others' instigation. Either way it is an indictable offence. For how does the man whose wickedness is his own do less wrong than he who is the mere minister of other men's wickedness? To the sufferers the loss is the same. I implore you, therefore, that Dorotheus may have his corn returned by the men by whom he has been robbed, and that they may not be allowed to lay the guilt of their outrage on other men's shoulders. If you grant me my request I shall reckon the value of the boon conferred by your excellency in proportion to the necessity of providing one's self with food. (LXXXVI)

In the same year, 372, Basil again used the prestige of his office and his own good reputation on behalf of people unable to help themselves. He sounds like Pliny writing to Trajan when, in a self-effacing manner, he asks a Roman official, the prefect Modestus, to reduce the taxes paid by those who live in the district of Mt. Taurus.

> In kindly condescending to come down to me you give me great honour and allow me great freedom; and these in like, aye and in greater, measure, I pray that your lordship may receive from our good Master during the whole of your life. I have long wanted to write to you and to receive honour at your hands, but respect for your great dignity has restrained me, and I have been careful lest I should ever seem to abuse the liberty conceded to me. Now, however, I am forced to take courage, not only by the fact of my having received permission from your incomparable excellency to write, but also by the necessity of the distressed. If, then, prayers of even the small are of any avail with the great, be moved, most excellent sir, of your good will to grant relief to a rural population now in pitiable case, and give orders that the tax of iron, paid by the inhabitants of iron-producing Taurus, may be made such as it is possible to pay. Grant

> this, lest they be crushed once for all, instead of being of lasting service to the state. I am sure that your admirable benevolence will see that this is done. (CX)

Basil was thus caught up precisely in those problems which some other churchmen sought to escape. One episode revealed how bishops in Cappadocia were at times treated as politicians rather than spiritual shepherds. Basil took part in the ordination of a slave as bishop without the permission of the wealthy mistress, Simplicia, who resented the loss of her servant. She in turn threatened to send her eunuchs to harass Basil, and in an uncharacteristically rude-sounding letter to her, in 372 or 373, he described her emissaries as "a disgraceful and detestable set of eunuchs; neither woman nor man, lustful, envious, ill-bribed, passionate, effeminate, slaves of the belly, mad for gold, ruthless, grumbling about their dinner, inconstant, stingy, greedy, insatiable, savage, jealous. What more need I say? At their very birth they were condemned to the knife" (CXV). Uncharitable, to be sure, but likely a common view of these unfortunate people at the time. That their mistress was said to be a heretic would not have helped matters any.

Basil, as mentioned a staunch defender of orthodoxy, was one of the leaders in the fight against the Arians. His letter to the Alexandrians in 373, when Valens ruled the east, showed his outrage and his sympathy for their plight as the victims of Arian persecutors, who also, of course, called themselves Christians.

> I have already heard of the persecution in Alexandria and the rest of Egypt, and, as might be expected, I am deeply affected. I have observed the ingenuity of the devil's mode of warfare. When he saw that the Church increased under the persecution of enemies and flourished all the more, he changed his plan. He no longer carries on an open warfare, but lays secret snares against us, hiding his hostility under the name which they bear, in order that we may both suffer like our fathers, and, at the same time, seem not to suffer for Christ's sake, because our persecutors too bear the name of Christians. With these thoughts for a long time we sat still, dazed at the news of what had happened, for, in sober earnest, both our ears tingled on hearing of the shameless and inhuman heresy of your persecutors. They have reverenced neither age, nor services to society, nor people's affection. They inflicted torture, ignominy, and exile; they plundered all the property they could find; they were careless alike of human condemnation and of the awful retribution to come at the hands of the righteous Judge. All this has amazed me and all but driven me out of my senses. (CXXXIX)

In a letter to the bishops of the west in 376, Basil hopes they will appeal to the western emperor Gratian to intervene against these persecutions.

> To his brethren truly God-beloved and very dear, and fellow ministers of like mind, the bishops of Gaul and Italy, [from] Basil, bishop of Caesarea in Cappadocia. . . . One chief object of our desire is that through you the state of confusion in which we are situated should be made known to the emperor [Gratian] of your part of the world. If this is difficult, we beseech you to send envoys to visit and comfort us in our affliction, that you may have the evidence of eyewitnesses of those sufferings of the East which cannot be told by word of mouth; because language is inadequate to give a clear report of our condition. . . . No malefactor is doomed without proof, but bishops have been convicted on calumny alone, and are consigned to penalties on charges wholly unsupported by evidence. Some have not even known who has accused them, nor been brought before any tribunal, nor even been falsely accused at all. They have been apprehended with violence late at night, have been exiled to distant places, and, through the hardships of these remote wastes, have been given over to death. (CCXLIII)

Ironically, it was not the western bishops who helped Basil so much as the Goths who defeated and killed Valens at the momentous battle of Adrianople, 9 August 378. They, too, felt themselves much wronged by this ruler, for although given land within the empire in return for their services, they were denied promised food, and their children were liable to be stolen and sold as slaves. When they rebelled and cut down Valens, they were the first of the barbarian peoples to defeat Roman legions inside the empire.

Basil usually had little to say about affairs in the empire not germaine to the church, but one letter, very likely written in 377, mentioned the turbulence and dangers in Thrace prior to the battle of Adrianople. Although it was a military disaster for Rome, the successor to Valens was the devout Theodosius (appointed by Gratian), who strictly adhered to the Nicene Creed and so was a vigorous defender of the orthodox position that Basil championed. In 380, he removed the Arian bishop of Constantinople and gave his support to Basil's friend Gregory of Nazianzus for the chair. But the Arians were not easily silenced, and Theodosius's orders against them became increasingly harsh. Some of the more radical ones were even sentenced to death. As the beliefs of the emperors shifted, so did the direction of the persecutions.

Early in Theodosius's reign, non-Christians continued in their traditional practices, but in 391 the emperor ordered all the temples of the old gods to be closed and, in effect, made Christianity the state religion. Prominent pagans, however, especially brilliant orators, were not much affected by this historic edict.

Under Theodosius, the famed Libanius (ca. 314 to ca. 393), who had been a friend of the pagan emperor Julian, continued to be an influential figure attracting both pagan and Christian students while teaching rhetoric in his native Antioch. In the letters exchanged with Basil, the subject of religion was handled gently. It seems likely that Basil had once studied rhetoric under Libanius, and their friendship was renewed in a letter (CCCXXXV) in which Basil says he is doing a favor for the son of a friend by sending him to study with Libanius. Back came a reply which included Libanius's highly favorable impressions of Basil as a young man.

> After some little time a young Cappadocian has reached me. One gain to me is that he is a Cappadocian. But this Cappadocian is one of the first rank. This is another gain. Further, he brings me a letter from the admirable Basil. This is the greatest gain of all. You think that I have forgotten you. I had great respect for you in your youth. I saw you vying with old men in self-restraint, and this in a city teeming with pleasures. I saw you already in possession of considerable learning. Then you thought that you ought also to see Athens, and you persuaded Celsus to accompany you. Happy Celsus, to be dear to you! Then you returned, and lived at home, and I said to myself, What, I wonder, is Basil about now? To what occupation has he betaken himself? Is he following the ancient orators, and practising in the courts? Or is he turning the sons of fortunate fathers into orators? Then there came those who reported to me that you were adopting a course of life better than any of these, and were, rather, bethinking you how you might win the friendship of God than heaps of gold, I blessed both you and the Cappadocians; you, for making this your aim; them, for being able to point to so noble a fellow-countryman. (CCCXXXVI)

Such a letter undercuts the notion of Christians and pagans altogether at odds. The common ground, of course, was the classical culture of their ancestors, the study of which still eases sharp differences, where given the chance.

Basil's friendly relations with the pagan Libanius were in sharp contrast to his hostility toward certain of his own religion. An abomination of the times, according to Basil, was the influence of power brokers in the affairs of the church. They were installing their incompetent agents as bishops. Here, in part, is what he wrote to Eusebius, bishop of Samosata, in 376. There are, in all, twenty-two letters sent to this friend, who lived about 260 miles away.

> The Lord has granted me the privilege of now saluting your holiness by our beloved and very reverend brother, the presbyter Antiochus, of exhorting you to pray for me as you are wont, and offering in our communication by letter some consolation for our long separation. And, when you pray, I ask you to beg from the Lord this as the first and greatest boon, that I may be delivered from vile and wicked men, who have gained such power over the people that now I seem to see, indeed, a repetition of the events of the taking of Jerusalem. For the weaker grow the Churches the more does men's lust for power increase. And now the very title of bishop has

> been conferred on wretched slaves, for no servant of God would choose to come forward in opposition to claim the see;—no one but miserable fellows like the emissaries of Anysius the creature of Euippius, and of Ecdicius of Parnassus: whoever has appointed him has sent into the Churches a poor means of aiding his own entry into the life to come.
>
> They have expelled my brother from Nyssa, and into his place have introduced hardly a man— a mere scamp worth only an obol or two, but, so far as regards the ruin of the faith, a match for those who have put him where he is.
>
> At the town of Doara they have brought shame upon the poor name of bishop, and have sent there a wretch, an orphans' domestic, a runaway from his own masters, to flatter a godless woman, who formerly used George as she liked, and now has got this fellow to succeed him.
>
> And who could properly lament the occurrences at Nicopolis? That unhappy Fronto did, indeed, for a while pretend to be on the side of the truth, but now he has shamefully betrayed both the faith and himself, and for the price of his betrayal has got a name of disgrace. He imagines that he has obtained from these men the rank of bishop; in reality he has become, by God's grace, the abomination of all Armenia. (CCXXXIX)

Basil's complaint about outsiders interfering in the church might fairly have been put on the grounds that there was enough politics inside the church to begin with. This was a point that might have been argued by his friend Gregory of Nazianzus, the third of the so-called Cappodician fathers.

Gregory of Nazianzus

Basil and Gregory had been close friends since their student days in Caesarea, the capital of Cappadocia, and later in Athens. They had much in common. Both came from well-educated, Christian families, rich in land and prestige. Basil was a native of Caesarea where they first met. Gregory (ca. 329 to 389) was born in the village of Arianzus, near the episcopal seat of Nazianzus, where, in that day and age, there was no objection to his father presiding as a bishop.

As will happen between young men in their student days, Basil and Gregory shared high ideals. Given the times, they talked about sharing a future life of philosophical contemplation. That, at least, is what Gregory thought. As it turned out, Basil proved to be decidedly more ambitious and aggressive than was at first apparent. After five years in Athens, Basil returned to Caesarea to teach rhetoric, but two years later was baptized, and at that point abruptly turned from the world. He then began an ascetic existence amid the beauties of nature, which he invited his friend Gregory to share, as related in letter XIV quoted earlier. It was with those who gathered around him that he worked out the fundamentals that became the basis for the famous Basilian Rule.

Ironically, however, before long he left the quiet life of a monk to take up the active role of a priest to which he was ordained in 364. During the following years, his skills as an administrator under an ineffectual bishop of Caesarea brought him recognition as a possible successor. When Eusebius died in 370, Basil sought the bishop's chair, but his fervent efforts to win election dismayed his old friend Gregory. Basil actually resorted to feigning ill-health, even being near death, in order to get his more retiring friend to come to help him. When Gregory learned the truth, he was shocked and wrote to Basil that their sacred friendship had been violated, in that "our life and our rule and everything is common to us both, who have been so closely associated by God from the first." He added: "For I must say this also, I wondered whether you remembered that such nominations are worthy of the most religious, not of the more powerful, nor of those most in favor with the multitude" (XL). Basil, encouraged by less idealistic associates, likely saw his election as necessary to the well-being of the church in Caesarea and thus his behavior was in a good cause. In any event, given his friend's attitude, he could be relieved that he had the full support of the actual bishop of Nazianzus, Gregory's father, who, though truly ill, did come to vote. Actually, Gregory himself wrote letters in Basil's behalf, but he refused to support him in person.

Gregory's years after Athens were similar to those of Basil in that he, too, taught rhetoric for a time and then, after baptism, decided on a monastic life. He did not follow Basil in being ambitious for a greater role in church affairs. It was his father who, in 361, having other plans for him, insisted he be ordained as a priest and make himself useful. Rosemary R. Ruether, in her learned study *Gregory of Nazianzus, Rhetor and Philosopher*, says: "The issue between the active and the contemplative life . . . was to remain a fundamental tension throughout Gregory's life, and the pattern of flight[4] and return was to become a characteristic motif of his career."[5] It was, of course, a source of conflict with his father and with Basil, who in his new position again sought to make use of him.

The year after Basil's election as the bishop of Caesarea, Cappadocia was divided into two provinces. Officially, it was for administrative (perhaps taxation) purposes, but the decision was viewed suspiciously for another reason. Much to Basil's discomfort, the Arians actually had the upper hand in the eastern half of the empire. As has been mentioned, Valens, who had governed the area from 369 to 379, was himself an Arian and used his power to support his beliefs. It was therefore surmised that the strongly orthodox Cappadocia was divided as a means of undermining its unity.

Basil's efforts to consolidate his own power meant placing appointees where they could bolster his influence. His younger brother was made bishop of Nyssa, and a new bishopric in a small crossroads named Sasima was established for Gregory. Ruether says: "Gregory was deeply offended by this action on Basil's part. The town of Sasima was most disagreeably situated. It was scarcely a town at all, but a kind of staging-post in a melancholy, waterless tract of countryside. Gregory, in his poem on his life, expresses his distaste for this vile little backwater in no uncertain terms" (p. 36). Obviously, he thought himself a pawn, and said so in this passage from a caustic letter to Basil.

> Do leave off speaking of me as an ill-educated and uncouth and unfriendly man, not even worthy to live, because I have ventured to be conscious of the way in which I have been treated. You yourself would admit that I have not done wrong in any other respect, and my own conscience does not reproach me with having been unkind to you in either great or small matters; and I hope it never may. I only know that I saw that I have been deceived—too late indeed, but I saw it—and I throw the blame on your throne, as having on a sudden lifted you above yourself; and I am weary of being blamed for faults of yours, and of having to make excuses for them to people who know both our former and our present relations. . . . I shall gain this only from your friendship, that I shall learn not to trust in friends, or to esteem anything more valuable than God. (XLVIII)[6]

Although reluctantly consecrated as a bishop in a ceremony at which Basil, undaunted, officiated, Gregory did not take up his post in Sasima. Basil called him lazy. Gregory thought himself high-minded and in this letter to Basil shows his awareness of a growing problem in the church.

> You accuse me of laziness and idleness, because I did not accept your Sasima, and because I have not bestirred myself like a Bishop, and do not arm you against each other like a bone thrown into the midst of dogs. My greatest business always is to keep free from business. And to give you an idea of one of my good points, so much do I value freedom from business, that I think I might even be a standard to all men of this kind of magnanimity, and if only all men would imitate me the Churches would have no troubles; nor would the faith, which every one uses as a weapon in his private quarrels, be pulled in pieces. (XLIX)

In spite of Gregory's obstinacy about Sasima, he had refused overtures from Basil's chief rival, Anthimus, and sought to make peace between the two. However, because of his blunt, honest, but impolitic manner of speech, he only succeeded in making both of them angry with him.

In his letters, Gregory frequently said he wished to be left alone to read and to write. Rosemary Ruether says that the orations he wrote "became the standard of orthodoxy in later generations, and were introduced as such in the records of later Church councils. For this, he, with St. John the Evangelist, became honoured in

Peter Paul Rubens (1577–1640), *St. Gregory of Nazianzus* (1621). Oil on wood, 19¾x25¾". Albright-Knox Art Gallery, Buffalo, N.Y. George B. Mathews Fund, 1952.

the Eastern Church by the title of 'Theologos,' as the ones who, above all, gave the correct understanding to the nature of the Deity" (p. 42).

Gregory's experience at various conventions of the clergy led him to believe they were generally fruitless, creating more problems than they solved. But he did agree with Basil in being strongly committed to the orthodox position. He was therefore, after more years in monastic retirement, persuaded to travel in 379 to Constantinople to take on the Arians. He was even for a time made bishop of that great metropolis by Theodosius, but his awkwardness and distaste for the job meant it would be a brief tenure.

On his arrival in Constantinople, he was greeted by mobs of Arian rioters, who even threw stones at him during a church service. Gregory was not a man for throwing them back. His good friend, Theodore, bishop of Tyana, who had also been attacked, wanted to punish the perpetrators of this disgrace, but Gregory wrote a letter outlining the old-new idea of conquest by kindness.

> I hear that you are indignant at the outrages which have been committed on us by the Monks and the Mendicants. And it is no wonder, seeing that you never yet had felt a blow, and were without experience of the evils we have to endure, that you did feel angry at such a thing. But we as ex-

perienced in many sorts of evil, and as having had our share of insult, may be considered worthy of belief when we exhort Your Reverence, as old age teaches and as reason suggests. Certainly what has happened was dreadful, and more than dreadful – no one will deny it: that our altars were insulted, our mysteries disturbed, and that we ourselves had to stand between the communicants and those who would stone them, and to make our intercessions a cure for stonings; that the reverence due to virgins was forgotten, and the good order of monks, and the calamity of the poor, who lost even their pity through ferocity. But perhaps it would be better to be patient, and to give an example of patience to many by our sufferings. For argument is not so persuasive of the world in general as is practice, that silent exhortation.

We think it an important matter to obtain penalties from those who have wronged us: an important matter, I say (for even this is sometimes useful for the correction of others) – but it is far greater and more Godlike, to bear with injuries. For the former course curbs wickedness, but the latter makes men good, which is much better and more perfect than merely being not wicked. Let us consider that the great pursuit of mercifulness is set before us, and let us forgive the wrongs done to us that we also may obtain forgiveness, and let us by kindness lay up a store of kindness. (LXXVII)

The quiet but good advice in this and other letters probably explains why so many people felt Gregory should play a more active role in the church. But he was to them, inevitably, a disappointment. He lacked the drive to be an effective statesman, and his dislike of politics was genuine. During the last years of his life he found the peace he was seeking in his native Nazianzus, where he devoted himself to writing religious poetry and corresponding with friends and relatives. His sister Gorgonia's grandson, Nicobolus, was a special favorite, and he wrote to him about the rules for writing a good letter. After some obvious remarks in which he says a letter should be neither too long nor too short depending on its content, he speaks of clarity and gracefulness of style, including perhaps some humor. The letter includes this passage: "My final remark shall be one which I heard a clever man make about the eagle, that when the birds were electing a king, and came with various adornment, the most beautiful point about him was that he did not think himself beautiful. This point is to be especially attended to in letter-writing, to be without adventitious ornament and as natural as possible" (LI). Very likely it was this grand-nephew who eventually collected and preserved Gregory's letters.

The Cappadocian Fathers passed from the scene on the eve of major developments. Basil died in 379, and his old friend Gregory of Nazianzus wrote a panegyric for the occasion. Gregory himself passed away about ten years later and only a few years before Theodosius, the last sole emperor of Rome, who, as has been mentioned, made Christianity the state religion. Theodosius died in 395 and, at about that time, so did Basil's younger brother, Gregory of Nyssa. When Theodosius's sons took over, Arcadius in the east and Honorius in the west, they appeared to rule as partners, but the empire was, in fact, thereafter irretrievably divided. The church, now triumphant, would one day also become divided between east and west, but not yet.

IX AUSONIUS AND PAULINUS

Old Friends Gone Separate Ways

DURING Julian's short reign, a teacher in Gaul named Ausonius was busily telling his students among the aristocracy to be mindful of their heritage and future responsibilities as leaders in their communities. One of them, Paulinus, was a disappointment. He became a monk and at the same time something of a stranger to his old teacher. Raymond Van Dam, in ***Leadership and Community in Late Antique Gaul***, suggests that the story of Ausonius and Paulinus could be used to develop "the fundamental transition from a pagan, Roman Gaul to a Christian, medieval Gaul."[1] In this chapter, their letters help to tell the story.

Ausonius

When Julian died, the man in charge of his personal guard, Flavius Jovian, was chosen by the army to succeed him. His decision to make a generous concession of territory to the Persians, in return for peace, was not popular. But his death after eight months, perhaps accidentally from a poorly vented stove, gave the army another, better choice. In February 364, a tough, hard-working Pannonian officer, Valentinian, was hailed as Augustus. In March, he appointed his brother Valens as co-emperor. It had long been evident that one man could not oversee all the problems in the empire. Valentinian took the western half as his domain, and in his reign from 364 to 375 he successfully held the Rhine and Danube frontiers.

Ammianus's account of the period makes two points worth mentioning. First, he described how Roman officers by their treachery or downright stupidity brought

machus insisted that she be punished the same as vestals who had broken their oaths from the earliest times. That meant being buried alive.

Symmachus's staunch defense of paganism did not hinder his usefulness as an administrator when he was appointed to be prefect. In this capacity, he was the emperor's man in Rome—the middle man between the emperor and the Senate and the people. Communications in either direction went through him. Actually, he had a jurisdiction covering the surrounding area of up to a hundred miles. As the letters to follow will show, he was concerned not just with law and order, but every facet of city life from its food supply to its entertainments. In time-honored fashion, the presence of lictors who preceded him announced his importance.

It was as prefect, on behalf of himself and the Senate, that he sent to Valentinian II a letter asking that the Altar of Victory be restored. Why offend the gods by removing this important part of Roman tradition, particularly at a time when the barbarians are strong? Can there not be tolerance for more than one faith?

Occasionally, in these letters, Symmachus adopts the formality of "your Divinities" or "Lords," as if addressing the emperors ruling jointly, but Valentinian II, supreme in the west, was the emperor to whom he actually would have been speaking, or, to be practical, it was likely this emperor's advisers.

> Grant, I beg you, that what in our youth we took over from our fathers, we may in our old age hand on to posterity. The love of established practice is a powerful sentiment; the action of the late Emperor Constantius quite rightly did not stand good for long. You should not adopt any precedent which you have discovered to have been quickly set aside. We are safeguarding the perpetuity of your good name, ensuring that future ages will not find it necessary to reverse your measures.
>
> . . . Everyone has his own customs, his own religious practices; the divine mind has assigned to different cities different religions to be their guardians. Each man is given at birth a separate soul; in the same way each people is given its own special genius to take care of its destiny. To this line of thought must be added the argument derived from "benefits conferred," for herein rests the most emphatic proof to man of the existence of the gods. Man's reason moves entirely in the dark; his knowledge of divine influences can be drawn from no better source than from the recollection and the evidences of good fortune received from them. If long passage of time lends validity to religious observances, we ought to keep faith with so many centuries, we ought to follow our forefathers who followed their forefathers and were blessed in so doing.
>
> . . . And so we ask for peace for the gods of our fathers, for the gods of our native land. It is reasonable that whatever each of us worships is really to be considered one and the same. We gaze up at the same stars, the sky covers us all, the same universe compasses us. What does it matter what practical system we adopt in our search for the truth? Not by one

> avenue only can we arrive at so tremendous a secret. But this is the kind of case for men to put with time on their hands; at the moment it is prayers that we present to you, not debating arguments. . . . We ask for that establishment of religious practices which preserved the Empire for the late father of your Divinities, which furnished a fortunate Emperor with legitimate heirs. From his citadel among the stars that elder Emperor [Valentinian I] looks down upon the tears of priests and believes that he has come under blame now that the custom which he himself was glad to preserve has been broken. Give your late brother [Gratian] the satisfaction that a policy which was not really his has now been corrected; cover up an act which he did not realize had displeased the senate—for indeed it is agreed that the delegation sent to him by the senate was denied access to his presence with the deliberate purpose of keeping him ignorant of public opinion. It would do much to redeem the reputation of earlier times if without hesitation you cancelled a policy of which indubitably the Emperor was not the author. (3)[2]

Symmachus's letters were written four centuries after those of Cicero, but in places they read as if written on the same day. Both use examples from the earliest centuries of Rome's history to bolster their arguments for holding to tradition. The Emperor Gratian had ordered the prefect of Rome to ride in an elaborate carriage on official occasions. Symmachus protests to Valentinian II, Gratian's half brother and successor, that this pretentiousness, a mere gain in pomp, will be resented by ordinary people as a loss of moral strength. The events of long ago proved to him, as they had to famed Livy and Cicero, that when the traditions of the Romans remained unchanged, so did their character.

> If the Roman world were still enjoying the presence of your Clemencies' brother the late Emperor, I should not keep silence about the matter which I now venture to bring to your notice, who are the guardians of his good name: I do it with the sense of dedication which makes it fitting for a prefect to set loyalty before flattery, my Lords Emperors. It was believed, but quite wrongly, that the use of a foreign and pretentious type of conveyance elevated the office of urban prefect to the height of distinction. At the time the kindly disposition of your predecessor was won over to this novel decision only by the desire that a richly furnished equipage should carry in procession the holder of a long-established magistracy. But a temperate glorification of it which will regret no measure it takes rejects outward trappings of that kind; if we let anything be added to usual methods, we are admitting that up till now they were inadequate. The eyes of ordinary citizens look for a dignified form of conveyance, and the Roman people believes that a prefecture is on the decline if it has attracted to itself more recent standards of taste. God forbid that the ruler of a free city, dedicated to freedom, should be conveyed in a fashion more suited to Salmoneus of

> Elis. We care nothing for marvels of display. This Rome of yours does not tolerate anything likely to encourage pride: for it has not forgotten, as you know, its spendid ancestors to whom the arrogance of a Tarquin and the chariot even of a Camillus gave such offence; a great man though he was, his chariot drawn by four white horses procured for him a miserable exile. On the other hand when Publicola lowered his own power the act brought him much honour; for he dipped his consul's axe in the presence of an assembly of the citizens and he diminished the pinnacle of his own glory in order that he might elevate the freedom of the citizen-body. Let us then be held in regard for our character rather than for our trappings. We do not censure this novel concession, but we value more the good things we already have. Get rid of this conveyance; its array may be more spectacular, but we have always preferred the kind whose use is the more ancient. (4)

Whether Symmachus realized it or not, there were remarks about everyday matters in his own letters that point to a gradual dissolution of old-time habits. For example, he complains that those best qualified for public office were least inclined to serve. Gone are the days when a place in the government was the top choice of ambitious men. He might have had Pliny the Younger in mind.

In the second century, Pliny had written from the province of Bithynia to the Emperor Trajan asking his advice and, sometimes, pleasantly, offering some of his own. Now, in the fourth century, Symmachus had a suggestion about improving the administration of Rome itself. He asked for better officials even if it meant appointing people without their consent.

> My love for your reign, my care for the state join my sense of loyalty in preventing me from hiding things which ought to be put right, my Lords Emperors. The highest interests of the civil administration pertain to the prefecture of the city. Certain departments of it are entrusted to minor offices; to supervise them hard-working and properly proved men should have been appointed so that each employee could carry out his duties irreproachably and smoothly. That is the kind of man that the public interest now expects from the good judgment of your Divinities. I do not want to blame those now occupying the posts; it satisfies my anxiety if you will give these responsibilities within the city walls to better men. For it is on my shoulders that the burden of the whole administration lies; the rest sink under it; they were men whom your Clemencies' absorption in many other matters prevented you from proving. These prosperous times possess men more worthy of the posts; indeed there is a rich vein of really good men. You will serve the interests of the city better in the future if you appoint men even against their will. (17)

Throughout Roman times finding enough food to feed a large urban population was a constant problem. And woe to public officials who failed to provide it. Symmachus, though privately contemptuous of the mob, was well aware that shortages could lead to violence. On one occasion, he was himself almost chased from the city. There were those of the well-to-do who left voluntarily, and Symmachus thought about sending his children to one of his country houses for safety's sake. It has often been the fate of populous cities to be dependent on outside help. As the prefect of Rome, Symmachus's chief duty was to convince the emperor of the seriousness of the need. In the following letter to Valentinian II there is some dignified begging for grain.

> Your good fortune promises the Eternal City a plentiful supply of its usual maintenance, my Lords Emperors, but we ought to be made safe in fact, not in expectation. That can easily be done the moment your Clemencies' care of things has regard for this side of your administration as well as others. The summer is far advanced: very little has been shipped from African harbours and we experience a touch of fear, not groundless, that the corn supply has got into serious difficulties: for this reason I beg and beseech your Perennities, who are the safeguard of our welfare, that a pretty stern dispatch may prod into action the African magistrates and the *notarius* to whom your Eternities have entrusted the transportation of grain: I ask you to send some energetic men to produce in visible form, while sailing is still feasible, the cargoes to which we are accustomed for the victualling of the city. Your reign, your divine qualities of character, demand that one of your first and principal cares should be freedom from care for the Roman people. Ships will make the voyages we desire and will arrive full, and a numerous and heavily laden fleet will enter Roman harbours once your Divinities' favorable help wafts them along. (18)

Symmachus had been careful to point out that it was for the Eternal City that grain was to be supplied by the provinces. But another letter (40) makes plain that more than the distribution of food was involved. For instance, a nearby city might be allotted some of its neighbor's grain supplies in return for supplying the capital with wood. That city might in turn owe some of its allotment to yet a third community. Thus a chain reaction was in effect, and changes in amounts due or any breakdown in the process, could prompt a crisis.

There was more bad news. The Eternal City was in debt, possibly due to mismanagement, but in any event in dire need of more money. How many similar requests from other cities was Valentinian II receiving? More and more demands were made and, as revenues dwindled, the empire was headed for bankruptcy.

> You alone are able to rescue the expenditure side of the Eternal City's accounts from being unable to make further payments, my Lords Emperors. The magistrates with powers subordinate to your Majesties can bring relief

> only to troubles of moderate severity; they are overwhelmed by the sheer size of a big crisis.
>
> And so we fly to your Divinities, who restore health to things, and we beg for a generous grant to the treasury of the Roman people. For some time now the provinces appointed for the purpose have contributed nothing of their usual revenues; hence the fear is justified that, if the subventions lapse, ordinary needs will be neglected which up till now low-grade officials of the department have been able to meet only by running up debts, as they complain. Also, the venerable senate was consulted but was unable of its own resources to alleviate the distress and therefore begged the help of your Perennities. A statement has been produced setting out the revenues which the commissariats of Spain and Alexandria should bring in; my conscientious department has summarized the items of expenditure which may be approved. I ask that, when you have examined according to your pleasure all the attached documents, you will extend swift relief to the public interest. The situation is pressing and the usual contribution of funds cannot be refused. Therefore be graciously pleased to furnish aid, as is your habit. Your sense of duty makes you bestow new benefactions on the Roman people; keep up also the old benefactions and deign to grant to your city both what past omissions have withheld from us and also what our future needs look for. (37)

If twentieth-century nations find themselves with stupendous deficits, rampant inflation, bureaucratic stagnation, inefficiency, and corruption, can it be much of a surprise that the ancient Roman Empire suffered the same problems, with neither sophisticated communications, nor controls, nor elaborate studies to advise them such as modern-day economists produce. But fourth-century emperors were trying to cure obvious abuses. Clues to their efforts are gleaned from the Theodosian Code, a codification of all the laws since 312, prepared in 438 under Theodosius II, who reigned an extraordinary forty-two years in the eastern Roman Empire, from 408 to 450. The biggest problem was the inability of the central government to enforce the laws put in place with good intentions. At the top level, large landowners, living far from the centers of power, found they could ignore the government even to the extent of not paying taxes, or at least delaying payment interminably. At a lower level, the horses serving in the state courier system were going hungry because somebody was pocketing the feed money. The government's own tax system was unfair and grossly mismanaged.

As a landowner, Symmachus complained about his costs. At the same time, in his official capacity in Rome, he was asking the emperor for subsidies. Where did he think the money was coming from? And was he aware of how many were cheating the state? Although he was paying his taxes, others of his class, because of ineffective administration and bribery of tax collectors, did not pay their share. The burden was therefore falling most heavily on a dwindling middle class, and as more of that group abandoned the land there was a worse future for those left. By trying to meet the expenses of defense, subsidies to cities, and support for a bureaucratic system increasing in size and inefficiency, the empire was taxing itself out of existence. At the same time, the government's effort to control its own officials was a failure. Descriptions of the abuse of local farmers by agents of the central government, who had the muscle of garrisoned soldiers to back them up, are reminiscent of the charges Cicero had made a long time ago about the rule of Verres in the first Roman province of Sicily.

The small farmer, unable to compete, sold out or, if he owed money to a powerful neighbor, lost out to him and became his tenant. On the positive side, the new arrangement meant some financial security and protection in case of local troubles. On the other hand, although he might not himself be a serf, with his body legally bound to the soil, that was where his descendants were headed. It was in the rural areas, where most Romans lived, that the signposts to medieval times are most evident. Life in the cities remained much the same as it always had. That is likely why Symmachus didn't say more about the disastrous economic conditions of his time. He didn't see them with the hindsight we have. To him, day-to-day events looked the same. For instance, the people, once fed, still wanted to be entertained. The old theme of "bread and circuses" went on, for gladiatorial contests remained too popular for even a Christian emperor to forbid them. Another letter, for the attention of Valentinian II, asks for public shows.

> The Roman people looks for outstanding benefactions from your Divinities, but, my Lords Emperors, it now asks again for those which your Eternities voluntarily promised: for it regards them as owed. Not that if feels any doubt that they are to be rendered to it—for we can trust nothing with greater confidence than the undertaking of good emperors—but it does not wish, by not making an immediate demand, to give the impression of dissatisfaction with what is offered. And so it begs that your Clemencies, after granting those subsidies which your generosity has made towards our sustenance, should furnish also the enjoyments of chariot races and dramatic performances to be held in the circus and in Pompey's theatre. The city delights in these entertainments and your promise has awakened anticipation. Every day messengers are awaited to confirm that these promised shows will soon arrive at the city; reports on charioteers and on horses are being collected; every conveyance, every ship is rumoured to have brought in theatrical artists. Nevertheless it is affection for your Perennities, not avidity for entertainment, that has whetted the longings of the populace. Give for this moment what is asked of you so that in the future room may be left for all the other things which without limit you will bestow. (6)

Symmachus took little interest in philosophy and did not, as Cicero had, condemn the cruelty of the games. The shows were part of the old tradition he so treasured. That he was enthusiastic about them is evident from his correspondence with his friends, who were mostly prominent people of the day. But the hundreds of letters he wrote offer surprisingly little hard information to historians. However, standard works such as T. R. Glover's *Life and Letters in the Fourth Century* and Samuel Dill's *Roman Society in the Last Century of the Western Empire* or more recently *The Later Roman Empire, A.D. 284–602* by A. H. M. Jones make good use of sparse material. The letters, for instance, tell of Symmachus's efforts to get the best chariot drivers. He was also proud to have helped to provide exotic beasts and writes of the difficulty of transporting animals, including crocodiles that refused to eat. Other animals died or were injured en route.

Symmachus was particularly upset when twenty-nine Saxon prisoners strangled each other in their cells rather than fight in the arena to entertain the citizens of Rome—a story that recalls Seneca's remarks, three centuries earlier, about gladiators committing suicide.

In his passion for spectacle and his lack of sympathy for slaves, Symmachus was the inheritor of old Roman attitudes. But his private life, as seen in his letters, adds balance to the dismal picture of a dissolute Roman society as described by Ammianus Marcellinus or as viewed from the perspective of St. Jerome. The scholarly Jerome, working long hours in his monastery in Bethlehem, had no interest in family life. Symmachus, on the other hand, shows great love for his daughter and son, and in the time-honored sign of family affection, he never forgot a birthday. F. Homes Dudden's *The Life and Times of St. Ambrose* calls Symmachus "a good example of the 'pagan gentleman and official,'" and adds, "He had a strong sense of duty, a still stronger sense of deportment, and no sense at all of humour."[3]

A persistent theme in Roman literature is the notion of the idyllic countryside, free from trouble. This was always in a world of poetry rather than fact, and by the fourth century those who were safe in the country had strong houses that began to look like castles. Both Ausonius and Symmachus spoke of the fear of being trapped by outlaws on the road. By their time, such a state of affairs was taken for granted.

As usual there were those who turned to crime because they wanted to and others because they thought they had to. A sinking economy, without social welfare programs, left many desperate men to their own devices. The ineffective government, short on law enforcement, left the public undefended.

In early 385, Symmachus gave up his post as prefect of Rome. In *Prefect and Emperor*, R. H. Barrow says Symmachus's last months in office were unhappy because "the Christian party at court had increased its influence; direct attack and underhand intrigue against the prefect and his administration and the pagan cause which he supported became more common."[4]

In the years to follow, his occasional political connections were also unsuccessful. He supported two ill-fated usurpers, Maximus and Eugenius. References to them would be among those items a watchful son cut out of the collection of letters. Despite such unfortunate episodes, Symmachus was named a consul of Rome in 391. Though by now a mere honor, the appointment was still a tribute to his reputation. As an elder statesman his opinions always counted for something, but more and more of his time was spent on his rural estates.

Toward the end of his life, Symmachus wrote to his son about the dangers of travel, but, as it happened, he was more threatened by a serious kidney ailment. His death, sometime between 402 and 404, took from the scene the foremost orator of the day, a polite and prominent gentleman, a leader of the old guard. In the best Roman tradition, he was mourned by a loving and respectful son.

Ambrose

In the late fourth century, Greek subjects of the Roman emperor did not appreciate having Gothic officers serving as officials in their districts. Those living in Thessalonica, a major city in northern Greece, liked it even less when in 390, Botheric, the Teutonic military commandant, arrested a popular charioteer on charges of immorality. An outraged mob, seeking the release of their hero, rioted, murdered Botheric, and dragged his lifeless body through the streets. The Emperor Theodosius was determined on an indiscriminate massacre of these unruly people. That was the course past emperors had taken when provincials defied them. But now there was a new power to be reckoned with. Ambrose, the bishop of Milan, was strenuously opposed to such brutality.

Traditionally, priests in the Roman state religion had been public officials with no great political power. The servants of the Christian God were a different sort. They were independent of the government, often charismatic, and as Christianity grew stronger in the fourth century, bishops became major political figures. When Ambrose heard that Theodosius's order had been carried out, he denounced the emperor for his sinfulness.

Actually, Theodosius had earlier relented and withdrawn his order, but it was too late. Soldiers had already attacked a crowd gathered at the arena and approximately seven thousand people were slain. The horrified Ambrose sent a private letter in his own hand to Theodosius, informing him that he was not to partake of holy sacraments. One may well imagine the reaction of earlier emperors to such a letter. But Theodosius, a believing Christian, did public penance so that he could be readmitted to the church.

Thus Ambrose, without an army or official standing, brought to heel a mighty emperor. The emperor could govern only this world. Ambrose held the keys to the kingdom of heaven. In his letter to Theodosius, written in 390, he offered the choice between salvation and damnation. Underneath the kindness there was an unmistakable awareness of the power he possessed. The letter mentions "heavenly signs." Whether

Peter Paul Rubens (1577–1640), *Saint Ambrose and the Emperor Theodosius.* Courtesy of the Kunsthistorisches Museum, Vienna.

Ambrose interpreted a comet which appeared that year as one of them is not certain. The story that the bishop in person confronted the emperor at a church door and refused him admittance is also debated and may simply be a later extrapolated dramatization of a momentous quarrel. It is nevertheless the subject of one of Ruben's famous historical paintings.

Understand this, august Emperor! I cannot deny that you are zealous for the faith; I do not disavow that you have a fear of God—but you have a natural vehemence which you quickly change to pity when one endeavors to soothe it. When one stirs it up, you so excite it that you can hardly check it. If only no one would enkindle it, if no one would arouse it! This I gladly commend to you: Restrain yourself, and conquer by love of duty your natural impetuousity. . . .

The affair which took place in the city of Thessalonica and with no precedent within memory, that which I could not prevent from taking place, which I had declared would be most atrocious when I entered pleas against it so many times, and which you yourself, by revoking it too late, manifestly considered to have been very serious, this when done I could not extenuate. It was first heard of when the synod had met on the arrival of Gallican bishops. No one failed to lament, no one took it lightly. Your being in fellowship with Ambrose was not an excuse for your deed; blame for what had been done would have been heaped upon me even more had no one said there must needs be a reconciliation with our God.

Are you ashamed, O Emperor, to do what King David the Prophet did, the forefather of the family of Christ according to the flesh? He was told that a rich man who had many flocks had seized and killed a poor man's one ram on the arrival of a guest, and recognizing that he himself was being condemned in this tale, for he had himself done so, he said: 'I have sinned against the Lord.' Do not be impatient, O Emperor, if it is said to you: 'You have done what was declared to King David by the prophet.' For if you listen carefully to this and say: 'I have sinned against the Lord,' if you repeat the words of the royal Prophet: 'Come, let us adore and fall down before him, and weep before our Lord who made us,' it will be said also to you: 'Since you repent, the Lord forgives you your sin and you shall not die.' . . .

Holy Job, also powerful in this world, says: 'I have not hid my sin, but declared it before all the people.' To fierce King Saul his own son Jonathan said: 'Sin not against thy servant David,' and 'Why wilt thou sin against innocent blood by killing David, who is without fault?' Although he was a king, he sinned if he killed the innnocent. Finally, even David, when he was in possession of his kingdom and had heard that an innocent man named Abner was slain by Joab, the leader of his army, said: 'I and my kingdom are innocent now and forever of the blood of Abner the son of Ner,' and he fasted in sorrow.

These things I have written not to disconcert you but that the examples of kings may stir you to remove this sin from your kingdom, for you will remove it by humbling your soul before God. You are a man, you have met temptation—conquer it. Sin is not removed except by tears and

what is known as the Investiture Conflict of the Middle Ages, when there were struggles between popes and kings over appointments of churchmen who were at the same time landholders within the feudal system and so had dual responsibilities.

> Alleging that he was acting at your command, the tribune and notary Dalmatius came to me and asked that I choose judges just as Auxentius has done. Yet he has not indicated the names of those who have been demanded. But he adds that there will be a discussion in the consistory, and the judgment of your Piety will be the deciding factor.
>
> To this I am making, as I think, a suitable response. No one should find that I am being insolent when I assert that your father of august memory not only gave his answer by word of mouth, but sanctioned by law this truth: In a matter of faith or of any Church regulation the decision should be given by him who is neither unsuited to the task nor disqualified by law. There are the words of his decree; in other words, he wished priests to make judgments regarding priests. In fact, if a bishop were accused of any charge and the case of his character needed to be examined, he wished these matters to belong to the judgment of bishops.
>
> Who, then, has given your Clemency an insolent answer? One who wishes you to be like your father, or one who wishes you to be unlike him? . . .
>
> By God's favor you will reach a ripe old age, and then you will realize what kind of a bishop subjects his priestly power to the laity. By God's favor your father, a man of ripe old age, said: 'It does not belong to me to judge between bishops', your Clemency now says: 'I must be the judge.' He, although baptized, thought he was unfit for the burden of such a judgment; your Clemency, who must still earn the sacrament of baptism, takes to yourself a judgment concerning faith, although you are unacquainted with the sacraments of that faith. (9)

In his own day, Ambrose used the great spiritual prestige of the church to strike relentlessly at his enemies. First and foremost were the pagans. Throughout the fourth century, defenders of the old gods had rallied support among the common people and raised their voices in debate in the imperial court. As has been noted in the previous section, as late as 384, Symmachus had led a group of Roman senators in petitioning Valentinian II to restore to the Senate its ancient Altar of Victory and certain other privileges. It was Ambrose who helped the young emperor to steel himself against this pressure from the Senate.

Reminding Valentinian of earlier persecutions of Christians by the pagans, Ambrose had no doubt as to what was right and, into the bargain, took a rather patronizing tone toward the young emperor. Symmachus had argued that Rome needed her ancient rites so that the gods would protect her as they always had. Ambrose replied that no gods had favored Rome, and in any case, her enemies had also worshiped the gods. And where were the gods during Rome's defeats? Symmachus had also asked to maintain the seven vestal virgins, but how did they compare, Ambrose wanted to know, to a whole world of Christian virtue? Moreover, he asserted, Symmachus spoke for only a small group, and most Romans no longer supported pagan views. Here are major passages from two letters Ambrose wrote to the thirteen-year-old Valentinian. The first was sent in the summer of 384.

> Let no one take advantage of your youth; if it is a pagan who makes these demands, he ought not ensnare your mind in the meshes of superstition, but by his zeal he should teach and instruct you how to be zealous for the true faith since he defends untruth with so much zeal. I agree that we must be respectful of the true merits of men of distinction, but it is certain that God should be preferred to all men. . . .
>
> A decree like this cannot be enforced without sacrilege. I beg you not to make such a decree, nor pass a law, nor sign a decree of this sort. As a priest of Christ, I appeal to your faith. All priests would make the appeal with me if the sudden news which came to their ears were not unbelievable that such a measure was suggested in your council or demanded by the Senate. Do not let it be said that the Senate demanded this, A few pagans are usurping the name which is not theirs. When the same thing was tried about two years ago, Damasus, the holy bishop of the Roman Church, elected by God's judgment, sent me a counter-petition which the Christian senators had given him. In great numbers they protested that they had made no such demand, that they did not agree with such requests of the pagans or give their assent. In public and in private they murmured that they would not come to the Senate if such a measure were decreed. Is it dignified in your day, a Christian day, that Christian Senators be deprived of their dignity so that heathens may have deference paid to their unholy will? I sent this memorandum to the brother of your Clemency, wherein was clear evidence that the Senate had made no provision for the upkeep of superstition.
>
> Perhaps it may be said: 'Why were they not present in the Senate when such proposals were being made?' They say clearly enough what they wish, by not being present; they have said enough by speaking to the emperor. Yet it is strange to us that they take from private individuals at Rome the liberty of resisting, while they are unwilling that you be free to withhold ordering what you do not approve and to maintain what you feel is right.
>
> Mindful, therefore, of the commission lately laid upon me I again call upon your faith, I call upon your judgment. Do not think that you have to give an answer favorable to the pagans, nor join to your answer in such a matter the sacrilege of your signature. Refer with assurance to the father of your Piety, Emperor Theodosius, whom you have been accustomed to

consult in almost all matters of great importance. Nothing is of more importance than religion; nothing is more exalted than faith.

If this were a civil case, the opposing party would be guaranteed the right of reply. It is a religious case, and I, the bishop, am using that right. Let a copy of the appeal be given me, and I will answer more fully. And may it seem fit to you to consult your faith's opinion on all these matters. Certainly, if any other decision is reached, we bishops cannot tranquilly allow it and pretend not to notice. You will be allowed to come to the church, but either you will find there no priest or you will find one who will gainsay you.

What will you answer the priest who says to you: 'The Church does not want your gifts because you have adorned the heathen temples with gifts. The altar of Christ spurns your gifts since you have made an altar for idols. Yours is the voice, yours the hand, yours the signature, yours the work. The Lord Jesus scorns and spurns your worship since you have worshipped idols, for He said to you: "You cannot serve two masters." Virgins consecrated to God have no privileges from you, and do Vestal virgins lay claim to them? Why do you ask for God's priests to whom you have brought the unholy demands of the pagans? We cannot be associated with another's error.' . . .

Wherefore, O Emperor, you see that if you decree anything of this kind you will offer injury first to God and then to your father and brother; I beg you do what you know will benefit your own salvation before God. (7)

Ambrose sent the second letter in the fall of 384.

The illustrious prefect of the city, Symmachus, has made an appeal to your Clemency that the altar which was removed from the Senate House in the city of Rome be restored to its place. You, O Emperor, still young in age, a new recruit without experience, but a veteran in faith, did not approve the appeal of the pagans. The very moment I learned this I presented a request in which, although I stated what seemed necessary to suggest, I asked that I be given a copy of the appeal.

Not doubtful, therefore, regarding your faith, but foreseeing the care that is necessary, and being confident of a kindly consideration, I am answering the demands of the appeal with this discourse, making this one request that you will not expect eloquence of speech but the force of facts. For, as holy Scripture teaches, the tongue of the wise and studious man is golden, decked with glittering words and shining with the gleam of eloquence, as though some rich hue, capturing the eyes of the mind by the comeliness of its appearance, dazzling in its beauty. But this gold, if you examine it carefully, though outwardly precious, within is a base metal. Ponder well, I beg you, and examine the sect of the pagans. They sound weighty and grand; they support what is incapable of being true; they talk of God, but they adore a statue.

The distinguished prefect of the city has brought forth in his appeal three points which he considers of weight; namely, that (according to him) Rome is asking again for her ancient rites, that the priests and Vestal virgins should be given their stipends, and since these stipends have been refused to the priests there has been general famine.

According to the first proposal, as he says, Rome is shedding tears with sad and mournful complaints, asking again for her ancient ceremonies. The sacred objects, he says, drove Hannibal from the city and the Senones from the Capitol. But at the same time as the power of the sacred objects is proclaimed, their weakness is betrayed. Hannibal reviled the sacred objects of the Romans for a long time, and while the gods warred against themselves the conqueror reached the city's walls. Why did they allow themselves to be besieged when the weapons of their gods did battle for them?

Why should I make mention of the Senones, whom, when they penetrated the innermost recesses of the Capitol, the Roman forces could not have withstood had not a goose (with its frightened cackling) betrayed them. See what sort of protectors guard the Roman temples. Where was Jupiter at that time? Was he making a statement through a goose?

Why do I refuse to admit that their sacred objects warred in behalf of the Romans? Hannibal, too, worshiped the same gods. Let them choose whichever they wish. If these sacred objects conquered in the Romans, then they were overcome in the Carthaginians. If they triumphed in the Carthaginians, they certainly did not help the Romans. . . .

Let the Vestal virgins, he says, keep their privileged state. Let men say this who are not able to believe what virginity can do without reward. Let them derive encouragement from gainful means, having no confidence in virtue. How many virgins get the rewards promised to them? About seven Vestal virgins are accepted. Lo! that is the whole number of those attracted by fillets and chaplets for the head, or purple-dyed robes, the pomp of a litter surrounded by a group of attendants, the greatest privileges, great gains, and a set period of virginity.

Let them raise the eye of the mind and of the body and see a nation of modesty, a people of purity, an assembly of virginity. Fillets are not the adornment of the head but a veil in common use, ennobled by chastity. The finery of beauty is not sought after, it is relinquished. There are none of those purple insignia, no charming luxuries, but rather the practice of fasts, no privileges, no gains. All are such, in fine, that you would think enjoyment restrained while duties are performed. But while *they* perform their duty, enjoyment grows apace. Chastity mounts by its own sacrifices.

That is not virginity which is bought for a price and not kept through a desire for the virtue. That is not purity which is paid for with money at an auction and only for a time. Chastity's chief victory is to conquer the desire for wealth because eagerness for gain is a temptation to modesty. Let us grant that bountiful provisions should be given to virgins. What amounts will overflow upon Christians! What treasury will supply such riches? Or if they think that only Vestals should be given grants, are they not ashamed that they claimed the whole for themselves under heathen emperors and do not think that under Christian princes we should have a like share?

They complain also that public support is not being duly granted to their priests and ministers. What a storm of words has sounded on this point! On the other hand, under recent laws we were denied even the inheritance of private property, and no one is complaining. We do not think that is an injury because we do not grieve over losses. If a priest seeks the privilege of declining the municipal burden, he has to give up the paternal and ancestral ownership of all his property. If the heathens suffered this, how would they urge their complaint, if the priest had to buy free time for the exercise of his ministry by the loss of his patrimony, and purchase the power of exercising his public ministry at the expense of all his private means! In addition, alleging his vigils for the common safety, he must console himself with the reward of domestic poverty, because he has not sold his service but has obtained a favor. . . .

I have answered those who provoked me as though I had not been provoked, for my object was to refute the appeal, not to expose superstition. But let their very appeal, O Emperor, make you more cautious. After saying that of former princes, the earlier ones practiced the cult of their fathers, and the later ones did not abolish them, it was claimed in addition that if the religious practice of older princes did not set a pattern, the act of overlooking them on the part of the later ones did. This showed plainly what you owe to your faith, that you should not follow the pattern of heathen rites, and to your affection, that you should not set aside the decrees of your brother. If in their own behalf only they have praised the permission of those princes who, although they were Christians, did not abolish the heathen decrees, how much more ought you to defer to your brotherly affection, so that you who must overlook some things, even though you do not approve them, should not abrogate your brother's decrees; you should maintain what you judge to be in agreement with your own faith and the bond of brotherhood. (8)

The success of the church's campaign against the old gods is seen in the laws of 391 to 392, which outlawed the practice of paganism and left Christianity as the sole legal religion of the empire. Technically, it was their ritualism that was banned, not the pagans themselves. But if Ambrose had had his way, all idol-worshipers would have been excluded from a totally orthodox empire. The next out would be the heretics.

By the late fourth century, the foremost heresy of the day, Arianism, was losing its strength in the west, but the orthodox, who held the authorized view of the Trinity, promulgated at Nicaea, could not yet afford to relax entirely. The Empress Justina, widowed mother of Valentinian II, headed a powerful faction in the court at Milan. It would seem that she was ambitious and jealous of the bishop's strong influence over her son. Dudden's comprehensive two-volume study of Ambrose says of Justina: "Perhaps only two things can be said of her with absolute certainty—she was an Arian in faith and she detested Ambrose" (p. 270).

In a letter to his sister Marcellina, at Easter in 386, Ambrose relates his continuing efforts, despite a threat of violence or exile, to prevent the Arians from having a church in Milan (60). A large majority of the population and many soldiers supported him.

The newly discovered skeletons of the martyrs Gervasius and Protasius (reputedly from the time of Nero)[6] greatly strengthened Ambrose's hand in his continuing struggle with the Arians in Milan, including Justina and her friends at court. The popular belief in the miraculous powers of these relics, discovered in excavations which Ambrose had ordered in the summer of 386, gave the bishop all the edge he needed. Justina and others might sneer and say it was a contrived event, but Ambrose obviously shared the current reverence for holy relics. In a letter to his sister Marcellina, he described the wonderous finding in the basilica in Milan. Marcellina and her mother had moved to Rome after Ambrose's father's death, and the daughter, early in life, had taken a vow of virginity. Ambrose respectfully addresses her as "your Holiness," despite their blood relationship.

> Ordinarily, I do not leave your Holiness unacquainted with the events taking place here in your absence. You should know, then, that we have found some holy martyrs. When I had consecrated the basilica, many persons with one accord began appealing to me, saying: 'Consecrate this as you did the Roman basilica.' 'I will,' I said, 'if I find relics of martyrs.' And at once I was seized, as it were, with a great presentiment of some sort of divine sign.
>
> In short, the Lord bestowed His favor. Even the clergy were afraid when I bade them clear away the ground in the spot before the grating of Sts. Felix and Nabor. I found encouraging signs. And when certain persons were brought forward to have my hands laid on them [in blessing], the holy martyrs began driving away [the evil spirit], so that before I had said anything one woman was seized and thrown forward at the holy burial place. We found two men of wondrous stature, such as ancient ages bore. The bones were all intact and there was much blood. A great throng of people was

> there during these two days. In short, we arranged everything in orderly fashion. As it was close to evening, we transferred them to the basilica of Fausta. All that night watch was kept and blessings were given. The next day we transferred them to that which is called the Ambrosian Basilica. While they were being transferred a blind man was cured. (61)

Finally, the third group Ambrose would expel from the empire, if he could, were the Jews. They, along with pagans and heretics, should certainly be refused marriage to orthodox Christians. His strong attitude toward the Jews was evident in a clash with the Emperor Theodosius that preceded the conflict in 390 over the massacre in Thessalonica. In 388, in Callinicum, a town on the Euphrates River in Mesopotamia, a mob led by fanatical monks, with the encouragement of the local bishop, burned a synagogue. To maintain law and order, Theodosius ordered that the monks be punished and that the bishop pay for the rebuilding of the edifice. Ambrose strongly opposed this decision and reprimanded the emperor in the following letter in December 388. Ambrose insisted that the burning of the synagogue was justified if only for revenge's sake, for the Jews had in the past burned certain of the church's basilicas.

> I am continually beset with almost unending cares, O most blessed Emperor, but never have I felt such anxiety as now, for I see that I must be careful not to have ascribed to me anything resembling an act of sacrilege. I beg you, therefore, give ear with patience to what I say. For, if I am not worthy of a hearing from you, I am not worthy of offering sacrifice for you, I to whom you have entrusted the offering of your vows and prayers. Will you yourself not hear one whom you wish heard when he prays in your behalf? . . .
>
> It is not fitting for an emperor to refuse freedom of speech, or for a bishop not to say what he thinks. There is no quality in you emperors so popular and so lovable as the cherishing of liberty even in those whom you have subdued on the battlefield. In fact, it spells the difference between good and bad emperors that the good love liberty; the bad, slavery. And there is nothing in a bishop so fraught with danger before God, so base before men, as not to declare freely what he thinks. . . . .
>
> I would rather, O Emperor, have partnership with you in good deeds than in evil. Therefore, the bishop's silence should be disagreeable to your Clemency; his freedom, agreeable. You are involved in the peril of my silence, but you are helped by the boon of my freedom. I am not, then, intruding in bothersome fashion where I have no obligation; I am not interfering in the affairs of others; I am complying with my duty; I am obeying the commands of our God. This I do, first of all, out of love for you, in gratitude to you, from a desire to preserve your well-being. If I

am not believed or am forbidden a hearing, I speak, nonetheless, for fear of offending God. . . .

I know that you are God-fearing, merciful, gentle, and calm, that you have the faith and fear of God in your heart, but often some things escape our notice. Some persons have zeal for God, but not according to knowledge. Care must be taken, I think, lest this condition steal upon pious souls. I know your devotion to God, your leniency toward men. I myself am indebted to you for many kind favors. Therefore, I fear the more, I am the more anxious lest you condemn me later in your judgment for the fault you did not avoid, because of my want of openness and my flattery of you. If I saw you sinning against me, I would not have to be silent, for it is written: "If thy brother sin against thee, first take hold of him, then rebuke him before two or three witnesses. If he refuse to hear thee, tell the Church." Shall I, then, keep silence in the cause of God? Let us then consider wherein lies my fear.

It was reported by a count [name unknown] of military affairs in the East that a synagogue was burned [at Callinicum], and this at the instigation of a bishop. You gave the order for those who were involved to be punished and the synagogue rebuilt at the bishop's expense. . . . This, I ask, O Emperor, that you rather take your vengeance on me, and, if you consider this a crime, attribute it to me. Why pronounce judgment on those who are far away? You have someone at hand, you have someone who admits his guilt. I declare that I set fire to the synagogue, at least that I gave the orders, so that there would be no building in which Christ is denied. If the objection is raised that I did not burn the synagogue here, I answer that its burning was begun by God's judgment [lightning ?] and my work was at an end. If you want the truth, I was really remiss, for I did not think such a deed was to be punished. Why should I have done what was to be without one to punish, and without reward? These words cause me shame but they bring me grace, lest I offend the most high God.

Let no one call the bishop to task for performing his duty:that is the request I make of your Clemency. And although I have not read that the edict was revoked, let us consider it revoked. What if other more timid persons should, through fear of death, offer to repair the synagogue at their expense, or the count, finding this previously determined, should order it to be rebuilt from the funds of Christians? Will you, O Emperor, have the count an apostate, and entrust to him the insignia of victory, or give the labarum, which is sanctified by Christ's name, to one who will rebuild a synagogue which knows not Christ? Order the labarum carried into the synagogue and let us see if they [the Jews] do not resist.

Shall a place be provided out of the spoils of the Church for the disbelief of the Jews, and shall this patrimony, given to Christians by the favor of

Christ, be transferred to the treasuries of unbelievers? We read that, of old, temples were reared for idols from the plunder taken from the Cimbrians and from the spoils of the enemy. The Jews will write on the front of their synagogue the inscription: "The Temple of Impiety, erected from the spoils of the Christians."

Is your motive a point of discipline, O Emperor? Which is of more importance: a demonstration of discipline or the cause of religion? The maintenance of civil law should be secondary to religion.

Have you not heard how, when Julian had ordered the Temple of Jerusalem rebuilt, those who were clearing the rubbish were burned by fire from heaven? Are you not afraid that this will also happen now? In fact, you should never have given an order such as Julian would have given. . . .

There is really no adequate cause for all this commotion, people being punished so severely for the burning of a building, and much less so, since a synagogue has been burned, an abode of unbelief, a house of impiety, a shelter of madness under the damnation of God Himself. For we read by the mouth of Jeremias, the Lord our God speaking: "And I will do to this house in which my name is called upon, and which you trust, and to the place which I have given you and your father, as I did to Silo. And I will cast you away from before my face, as I have cast away all your brethren, the whole seed of Ephraim. Therefore do not thou pray for this people, nor show mercy for them and so not approach me for them; for I will not hear thee. Seest thou not what they do in the cities of Juda?" God forbids us to make intercession for those that you think should be vindicated.

If I were pleading according to the law of the nations, I would mention how many of the Church's basilicas the Jews burned in the time of Julian, two at Damascus–one of which is scarcely yet repaired, and that at the expense of the Church, not of the synagogue–while the other basilica is still a rough heap of unsightly ruins. Basilicas were burned at Gaza, Ascalon, Beirut, in fact, almost all over that region, and no one demanded punishment. A basilica of surpassing beauty at Alexandria was burned by heathens and Jews, but the Church was not avenged, and shall the synagogue be avenged? . . .

Will you grant the Jews this triumph over God's Church? this trophy over Christ's people? these joys, O Emperor, to unbelievers? this festival to the synagogue? this grief to the Church? The Jewish people will put this solemnity among their feast days, and doubtless they will rank it with their triumphs over the Amorites and the Canaanites, or their deliverance from Pharao, the king of Egypt, or from the hand of Nabuchodonosor, the king of Babylon. They will have this solemnity marking the triumphs they have wrought over the people of Christ.

And although they refuse to be bound by the laws of Rome, thinking them outrageous, they now wish to be avenged, so to speak, by Roman laws. Where were those laws when they set fire to the domes of the sacred basilicas? If Julian did not avenge the Church, because he was an apostate, will you, O Emperor, avenge the harm done the synagogue, because you are a Christian? . . .

How important it is for you, O Emperor, not to feel bound to investigate or punish a matter which no one up to now has investigated or punished! It is a serious matter to jeopardize your faith in behalf of the Jews. When Gideon had slain the sacred calf, the heathens said: "Let the gods themselves avenge the injury done to them." Whose task is it to avenge the synagogue? Christ whom they slew, whom they denied? Or will God the Father avenge those who did not accept the Father, since they did not accept the Son? . . .

Now, O Emperor, I beg you not to hear me with contempt, for I fear for you and for myself, as says the holy man: "Wherefore was I born to see the ruin of my people," that I should commit an offense against God? Indeed, I have done what I could do honorably, that you might hear me in the palace rather than make it necessary to hear me in the Church. (2)

That concluding remark, " . . . make it necessary to hear me in the Church," had an ominous sound. Although Theodosius had decided to have the state bear the expense of rebuilding the synagogue, Ambrose would not agree even to that and furthermore demanded amnesty for all the Christians involved. After the bishop delivered a sermon against any compromise, Theodosius was forced to give in entirely. Dudden argues that, at the time, the capitulation was less for religious reasons than for political ones. The popular and powerful Ambrose was capable of stirring up the citizenry, even soldiers, against him, and given what was at issue, the emperor preferred to back down. Had he been confronted by an eastern bishop, the result might have been different, for Constantine had presided over the Council of Nicaea in 325 and thereafter, in the east, churchmen were more in the habit of pleading with emperors than condemning them.

When Gothic attacks on Thessalonica failed, Ambrose attributed the safety of the city to miracles and the prayers of its saintly Bishop Acholius, rather than merely to the valor of its defenders. The barbarian invasions provided yet another opportunity for testimonials of faith. His perspective, shared by others at the time, is missing from modern textbook accounts of those days. They simply say that Valentinian I made his narrow-minded, if not stupid, brother Valens the emperor of the east, and it proved to be a disaster. The Visigoths, fleeing from the more fearsome Huns, asked in 376 to be admitted to the empire on peaceful terms as farmers and soldiers. Valens allowed them in, but they were subsequently so badly treated, being denied the food they were promised and having their children enslaved, that they revolted. The battle of Adrianople in 378 was memorable. For the first time, Roman legions were defeated by barbarians inside the empire. Valens himself was killed and his body never found. This was the catastrophe which prompted Gratian to promote the more able Theodosius to be the ruler of the eastern half of the empire. He eventually, in 382, made peace with the Goths.

Passages from a letter of condolence Ambrose sent to "all the beloved clergy and people of Thessalonica" after Bishop Acholius had died in 382 put his own interpretation on recent events. Speaking of the Goths, he wrote:

> The saintly Acholius by his prayers drove the victors from Macedonia. Do we not see it was by a higher power that from where there was no soldier they were routed without a soldier? Is it not blindness for them to have fled whom no one pursued? Truly the saintly Acholius was attacking and engaging them, not with swords but with prayers, not with spears but by his merits. (37)

Ambrose could praise the "saintly Acholius," but his own standing in the east was far less auspicious. He was obviously so convinced of the rightness of his own orthodox position that he was at times awkward and overreaching with his eastern colleagues, among whom Arianism was very strong. His greatest successes came with those who came under the spell of his presence.

As the dominant bishop in northern Italy, Ambrose was often involved in momentous events. Valentinian II, who reigned 375 to 392, twice sent him as envoy to the usurper Magnus Maximus, who, after the murder of Gratian, allowed his troops at Trier to hail him as emperor. Ambrose seemed the right man for the mission on behalf of the young emperor, for Maximus was staunchly orthodox and, in fact, after being recognized by Theodosius, was the first emperor to put heretical Christians to death.

Ambrose's first visit was in the winter of 383–384. In his second visit, in 385 or 386, Maximus was undoubtedly pleased that Ambrose was bringing his brother, Marcellinus, back to him, but insisted that Valentinian come in person to Trier to negotiate peace. It was a concession the court in Milan politely evaded.

Although Ambrose had the first time been received by Maximus in public audience rather than in private chambers, he was on the second occasion openly displeased with such an arrangement. As elsewhere in the following letter, a complaint about protocol reveals Ambrose's sense of propriety, or maybe his pride. The role he played in these missions showed what an important personage he had become, but his trips on behalf of peace were not really successful.

The letter, written to Valentinian in 386, describes the meeting in which the bishop seems to boast of the blunt manner in which he accused Maximus of various misdeeds. He also snubbed the bishops who supported Maximus. A reference to barbarians in the imperial service is a sign of the times.

> You have had such confidence in my recent embassy that no report of it was demanded of me. It was sufficiently clear from my having stayed

some days in Gaul that I did not accept the terms favorable to Maximus or agree with those which favored his will rather than peace. Moreover, you would never have sent me on a second embassy unless you had approved the first. But, inasmuch as I was forced to the necessity of contesting with him on my arrival, I have determined to give an account of my embassy in this letter so that no one's report will confuse the false with the true before, on my return, I make a clear and trustworthy account of the truth.

The day after I arrived at Trier I went to the palace. The grand chamberlain Gallicanus, a royal eunuch, came out to me. I asked the privilege of entering; he asked if I had an imperial order from your Clemency. I answered that I did. He retorted that I could be interviewed only in the consistory. I replied that this was not customary for one of the episcopal rank and, in fact, that there were certain matters of which I had to speak in earnest with the prince. In short, he went and consulted him, but maintained that the conditions would have to hold, so that it became clear that even his first remarks had been prompted by the other's wishes. I remarked that it was not in keeping with my office, but that I would not fail the embassy entrusted to me. I was happy to be humbled, especially on your behalf and in the performance of a duty which involved the affection you bear your brother.

As soon as he was seated in the consistory, I entered; he arose to give me the kiss of greeting; I was standing with the members of the consistory. Some began urging me to step forward; he began summoning me. I said: "Why would you greet with a kiss one whom you do not know? If you knew me you would not see me here." "Bishop," he said, "you are greatly upset." "Not by the insult," I answered, "but by the embarrassment of standing in a place where I do not belong." "You came into the consistory," he said, "on your first embassy." "That was not my fault," I said, "but the fault of the one who summoned me; I merely came in answer to the summons." "Why did you come?" he asked. "Because," I replied, "at that time I was asking for peace for one who was weaker than you, but I do so now for one who is your equal." "Equal by whose kindness?" he asked. "That of almighty God," said I, "for He preserved for Valentinian the kingdom He had given him."

The letter then continues with a lengthy description of the wrangling that went on between Ambrose and Maximus, and finally concludes with this passage:

Later, when he observed that I stayed aloof from the bishops who were in his service and who were asking that certain persons, heretics, should be put to death, he became very angry and ordered me to leave at once. I went, although several thought I would not escape his ambushes. I was overwhelmed with sorrow finding that the old bishop, Hyginus, though he had but the last breath of life left in him, was being sent into exile. When I approached some of his men and begged them not to allow him to be driven forth without clothing, without a bed to lie on, I was myself driven out.

This is the account of my embassy. Farewell, O Emperor, and be on your guard against a man who is cloaking war under the mask of peace. (10)

Ambrose's prediction proved to be true. Valentinian II was forced to flee Italy and was not restored until Theodosius, the eastern ruler, had twice defeated Maximus, and finally executed him in 388. Four years later, Valentinian was murdered by Richimer and Arbogast, two barbarian courtiers who brought about the accession of Eugenius as emperor in the west. This was done without the approval of Theodosius, who was, however, slow to respond, and in the summer of 393 Eugenius and Arbogast invaded Italy.

About this event, Ambrose and Theodosius had no misunderstanding. Ambrose was opposed to Eugenius because he saw him as a danger to peace and also was suspicious of his sympathy to paganism. After all, Arbogast and Richimer were pagans, and Eugenius was only a lukewarm Christian. So, while Ambrose responded diplomatically to Eugenius's invasion by maintaining a correspondence with him, he at the same time kept moving from place to place (Bologna, Florence) so as to avoid his troops. The following letter, written in the summer of 393, is a forthright but very respectful message to Eugenius justifying Ambrose's course of action. By mentioning his confrontations with Valentinian and Theodosius and their submission to his wishes, Ambrose was obviously, if in a subtle way, again talking about excommunication.

My reason for leaving [Milan] was the fear of the Lord to whom I direct all my acts, as far as possible, never turning my mind from Him nor considering any man's favor of more worth than the grace of Christ. By preferring God to everyone else I harm no one, and trusting in Him I have no fear of telling your majesties, the emperors, what I feel with my own conviction. Thus I shall not refrain from saying to you, most clement Emperor, what I have never refrained from saying to other emperors. . . . when your Clemency assumed the government of the Empire [August 392] . . . donations were found to have been made to distinguished citizens of the heathen religion. Perhaps, O august Emperor, it may be said that you yourself did not make the donations to the temples, but merely gave benefits to men who deserved well of you. . . .

The imperial power is great, but consider, O Emperor, how great God is. He sees the hearts of all; He probes their inmost conscience; He knows all things before they come to pass; He knows the innermost secrets of

> your heart. You do not allow yourself to be deceived; do you expect to hide anything from God? Has this thought not occurred to you? Although they persisted in their requests, was it not your duty, O Emperor, out of reverence for the most high, true, and living God, to oppose them still more persistently and to refuse what was harmful to the holy law? . . . Since I am deeply respectful of a private individual, why should I not be so of the emperor? Just as you wish to be held in respect, allow us to respect Him from whom you would like to prove that your authority is derived. (11)

By 394, Theodosius had made up his mind to put an end to this new usurper in the west and in September of that year defeated and beheaded Eugenius. A few days later, Arbogast, who had not been captured, committed suicide. Only a few months later, in January of 395, the mighty Theodosius himself fell ill and died. Ambrose gave the funeral oration before the body was taken to Constantinople for burial.

In the last two years of his own life, Ambrose was apparently less active in wordly affairs, but as zealous as he had always been on behalf of his strong religious beliefs. He was delighted to hear that Paulinus of Nola and his wife Therasia had decided to live as ascetics. (see Chapter IX) He was himself given to frequent periods of fasting and even more frequent periods of prayer. In a letter to a bishop named Sabinus, written in 395, he responded to criticism from those who viewed the ascetic lifestyle as peculiar and shameful. It was, in fact, not more shameful than the practices of other religions in Rome, or indeed of the performances in the theater. Biblical heroes, such as David, gladly endured public censure when performing unpopular acts in the name of religion.

> I have learned that Paulinus, second to none of the Aquitanians in luster of birth, has sold his and his wife's possessions, and has taken up these practices of faith that he is giving his property to the poor by changing it into money, while he, poor now instead of rich, as if relieved of a heavy burden, has said farewell to home, country, and kindred in order to serve God with greater zeal. Word has it that he has chosen a retreat in the city of Nola where he will pass his days out of reach of the tumult of the world. His wife [Therasia], too, closely followed the example of his zeal and virtue, not objecting to her husband's resolve. She has transferred her property to the jurisdiction of others and is following her husband, where, perfectly content with his little patch of ground, she will comfort herself with the riches of religion and charity. They have no children [a baby son had died after eight days], but their desire is a posterity of good deeds.
>
> What will our leading citizens say when they hear this? It is unthinkable that a man of such family, such background, such genius, gifted with such eloquence, should retire from the Senate and that the succession of so no-

ble a family should be broken. Although in performing the rites of Isis they shave their heads and eyebrows, they yet call it a shameful thing for a Christian out of devotion to his holy religion to change his apparel. . . . David was not ashamed when he danced before the Ark of the Covenant in the presence of all the people. Isaias was not ashamed, for he went naked and barefoot through the crowd, proclaiming heavenly prophecies.

As a matter of fact, what is actually so embarrassing as the gestures of actors and the twining of their limbs in womanly fashion? Lewd dancing is the companion of wantonness and the pastime of riotous living. What did he [David] mean by singing: "Clap your hands, all ye people?" Obviously, if we consider his bodily actions, we realize that he clapped his hands, dancing with women and stamping with unbecoming sounds. Of Ezechiel, too, it was said: "Strike with the hand and stamp with the foot."

Yet, these actions of the body, though unseemly when viewed in themselves, become reverential under the aspect of holy religion, so that those who censure them drag their own souls into the net of censure. Thus, Michol censured David for dancing and said: "How glorious was the king of Israel today, for he uncovered himself today before the eyes of his handmaids." And David answered her: "I will play before the Lord who chose me rather than my father, and than all his house, and commanded me to be ruler over his people of Israel. And I will play before the Lord and I will thus be uncovered and I will be mean in thy eyes, and with the handmaids, to whom you said I was uncovered, I shall be honored." (28)

To Ambrose marriage was honorable, but virginity was better. He defended the doctrine of the miraculous virgin birth, which was not accepted by all Christians. Ambrose had grown up in a household presided over by an extremely devout mother and sister. In a chapter entitled, "Women in the Fourth Century and Ambrose's Work Among Them," Dudden writes that Ambrose "considered it the duty of a bishop to sow the seeds of chastity and stir up zeal for virginity. He accordingly addressed himself with ardour to the congenial work of persuading young women to adopt the celibate life" (pp. 147–49). With such ardour, it seems, Ambrose even advised daughters to defy their parents if the latter were opposed to the bishop's teachings. Those who glorified the rigourously moral life had common enemies. Both Jerome and Ambrose denounced a priest named Jovinian, who in the 390s caused an uproar by teaching that no special benefit derived from living a spare existence. As usual, it was Ambrose who took the most telling action. He presided over a Synod of Milan in 393, where Jovinian's view was condemned as heresy. In the synod report to Pope Siricius the "raving of wolves" is countered with the following paragraph from a letter that reveals the strong feelings aroused in any debate over the concept of self-denial.

> They pretend that they are giving honor to marriage. What praise is possible to marriage if virginity receives no distinction? We do not say that marriage was not sanctified by Christ, since the Word of God says: "The two shall become one flesh" and one spirit. But we are born before we are brought to our final goal, and the mystery of God's operation is more excellent than the remedy for human weakness. Quite rightly is a good wife praised, but a pious virgin is more rightly preferred, for the Apostle says "He who gives his daughter in marriage does well, and he who does not give her does better. The one thinks about the things of God, the other about the things of the world." The one is bound by marriage bonds, the other is free from bonds; one is under the law, the other under grace. Marriage is good: through it the means of human continuity are found. But virginity is better: through it are attained the inheritance of a heavenly kingdom and a continuity of heavenly rewards. Through a woman distress entered the world; through a virgin salvation came upon it. Lastly, Christ chose Himself the special privilege of virginity and set forth the benefit of chastity, manifesting in Himself what He had chosen in His mother. (44)

It was the constancy of Ambrose's faith, the eloquence of his sermons, and the beauty of the hymns he composed that won the heart of Augustine, his most famous convert, whom he had baptized on the eve of Easter, 387. But they were never really strong friends, and Ambrose did not live long enough to read any of the books for which Augustine is famous. When Ambrose died on 4 April 397, after an illness of a few months, it would have been hard to imagine that Rome would be sacked by the Goths only thirteen years later. True to Ambrose's faith, Augustine's *City of God* found a heavenly purpose in that cataclysmic event. On a less lofty plane were his sometimes quarrelsome words addressed to the scholarly Jerome, whose letters are the subject of the next chapter.

XI
JEROME

Struggling with Himself, Satan, and Others

SIXTEEN hundred years ago, in A.D. 384, there was a bitter controversy in Rome over a girl of twenty who had starved herself to death. Blaesilla, of noble birth, had been encouraged to fast by an eminent Christian writer whom we know as St. Jerome. She might today be called anorexic. Although extreme conduct by young people is not unexpected at any time, the reasons change. In the fourth century, giving up food was not in search of a stylish figure; it meant rejecting the body altogether. Understandably, there are many who have no patience with such behavior. But Jerome's mind remained fixed about Blaesilla. In the following letter, written late in 384 to her mother, Paula, a close friend of his, he proclaims Blaesilla the victor in the struggle against Satan. He also criticizes Paula for exhibiting grief over the death of her daughter. Jerome's attitude is not only a key to the mind of the greatest scholar of the fourth century but also, of course, to a mentality that would prevail widely in the centuries to follow.

> Spare yourself, I beseech you, spare Blaesilla, who now reigns with Christ; as least spare Eustochium,[1] whose tender years and inexperience depend on you for guidance and instruction. Now does the devil rage and complain that he is set at naught, because he sees one of your children exalted in triumph. The victory which he failed to win over her that is gone he hopes to obtain over her who still remains. Too great affection towards one's children is disaffection towards God. Abraham gladly prepares to slay his only son, and do you complain if one child out of several has received her crown? I cannot say what I am going to say without a groan. When you were carried fainting out of the funeral procession, whispers such as these were audible in the crowd. "Is not this what we have often said. She weeps for her daughter, killed with fasting. She wanted her to marry again, that

> she might have grandchildren. How long must we refrain from driving these detestable monks out of Rome? Why do we not stone them or hurl them into the Tiber? They have misled this unhappy lady; that she is not a nun from choice is clear. No heathen mother ever wept for her children as she does for Blaesilla." What sorrow, think you, must not Christ have endured when he listened to such words as these! And how triumphantly must Satan have exulted, eager as he is to snatch your soul! Luring you with the claims of a grief which seems natural and right, and always keeping before you the image of Blaesilla, his aim is to slay the mother of the victresss, and then to fall upon her forsaken sister. I do not speak thus to terrify you. The Lord is my witness that I address you now as though I were standing at His judgment seat. Tears which have no meaning are an object of abhorrence. Yours are detestable tears, sacrilegious tears, unbelieving tears; for they know no limits, and bring you to the verge of death. You shriek and cry out as though on fire within, and do your best to put an end to yourself. But to you and others like you Jesus comes in His mercy and says: "Why weepest thou? the damsel is not dead but sleepeth." The bystanders may laugh him to scorn; such unbelief is worthy of the Jews. If you prostrate yourself in grief at your daughter's tomb you too will hear the chiding of the angel, "Why seek ye the living among the dead?" It was because Mary Magdalene had done this that when she recognized the Lord's voice calling her and fell at His feet, He said to her: "Touch me not, for I am not yet ascended to my Father:" that is to say, you are not worthy to touch, as risen, one whom you suppose still in the tomb. (XXXIX)[2]

Jerome questioned the value of family life. Today, secular influences take the blame for the breakdown of the family. Jerome's attack came from the religious side. He saw familial affection as a challenge to the love of God. Relations with his own family appear to have been strained early on.

They called him Hieronymos, or "the holy name," which we shorten to Jerome. He was born about 348 in Stridon, near modern Venice, and went to Rome to study at a young age, living there during the rule of Julian the Apostate. Jerome received an exceptional education under a teacher, Aelius Donatus, whose commentaries on classical authors became standard textbooks in the Middle Ages. Although baptized in Rome in 367, it was later, while continuing his studies in Treves (modern Trier), where the Emperor Valentinian I had his headquarters, that he turned forever toward a religious life. By the time he saw his family again, years later, he had committed himself to the monastic ideal. Some of his relations seem to have resented Jerome's decision, having hoped for a more conventional career. Difficulties with his sister were overcome when she decided to follow her brother's example and adopt the ascetic life (cf. letters VI and VII). Estrangement from a maternal aunt, Castorina, continued some time before he sought a reconciliation in 374. His brief letter to her combines a prayerful Christian message with a Roman legalistic note. About one-fourth is quoted from scripture, but at the end he says the very act of writing the letter has absolved him from any guilt in the matter, and he is now free. It is not certain what they were quarreling about, but there is no doubt that Jerome considered himself to be standing on the high ground.

> I renew the prayer which I made a year ago in a previous letter, that the Lord's legacy of peace may be indeed ours, and that my desires and your feelings may find favor in His sight. Soon we shall stand before His judgment seat to receive the reward of harmony restored or to pay the penalty for harmony broken. In case you shall prove unwilling—I hope that it may not be so—to accept my advances, I for my part shall be free. For this letter, when it is read, will insure my acquittal. (XIII)

That letter was written from Antioch in Syria, where Jerome continued his studies, particularly in theology and Greek. Then came a period from 374 or 375 to maybe 377—the chronology is uncertain—in which he put himself through a severe test of his desire for perfection. He adopted the life of monks who lived as hermits in caves on the edge of the Syrian desert. It was during this period that Jerome began to learn Hebrew from a converted Jew who had become a monk and was living nearby. The hardship of learning a difficult language was matched by the harshness of Jerome's private life. Taking up the monastic search for perfection meant abstaining from any bodily pleasure or activity that might deflect him from the path of heaven. Sexual acts were given up along with washing, either of the body or of clothing, and eating of any food beyond the barest necessities. But amid this extraordinarily spare life, Jerome continued to have problems with his "unhappy flesh." There is a vivid recollection of his experience in a very long letter addressed to Julia Eustochium, the younger sister of Blaesilla. It is actually an essay on the monastic way of life, probably written in the spring of 384. Although the essay is cast in the form of a letter, directing this personal material to a young girl was really a formality. Jerome was, as usual, saying what he wanted to say for his own sake. He mentions that he decided early on to live a monastic life not to gain time for the pursuit of learning, but because he had a great fear of hell (XXII). We can assume that he was more sensitive about the foolishness of his schooldays than were other young men of his age. "Wine and youth," he wrote, "between them kindle the fire of sensual pleasure. Why do we throw oil on the flame—why do we add fresh fuel to a miserable body which is already ablaze" (XXII).

Here is the passage in that same letter about what he had to endure in the desert.

> How often when I was living in the desert, in the vast solitude which gives to hermits a savage dwelling-place, parched by a burning sun, how often did I fancy myself among the pleasures of Rome! I used to sit alone because

> I was filled with bitterness. Sackcloth disfigured my unshapely limbs and my skin from long neglect had become as black as an Ethiopian's. Tears and groans were everyday my portion; and if drowsiness chanced to overcome my struggles against it, my bare bones, which hardly held together, clashed against the ground. Of my food and drink I say nothing; for even in sickness, the solitaries have nothing but cold water, and to eat one's food cooked is looked upon as self-indulgence. Now, although in fear of hell I had consigned myself to this prison, where I had no companions but scorpions and wild beasts, I often found myself amid bevies of girls. My face was pale and my frame chilled with fasting; yet my mind was burning with desire, and the fires of lust kept bubbling up before me when my flesh was as good as dead. Helpless, I cast myself at the feet of Jesus, I watered them with my tears, I wiped them with my hair: and then I subdued my rebellious body with weeks of abstinence. (XXII)

In the later Middle Ages, Jerome's dramatic struggle with the flesh was an inspiration to those who practiced what has been called "masochistic spirituality." Actually, however, overcoming the lust of the body was not as difficult for Jerome as giving up his love of pre-Christian writings. And, in fact, that struggle was one he seems to have lost. He was especially fond of the writings of Cicero, as was St. Augustine, but he came to feel that his study of such works kept him from full devotion to God. In another passage from the same letter (XXII), he described a nightmare he had had, warning him against the pagan classics. At first, he was determined to give them up, but in a few years he went back to reading them again. Actually, what he really gave up was his belief in dreams, which later in life he denounced even as the prophets had.

> Many years ago, when for the kingdom of heaven's sake I had cut myself off from home, parents, sister, relations, and—harder still—from the dainty food to which I had become accustomed; and when I was on my way to Jerusalem to wage my warfare, I still could not bring myself to forego the library which I had formed for myself at Rome with great care and toil. And so, miserable man that I was, I would fast only that I might afterwards read Cicero. After many nights spend in vigil, after floods of tears called from my inmost heart, after the recollection of my past sins, I would once more take up Plautus. And when at times I returned to my right mind, and began to read the prophets, their style seemed rude and repellent. I failed to see the light with my blinded eyes; but attributed the fault not to them, but to the sun. While the old serpent was thus making me his plaything, about the middle of Lent a deep-seated fever fell upon my weakened body, and while it destroyed my rest completely—the story seems hardly credible—it so wasted my unhappy frame that scarcely anything was

El Greco (ca. 1548–ca. 1620), *Saint Jerome.* National Gallery of Art, Washington, D.C.; Chester Dale Collection.

> left of me but skin and bone. Meantime preparations for my funeral went on; my body grew gradually colder, and the warmth of life lingered only in my throbbing breast. Suddenly I was caught up in the spirit and dragged before the judgment seat of the Judge; and here the light was so bright, and those who stood around were so radiant, that I cast myself upon the ground and did not dare to look up. Asked who and what I was I replied: "I am a Christian." But He who presided said: "Thou liest, thou art a follower of Cicero and not of Christ. For 'where thy treasure is, there will thy heart be also.'" Instantly I became dumb, and amid the strokes of the lash—for He had ordered me to be scourged—I was tortured more severely still by the fire of conscience, considering with myself that verse, "In the grave who shall give thee thanks?" Yet for all that I began to cry and to bewail myself, saying: "Have mercy upon me, O Lord: have mercy upon me." Amid the sound of the scourges this cry still made itself heard. At last the bystanders, falling down before the knees of Him who presided, prayed that He would have pity on my youth, and that He would give me space to repent of my error. He might still, they urged, inflict torture on me, should I ever again read the works of the Gentiles. Under the stress of that awful moment I should have been ready to make even still larger promises than these. Accordingly I made oath and called upon His name, saying: "Lord, if ever again I possess worldly books, or if ever again I read such, I have denied Thee." Dismissed, then, on taking this oath, I returned to the upper world, and, to the surprise of all, I opened upon them eyes so drenched with tears that my distress served to convince even the incredulous. And that this was no sleep nor idle dream, such as those by which we are often mocked, I call to witness the tribunal before which I lay, and the terrible judgment which I feared. May it never, hereafter, be my lot to fall under such an inquisition! I profess that my shoulders were black and blue, that I felt the bruises long after I awoke from my sleep, and that thenceforth I read the books of God with a zeal greater than I had previously given to the books of men. (XXII)

According to a letter of 376 or 377, written to a local priest, Marcus, Jerome did not find the peace he was seeking in the desert. There were quarrels with other monks who suspected him of heresy. In any event he had decided to stop "rolling in sack-cloth and ashes."

> Every day I am asked for my confession of faith, as though when I was regenerated in baptism I had made none. I accept their formulas, but they are still dissatisfied. I sign my name to them, but they still refuse to believe me. One thing only will content them, that I should leave the country. I am on the point of departure. (XVII)

Foremost among the issues which so exercised the monks was whether God should be spoken of as having one hypostasis or three. Jerome, who would become a leading expert in exegesis, the interpretation of scripture, was not an original thinker when it came to complex theological matters. Submitting to authority, he wrote a letter (XV) to Pope Damasus asking him to decide the question and "to authorize me by letter to use or to refuse this formula of three hypostases."

Leaving behind the monks and their intellectual disputes, Jerome returned to Antioch, where he was ordained as a priest, although he never actually practiced as one. Wherever he went he could not escape the unseemly wranglings among clergymen. En route to Rome in 381, he spent time in Constantinople, where quarrels over the Arian doctrine were still raging. There he met and was much impressed by the orthodox bishop of brief tenure, Gregory of Nazianzus, whose letters are discussed in Chapter VIII along with those of Basil's brother, Gregory of Nyssa, whom Jerome also met in Constantinople.

Finally, it was in Rome from 382 to 385 that Jerome earned a reputation as a confidant of devout women among whom he set up study groups. His advice to these women was to give up searching for fulfillment in family life or even in the world at all. Since he eagerly promoted a life of spiritual detachment, much credit has been given to him for the idea of the convent. His influence on the wealthy noblewoman Paula and her daughters Blaesilla and Julia Eustochium has already been mentioned.

At the same time, he began his career as a scholar in earnest and, at the request of Pope Damasus, produced a revised text of the Gospels. Before the days of standardized printing, when all copies of books were hand written by scribes or slaves, individual copies contained numerous errors. Jerome's work was a remedy. There were, however, those who criticized his new translations, and the following letter shows how quick he was to be offended by these "contemptible creatures." It was written in 384 to Marcella, a wealthy widow. She was the first woman of high status in Rome to adopt a life of self-denial and was winning converts even before Jerome began his own local recruiting.

> After I had written my former letter, containing a few remarks on some Hebrew words, a report suddenly reached me that certain contemptible creatures were deliberately assailing me with the charge that I had endeavored to correct passages in the gospels, against the authority of the ancients and the opinion of the whole world. Now, though I might—as far as strict right goes—treat these persons with contempt (it is idle to play the lyre for an ass), yet lest they should follow their usual habit and reproach me with superciliousness, let them take an answer as follows: I am not so dull-witted nor so coarsely ignorant (qualities which they take for holiness, calling themselves the disciples of fishermen as if men were made holy by knowing nothing)—I am not, I repeat, so ignorant as to suppose that any of the

> Lord's words is either in need of correction or is not divinely inspired; but the Latin manuscripts of the Scriptures are proved to be faulty by the variations which all of them exhibit, and my object has been to restore them to the form of the Greek original, from which my detractors do not deny that they have been translated. If they dislike water drawn from the clear spring, let them drink of the muddy streamlet, and when they come to read the Scriptures let them lay aside the keen eye which they turn on woods frequented by game-birds and waters abounding in shellfish. Easily satisfied in this distance alone, let them, if they will, regard the words of Christ as rude sayings, albeit that over these so many great intellects have labored for so many ages rather to divine than to expand the meaning of each single word. Let them charge the great apostle with want of literary skill, although it is said of him that much learning made him mad.
>
> I know that as you read these words you will knit your brows, and fear that my freedom of speech is sowing the seeds of fresh quarrels; and that, if you could, you would gladly put your finger on my mouth to prevent me from even speaking of things which others do not blush to do. But, I ask you, wherein have I used too great license? Have I ever embellished my dinner plates with engravings of idols? Have I ever, at a Christian banquet, set before the eyes of virgins the polluting spectacle of Satyrs embracing bacchanals? Or, have I ever assailed any one in too bitter terms? Have I ever complained of beggars turned millionaires? Have I ever censured heirs for the funerals which they have given to their benefactors? The one thing that I have unfortunately said has been that virgins ought to live more in the company of women than of men, and by this I have made the whole city look scandalized and caused everyone to point at me the finger of scorn. (XXVII)

If there was anything human Jerome did not give up in his search for holiness, it was his bad temper. He frequently used name-calling and sarcasm to express his great anger, and a certain Helvidius was considered to be particularly hateful. This young monk declared the excessive attention given to the Virgin Mary to be a form of idolatry. To Jerome, Mary's virginity was the ideal to which young women should aspire. Helvidius favored marriage.

Some years later, when Jerome was working in his cell in Bethlehem, a former monk named Jovinian took it upon himself to write a tract denouncing the theory and practice of monasticism. He also joined Helvidius in contesting Jerome's view on marriage. Only fragments of his writings remain, but he had written much that made Jerome very unhappy. As it will happen, and especially as it happened with Jerome, strong feelings led to strong words that got him into trouble. He wrote two treatises against Jovinian, in which his language about marriage seemed to make it almost accountable as a sin. His friends in Rome recognized his excessive defense of virginity as being the root of the problem, but nevertheless, in the interest of the church, sought to suppress his attacks on Jovinian.

Caution therefore is necessary when reading Jerome's letters, for his vituperative language in certain passages prompts him to contradict what he says, with less heat, elsewhere. Here are selections from a letter written in 393 or 394 to Pammachius, one of those friends in Rome who had judged his two treatises to be immoderate. Jerome, still harsh on Jovinian, backtracks considerably on the subject of marriage and says he is even more generous than St. Paul.

Certain persons find fault with me because in the books which I have written against Jovinian I have been excessive (so they say) in praise of virginity and in depreciation of marriage; and they affirm that to preach up chastity till no comparision is left between a wife and a virgin is equivalent to a condemnation of matrimony. If I remember aright the point of the dispute, the question at issue between myself and Jovinian is that he puts marriage on a level with virginity, while I make it inferior; he declares that there is little or no difference between the two states, I assert that there is a great deal. Finally—a result due under God to your agency—he has been condemned because he has dared to set matrimony on an equality with perpetual chastity. Or, if a virgin and a wife are to be looked on as the same, how comes it that Rome has refused to listen to this impious doctrine? A virgin owes her being to a man, but a man does not owe his to a virgin. There can be no middle course. Either my view of the matter must be embraced, or else that of Jovinian. If I am blamed for putting wedlock below virginity, he must be praised for putting the two states on a level. If, on the other hand, he is condemned for supposing them equal, his condemnation must be taken as testimony in favor of my treatise. If men of the world chafe under the notion that they occupy a position inferior to that of virgins, I wonder that clergymen and monks—who both live celibate lives—refrain from praising what they consistently practise. They cut themselves off from their wives to imitate the chastity of virgins, and yet they will have it that married women are as good as these. They should either be joined again to their wives whom they have renounced, or, if they persist in living apart from them, they will have to confess—by their lives if not by their words—that, in preferring virginity to marriage, they have chosen the better course. . . .The Church, I say, does not condemn wedlock, but subordinates it. Whether you like it or not, marriage is subordinated to virginity and widowhood. Even when marriage continues to fulfil its function, the Church does not condemn it, but only subordinates it; it does not reject it, but only regulates it. It is in your power, if you will, to mount the second step of chastity. Why are you angry if, standing on the third and lowest step, you will not make haste to go up higher?

> Since, then, I have so often reminded my reader of my views; and since I have picked my way like a prudent traveller over every inch of the road, stating repeatedly that, while I receive marriage as a thing in itself admissible, I yet prefer continence, widowhood, and virginity, the wise and generous reader ought to have judged what seemed hard sayings by my general drift, and not to have charged me with putting forward inconsistent opinions in one and the same book. For who is so dull or so inexperienced in writing as to praise and to condemn one and the same object, as to destroy what he has built up, and to build up what he has destroyed; and when he has vanquished his opponent, to turn his sword, last of all, against himself? Were my detractors country bred or unacquainted with the arts of rhetoric or of logic, I should pardon their want of insight; nor should I censure them for accusing me if I saw that their ignorance was in fault and not their will. As it is, men of intellect who have enjoyed a liberal education make it their object less to understand me than to wound me, and for such I have this short answer, that they should correct my faults and not merely censure me for them. (XLVIII)

In another letter (XLIX), also to Pammachius, Jerome sees the need to suppress his treatise against Jovinian and proceeds to blame his detractors for the same excessiveness of language which, ironically, is part of his own problem.

Finally, in a third letter Jerome is unequivocal about marriage. Speaking of Jovinian—"an unlettered man of letters if ever there was one"—he writes: "In spite of all the lands and seas and peoples which lie between us, he must hear at least the echo of my cry, I do not condemn marriage, I do not condemn wedlock. Indeed—and this I say to make my meaning quite clear to him—I should like everyone to take a wife who, because they get frightened in the night, cannot manage to sleep alone" (L).

Jerome's chronic indigestion was not helped when another dissident, Vigilantius, began to denounce the fuss made over the bones of saints. Jerome, who defended the veneration of relics, had bitter words for what he considered pure perversity. But some of his problems were of a different sort. During the period 382 to 385 in Rome, a public outcry against him resulted from rumors about his prayer groups for women. He had to deny he was making any money. Animosity was also fueled by his perceived ambition to take over the papal chair recently left vacant—11 December 384—by the death of his friend Damasus, whose secretary he had been.

Certainly his popularity was not advanced by outspoken criticism of Roman society. Passages from the famous letter to Julia Eustochium (XXII), written with his usual pungent style, describe the peculiar activities of certain of his contemporaries who exhibited "plain signs of the devil." As in Cicero's day, letters continued to be copied and exchanged. This particular letter was no doubt widely circulated. J. N. D. Kelly in his *Jerome, His Life, Writings and Controversies* says that such a letter was likely, in part, written for the purpose of "exposing the rottenness which, as he saw it, was infecting great numbers of would-be Christians in Rome, including many clergy and professed ascetics."[3]

> Some women, it is true, disfigure their faces, that they may appear unto men to fast. As soon as they catch sight of any one they groan, they look down; they cover up their faces, all but one eye, which they keep free to see with. Their dress is sombre, their girdles are of sackcloth, their hands and feet are dirty; only their stomachs—which cannot be seen—are hot with food. Of these the psalm is sung daily: "The Lord will scatter the bones of them that please themselves." Others change their garb and assume the mien of men, being ashamed of being what they were born to be—women. They cut off their hair and are not ashamed to look like eunuchs. Some clothe themselves in goat's hair, and, putting on hoods, think to become children again by making themselves look like so many owls.
>
> But I will not speak only of women. Avoid men, also, when you see them loaded with chains and wearing their hair long like women, contrary to the apostle's precept, not to speak of beards like those of goats, black cloaks, and bare feet braving the cold. All these things are tokens of the devil. Such an one Rome groaned over some time back in Antimus; and Sopronius is a still more recent instance. Such persons, when they have once gained admission to the houses of the high-born, and have deceived "silly women laden with sins, ever learning and never able to come to the knowledge of the truth," feign a sad mien and pretend to make long fasts while at night they feast in secret. Shame forbids me to say more, for my language might appear more like invective than admonition. There are others—I speak of those of my own order—who seek the presbyterate and the diaconate simply that they may be able to see women with less restraint. Such men think of nothing but their dress; they use perfumes freely, and see that there are no creases in their leather shoes. Their curling hair shows traces of the tongs; their fingers glisten with rings; they walk on tiptoe across a damp road, not to splash their feet. When you see men acting in this way, think of them rather as bridegrooms than as clergymen. Certain persons have devoted the whole of their energies and life to the single object of knowing the names, houses, and characters of married ladies. I will here briefly describe the head of the profession, that from the master's likeness you may recognize the disciples. He rises and goes forth with the sun; he has the order of his visits duly arranged; he takes the shortest road; and, troublesome old man that he is, forces his way almost into the bedchambers of ladies yet asleep. If he sees a pillow that takes his fancy or an elegant table-cover—or indeed any article of household furniture—he praises it, looks admiringly at it, takes it into his hand, and complaining that he has nothing

> of the kind, begs or rather extorts it from the owner. All the women, in fact, fear to cross the news-carrier of the town. Chastity and fasting are alike distasteful to him. What he likes is a savory breakfast—say off a plump young crane such as is commonly called a cheeper. In speech he is rude and forward and is always ready to bandy reproaches. Wherever you turn he is the first man that you see before you. Whatever news is noised abroad he is either the originator of the rumor or its magnifier. He changes his horses every hour; and they are so sleek and spirited that you would take him for a brother of the Thracian king. (XXII)

The subject of marriage was a favorite with Jerome, and in the same letter he was concerned about more than a loss of virginity. He mentions "the drawbacks of marriage, such as pregnancy, the crying of infants, the torture caused by a rival, the cares of household management, and all those fancied blessings which death at last cuts short" (XXII). In another passage, he has a warning for spiritually minded young girls against spending time even with married women. Widows were to be avoided altogether, for they were likely spending less time grieving for a lost husband than looking for a new one. But Jerome's description of the ostentatious vices of Roman society may have been overstated, given his propensity to scold.

> Do not court the company of married ladies or visit the houses of the high-born. Do not look too often on the life which you despised to become a virgin. Women of the world, you know, plume themselves because their husbands are on the bench or in other high positions. And the wife of the emperor always has an eager throng of visitors at her door. Why do you, then, wrong your husband? Why do you, God's bride, hasten to visit the wife of a mere man? Learn in this respect a holy pride; know that you are better than they. And not only must you avoid intercourse with those who are puffed up by their husbands' honors, who are hedged in with troops of eunuchs, and who wear robes inwrought with threads of gold. You must also shun those who are widows from necessity and not from choice. Not that they ought to have desired the death of their husbands; but that they have not welcomed the opportunity of continence when it has come. As it is, they only change their garb; their old self-seeking remains unchanged. To see them in their capacious litters, with red cloaks and plump bodies, a row of eunuchs walking in front of them, you would fancy them not to have lost husbands but to be seeking them. Their houses are filled with flatterers and with guests. The very clergy, who ought to inspire them with respect by their teaching and authority, kiss these ladies on the forehead, and putting forth their hands (so that, if you knew no better, you might suppose them in the act of blessing), take wages for their visits. (XXII)

Jerome's comments on society add another dimension to the story of Rome during the years when Symmachus and Ambrose were quarreling over the Altar of Victory (see Chapter X). Augustine, too, was in Rome at the time, but there is no evidence that he and Jerome met, and their correspondence does not begin until some years later.

Jerome was under something of a cloud when he left Rome in 385 to set out on his last long journey, this time to the Holy Land, where, after a brief visit to Egypt, he settled down for the rest of his life. Bethlehem was chosen as the site for his new monastery. His friend Paula established a convent nearby.

The spiritual companionship of Jerome and the devout Paula gave rise to some earthbound speculation. In the following letter, Jerome defends the relationship by insisting that their fondness for each other is based solely on a mutual love of a spiritual life. They remained dear friends until her death in Jerusalem in 404. This letter, written in August 385, just before Jerome boarded a ship in Ostia, was addressed to a sister of the Marcella mentioned earlier. Asella, who could outmatch Jerome in her self-denial, lived in her room like those monks in their desert cells, but may have heard some of the rumors about Jerome which he says were circulating in Rome.

> Before I became acquainted with the family of the saintly Paula, all Rome resounded with my praises. Almost every one concurred in judging me worthy of the episcopate. Damasus, of blessed memory, spoke no words but mine. Men called me holy, humble, eloquent.
>
> Did I ever cross the threshold of a light woman? Was I ever fascinated by silk dresses, or glowing gems, or rouged faces, or display of gold? Of all the ladies in Rome but one had power to subdue me, and that one was Paula. She mourned and fasted, she was squalid with dirt, her eyes were dim from weeping. For whole nights she would pray to the Lord for mercy, and often the rising sun found her still at her prayers. The psalms were her only songs, the Gospel her whole speech, continence her one indulgence, fasting the staple of her life. The only woman who took my fancy was one whom I had not so much as seen at table. But when I began to revere, respect, and venerate her as her conspicuous chastity deserved, all my former virtues forsook me on the spot.
>
> Oh! envy, that dost begin by tearing thyself! Oh! cunning malignity of Satan, that dost always persecute things holy! Of all the ladies in Rome, the only ones that caused scandal were Paula and Melanium, who, despising their wealth and deserting their children, uplifted the cross of the Lord as a standard of religion. Had they frequented the baths, or chosen to use perfumes, or taken advantage of their wealth and position as widows to enjoy life and to be independent, they would have been saluted as ladies of high rank and saintliness. As it is, of course, it is in order to appear beautiful that they put on sackcloth and ashes, and they endure fasting and filth merely to go down into the Gehenna of fire! As if they could not perish

with the crowd whom the mob applauds! If it were Gentiles or Jews who thus assailed their mode of life, they would at least have the consolation of failing to please only those whom Christ Himself has failed to please. But, shameful to say, it is Christians who thus neglect the care of their own households, and disregarding the beams in their own eyes, look for motes in those of their neighbors. They pull to pieces every profession of religion, and think that they have found a remedy for their own doom, if they can disprove the holiness of others, if they can detract from every one, if they can show that those who perish are many, and sinners, a great multitude. . . .

I write this in haste, dear Lady Asella, as I go on board, overwhelmed with grief and tears; yet I thank my God that I am counted worthy of the world's hatred. . . . Men call me a mischief-maker, and I take the title as a recognition of my faith. For I am but a servant, and the Jews still call my master a magician. The Apostle [St. Paul] likewise, is spoken of as a deceiver. There hath no temptation taken me but such as is common to man. How few distresses have I endured, I who am yet a soldier of the cross! Men have laid to my charge a crime of which I am not guilty; but I know that I must enter the kingdom of heaven through evil report as well as through good.

Salute Paula and Eustochium, who, whatever the world may think, are always mine in Christ. Salute Albina, your mother, and Marcella, your sister; Marcellina also, and the holy Felicitas; and say to them all: "We must all stand before the judgment seat of Christ, and there shall be revealed the principle by which each has lived."

And now, illustrious model of chastity and virginity, remember me, I beseech you, in your prayers, and by your intercessions calm the waves of the sea. (XLV)

Letters written by the Romans to console persons for the loss of a relative or dear friend were longer than would be customary today, but Jerome's letter to Paula's daughter Eustochium, after her mother died, must be a candidate for one of the longest ever written. Two short passages here will suffice to represent the whole of it.

Making up her mind to dwell permanently in holy Bethlehem, she took up her abode for three years in a miserable hostelry; till she could build the requisite cells and monastic buildings, to say nothing of a guest house for passing travellers where they might find the welcome which Mary and Joseph had missed. . . . I call God to witness that I am no flatterer. I add nothing I exaggerate nothing. On the contrary, I tone down much that I may not appear to relate incredibilities. My carping critics must not insinuate that I am drawing on my imagination or decking Paula, like Aesop's crow, with the fine feathers of other birds. Humility is the first of Christian

> graces, and hers was so pronounced that one who had never seen her, and who on account of her celebrity had desired to see her, would have believed that he saw not her but the lowest of her maids. When she was surrounded by companies of virgins she was always the least remarkable in dress, in speech, in gesture, and in gait. From the time that her husband died until she fell asleep herself she never sat at meat with a man, even though she might know him to stand upon the pinnacle of the episcopate. She never entered a bath except when dangerously ill. Even in the severest fever she rested not on an ordinary bed but on the hard ground covered only with a mat of goat's hair; if that can be called rest which made day and night alike a time of almost unbroken prayer. Well did she fulfill the words of the psalter: "All the night make I my bed to swim; I water my couch with my tears!" (CVIII)

Paula, once a wealthy widow, had spent all her money. Jerome writes:

> Jesus is witness that Paula has left not a single penny to her daughter but, as I said before, on the contrary a large mass of debt; and, worse even than this, a crowd of brothers and sisters whom it is hard for her to support but whom it would be undutiful to cast off. Could there be a more splendid instance of self-renunciation than that of this noble lady who in the fervour of her faith gave away so much of her wealth that she reduced herself to the last degree of poverty? (CVIII)

Jerome's love of the devoted women who shared his ideals is unquestioned, but his overkill in bitter attacks on others made him many enemies and even upset his friends. Being a crusader, he remained unmoved. His mission was to defend the church amid controversies that seized people's emotions with far greater intensity at the time than is usual in western societies today. From his monastery in Bethlehem he exchanged letters with churchmen in which he rails against heretics, nonbelievers, and even loyal Christians who disagreed with him about anything. Only those who defended strict orthodoxy the way he did were praised.

The animosity Jerome incurred convinced him that he was fighting a good fight. The brilliance of his scholarship during the years in Bethlehem also sustained him. In the major work of his life, for which he is best known, he used both Hebrew and Greek in his translations of the scriptures into the Latin Bible, the Vulgate, a treasure of the Roman Catholic Church.

A letter to Pope Theophilus in 405 is somewhat more personal and lacking in the usual extended preachments. Jerome mentions the hardships he endured while pursuing his scholarly work. There is also an instructive paragraph about the increasing sanctity of "holy things," in keeping with Jerome's promotion of relics destined for such importance in the medieval church.

> My delay in sending back to your holiness your treatise translated into Latin is accounted for by the many interruptions and obstacles that I have met with. There has been a sudden raid of the Isaurians; Phoenicia and Galilee have been laid waste; Palestine has been panic-stricken, and particularly Jerusalem; we have all been engaged in making not books but walls. There has also been a severe winter and an almost unbearable famine; and these have told heavily upon me who have the charge of many brothers. Amid these difficulties the work of translation went on by night, as I could save or snatch time to give to it. . . .
>
> I admire in your work its practical aim, designed as it is to instruct by the authority of scripture ignorant persons in all the churches concerning the reverence with which they must handle holy things and minister at Christ's altar; and to impress upon them that the sacred chalices, veils, and other accessories used in the celebration of the Lord's passion are not mere lifeless and senseless objects devoid of holiness, but that rather, from their association with the body and blood of the Lord, they are to be venerated with the same awe as the body and the blood themselves. (CXIV)

The amount of work Jerome did under the circumstances is truly amazing. If Cyprian's master was Tertullian, Jerome's was Origen (ca A.D. 185 to ca. 254), seventy of whose works he translated into Latin. Origen was Jerome's major predecessor in studying the translations of the Hebrew scriptures and a controversial figure, particularly for his allegorical interpretations and novel theological suggestions. Jerome did not agree with all the directions of Origen's thought, but he took on the few "rabid hounds" who sought unjustly to sully that illustrious scholar's reputation (XXXIII).

Jerome's protection of his own reputation was evident in a correspondence with Augustine, which began in 394 or 395. Beneath his sincere, if cranky, piety, there lurked a devilishly dry wit. The barbs in a delightful exchange of letters are like so many fishhooks in a basket of flowers. The letters to follow take these two remarkable men out of their saintly niches and place them alongside modern scholars whose polite, if tense, exchanges appear in scholarly journals. A letter Jerome wrote to Augustine in 404 exhibits the testiness with which he puts down a possible rival.

> You are sending me letter upon letter, and often urging me to answer a certain letter of yours, a copy of which, without your signature, had reached me through our brother Sysinnius, deacon, as I have already written, which letter you tell me that you entrusted first to our brother Profuturus, and afterwards to someone else; but that Profuturus was prevented from finishing his intended journey, and having been ordained a bishop, was removed by sudden death; and the second messenger, whose name you do not give, was afraid of the perils of the sea, and gave up the voyage which he had

intended. These things being so, I am at a loss to express my surprise that the same letter is reported to be in the possession of most of the Christians in Rome, and throughout Italy, and has come to every one but myself, to whom alone it was ostensibly sent. I wonder at this all the more, because the brother Sysinnius aforesaid tells me that he found it among the rest of your published works, not in Africa, not in your possession, but in an island of the Adriatic some five years ago.

True friendship can harbour no suspicion; a friend must speak to his friend as freely as to his second self. Some of my acquaintances, vessels of Christ, of whom there is a very large number in Jerusalem and in the holy places, suggested to me that this had not been done by you in a guileless spirit, but through desire for praise and celebrity, and *eclat* in the eyes of the people, intending to become famous at my expense; that many might know that you challenged me, and I feared to meet you; that you had written as a man of learning, and I had by silence confessed my ignorance, and had at last found one who knew how to stop my garrulous tongue. I, however, let me say it frankly, refused at first to answer your Excellency, because I did not believe that the letter, or as I may call it (using a proverbial expression), the honeyed sword, was sent from you. Moreover, I was cautious lest I should seem to answer uncourteously a bishop of my own communion, and to censure anything in the letter of one who censured me, especially as I judged some of its statements to be tainted with heresy. . . .

Wherefore, as I have already written, either send me the identical letter in question subscribed with your own hand, or desist from annoying an old man, who seeks retirement in his monastic cell. If you wish to exercise or display your learning, choose as your antagonists, young, eloquent, and illustrious men, of whom it is said that many are found in Rome, who may be neither unable nor afraid to meet you, and to enter the lists with a bishop in debates concerning the Sacred Scriptures. As for me, a soldier once, but a retired veteran now, it becomes me rather to applaud the victories won by you and others, than with my worn-out body to take part in the conflict; beware lest, if you persist in demanding a reply, I call to mind the history of the way in which Quintus Maximus by his patience defeated Hannibal, who was, in the pride of youth, confident of success. . . .

As to your calling God to witness that you had not written a book against me, and of course had not sent to Rome what you had never written, adding that, if perchance some things were found in your works in which a different opinion from mine was advanced, no wrong had thereby been done to me, because you had, without any intention of offending me, written only what you believed to be right; I beg you to hear me with patience. You never wrote a book against me: how then has there been brought to me a copy, written by another hand, of a treatise containing a rebuke administered to me by you? How comes Italy to possess a treatise of yours which you did not write? Nay, how can you reasonably ask me to reply to that which you solemnly assure me was never written by you? Nor am I so foolish as to think that I am insulted by you, if in anything your opinion differs from mine. . . . For it does not become me, who have spent my life from youth until now, sharing the arduous labours of pious brethren in an obscure monastery, to presume to write anything against a bishop of my own communion, especially against one whom I had begun to love before I knew him, who also sought my friendship before I sought his, and whom I rejoiced to see rising as a successor to myself in the careful study of the Scriptures. Wherefore either disown that book, if you are not its author, and give over urging me to reply to that which you never wrote; or if the book is yours, admit it frankly; so that if I write anything in self-defence, the responsibility may lie on you who gave, not on me who am forced to accept, the challenge. . . . I tell you again, without reserve, what I feel: you are challenging an old man, disturbing the peace of one who asks only to be allowed to be silent, and you seem to desire to display your learning. It is not for one of my years to give the impression of enviously disparaging one whom I ought rather to encourage by approbation. And if the ingenuity of perverse men finds something which they may plausibly censure to the writings even of evangelists and prophets, are you amazed if, in your books, especially in your exposition of passages in Scripture which are exceedingly difficult of interpretation, some things be found which are not perfectly correct? This I say, however, not because I can at this time pronounce anything in your works to merit censure. For, in the first place, I have never read them with attention; and in the second place, we have not beside us a supply of copies of what you have written, excepting the books of Soliloquies and Commentaries on some of the Psalms; which, if I were disposed to criticise them, I could prove to be at variance, I shall not say with my own opinion, for I am nobody, but with the interpretation of the older Greek commentators.

Farewell, my very dear friend, my son in years, my father in ecclesiastical dignity; and to this I most particularly request your attention, that henceforth you make sure that I be the first to receive whatever you may write to me. (LXXII)[4]

Augustine's reply in the same year was also not lacking in subtlety, as the following passage shows.

I answer . . . the letter which you have deigned to send me by our holy son Asterius, in which I have found many proofs of your most kind goodwill to me, and at the same time some signs of your having in some

> measure felt aggrieved by me. In reading it, therefore, I was no sooner soothed by one sentence than I was buffeted in another; my wonder being especially called forth by this, that after alleging, as your reason for not rashly accepting as authentic the letter from me of which you had a copy, the fact that, offended by your reply, I might justly remonstrate with you, because you ought first to have ascertained that it was mine before answering it, you go on to command me to acknowledge the letter frankly if it is mine, or send me a more reliable copy of it, in order that we may, without any bitterness of feeling, address ourselves to the discussion of scriptural doctrine. For how can we engage in such discussion without bitterness of feeling, if you have made up your mind to offend me? Or, if your mind is not made up to this, what reason could I have had, when you did not offend me, for justly complaining as having been offended by you, that you ought first to have made sure that the letter was mine, and only then to have replied, that is to say, only then to have offended me? (LXXIII)

Only rarely do passages in Jerome's letters mention current events. But in another of his long letters of consolation, written in 396 to his friend Heliodorus, he reminds him of the current ills of the day from which a recently deceased nephew, Nepotian, has now escaped. The barbarians have breached the frontier in numerous places and driven deep into the empire. "The Roman world is falling," he says and then, not unexpectedly, with eagerness, insists that all such ills were punishment for the sins of men.

> I shudder when I think of the catastrophes of our time. For twenty years and more the blood of Romans has been shed daily between Constantinople and the Julian Alps. Scythia, Thrace, Macedonia, Dardania, Dacia, Thessaly, Achaia, Epirus, Dalmatia, the Pannonias—each and all of these have been sacked and pillaged and plundered by Goths and Sarmatians, Quades and Alans, Huns and Vandals and Marchmen. How many of God's matrons and virgins, virtuous and noble ladies, have been made the sport of these brutes! Bishops have been made captive, priests and those in minor orders have been put to death. Churches have been overthrown, horses have been stalled by the altars of Christ, the relics of martyrs have been dug up. . . . The Roman world is falling: yet we hold up our heads instead of bowing them. What courage, think you, have the Corinthians now, or the Athenians or the Lacedaemonians or the Arcadians, or any of the Greeks over whom the barbarians bear sway? I have mentioned only a few cities, but these once the capitals of no mean states. The east, it is true, seemed to be safe from all such evils: and if men were panic-stricken here, it was only because of bad news from other parts. But lo! in the year just gone by the wolves (no longer of Arabia but of the whole North) were let loose

> upon us from the remotest fastnesses of Caucasus and in a short time overran these great provinces. What a number of monasteries they captured! What many rivers they caused to run red with blood! They laid siege to Antioch and invested other cities on the Halys, the Cydnus, the Orontes, and the Euphrates. They carried off troops of captives. Arabia, Phoenicia, Palestine and Egypt, in their terror fancied themselves already enslaved . . . It is our sins which make the barbarians strong, it is our vices which vanquish Rome's soldiers: and, as if there were here too little material for carnage, civil wars have made almost greater havoc among us than the swords of foreign foes. . . .
>
> But I have gone beyond the office of a consoler, and while forbidding you to weep for one dead man I have myself mourned the dead of the whole world. Xerxes the mighty king who razed mountains and filled up seas, looking from high ground upon the untold host, the countless army before him, is said to have wept at the thought that in a hundred years not one of those whom he then saw would be alive. Oh! if we could but get up into a watch-tower so high that from it we might behold the whole earth spread out under our feet, then I would shew you the wreck of a world, nation warring against nation and kingdom in collision with kingdom; some men tortured, others put to the sword, others swallowed up by the waves, some dragged away into slavery; here a wedding, there a funeral; men born here, men dying there; some living in affluence, others begging their bread; and not the army of Xerxes, great as that was, but all the inhabitants of the world, alive now but destined soon to pass away. Language is inadequate to a theme so vast and all that I can say must fall short of the reality. (LX)

In 399, Jerome, writing to his friend Oceanus, reported his alarm at hearing that the Huns were advancing from the direction of the Caucasus toward Jerusalem. Not his own life, but the chastity of the virgins with him was the primary concern. Fortunately the Huns never arrived.

> News came that the hordes of the Huns had poured forth all the way from Maeotis [Sea of Azov] . . . and that, speeding hither and thither on their nimble-footed horses, they were filling all the world with panic and bloodshed. The Roman army was absent at the time, being detained in Italy on account of the civil wars. Of these Huns Herodotus tells us that under Darius King of the Medes they held the East in bondage for twenty years and that from the Egyptians and Ethiopians they exacted a yearly tribute. May Jesus avert from the Roman world the farther assaults of these wild beasts! Everywhere their approach was unexpected, they outstripped rumour in speed, and, when they came, they spared neither religion nor rank nor age,

> even for wailing infants they had no pity. Children were forced to die before it could be said that they had begun to live; and little ones not realizing their miserable fate might be seen smiling in the hands and at the weapons of their enemies. It was generally agreed that the goal of the invaders was Jerusalem and that it was their excessive desire for gold which made them hasten to this particular city. Its walls uncared for in time of peace were accordingly put in repair. Antioch was in a state of siege. Tyre, desirous of cutting itself off from the land, sought once more its ancient island. We too were compelled to man our ships and to lie off the shore as a precaution against the arrival of our foes. No matter how hard the winds might blow, we could not but dread the barbarians more than shipwreck. It was not, however, so much for our own safety that we were anxious as for the chastity of the virgins who were with us. (LXXVII)

In 412, Jerome offers a vivid picture of the Visigoths, under Alaric, taking Rome two years earlier. There follows a passage from a letter written to Principia, another woman who had taken up Bible study in Rome and who looked to Jerome for guidance. Most of the letter is a tribute to Marcella, who appears to have died during the famine that overwhelmed Rome at the same time.

> A dreadful rumour came from the west. Rome had been besieged [408] and its citizens had been forced to buy their lives with gold. Then thus despoiled they had been besieged again [410] so as to lose not their substance only but their lives. My voice sticks in my throat; and, as I dictate, sobs choke my utterance. The City which had taken the whole world was itself taken; [410] nay more famine was beforehand with the sword and but few citizens were left to be made captives. In their frenzy the starving people had recourse to hideous food; and tore each other limb from limb that they might have flesh to eat. Even the mother did not spare the babe at her breast. (CXXVII)

In Jerome's letters, such calamitous events took up little space amid voluminous passages giving advice. For example, writing to a young Gallic monk named Rusticus, he gladly described some of the fine points of the monastic life. The moderate tone of his letter written in A.D. 411 is many years away from the explicit self-torture described in the earlier account of his life in the desert. In fact, Jerome would spare this young man such an experience and advises him to live in a monastery with other monks.

> If for your part you desire to be a monk and not merely to seem one, be more careful of your soul than of your property; for in adopting a religious profession you have renounced this once for all. Let your garments be squalid to shew that your mind is white; and your tunic coarse to prove

that you despise the world. But give not way to pride lest your dress and language be found at variance. Baths stimulate the senses and must, therefore, be avoided; for to quench natural heat is the aim of chilling fasts. Yet even these must be moderate, for, if they are carried to excess, they weaken the stomach and by making more food necessary to it promote indigestion, that fruitful parent of unclean desires. A frugal and temperate diet is good for both body and soul.

See your mother as often as you please but not with other women, for their faces may dwell in your thoughts. . . .

The maidservants who attend upon her you must regard as so many snares laid to entrap you; for the lower their condition is the more easy it is for you to effect their ruin. John the Baptist had a religious mother and his father was a priest. Yet neither his mother's affection nor his father's wealth could induce him to live in his parent's house at the risk of his chastity. He lived in the desert, and seeking Christ with his eyes refused to look at anything else. His rough garb, his girdle made of skins, his diet of locusts and wild honey were all alike designed to encourage virtue and continence. The sons of the prophets, who were the monks of the Old Testament, built for themselves huts by the waters of Jordan and forsaking the crowded cities lived in these on pottage and wild herbs. As long as you are at home make your cell your paradise, gather there the varied fruits of scripture, let this be your favourite companion and take its precepts to your heart. . . .

The first point to be considered is whether you ought to live by yourself or in a monastery with others. For my part I should like you to have the society of holy men so as not to be thrown altogether on your own resources. For if you set upon a road that is new to you without a guide, you are sure to turn aside immediately either to the right or to the left, to lay yourself open to the assaults of error, to go too far or else not far enough, to weary yourself with running too fast or to loiter by the way and to fall asleep. In loneliness pride quickly creeps upon a man: if he has fasted for a little while and has seen no one, he fancies himself a person of some note; forgetting who he is, whence he comes, and whither he goes, he lets his thoughts riot within and outwardly indulges in rash speech. . . . Do I condemn a solitary life? By no means: in fact I have often commended it. But I wish to see the monastic schools turn out soldiers who have no fear of the rough training of the desert, who have exhibited the spectacle of a holy life for a considerable time, who have made themselves last that they might be first, who have not been overcome by hunger or satiety, whose joy is in poverty, who teach virtue by their garb and mien, and who are too conscientious to invent—as some silly men do—monstrous stories of struggles with demons, designed to magnify their heroes in the eyes of the crowd and before all to extort money from it.

> If I wish you then not to live with your mother, it is for the reasons given above, and above all for the two following. If she offers you delicacies to eat, you will grieve her by refusing them; and if you take them, you will add fuel to the flame that already burns within you. Again in a house where there are so many girls you will see in the daytime sights that will tempt you at night. Never take your hand or your eyes off your book; learn the psalms word for word, pray without ceasing, be always on the alert, and let no vain thoughts lay hold upon you. Direct both body and mind to the Lord, overcome wrath by patience, love the knowledge of scripture, and you will no longer love the sins of the flesh. Do not let your mind become a prey to excitement, for if this effects a lodgment in your breast it will have dominion over you and will lead you into the great transgression. Always have some work on hand, that the devil may find you busy.

Jerome also had strong opinions on how to raise a little girl who had been committed to a religious life. In Chapter VI, it was mentioned how the ancient Phoenicians of Carthage had offered up to Baal their children as human sacrifices. To see the dedication of a young girl to a life of virginity as a refined parallel is of course a wordly view quite out of context with the religiosity of Jerome's time. When this girl's father Gaudentius, writing from Rome, asked for advice, Jerome replied that Pacatula must continue to be isolated from the world and thus from all its temptations. This letter, written in 413, also shows how much the taking of Rome by the Visigoths had affected Jerome, for again he includes a passage on that event.

> Some mothers when they have vowed a daughter to virginity clothe her in sombre garments, wrap her up in a dark cloak, and let her have neither linen nor gold ornaments. They wisely refuse to accustom her to what she will afterwards have to lay aside. . . .
>
> A girl should associate only with girls, she should know nothing of boys and should dread even playing with them. She should never hear an unclean word, and if amid the bustle of the household she should chance to hear one, she should not understand it. Her mother's nod should be to her as much a command as a spoken injunction. She should love her as her parent, obey her as her mistress, and reverence her as her teacher. She is now a child without teeth and without ideas, but, as soon as she is seven years old, a blushing girl knowing what she ought not to say and hesitating as to what she ought, she should until she is grown up commit to memory the psalter and the books of Solomon; the gospels, the apostles and the prophets should be the treasure of her heart. She should not appear in public too freely or too frequently attend crowded churches. All her pleasure should be in her chamber. She must never look at young men or turn her eyes upon curled fops; and the wanton songs of sweet voiced girls which wound

> the soul through the ears must be kept from her. The more freedom of access such persons possess, the harder is it to avoid them when they come. . . . I am ashamed to say it and yet I must; high born ladies who have rejected more high born suitors cohabit with men of the lowest grade and even with slaves. Sometimes in the name of religion and under the cloak of a desire for celibacy they actually desert their husbands in favour of such paramours. You may often see a Helen following her Paris without the smallest dread of Menelaus. Such persons we see and mourn for but we cannot punish, for the multitude of sinners procures tolerance for the sin.
>
> The world sinks into ruin: yes! but shameful to say our sins still live and flourish. The renowned city, the capital of the Roman empire, is swallowed up in one tremendous fire; and there is no part of the earth where Romans are not in exile. Churches once held sacred are not but heaps of dust and ashes; and yet we have our minds set on the desire of gain. We live as though we are going to die tomorrow; yet we build as though we are going to live always in this world. Our walls shine with gold, our ceilings also and the capitals of our pillars; yet Christ dies before our doors naked and hungry in the persons of His poor. (CXXVIII)

The strictness of Jerome's own life undoubtedly sharpened the rebuke delivered to a lecherous deacon named Sabinianus who lived in Bethlehem. If Jerome has the story right, then surely on this occasion there was a good cause for his well-attested irritability.

The letter is of uncertain date.

> Have mercy I beseech you upon your soul. Consider that God's judgment will one day overtake you. Remember by what a bishop you were ordained. The holy man was mistaken in his choice; but this he might well be. For even God repented that he had anointed Saul to be king. Even among the twelve apostles Judas was found a traitor. And Nicolas of Antioch—a deacon like yourself—disseminated the Nicolaitan heresy[5] and all manner of uncleanness. I do not now bring up to you the many virgins whom you are said to have seduced, or the noble matrons who have suffered death[6] because violated by you, or the greedy profligacy with which you have hied through dens of sin. For grave and serious as such sins are in themselves, they are trivial indeed when compared with those which I have now to narrate. How great must be the sin beside which seduction and adultery are insignificant? Miserable wretch that you are! when you enter the cave wherein the Son of God was born, where truth sprang out of the earth and the land did yield her increase, it is to make an assignation. Have you no fear that the babe will cry from the manger, that the newly delivered virgin will see you, that the mother of the Lord will behold you? The angels cry aloud, the

Raphael (Raffaello Sanzio, 1483–1520), *St. Jerome Punishing the Heretic Sabinian.* The North Carolina Museum of Art, Raleigh. Gift of Mrs. Nancy Susan Reynolds, the Sarah Graham Kenan Foundation, Julius H. Weitzner, and Museum Purchase Fund. The scene is of a miracle. St. Jerome, appearing as a cardinal, which of course he never was, arrives in time to prevent the beheading of his supporter bishop Sylvan and prompting the head of the bishop's enemy Sabinian to fall off instead.

> shepherds run, the star shines down from heaven, the wise men worship, Herod is terrified, Jerusalem is in confusion, and meantime you creep into a virgin's cell to seduce the virgin to whom it belongs. I am filled with consternation and a shiver runs through me, soul and body, when I try to set before your eyes the deed that you have done. (CXLVII)

In 417, the devils Jerome had to contend with were heretics. For several years the writings of Pelagius, a British monk living in Rome, had advanced the idea that man by his own efforts could overcome sin and so achieve salvation. If that was true, what need was there for the redemption of Christ? Pelagius and his followers had not yet shifted out of the "man-centered" Graeco-Roman view into the medieval dependency on God (and the church). The intensity of the controversy led local Pelagians, perhaps led by Pelagius himself, to riot against the stern opposition of Jerome and his fellow monks and even to destroy their monastery. The bishop of Jerusalem, himself sympathetic to the Pelagian position, was censured in 417 by Pope Innocent for having failed to take a stronger stand against violence. According to Kelly, "Innocent was quick to exploit the welcome opportunity for asserting the papal supremacy in the east" (p. 322). Innocent's letter ended with this sentence: "If nothing is done, the law of the Church on the subject of injuries may compel the person who has failed to defend his flock to shew cause for his negligence" (CXXXVII). It appears, however, that the offending John died before that warning reached him.

In a letter to Riparius, a priest in Gaul, who had reported Vigilantius's teachings against relics, Jerome calls his new enemy, Pelagius, a "Catiline"—the ringleader of the conspiracy during Cicero's consulship in 63 B.C. and so a threat to the state. Pelagius was now, in A.D. 417, no less a danger to the church.

In the following year, a convocation of bishops meeting in Carthage denounced and outlawed Pelagianism. Augustine, the bishop of Hippo, was largely responsible for bringing this about. Jerome's former peevishness toward him gave way to high praise.

The fight with Pelagius was Jerome's last battle. His health, never vigorous, finally failed him and he died in 419 or 420. There is no doubt he was buried in Bethlehem. His tomb is where he wanted it to be, which is near the very spot where he believed Jesus was born. Augustine, whose letters are the subject of the next chapter, survived Jerome by about ten years.

XII
AUGUSTINE

A Giant of Mind and Faith

IN the ancient world, western man was inspired by the Greek experience to think about who he was and what he could do for himself. In the Middle Ages, the questions became who God was, and what could be done for Him. In the earlier time, Diogenes, lantern in hand, looking for an honest man, sought tranquillity on his own. Later, St. Francis, serving his fellowman, sought to please the Almighty. The voice that most strongly influenced that shift in thinking belonged to St. Augustine, a prolific writer, who unreservedly established the dependency of lowly man on his omnipotent Maker. He had a crucial impact on the future of Christian theology, including Calvinism, and on the political ascendancy of the Roman papacy in the Middle Ages.

Ironically, if anybody obscures the view of Augustine's pivotal role in history, it is Augustine himself. His most popular book, the *Confessions*, is an account of his troubled days as a youth culminating in a famous garden scene where a passage from St. Paul (Rom. 13.13, 14) led to his baptism as a Christian.

This spiritual autobiography, personal and dramatic, has always won more attention than Augustine's major work, *The City of God*. It was the latter, written over a period of fifteen years, which established the idea of a holy city, the church, through which Christ ruled over the earthly city, the Roman Empire. That lengthy thesis foreshadowed the church supreme in later centuries when popes wielded enormous power over a submissive Europe. In his own time, Augustine voiced his authoritarian views in a bitter struggle with Christians who strayed from the orthodoxy of the Roman church. He had once been bothered by doubts himself and was then tolerant of various opinions, but when he became an official in the church he found it necessary, as might be expected, to take a different stand. For their own good, others were not entitled to the freedom he had himself once enjoyed.

The Roman government, until A.D. 311, had persecuted the Christians so that unity within the empire could be maintained. Should the Christians now do the same to heretics so that the unity of the church could be maintained? At least one bishop is recorded as favoring the death sentence for dissidents. That was not true of Augustine, but in a letter written in 408 to Vincentius, for many years one of the companions of Jerome, he clearly thought force should be used and gave God's censure of the Hebrews as a precedent.

> We already rejoice in the correction of many who hold and defend the Catholic unity with such sincerity, and are so glad to have been delivered from their former error, that we admire them with great thankfulness and pleasure. Yet these same persons, under some indescribable bondage of custom, would in no way have thought of being changed to a better condition, had they not, under the shock of this alarm, directed their minds earnestly to the study of the truth; fearing lest, if without profit, and in vain, they suffered hard things at the hands of men, for the sake not of righteousness, but of their own obstinacy and presumption, they should afterwards receive nothing else at the hand of God than the punishment due to wicked men who despised the admonition which He so gently gave and His paternal correction; and being by such reflection made teachable, they found not in mischievous or frivolous human fables, but in the promises of the divine books, that universal Church which they saw extending according to the promise throughout all nations: just as, on the testimony of prophecy in the same Scriptures, they believed without hesitation that Christ is exalted above the heavens, though He is not seen by them in His glory. . . . Not every one who is indulgent is a friend; nor is every one an enemy who smites. Better are the wounds of a friend than the proffered kisses of an enemy. It is better with severity to love, than with gentleness to deceive. . . . Who can love us more than God does? And yet He not only gives us sweet instruction, but also quickens us by salutary fear, and this unceasingly. Often adding to the soothing remedies by which He comforts men the sharp medicine of tribulation, He afflicts with famine even the pious and devout [Hebrew] patriarchs, disquiets a rebellious people by more severe chastisements, and refuses, though thrice besought, to take away the thorn in the flesh of the apostle, that He may make His strength perfect in weakness. Let us by all means love even our enemies, for this is right, and God commands us so to do, in order that we may be the children of our Father who is in heaven, "who maketh His sun to rise on the evil and on the good, and sendeth rain on the just and on the unjust." But as we praise these His gifts, let us in like manner ponder His correction of those whom He loves.
>
> You are of opinion that no one should be compelled to follow righteousness; and yet you read that the householder said to his servants, "Whom-

> soever ye shall find, compel them to come in." You also read how he who was at first Saul, and afterwards Paul, was compelled, by the great violence with which Christ coerced him, to know and to embrace the truth; for you cannot but think that the light which your eyes enjoy is more precious to men than money or any other possession. This light, lost suddenly by him when he was cast to the ground by the heavenly voice, he did not recover until he became a member of the Holy Church. You are also of opinion that no coercion is to be used with any man in order to [prompt] his deliverance from the fatal consequences of error; and yet you see that, in examples which cannot be disputed, this is done by God, who loves us with more real regard for our profit than any other can; and you hear Christ saying, "No man can come to me except the Father draw him," which is done in the hearts of all those who, through fear of the wrath of God, betake themselves to Him. (XCIII)[1]

Those looking for a justification for the use of force in good causes can find it in that letter. On the other hand, there are letters that satisfy the quest for non-violence. For instance, a certain Publicola wrote to Augustine (letter XLVI) in 398, asking how to behave in a series of eighteen situations involving pagans. One of them was: "If a Christian is on the point of being killed by a barbarian or a Roman, ought he to kill the aggressor to save his own life?" Augustine's response included the following passage: "As to killing others in order to defend one's own life, I do not approve of this, unless one happen to be a soldier or public functionary acting, not for himself, but in defence of others or of the city in which he resides, if he act according to the commission lawfully given him, and in the manner becoming his office" (XLVII).

The great many books written by Augustine are almost forbidding in their breadth—a vast resource for scholarly careers and innumerable doctoral dissertations. It is the letters of this great theologian which bring him back on the human side. As already seen, there were contradictory views in his writings resulting from conflicting goals. Other letters show Augustine, like the rest of us, becoming upset, giving in to his emotions; in short, having his ups and downs. His younger days were the hardest.

Aurelius Augustinus was born on 13 November 354, at Thagaste, modern Souk Ahras in Algeria, in the Roman province of Numidia. He began his advanced studies in Carthage, the major city of the area, and being in his late teens, busied himself in search of excitement. Later he admitted to bragging about more exploits than actually occurred, but there is no doubt that he took a concubine by whom he had an illegitimate son, born in 372. As he grew older, there was much remorse about his earlier life. A sense of guilt was, in part, the reason he joined the Manichaeans, a cult noted for its moral strictness. The elite members took a vow of celibacy, but Augustine had not yet reached that point.

The founder of the religion, Mani, a Persian, had a special answer for the problem of evil. He said that there were two ruling principles: one good and one evil. Here was a solution to the bothersome question as to why one God Almighty could allow such horrors as Augustine saw in the sensible world. He remained a Manichaean for nine years, during which time he was teaching in Carthage. Eventually, however, he became disenchanted with the extremism of this system, and for a couple of years lapsed into skepticism. That was followed by his eventual attraction to Neoplatonism, for Plotinus's teachings introduced him to a different answer to his problem. Evil was nothing. It was simply the absence of God, of good. This belief in the perfect God never left him. Nor did the notion of a mystical union when his restless heart would find an eternal rest with the Almighty.

It was in Rome, where Augustine went to teach, that he met and impressed Symmachus (see Chapter X), who, in 385, recommended him for a teaching position in Milan. There he listened to the persuasive preaching of the bishop Ambrose. At the same time, his letters betray an inner turmoil. They show Augustine disgruntled and dissatisfied with the way things happen to be. Self-conscious about his own busy search for truth in 386, he deplored the indolence of others: "Such is the indisposition to strenuous exertion, and the indifference to the liberal arts, that so soon as it is noised abroad that, in the opinion of the most acute philosophers, truth is unattainable, men send their minds to sleep, and cover them up for ever" (I). Wisdom could not be acquired without hard work. With high-minded resolve he argued that the attainment of wisdom was the only true path to happiness (III). But what was happiness anyway? How could he be happy, he wondered, when there was so much he did not know. A letter written, in 387, to a friend of his youth, Nebridius, is typical of the way Augustine saw himself and his gradual spiritual development. The influence of Plato, with an emphasis on things eternal over those that are temporal, is obvious. So, too, is St. Paul's declaration of the survival of the things that are not seen over those that are.

> It is very wonderful how completely I was taken by surprise, when, on searching to discover which of your letters still remained unanswered, I found only one which held me as your debtor,—that, namely, in which you request me to tell you how far in this my leisure, which you suppose to be great, and which you desire to share with me, I am making progress in learning to discriminate those things in nature with which the senses are conversant, from those about which the understanding is employed. But I suppose it is not unknown to you, that if one becomes more and more fully imbued with false opinions, the more fully and intimately one exercises himself in them, the corresponding effect is still more easily produced in the mind by contact with truth. Nevertheless my progress, like our physical development, is so gradual, that it is difficult to define its steps distinctly, just as though there is a very great difference between a boy and a young man, no one, if daily questioned from his boyhood onward, could at any one date say that now he was no more a boy, but a young man.

I would not have you, however, so to apply this illustration as to suppose that, in the vigour of a more powerful understanding, I have arrived as it were at the beginning of the soul's manhood. For I am yet but a boy, though perhaps, as we say, a promising boy, rather than a good-for-nothing. For although the eyes of my mind are for the most part perturbed and oppressed by the distractions produced by blows inflicted through things sensible, they are revived and raised up again by that brief process of reasoning: "The mind and intelligence are superior to the eyes and the common faculty of sight; which could not be the case unless the things which we perceive by intelligence were more real than the things which we perceive by the faculty of sight." I pray you to help me in examining whether any valid objection can be brought against this reasoning. By it, meanwhile, I find myself restored and refreshed; and when, after calling upon God for help, I begin to rise to Him, and to those things which are in the highest sense real, I am at times satisfied with such a grasp and enjoyment of the things which eternally abide, that I sometimes wonder at my requiring any such reasoning as I have above given to persuade me of the reality of those things which in my soul are as truly present to me as I am to myself.

Please look over your letters yourself, for I own that you will be in this matter at greater pains than I, in order to make sure that I am not perchance unwittingly still owing an answer to any of them: for I can hardly believe that I have so soon got from under the burden of debts which I used to reckon as so numerous; albeit, at the same time, I cannot doubt that you have had some letters from me to which I have as yet received no reply. (IV)

To this troubled mind, Christianity eventually offered the most successful therapy of the age. The emotional episode in the garden, as told in his *Confessions*, led to his baptism by Ambrose at Easter in 387. When he wrote this story of his life to 388, he natually saw events as the unfoldment of a divine plan for his salvation. Augustine's mother, Monica, a devout Christian with whom he was very close, saw the baptism of her son as the fulfillment of her prayers. Unfortunately, she did not live to see him ordained a priest in 391 and then become a bishop in 395.

There are extant over 250 letters written either by Augustine or to him. Many tell of the daily life of the time and the burdens of a hard working bishop in Hippo in North Africa. Augustine, humbly and predictably, described himself as a servant of God (CLXXXVI). He also had an understandably human need to be appreciated, and he reminds the people of Hippo that he has devoted himself entirely to working for them (CXXII).

A letter written in 413 captures the spirit of his age. Augustine expressed his delight that the daughter of the distinguished family of Anicius was being consecrated to a life of virginity.

> Who can declare in words, or expound with adequate praises, how incomparably greater is the glory and advantage gained by your family in giving to Christ women consecrated to His service, than in giving to the world men called to the honours of the consulship? For if it be a great and noble thing to leave the mark of an honoured name upon the revolving ages of this world, how much greater and nobler is it to rise above it by unsullied chastity both of heart and of body! Let this maiden, therefore, illustrious in her pedigree, yet more illustrious in her piety, find greater joy in obtaining, through espousals to her divine Lord, a pre-eminent glory in heaven, than she could have had in becoming, through espousal to a human consort, the mother of a line of illustrious men. This daughter of the house of Anicius has acted the more magnanimous part, in choosing rather to bring a blessing on that noble family by forbearing from marriage, than to increase the number of its descendants, preferring to be already, in the purity of her body, like unto the angels, rather than to increase by the fruit of her body the number of mortals. For this is a richer and more fruitful condition of blessedness, not to have a pregnant womb, but to develop the soul's lofty capacities; not to have the breasts flowing with milk, but to have the heart pure as snow; to travail not with the earthly in the pangs of labour, but with the heavenly in persevering prayer. May it be yours, my daughters, most worthy of the honour due to your rank, to enjoy in her that which was lacking to yourselves; may she be steadfast to the end, abiding in the conjugal union that has no end. (CL)

Augustine was a Roman citizen with goals very different from those of his forefathers. There were many men who thought as he did or took an even more extreme position. In Syria in the first half of the fifth century, there lived a young man who would become the first and most famous of the pillar saints, Simeon Stylites (from *stylos*, pillar). According to tradition, he spent the last thirty years of his life, from 429 to 459, sitting on a platform sixty feet high. Pilgrims came to stare at him in awe. And what would Julius Caesar have thought of that? Or how would Cicero have rated this new hero seeking a greater prize than one for statesmanship?

Augustine, although never reclusive like Jerome, developed a similar admiration for those who were. In one of his letters, written in 423, he set forth an elaborate series of rules for women in a nunnery. For those unfamiliar with this aspect of the Christian experience, the letter describes the Spartan discipline of such a life. There is also a determination to break down class barriers. The members of the community are urged to spy on one another—a mischief common to all collectivistic arrangements where conformity is the rule and individualism discouraged. Obviously, at the time, focusing on high moral principles helped to mask the unfortunate side effects which the modern observer sees at work.

The rules which we lay down to be observed by you as persons settled in a monastery are these:—

First of all, in order to fulfil the end for which you have been gathered into one community, dwell in the house with oneness of spirit, and let your hearts and minds be one in God. Also call not anything the property of any one, but let all things be common property, and let distribution of food and raiment be made to each of you by the prioress,—not equally to all, because you are not all equally strong, but to every one according to her need. For you read in the Acts of the Apostles: "They had all things common: and distribution was made to every man according as he had need." Let those who had any worldly goods when they entered the monastery cheerfully desire that these become common property. Let those who had no worldly goods not ask within the monastery for luxuries which they could not have while they were outside of its walls; nevertheless, let the comforts which the infirmity of any of them may require be given to such, though their poverty before coming in to the monastery may have been such that they could not have procured for themselves the bare necessaries of life; and let them in such case be careful not to reckon it the chief happiness of their present lot that they have found within the monastery food and raiment, such as was elsewhere beyond their reach. . . .

Keep the flesh under by fastings and by abstinence from meat and drink, so far as health allows. When any one is not able to fast, let her not, unless she be ill, take any nourishment except at the customary hour of repast. From the time of your coming to table until you rise from it, listen without noise and wrangling to whatever may be in course read to you; let not your mouths alone be exercised in receiving food, let your ears be also occupied in receiving the word of God. . . . Though a passing glance be directed towards any man, let your eyes look fixedly at none; for when you are walking you are not forbidden to see men, but you must neither let your desires go out to them, nor wish to be the objects of desire on their part. For it is not only by touch that a woman awakens in any man or cherishes towards him such desire, this may be done by inward feelings and by looks. And say not that you have chaste minds though you may have wanton eyes, for a wanton eye is the index of a wanton heart. And when wanton hearts exchange signals with each other in looks, though the tongue is silent, and are, by the force of sensual passion, pleased by the reciprocation of inflamed desire, their purity of character is gone, though their bodies are not defiled by any act of uncleanness. Nor let her who fixes her eyes upon one of the other sex, and takes pleasure in his eye being fixed on her, imagine that the act is not observed by others; she is seen assuredly by those by whom she supposes herself not to be remarked. But even though she should elude notice, and be seen by no hu-

> man eye, what shall she do with that Witness above us from whom nothing can be concealed? . . .
>
> And if you perceive in any one of your number this forwardness of eye, warn her at once, so that the evil which has begun may not go on, but be checked immediately. But if, after this admonition, you see her repeat the offence, or do the same thing on any other subsequent day, whoever may have had the opportunity of seeing this must now report her as one who has been wounded and requires to be healed, but not without pointing her out to another, and perhaps a third sister, so that she may be convicted by the testimony of two or three witnesses, and may be reprimanded with necessary severity. And do not think that in thus informing upon one another you are guilty of malevolence. For the truth rather is, that you are not guiltless if by keeping silence you allow sisters to perish, whom you may correct by giving information of their faults. For if your sister had a wound on her person which she wished to conceal through fear of the surgeon's lance, would it not be cruel if you kept silence about it, and true compassion if you made it known? How much more, then, are you bound to make known her sin, that she may not suffer more fatally from a neglected spiritual wound. But before she is pointed out to others as witnesses by whom she may be convicted if she deny the charge, the offender ought to be brought before the prioress, if after admonition she has refused to be corrected, so that by her being in this way more privately rebuked, the fault which she has committed may not become known to all the others. If, however, she then deny the charge, then others must be employed to observe her conduct after the denial, so that now before the whole sisterhood she may not be accused by one witness, but convicted by two or three. When convicted of the fault, it is her duty to submit to the corrective discipline which may be appointed by the prioress or the prior. If she refuse to submit to this, and does not go away from you of her own accord, let her be expelled from your society. For this is not done cruelly but mercifully, to protect very many from perishing through infection of the plague with which one has been stricken. (CCXI)

Augustine shared with Jerome a penchant for giving women advice and deplored the use of makeup, even by those who were married, as a form of deception (CCXLV). He is more famous, of course, for the answers he gave to numerous questions on Christian doctrine, which he received from all parts of the empire. Some of his responses are actually essays on the order of those Seneca wrote.

Much of Augustine's time had to be given to administrative duties, including making unpopular decisions. For instance, in 405 he wrote a letter to a fellow bishop whose brother he had assigned to duties in a remote area. Priestly guidance was needed outside the cities, and this man was particularly valuable because he could preach in the native Punic tongue. But Augustine says we all have sacrifices to make:

> However strong be the bond of kindred between brothers, it does not surpass the bond by which my brother[2] Severus and I are united to each other, and yet you know how rarely I have the happiness of seeing him. And this has been caused neither by his wish nor by mine, but because of our giving to the claims of our mother the Church precedency above the claims of this present world, out of regard to that coming eternity in which we shall dwell together and part no more. (LXXXIV)

The letter was brought to a close with studied politeness in the following way: "For you will do me no small favor if you do not burden me with any further request upon this subject, lest I should have occasion to appear anything more than somewhat hard-hearted to you, whom I revere for your holy benignity of disposition."

Augustine's insistence that a priest must be able to use the language of the local people was part of his interest in his parishes. Another letter, written in 410 to Fortunatus, bishop of Cirta, tells how Augustine personally intervened to help a sharecropper against a harsh landowner. It is to be noted that the church offered sanctuary for political and social causes even as some religious groups still do: "Your Holiness is well acquainted with Faventius, a tenant on the estate of the Paratian forest. He, apprehending some injury or other at the hands of the owner of that estate, took refuge in the church at Hippo, and was there, as fugitives are wont to do, waiting till he could get the matter settled through my mediation" (CXV).

Augustine's writings, the work of forty years, are the major historical sources for the splinter movements which gave the Church so much worry. Especially troublesome were two heresies: Donatism and Pelagianism.

The Donatist heresy had originated in North Africa in the third century, and in Augustine's time its adherents were still numerous there. Briefly, Donatism was named after a bishop of Carthage whose followers considered themselves to be the upholders of the true Christian church because in puritanical fashion they declared that the sacraments given by immoral priests were invalid. Especially rejected were the acts of *traditores*, clergymen who in time of persecution had given up the Holy Scriptures to be burned. But whatever reasons the Donatists gave for exclusion, Augustine opposed them, for they made God's sacraments contingent on the behavior of mortal men, and evil ones at that. To Augustine, the priest was merely a vessel for divine grace. Here was the exaltation of God and demotion of man which greatly inspired Calvin. There was also a serious practical objection to Donatism. To make the validity of the sacraments rely on the private lives of clergymen would leave the faithful forever in doubt as to whether they had truly been baptized, married, or whatever.

Some of Augustine's letters on the Donatist question have a conciliatory tone.

Sandro Botticelli (ca. 1444–1510), the *St. Augustine* fresco in the Church of Ognissanti, Florence. Photograph courtesy of Alinari/Art Resource, New York, N.Y.

In a letter of 396 to Crispinus, the Donatist bishop of Calama, he invited him to debate in public the controversy involving about eighty people of Mappalia whom the Donatists had forcibly rebaptized (LVI). They had, of course, been first baptized by clergymen who for one reason or another were unacceptable to the Donatists. Even one rebaptized person was a cause for pain to Augustine, and in a letter (XXXIV) written in 396 to a fellow bishop, Eusebius, the Donatists were made to look a bad lot indeed. A man who regularly beat his mother fled to the Donatists, who, happy to have another recruit, rebaptized him, much to Augustine's horror. The stringent tone of the letter, which sought to arouse Eusebius to the dangers of Donatism, was in keeping with the seriousness with which such matters were viewed in those times, but was not necessarily indicative of Augustine's true temperament. From other sources, he seems to have been a kindly man much beloved by those who knew him.

Later in 399 or 400, Augustine wrote to Crispinus to ask for a discussion of the basic theological differences between them. But the opening of the letter, indicating the difficulty they had even addressing each other, shows how far they had to go.

> I have adopted this plan[3] in regard to the heading of this letter, because your party are offended by the humility which I have shown in the salutations prefixed to others. I might be supposed to have done it as an insult to you, were it not that I trust that you will do the same in your reply to me. Why should I say much regarding your promise at Carthage, and my urgency to have it fulfilled? Let the manner in which we then acted to each other be forgotten with the past, lest it should obstruct future conference. Now, unless I am mistaken, there is, by the Lord's help, no obstacle in the way: we are both in Numidia, and located at no great distance from each other. I have heard it said that you are still willing to examine, in debate with me, the question which separates us from communion with each other. See how promptly all ambiguities may be cleared away: send me an answer to this letter if you please, and perhaps that may be enough, not only for us, but for those also who desire to hear us; or if it is not, let us exchange letters again and again until the discussion is exhausted. For what greater benefit could be secured to us by the comparative nearness of the towns which we inhabit? I have resolved to debate with you in no other way than by letters, in order both to prevent anything that is said from escaping from our memory, and to secure that others interested in the question, but unable to be present at a debate, may not forfeit the instruction. You are accustomed, not with any intention of falsehood, but by mistake, to reproach us with charges such as may suit your purpose, concerning past transactions, which we repudiate as untrue. (LI)

In another letter (LXXXVIII) Augustine speaks of violent outbursts between the traditional Christian community and the so-called Circumcelliones,[4] fanatical

Donatists who went from house to house provoking trouble. It is customary to think of this period as a time of antagonisms between pagans and Christians, but the following passage brings to mind the pagan historian Ammianus Marcellinus's famous remark that "no wild beasts are such enemies to mankind as are most of the Christians in their deadly hatred of one another."[5]

Writing in 406 to Januarius, bishop of Casae Nigrae in Numidia, who headed the Donatists at the time, Augustine admitted that his conciliatory attitude, whereby he hoped to win men over by peaceful debate, had not been successful, and he finally decided to accept the Emperor Honorius's solution of 405, which was to use the force of civil law against them. That included the confiscation of their property.

> You have therefore no ground for complaint against us: nay more, the clemency of the Catholic Church would have led us to desist from even enforcing these decrees of the emperors, had not your clergy and Circumcelliones, disturbing our peace, and destroying us by their most monstrous crimes and furious deeds of violence, compelled us to have these decrees revived and put in force again. For before these more recent edicts of which you complain had come into Africa, these desperadoes laid ambush for our bishops on their journeys, abused our clergy with savage blows, and assaulted our laity in the same most cruel manner, and set fire to their habitations. A certain presbyter who had of his own free choice preferred the unity of our Church, was for so doing dragged out of his own house, cruelly beaten without form of law, rolled over and over in a miry pond, covered with a matting of rushes, and exhibited as an object of pity to some and of ridicule to others, while his persecutors gloried in their crime; after which they carried him away where they pleased, and reluctantly set him at liberty after twelve days. When Proculeianus[6] was challenged by our bishop concerning this outrage, at a meeting of the municipal courts, he at first endeavoured to evade inquiry into the matter by pretending that he knew nothing of it; and when the demand was immediately repeated he publicly declared that he would say nothing more on the subject. And the perpetrators of that outrage are at this day among your presbyters, continuing moreover to keep us in terror, and to persecute us to the utmost of their power. (LXXXVIII)

One reason Augustine failed wth less harsh measures was because more than religious matters were involved. The Donatists, at times in the majority in North Africa, found their strength among the poor and less educated. But not all of these people were attracted on doctrinal grounds. The Donatist movement was, in part, a rebellion against poor economic conditions. The established church, benefiting from the gifts of emperors and legacies of the rich, was a landowner and employer, which, given the conditions of the times, meant oppressor. Even the use of ornate salutations with which churchmen prefaced their letters (over which Augustine and Crispinus were quarreling) showed a prospering church assembling the decorations of power. Historically then, the church, as an institution growing in wealth and power, came to be at odds with a Gospel-related brotherhood of man which sought the ending of class distinctions. Moreover, as time passed, the weakness of the central government in Rome left vast domains, under wealthy landlords, for all practical purposes independent of imperial rule. These estates might have several small churches and even a bishop over them accounting for an inordinate number of such clergymen who, with a stake in local order, would be likely targets for disgruntled Donatists.

The support of the emperor gave the church the victory it wanted. At the same time it is likely that more Donatists were cut down by the swords of the Vandals than by any of Augustine's sharp words, which were, of course, focused on their religious practices. Actually, the Donatists did not disappear entirely until the Arab conquest in the seventh century. (Another separate group of Christians, the Copts in Egypt, survived. These people belonged to a Church they believed to be founded by St. Mark in Alexandria rather than the one following St. Peter in Rome. Thus, the Coptic church was a regional division in Christianity separate from the universal claims of the Roman church which Augustine promoted. It still is.)

The other major heresy Augustine had to combat was Pelagianism, which had given so much trouble to Jerome. Practically speaking, it was not so serious a matter as Donatism, for its appeal was more intellectual and of less consequence to the devout. Still, the notion that a man could achieve perfection through his own unaided efforts was an obvious attack on Augustine's central idea of dependency on God and His church. As mentioned earlier, it was Augustine's leadership in the campaign to outlaw Pelagianism that so greatly pleased Jerome. On Pelagius, they could agree even if earlier Jerome's temper was sorely tested by Augustine's unsolicited advice about his translations.

Although acclaimed for his theological writings, Augustine was not an accomplished linguist. Nevertheless, in a letter written in 394 or 395, he presumed to advise Jerome about his Latin translation of the Hebrew scriptures from the original texts. Why not use the Septuagint, the widely used third century B.C. Greek translation named for the seventy scholars who according to tradition worked in miraculous harmony?

> We therefore, and with us all that are devoted to study in the African churches, beseech you not to refuse to devote care and labour to the translation of the books of those who have written in the Greek language most able commentaries on our Scriptures. You may thus put us also in possession of these men, and especially of that one whose name you seem to have singular pleasure in sounding forth in your writings [Origen]. But I beseech you not to devote your labour to the work of translating into Latin the sacred canonical books, unless you follow the method in which you have translated Job, viz. with the addition of notes, to let it be seen plainly

> what differences there are between this version of yours and that of the Seventy, whose authority is worthy of highest esteem. For my own part, I cannot sufficiently express my wonder that anything should at this date be found in the Hebrew MSS. which escaped so many translators perfectly acquainted with the language. I say nothing of the Seventy, regarding whose harmony in mind and spirit, surpassing that which is found in even one man, I dare not in any way pronounce a decided opinion, except that in my judgment, beyond question, very high authority must in this work of translation be conceded to them. I am more perplexed by those translators who, though enjoying the advantage of labouring after the Seventy had completed their work, and although well acquainted, as it is reported, with the force of Hebrew words and phrases, and with Hebrew syntax, have not only failed to agree among themselves, but have left many things which, even after so long a time, still remain to be discovered and brought to light. Now these things were either obscure or plain: if they were obscure, it is believed that you are as likely to have been mistaken as the others; if they were plain, it is not believed that they [the Seventy] could possibly have been mistaken. (XXVIII)

In another letter to Jerome, written in 403, Augustine makes a complaint that sounds familiar in the present time of up-to-date prayer books and colloquial scripture. It seems that a reading of Jerome's version of the ***Book of Jonah*** had sparked an unpleasant upheaval in one of the churches. The worshipers wanted to hear the same words they had always heard, and if they didn't hear them it was the bishop who would go.

> For my part, I would much rather that you would furnish us with a translation of the Greek version of the canonical Scriptures known as the work of the Seventy translators. For if your translation begins to be more generally read in many churches, it will be a grievous thing that, in the reading of Scripture, differences must arise between the Latin Churches and the Greek Churches, especially seeing that the discrepancy is easily condemned in a Latin version by the production of the original in Greek, which is a language very widely known; whereas, if any one has been disturbed by the occurrence of something to which he was not accustomed in the translation taken from the Hebrew, and alleges that the new translation is wrong, it will be found difficult, if not impossible, to get at the Hebrew documents by which the version to which exception is taken may be defended. And when they are obtained, who will submit to have so many Latin and Greek authorities pronounced to be in the wrong? Besides all this, Jews, if consulted as to the meaning of the Hebrew text, may give a different opinion from yours: in which case it will seem as if your presence were indispensable, as being

> the only one who could refute their view; and it would be a miracle if one could be found capable of acting as arbiter between you and them.
>
> A certain bishop, one of our brethren, having introduced in the church over which he presides the reading of your version, came upon a word in the book of the prophet Jonah, of which you have given a very different rendering from that which had been of old familiar to the senses and memory of all the worshippers, and had been chanted for so many generations in the church. Thereupon arose such a tumult in the congregation, especially among the Greeks, correcting what had been read, and denouncing the translation as false, that the bishop was compelled to ask the testimony of the Jewish residents (it was in the town of Oea). These, whether from ignorance or from spite, answered that the words in the Hebrew MSS. were correctly rendered in the Greek version, and in the Latin one taken from it. What further need I say? The man was compelled to correct your version in that passage as if it had been falsely translated, as he desired not to be left without a congregation—a calamity which he narrowly escaped. From this case we also are led to think that you may be occasionally mistaken. You will also observe how great must have been the difficulty if this had occurred in those writings which cannot be explained by comparing the testimony of languages now in use. (LXXI)

When Jerome, in 404, sent back a reply to these two letters the first of which took nine years to reach him, he politely suggested that Augustine didn't know what he was talking about.

> You ask why a former translation which I made of some of the canonical books was carefully marked with asterisks and obelisks, whereas I afterwards published a translation without these. You must pardon my saying that you seem to me not to understand the matter: for the former translation is from the Septuagint; and wherever obelisks are placed, they are designed to indicate that the Seventy have said more than is found in the Hebrew. But the asterisks indicate what has been added by Origen from the version of Theodotion. In that version I was translating from the Greek: but in the later version, translating from the Hebrew itself, I have expressed what I understood it to mean, being careful to preserve rather the exact sense than the order of the words. I am surprised that you do not read the books of the Seventy translators in the genuine form in which they were originally given to the world, but as they have been corrected, or rather corrupted, by Origen, with his obelisks and asterisks; and that you refuse to follow the translation, however feeble, which has been given by a Christian man, especially seeing that Origen borrowed the things which he had added from the edition of a man who, after the passion of Christ, was a

> Jew and a blasphemer. Do you wish to be a true admirer and partisan of the Seventy translators? Then do not read what you find under the asterisks; rather erase them from the volumes, that you may approve yourself indeed a follower of the ancients. If, however, you do this, you will be compelled to find fault with all the libraries of the Churches; for you will scarcely find more than one M.S. here and there which has not these interpolations. . . . You tell me that I have given a wrong translation of some word in Jonah, and that a worthy bishop narrowly escaped losing his charge through the clamorous tumult of his people, which was caused by the different rendering of this one word. At the same time, you withhold from me what the word was which I have mistranslated; thus taking away the possibility of my saying anything in my own vindication, lest my reply should be fatal to your objection. (LXXV)

As in Jerome's correspondence, Augustine's letters do occasionally relate some news of the day. For instance, it is evident that Christians in North Africa were still not free from sudden attacks by pagans (L and XC). In the long term, of course, there was much more to fear from the barbarians. Being kept informed of events abroad, Augustine, in a letter of late 408 or early 409 to the "very devout Italica," refers to the first Gothic attacks on Rome in 408. He insists that Christians everwhere must share in the grief of those who suffer in the conflict in the capital. Indeed, soon most of them would.

> To this last letter, just now received, I lose no time in promptly replying, because your Excellency's agent has written to me that he can send my letter without delay to Rome. By his letter we have been greatly distressed, because he has taken pains to acquaint us with the things which are taking place in the city [Rome] or around its walls, so as to give us reliable information concerning that which we were reluctant to believe on the authority of vague rumors. In the letters which were sent to us previously by our brethren, tidings were given to us of events, vexations and grievous, it is true, but much less calamitous than those of which we now hear. I am surprised beyond expression that my brethren the holy bishops did not write to me when so favourable an opportunity of sending a letter by your messengers occurred, and that your own letter conveyed to us no information concerning such painful tribulation as has befallen you—tribulation which, by reason of the tender sympathies of Christian charity, is ours as well as yours. (XCIX.1–2)

North Africa was safe from the northern marauders for a time, but in 429, the Vandals, under their king Geiseric, invaded. A Roman general, Boniface, appears to have played a dual role in the event. First, while serving in North Africa, and unhappy about the treatment he received from the Emperor Honorius, he may actually have invited the Vandals to come from Spain. When his affairs at home were settled, however, he turned on his former allies and sought to drive them out, without success.

Boniface was well known to Augustine, who nevertheless had little to say about military affairs. There is, however, a letter written much earlier, in 418, wherein he reminded Boniface that he should maintain his devotion to God and added a familiar argument about why wars should be fought.

> Think, then, of this first of all, when you are arming for the battle, that even your bodily strength is a gift of God; for, considering this, you will not employ the gift of God against God. For, when faith is pledged, it is to be kept even with the enemy against whom the war is waged, how much more with the friend for whom the battle is fought! Peace should be the object of your desire; war should be waged only as a necessity, and waged only that God may by it deliver men from the necessity and preserve them in peace. For peace is not sought in order to the kindling of war, but war is waged in order that peace may be obtained. Therefore, even in waging war, cherish the spirit of a peacemaker, that, by conquering those whom you attack, you may lead them back to the advantages of peace; for our Lord says: "Blessed are the peacemakers; for they shall be called the children of God." If, however, peace among men be so sweet as procuring temporal safety, how much sweeter is that peace with God, which procures for men the eternal felicity of the angels! Let necessity, therefore, and not your will, slay the enemy who fights against you. As violence is used towards him who rebels and resists, so mercy is due to the vanquished or the captive, especially in the case in which future troubling of the peace is not to be feared. (CLXXXIX)

A letter (CCXX) written to Boniface in 427 praised the general's good qualities but took him to task for remarrying after his first wife died. The sullying of chastity was worsened by the fact that the woman was an Arian before her marriage. Only after a long discussion on that subject did Augustine mention briefly the deteriorating military situation. Again, however, the problem was primarily religious. Calamities resulted from sin. Man should occupy himself with spiritual things.

With the Vandal pressure growing, Augustine responded to the query of Bishop Honoratus of Thiaba in Mauritania as to whether the clergy ought to flee. He answered that a clergyman should escape only when he was singled out for persecution. It would be wrong to flee merely because of fear. The clergy should continue to minister to their flock as long as the people wished to remain. Augustine's letter, written in 428 or 429, indicates what some people were thinking about as the provinces were falling to the barbarians—and the last year in which an emperor of Rome was named was less than fifty years away.

> I thought that by sending to your Grace a copy of the letter which I wrote to our brother and co-bishop Quodvultdeus, I had earned exemption from the burden which you have imposed upon me, by asking my advice as to what you ought to do in the midst of the dangers which have befallen us in these times. For although I wrote briefly, I think that I did not pass over anything that was necessary either to be said by me or heard by my questioner in correspondence on the subject: for I said that, on the one hand, those who desire to remove, if they can, to fortified places are not to be forbidden to do so; and, on the other hand, we ought not to break the ties by which the love of Christ has bound us as ministers not to forsake the churches which it is our duty to serve. The words which I used in the letter referred to were: "Therefore, however small may be the congregation of God's people among whom we are, if our ministry is so necessary to them that it is a clear duty not to withdraw it from them, it remains for us to say to the Lord, 'Be Thou to us a God of defence, and a strong fortress.'" . . . What, then, shall we say to the position which you thus state in your former epistle:—"I do not see what good we can do to ourselves or to the people by continuing to remain in the churches, except to see before our eyes men slain, women outraged, churches burned, ourselves expiring amid torments applied in order to extort from us what we do not possess"? God is powerful to hear the prayers of His children and to avert those things which they fear; and we ought not, on account of evils that are uncertain, to make up our minds absolutely to the desertion of that ministry, without which the people must certainly suffer ruin, not in the affairs of this life, but of that other life which ought to be cared for with incomparably greater diligence and solicitude. . . . the minister who flees when the consequence of his flight is the withdrawal from Christ's flock of that nourishment by which its spiritual life is sustained, is an "hireling who seeth the wolf coming, and fleeth because he careth not for the sheep." . . . With love, which I know to be sincere, I have now written what I believe to be true on this question, because you asked my opinion, my dearly beloved brother; but I have not enjoined you to follow my advice, if you can find any better than mine. Be that as it may, we cannot find anything better for us to do in these dangers than continually beseech the Lord our God to have compassion on us. And as to the matter about which I have written, namely, that ministers should not desert the churches of God, some wise and holy men have by the gift of God been enabled both to will and to do this thing, and have not in the least degree faltered in the determined prosecution of their purpose, even though exposed to the attacks of slanderers. (CCXXVIII)

Among the last of Augustine's extant letters is one written when this giant of mind and faith had grown frail in body. He wrote during his final winter, 429–430, that the feebleness of old age prevented a visit to his friend Nobilius, who is otherwise unknown.

> So important is the solemnity at which your brotherly affection invites me to be present, that my heart's desire would carry my poor body to you, were it not that infirmity renders this impossible. I might have come if it had not been winter; I might have braved the winter if I had been young: for in the latter case the warmth of youth would have borne uncomplainingly the cold of the season; in the former case the warmth of summer would have met with gentleness the chill languor of old age. For the present, my lord most blessed, my holy and venerable partner in the priestly office, I cannot undertake in winter so long a journey, carrying with me as I must the frigid feebleness of very many years.[7] I reciprocate the salutation due to your worth, on behalf of my own welfare I myself beseech the Lord God to grant that the prosperity of peace may follow the dedication of so great an edifice to His sacred service. (CCLXIX)

Augustine died in 430, three months after the Vandals began besieging Hippo. The city fell after fourteen months.

So ended the life of the greatest of the church fathers. Do we ever catch a glimpse of humor beneath his ponderous writings and heavy reputation? Yes, at least once. In a letter to Jerome, in 415, when writing about the investigation of sin and the hope of salvation, Augustine repeated a charming old story:

> A man had fallen into a well where the quantity of water was sufficient to break his fall and save him from death, but not deep enough to cover his mouth and deprive him of speech. Another man approached, and on seeing him cries out in surprise: "How did you fall in here?" He answers: "I beseech you to plan how you can get me out of this, rather than ask how I fell in." So . . . it is sufficient for the soul . . . that we know the way in which it is saved, even though we should never know the way in which it came into that wretched condition. (CLXVII)

XIII
SYNESIUS OF CYRENE

The Reluctant Bishop

THE sainted Jerome and Augustine are famous for their unwavering faith. One of their contemporaries, a bishop named Synesius, was not so sure. He was even uncertain about the Resurrection. His reservations made him an unlikely choice for church office, and there is little wonder that he hesitated in accepting one. Yet, even today, for an occasional bishop, the possibility of dutiful service might outweigh a private conclusion.

In the fourth century, religious leaders such as Jerome and Augustine, combining extraordinary talent with pious zeal, were, as always, rare. At the same time, the growing church needed skilled administrators. Resourceful men, even those shaky in their faith, found themselves chosen to be bishops, and Synesius, a native of Cyrene[1] in North Africa, was one of them. His 156 letters show a notable lack of interest in church politics or polemics. Nor did Synesius consider himself any less of a Christian for lacking a Jerome-style struggle with himself about reading the classics. On the contrary, he felt that it was his love of philosophy that bound him to godliness and virtue. The hymns and poems he wrote are flavored with classical allusions and Christian doctrine. He quotes Plato well over one hundred times.

Synesius was born of Greek descent, sometime between 365 and 370, into a family that was not Christian. Income from the family's property was sufficient to allow a traditional education in the classics and support his leisurely study of philosophy, and he had time for writings that show the range of interests. A book *On Dreams* is extant, as is a philosophical *Egyptian Tale* and an oration *On Kingship*, in which Synesius, a stout defender of old Roman values, denounces the Goths and their influence at the court in Constantinople. In addition, he wrote, tongue in cheek, a *Eulogy on Baldness*, which proclaims such a condition to be a sign of intellect, Synesius himself having begun to go bald at an early age.

Although Synesius proudly claimed descent from ancient Spartan royalty, he was planning a trip to Athens when he wrote the following letter to his older brother, Euoptius, with whom he was always close and, indeed, to whom he wrote most of the letters.

> A great number of people, either private individuals or priests, by moulding dreams, which they call revelations, seem likely to do me harm when I am awake, if I do not happen with all speed to visit sacred Athens. Whenever, then, you happen to meet a skipper sailing for the Piraeus, write to me, as it is there that I shall receive my letters. I shall gain not only this by my voyage to Athens—an escape from my present evils, but also a relief from doing reverence to the learning of those who come back from Athens. They differ in no wise from us ordinary mortals. They do not understand Aristotle and Plato better than we, and nevertheless they go about among us as demi-gods among mules, because they have seen the Academy, the Lyceum, and the Poecile where Zeno gave his lectures on philosophy. However, the Poecile no longer deserves its name, for the proconsul has taken away all the pictures, and has thus humiliated these men's pretensions to learning. (54)[2]

Athens was a disappointment. Later, he remarked on his preference for Alexandria, where, beginning about 394, he had studied with Hypatia, one of the famous women of antiquity, a renowned teacher of mathematics and philosophy, particularly Neoplatonism. In another letter to his brother he wrote, "Today Egypt has received and cherishes the fruitful wisdom of Hypatia. Athens was aforetime the dwelling-place of the wise: today the bee-keepers alone bring it honour" (136).

Another of Synesius's letters to his brother detailed the hazards of sea travel. Although an account of a nearly disastrous voyage, the story is at times amusing. It seems that a heavy storm struck his ship on a Friday night, and among the crew were many Jews who, along with the Jewish captain, would make no effort to rescue the ship on their Sabbath, until the direst extremity was reached. The letter is not only a good example of Synesius's lighthearted manner, but of his relative tolerance in religious matters. No doubt one of the reasons for his popularity was that although at times abrupt in his speech, he was not a mean-spirited man.

> Although we started from Bendideum at early dawn, we had scarcely passed Pharius Myrmex by noonday, for our ship went aground two or three times in the bed of the harbour. This mishap at the very outset seemed a bad omen, and it might have been wiser to desert a vessel which had been unlucky from the very start. . . . Hear my story then, that you may have no further leisure for your mocking wit, and I will tell you first of all how our crew made up. Our skipper was fain of death owing to his bankrupt condition; then besides him we had twelve sailors, thirteen in all! More than half of them, including the skipper, were Jews—a graceless race

and fully convinced of the piety of sending to Hades as many Greeks as possible. The remainder were a collection of peasants who even as late as last year had never gripped an oar, but the one batch and the other were alike in this, that every man of them had some personal defect. . . . We had embarked to the number of more than fifty, about a third of us being women, most of them young and comely. Do not, however, be too quick to envy us, for a screen separated us from them and a stout one at that, the suspended fragment of a recently torn sail, to virtuous men the very wall of Semiramis. Nay, Priapus himself might well have been temperate had he taken passage with Amarantus, for there was never a moment when this fellow allowed us to be free from fear of the uttermost danger. . . . as the hours passed the seas increased continually in volume. Now it so happened that this was the day on which the Jews make what they term the "Preparation," and they reckon the night, together with the day following this, as a time during which it is not lawful to work with one's hands. They keep this day holy and apart from the others, and they pass it in rest from labour of all kinds. Our skipper accordingly let go the rudder from his hands the moment he guessed that the sun's rays had left the earth, and throwing himself prostrate, "Allowed to trample on him what sailor so desired" [Sophocles, *Ajax*].

We who at first could not understand why he was thus lying down, imagined that despair was the cause of it all. We rushed to his assistance and implored him not to give up the last hope yet. Indeed the hugest waves were actually menacing the vessel, and the very deep was at war with itself. Now it frequently happens that when the wind has suddenly relaxed its violence, the billows already set in motion do not immediately subside; they are still under the influence of the wind's force, to which they yield and with which they battle at the same time, and the oncoming waves fight against those subsiding. I have every need of my store of flaming language, so that in recounting such immense dangers I may not fall into the trivial. To people who are at sea in such a crisis, life may be said to hang by a thread only, for if our skipper proved at such a moment to be an orthodox observer of the Mosaic law, what was life worth in the future? Indeed we soon understood why he had abandoned the helm, for when we begged him to do his best to save the ship, he stolidly continued reading his roll. Despairing of persuasion, we finally attempted force, and one staunch soldier—for many Arabs of the cavalry were of our company—one staunch soldier, I say, drew his sword and threatened to behead the fellow on the spot if he did not resume control of the vessel. But the Maccabean in very deed was determined to persist in his observances. However, in the middle of the night he voluntarily returned to the helm. "For now," he said, "we are clearly in danger of death, and the law commands." On this the tumult sprang up afresh, groaning of men and shrieking of women. All called upon the gods, and cried aloud; all called to mind those they loved. . . . Then some one loudly proclaimed that every one possessing gold should suspend it about the neck, and those who possessed it did so, as well as those who had anything of the value of gold. The women themselves put on their jewellery, and distributed cords to those who needed them: such is the time-honoured custom. Now this is the reason for it. It is a matter of necessity that the corpse from a shipwreck should carry with it the fee for burial, inasmuch as whosoever comes across the dead body and profits by it, will fear the laws of Adrastia [Nemesis], and will scarcely grudge sprinkling a little sand on the one who has given to him so much more in value. . . .

But day broke before all this had time to occur, and never, I know, did we behold the sun with greater joy. The wind grew more moderate as the temperature became milder, and thus, as the moisture evaporated, we were able to work the rigging and handle the sails. We were unable, it is true, to replace our sail by a new one, for this was already in the hands of the pawnbroker, but we took it in like the swelling folds of a garment, and lo, in four hours' time we who had imagined ourselves already in the jaws of death, were disembarking in a remote desert place, possessing neither town nor farm near it, only an expanse of open country of one hundred and thirty stadia. Our ship was riding in the open sea, for the spot was not a harbour, and it was riding on a single anchor. The second anchor had been sold, and a third Amarantus did not possess. When now we touched the dearly Beloved land, we embraced the earth as a real living mother. We sent up hymns of gratitude to Providence, as in our custom, and to all this we added a mention of the present good fortune by which we had been saved contrary to all expectation. Thus we waited two days until the sea should have abated its fury. When, however, we were unable to discover any way out by land, for we could find no one in the country, we decided to try our fortune again at sea.

As a consequence of another violent storm, their ship was run aground again. Synesius continues his story.

Now provisions began to run short. So little accustomed were we to such accidents and so little had we anticipated a voyage of such length, that we had not brought a sufficient stock and, what is more, we had not husbanded what he had on board. . . . Every one kept avariciously whatever he could get hold of, and no one gave a present to his neighbour, but now we have abundance, and this is how it all happened. The Libyan women would have offered even bird's milk to the women of our party. They bestowed upon them all the products of earth and air alike; to wit, cheeses, flour, barley cakes, lamb, poultry and eggs; one of them even made a present of a bustard, a bird of very delicious flavour. A yokel would call it at first sight a peacock. They bring these presents to the ship, and our women accept them and share them with those who wish it. At present they who go fishing have become generous—a man, a child, comes to me one after another, and makes me a present, now a fish caught on the line, invariably some dainty that the rocks produce. To please you I take nothing from the women, that there may be no truce between them and me, and that I may be in no difficulty about denial, when I have to abjure all connexion with them. And yet what was to hinder me from rejoicing in necessities? So much comes in from all sides. The kindness of the inhabitants of the country towards their women guests you probably attribute to their virtue alone. Such is not the case; and it is worth while to explain all this to you, particularly as I have so much leisure. The wrath of Aphrodite, it would seem, lies heavy on the land; the women are as unlucky as the Lemnians; their breasts are overfull and they have disproportionately large chests, so that the infants obtain nourishment held not by the mother's arm, but by her shoulder, the nipple being turned upwards. One might of course maintain that Ammon and the country of Ammon is as good a nurse of children as of sheep, and that nature has there endowed cattle and humanity alike with fuller and more abundant fountains of milk, and so to that end are ampler breasts or reservoirs needed. Now, when these women hear from men who have had commerce with others beyond the frontier, that all women are not like this, they are incredulous. So when they fall in with a foreign woman, they make up to her in every way until they have gained their object, which is to examine her bosom, and then the woman who has examined the stranger tells another, and they call one another like the Cicones, they flock together to the spectacle and bring presents with them. We happened to have with us a young female slave who came from Pontus. Art and nature had combined to make her more highly chiselled than an ant. All the stir was about this one, and she made much gain from the women, and for the last three days the richest in the neighbourhood have been sending for her, and have passed her on from one to the other. She was so little embarrassed that she readily exhibited herself in undress.

So much for my story. The divinity has shaped it for you in mingling the comic with the tragic element. I have done likewise in the account I have given you. I know this letter is too long, but as when with you face to face, so in writing to you I am insatiable, and as it is by no means certain that I shall be able to talk with you again, I take all possible pleasure in writing to you now. Moreover, by fitting the letter into my diary, about which I take great pains, I shall have the reminiscences of many days. . . . As for you, may you never trust yourself to the sea. Or at least, if you really must do so, let it not be at the end of the month.(4)

The extremes of religious behavior, so common at the time among Christians, were to Synesius unreasonable and tasteless. He and the students he met in Alexandria, who were to be his lifelong friends, had a more philosophical point of view. Still, it was not without some superciliousness. In one of the ten letters written to a fellow student, Herculian, he takes his friend to task for talking to uneducated people about subjects better left to the learned. Akin to Plato's philosopher-kings, there were a select few who would give guidance to all the rest. The letter was written in A.D. 402.

> You have not kept your promise, my dear friend, the promise which you made me that you would not reveal those things which ought to remain hidden. I have just listened to people who have come from you. They remembered some of your expressions, and they begged me to reveal the meaning to them. But according to my custom I did not pretend to them that I understood the writings in question, nor did I say that I knew them. You no longer need any warning from me, my dear Herculian, for it would not be enough to convince you. Rather look up the letter which Lysis the Pythagorean addressed to Hipparchus, and when you have found it, oblige me by reading it frequently. Perhaps you will then experience a complete change of mind in regard to your uncalled-for revelation. "To explain philosophy to the mob," as Lysis says in his somewhat Dorian dialect, "is only to awaken amongst men a great contempt for things divine." How often have I met, time and time again, people who, because they had rashly listened to some stately little phrases, refused to believe themselves the laymen that they really were!
>
> Full of vanity, they sullied sacred dogmas by pretending to teach what they had never succeeded in learning. They attached to themselves three or four followers to flatter them, men in no way different in their souls from the vulgar, and none of them such as are instructed through early education. It is a dreadful thing and full of guile, this conceit of wisdom, shrinking at nothing in the case of the ignorant, and daring all things thoughtlessly; for what could be more reckless than ignorance? (143)

There are seven letters addressed to his teacher Hypatia, and in one of them, written in 404, Synesius was critical of both pretentious philosophers and narrow-minded monks. There is also a passage in which he shows his great respect for Hypatia's judgment about a book he had written. She, too, was a writer, but, unfortunately, all her works have been lost.

> I have brought out two books this year. One of them as I was moved thereto by God Himself, the other because of the slander of men. Some of those who wear the white [philosopher] or dark [monk] mantle have maintained that I am faithless to philosophy, apparently because I profess grace and harmony of style, and because I venture to say something con-

cerning Homer and concerning the figures of the rhetoricians. In the eyes of such persons one must hate literature in order to be a philosopher, and must occupy himself with divine matters only. No doubt these men alone have become spectators of the knowable. This privilege is unlawful for me, for I spend some of my leisure in purifying my tongue and sweetening my wit. . . . There are certain men among my critics whose effrontery is only surpassed by their ignorance, and these are the readiest of all to spin out discussions concerning God. Whenever you meet them, you have to listen to their babble about inconclusive syllogisms. They pour a torrent of phrases over those who stand in no need of them, in which I suppose they find their own profit. The public teachers that one sees in our cities, come from this class. . . . You will, I think, recognize this easy-going tribe, which miscalls nobility of purpose. They wish me to become their pupil; they say that in a short time they will make me all-daring in questions of divinity, and that I shall be able to declaim day and night without stopping. The rest, who have more taste, are, as sophists, much more unfortunate than these. They would like to be famous in the same way, but fortunately for them they are incapable even of this. You know some who, despoiled at the office of the tax collector, or urged thereto by some one calamity, have become philosophers in the middle of their lives. Their philosophy consists in a very simple formula, that of calling God to witness, as Plato did, whenever they deny anything or whenever they assert anything. A shadow would surpass these men in uttering anything to the point; but their pretensions are extraordinary. Oh, what proudly arched brows! They support their beards with the hand. They assume a more solemn countenance than the statues of Xenocrates. . . . If you decree that I ought to publish my book, I will dedicate it to orators and philosophers together. The first it will please, and to the others it will be useful, provided of course that it is not rejected by you, who are really able to pass judgement. If it does not seem to you worthy of Greek ears, if, like Aristotle, you prize truth more than friendship, a close and profound darkness will overshadow it, and mankind will never hear it mentioned. . . .

So much for this matter. The other work God ordained and He gave His sanction to it, and it has been set up as a thank-offering to the imaginative faculties. It contains an inquiry into the whole imaginative soul, and into some other points which have not yet been handled by any Greek philosopher. But why should one dilate on this? This work was completed, the whole of it, in a single night, or rather, at the end of a night, one which also brought the vision enjoining me to write it. There are two or three passages in the book in which it seemed to me that I was some other person, and that I was one listening to myself amongst others who were present. Even now this work, as often as I go over it, produces a marvellous effect upon me, and a certain divine voice envelops me as in poetry.

> Whether this my experience is not unique, or may happen to another, on all this you will enlighten me, for after myself you will be the first of the Greeks to have access to the work. (154)

Synesius's comments on the shortcomings of philosophers and monks are more than matched by his caustic remarks about the poor quality of Roman provincial officials. During his time, the much-heralded reputation of the Romans for good government continued to decline. He was a witness to the ineffective handling of local problems. This was particularly true when the Ausurians, hostile tribesmen of the hinterland, were making forays into Cyrenaica. Synesius, ever conscious of his Roman citizenship, was defiant of marauders who "dared to attack Roman citizens." One of his letters to his brother contains sarcastic references to a buffoonish officer, Joannes, who had a talent for making excuses to cover his absences in times of danger.

> How often one sees the same men who are very courageous in peacetime, showing themselves cowardly at the moment of combat! This is to say, they are worthless everywhere. Thus it seems to me that every one should be thankful to war, for it is an exact touchstone of the blood in the heart of each one of us. It takes away many boasters, and returns them to us more temperate men. In the future, I think, we shall no longer see the guilty Joannes swaggering about the public square, and attacking with kicks and blows men of a peaceable disposition. Indeed, yesterday the proverb, or rather the oracle, received clear confirmation, for you certainly know it as an oracle, that: There be no long-haired men who are not degenerates.
>
> For some days now they have been warning us of the approach of the enemy. I thought that we ought to march out to meet these. The leader of the Balagritae drew up his forces, and sallied out with them. Then, having occupied the plain first, we waited. The enemy did not appear. In the evening we went away home each of us, after we had arranged to return upon the following day. During this time Joannes the Phrygian was nowhere; at least he was invisible, but he spread rumours in secret, at one moment that he has broken a leg and they have been obliged to amputate it, at another moment that he is suffering from asthma, later that some other untoward fate has overtaken him. Such tale-bearers kept drifting in from different sides, or so they pretended, the object being, no doubt, that no one should know into what retreat our man had slipped, or where he was concealed. And you should have heard them in the midst of their narrative deploring the unlucky misfortune with tears in their eyes. . . .
>
> For five days we had in vain sallied out in arms to find the enemy, but they were always at the frontier places which they were engaged in devastating. Then when Joannes was convinced that the enemy would not dare to come into the heart of the country, he himself appeared and is now

turning everything into confusion. He ill? Never! Why, he was even laughing at the people who believed such a story. He had come from a great distance, he said, I know not whence. He had been called there to bring assistance, and it was owing to this that the districts which had called on him were saved, for the enemy did not invade, terrified as they were at the mere rumour of the approach of Joannes. Once he had tranquillized everything there, he rushed up, so he said, to the menaced province. He is waiting for the barbarians, who may appear at any moment, so long as they were not aware of his presence, and so long as his name is not mentioned. So here he is, spreading confusion everywhere. He is claiming to be at the general's right hand, he is promising that in no time at all he will teach the art of victory. He is shouting "Front form! fall into line! form square to the flank!" In a word he is using all the words of the military professions without any knowledge of their meaning.

Thus some considered him a man of consequence and praised his talents, and were eager to become his pupils.

It was now late in the evening. It was time to pursue our attack. When we came down from the mountains, we pushed on in the plain . . . we saw some wretched creatures on horseback, men who, to judge from the look of them, had been pushed into battle merely by hunger, and were quite ready to risk their lives in order to possess themselves of our goods.

The moment that they saw us, as we also saw them, before they were within javelin throw, they jumped from their horses, as is their way, to give battle on foot. I was of the opinion that we ought to do the same thing, for the ground did not lend itself to cavalry manoeuvres. But our noble friend said he would not renounce the arts of horsemanship, and insisted on delivering a cavalry attack. What then? He pulls the horse's head sharply to the side, turns and flees away at full gallop, covers his horse with blood, gives it full rein, incites it with frequent application of spear, whip, and voice. I really do not know which of the two to admire the more, the horse or the rider, for if the horse galloped up hill and down hill and over rough country and smooth alike, cleared ditches and banks at a bound, the horseman, for his part, kept his seat in the saddle firm and unshaken. . . . On both sides the troops stood watching each other. Finally they drew off to the left and then we to the right, but at a walking pace and without haste, so that the retreat might not have the appearance of a flight.

Notwithstanding all these anxieties as we tried to find out where in the world Joannes was. He had galloped without reining up as far as Bombaea, and he remained hidden in the cave there, like a field-mouse in its hole. Bombaea is a mountain full of caverns, where art and nature have combined to form an impregnable fortress. It has long been celebrated, and justly; they often compare it to the subterranean vaults of Egypt. But to-day every

> one admits that there are no walls behind which one could be safer than at Bombaea, since even the most prudent of all men—I am too polite to say the most cowardly, the right word to use—has gone thither to hide himself, as to the surest refuge. The moment one enters this place, one is in a regular labyrinth, hard to get through, so that it by itself could provide places of refuge for Joannes. (104)

Generalizations about the decline and fall of the Roman Empire are well known. Synesius's letters are useful in focusing more precisely on what was going wrong in one corner of that world. Joannes was simply a local example of the incompetence and corruption of the imperial officialdom that contributed to the total collapse. In another letter to his brother, Synesius says that many of the soldiers stationed in the province were also unwilling to risk their lives for the native population. In the crisis, it was a man of the church who rallied the peasantry to their own defence.

> May all good things befall the priests of Axomis! While the soldiers were hiding themselves in the gorges of the mountains to take care of their precious lives, these priests called the peasants about them, and led them straight from the very church door against the enemy, and then they called upon God, and erected a trophy in the Myrtle Valley! This is a long ravine, deep and covered with forests. The barbarians, when they found no resistance in their way, rashly entered this dangerous defile, but they had to meet the valiant Faustus, the deacon of the church. This man, unarmed, when marching at the head of his troops, was himself the first to encounter a hoplite. He snatches up a stone, not to hurl it, but, holding it in his hand, and leaping upon him as with clenched fist he strikes the other violently on the temple. He knocks him down, strips him of his armour, and heaps many of the barbarians upon him. If any other man gave proof of courage in that battle, it is to Faustus that credit is due, both on account of his personal bravery, and for the orders which he gave at the critical moment.
>
> For my part, I would willingly give a victor's wreath to all those who participated in the engagement, and I would have their names proclaimed by the voice of a herald, for they were the first to do brave deeds, and to show panicstricken souls that the barbarians are not Corybantes nor the demons who serve Rhea, but men like ourselves, who can be wounded and killed. And if only we are men in such a crisis as this, even the second prize will be honourable. Fate perchance might accord us even the first, if instead of being fifteen irregulars lurking in a valley to forage, we were able to give battle in the open, in regular warfare, mass against mass. (122)

But a different letter to his brother suggests that such an incident may have been exceptional. If the soldiers did not show much spunk, neither did the provincials whom they were assigned to protect. Under the circumstances, why didn't more of these people do something to help themselves? The answer seems to be that the Romans, as occupiers of the country, had always favored a passive population. The resourcefulness, now so badly needed, was precisely what had been discouraged for so long.

> How sad it is to have only bad news to send when we write to each other, for, behold, the enemy has occupied Battia, he has attacked Aprosylis, he has burnt the threshing-floors, ravaged the fields, sold the women into slavery; and as to the men, there was no quarter given. Formerly they used to take away the little boys alive, but now, I suppose, they do not consider themselves sufficient in number to guard the booty, and at the same time to meet all the necessities of war, in case any one should attack them. However, none of us shows any indignation. We remain helpless in our homes. We always wait for our soldiers to defend us, and a sorry help they are! And, in spite of this, we are never done talking about the pay we give them and the privileges which they enjoy in time of peace, as if this were the moment to impeach them, and not the moment to hurl back the barbarians. When shall we have done with our useless chatter? When shall we act seriously? Let us collect our peasants, the tillers of the soil, to advance upon the enemy, to assure the safety of our wives, of our children, of our country, and also, I may add, of our soldiers. It will be a fine thing in time of peace to go about saying that we took care of the troops, and that we saved them. I am dictating this letter almost from my horse. I myself enrolled companies and officers with the resources I had at my disposal. I am collecting a very considerable body at Asusamas also, and I have given the Dioestae word to meet me at Cleopatra. Once we are on the march, and when it is announced that a young army has collected round me, I hope that many more will join us of their own free will. They will come from every side, the best men to associate themselves with our glorious undertaking, and the worthless to get booty. (125)

In a letter, A.D. 404 or 405,[3] to Olympius, another friend from his student days, Synesius had something to say about the uncertainties of the mail. He then went on to describe the problems of his battle-torn region. What he needs are bows and especially arrows.

> Just the other day, during the recent consulship of Aristaenetus and of—I don't know the name of his colleague—I received a letter sealed with your seal, and signed with your sacred name. But I conjecture it was a very old one, for it was worm-eaten, and the words for the most part were illegible. I wish very much that you would not content yourself with merely sending me one letter a year, as a sort of tribute, and that you would not take our

friend Syrus for your only postman. In this way nothing comes to me in its pristine freshness, everything seems stale. Do, therefore, as I do—no messenger of the Court changes his horses and leaves our city, without his bag being made heavier by some letter of mine addressed to your eloquent self. Whether all or only some of them give you my letters, may those who put them in your hands be ever blest! they are excellent men. But if they do otherwise, you will then be the wiser, inasmuch as you will not put faith in faithless men. But that I may not uselessly weary my secretary in dictating letters to him that you will never receive, I should like to be sure about this.

I shall in that case arrange things differently in future, and entrust them to Peter alone. I think Peter will bring on this letter through the agency of the sacred hand, for I am sending it from Pentapolis to our common teacher. She will choose the man by whom she wishes it to be conveyed, and her choice, I am sure, will fall upon the most trusted messenger. We do not know my dearest and best friend, if we shall ever have a chance of conversing together again. The cowardice of our generals has delivered up our country to the enemy without a single battle; there are no survivors except those of us who have seized fortified places. Those who have been captured in the plains have been butchered like victims for sacrifice. We are now afraid of a prolonged siege, lest it should compel most of the fortresses to surrender to thirst.[4] This is the reason why I did not answer your counter-charges on the subject of the presents. I had no leisure, for I was taken up with a machine which I am constructing, that we may hurl long-distance missiles from the turrets, stones of really substantial weight. I shall leave you, however, entirely at liberty to send me gifts, for of course Synesius must yield to Olympius, but they must not be gifts of a luxurious sort. I disapproved of the luxury of the quarters assigned to the company. Send me then, things that are useful for soldiers, such as bows and arrows, above all arrows with heads attached to them. As far as the bows are concerned, I can at a pinch buy them elsewhere, or repair those which I have already, but it is not easy to procure arrows, I mean really good ones. The Egyptian arrows that we have bulge at the knots and sink in between the knots, so that they deviate from their right course. They are like men starting in a foot-race, who from the very start are hampered and stumble; but those which are manufactured in your country are long and are deftly turned on the pattern of a single cylinder; and this means everything for the straight course of their flight. Now this is what you ought to send me, and at the same time some serviceable bits for my horses. That Italian horse whose praises you set forth in such beautiful language, I would have very gladly seen, if he will give us, as you promise, some excellent colts. However, at the end of your letter, in a postscript, I read that you were obliged to leave

> him at Seleucia, because the captain of your vessel refused to embark such a cargo on account of the bad weather; but as I recognize neither a style resembling your own, nor your hand, nor the precision of your script, I think I ought to warn you of the fact. It would be absurd if such a fine horse were preserved neither for you nor for me. (133)

Synesius did not become a baptized Christian until his mid-forties, although he seems to have been headed in that direction for many years. What his fellow citizens knew about him was that he had a spirited personality and a persuasive manner. In 399, they sent him to Constantinople to petition the Emperor Arcadius for an easing of taxes. While there, between 399 and 402, he enjoyed the company of many high-ranking Christians and may have been taking instructions in Christian teachings. En route home he spent some time in Alexandria and there married a woman from a prominent Christian family.

Eight years later, Cyrenaica, amid faltering leadership and widespread corruption, was again in danger of attack by marauders from the interior and faced with the threat of famine. Synesius's talents were needed. In 410, the same year in which Synesius was baptized, the death of the bishop of Ptolemais (modern Tolmeta), the chief town of the area, created a vacancy. Although Synesius was the obvious choice of the Christian population to fill the post, he was much troubled by the prospect. In a letter to his brother, he wrote frankly about his reservations. He was a philosopher and not a politician, he said. The office of bishop carried great responsibilities, and it was difficult to be truly worthy. He must be honest with himself and with those who had called him to the office. He was also worried about how it would affect his happy family life. There were three sons, although, as FitzGerald points out, Synesius's wife was such a "shadowy figure" that even her name has been lost from the record. Synesius admitted, too, that he was reluctant to give up his enjoyment of hunting. How could such a man share the conviction of Christians who renounced the world?

Synesius saw the Resurrection as an allegory, and he was never as successful as Augustine in freeing himself from Neoplatonic influence. That is why Jay Bregman's biography of Synesius speaks of "the philosophical religion which Synesius embraced."[5] Bregman's work uses, in addition to the letters, the other writings of Synesius in a study concentrating on a troubled bishop's effort to reconcile the philosophy of the past with the Christianity of the future. In Greek philosophy, the rejection of matter went back beyond Plato and Socrates, even to the Pythagoreans, and in that line of thought Synesius felt comfortable. Theoretically, according to his thinking, if all that counts is the spirit, what need is there for the body, alive, dead, or resurrected? Bregman writes: "I intend to demonstrate that Synesius was a Platonic 'philosopher-bishop' whose acceptance of Christianity was provisional and remained secondary to his commitment to Neoplatonism" (p. 5). FitzGerald, however, in his preface to the letters stated that it was his "own view that Synesius was at no time a Neoplatonist at heart, and that the early influences of his education were probably founded directly on Plato and the traditions of the Stoics" (p. 6).

In either case, the question remained: Could Synesius become a bishop without compromising his own convictions? Although his sincerity and honesty were surely in his favor, a wide gulf existed between his own position and what he felt others would expect of him.

The entire letter to his brother is given because it is the best way to understand Synesius, his character, what he thought, and how he expressed himself.

> I should be altogether lacking in sense, if I did not show myself very grateful to the inhabitants of Ptolemais, who consider me worthy of an honour to which I should never have dared to aspire. At the same time I ought to examine, not the importance of the duties with which they desire to entrust me, but merely my own capacity for fulfilling them. To see oneself called to a vocation which is almost divine, when after all one is only a man, is a great source of joy, if one really deserves it. But if, on the other hand, one is very unworthy of it, the prospects of the future are sombre. It is by no means a recent fear of mine, but a very old one, the fear of winning honour from men at the price of sinning against God.
>
> When I examine myself, I fail to find the capacity necessary to raise me to the sanctity of such a priesthood as this. I will now speak to you of the emotions of my soul: for I cannot speak to any one in preference to you who are so dear to me, and have been brought up with me. It is quite natural that you should share my anxieties, that you should watch with me during the night, and that by day we should search together whatever may bring me joy or turn sorrow away from me. Let me tell you, then, how my circumstances are, although you know in advance most of what I am going to say to you.
>
> I took up a light burden, and up to this moment I think I have borne it well. It is, in a word, philosophy. Inasmuch as I have never fallen too far below the level of the duties which it imposed upon me, people have praised me for my work. And I am regarded as capable of better things still, by those who do not know how to estimate in what directions my talents lie. Now, if I frivolously accept the dignity of the position which has been offered to me, I fear I may fail in both causes, slighting the one, without at the same time raising myself to the high level of the other. Consider the situation. All my days are divided between study and recreation. In my hours of work, above all when I am occupied with divine matters, I withdraw into myself. In my leisure hours I give myself up to my friends. For you know that when I look up from my books, I like to enter into every sort of sport. I do not share in the political turn of mind, either by nature or in my pursuits. [That statement seems to be at variance with his

own actions, however.] But the priest should be a man above human weaknesses. He should be a stranger to every sort of diversion, even as God Himself. All eyes are keeping watch on him to see that he justifies his mission. He is of little or no use unless he has made himself austere and unyielding towards any pleasure. In carrying out his holy office he should belong no longer to himself, but to all men. He is a teacher of the law, and must utter that which is approved by law. In addition to all this, he has as many calls upon him as all the rest of the world put together, for the affairs of all he alone must attend to, or incur the reproaches of all. Now, unless he has a great and noble soul, how can he sustain the weight of so many cares without his intellect being submerged? How can he keep the divine flame alive within him when such varied duties claim him on every side? I know well that there are such men. I have every admiration for their character, and I regard them as really divine men, whom intercourse with man's affairs does not separate from God. But I know myself also. I go down to the town, and from the town I come up again, always enveloped in thoughts that drag me down to earth, and covered with more stains than anybody could imagine. In a word, I have so many personal defilements of old date, that the slightest addition fills up my measure. My strength fails me. I have no strength and there is no health in me. I am not equal to confronting what is without me, and I am far from being able to bear the distress of my own conscience. If anybody asks me what my idea of a bishop is, I have no hesitation in saying explicity that he ought to be spotless, more than spotless, in all things, he to whom is allotted the purification of others.

In writing to you, my brother, I have still another thing to say. You will not be by any means the only one to read this letter. In addressing it to you, I wish above all things to make known to every one what I feel, so that whatever happens hereafter, no one will have a right to accuse me before God or before man, nor, above all, before the venerable Theophilus [the bishop of Alexandria]. In publishing my thoughts, and in giving myself up entirely to his decision, how can I be in the wrong? God himself, the law of the land, and the blessed hand of Theophilus himself have given me a wife. I, therefore, proclaim to all and call them to witness once for all that I will not be separated from her, nor shall I associate with her surreptitiously like an adulterer; for of these two acts, the one is impious, and the other is unlawful. I shall desire and pray to have many virtuous children. This is what I must inform the man upon whom depends my consecration. Let him learn this from his comrades Paul and Dionysius, for I understand that they have become his deputies by the will of the people.

There is one point, however, which is not new to Theophilus, but of which I must remind him. I must press my point here a little more, for beside his difficulty all the others are as nothing. It is difficult, if not quite impossible, that convictions should be shaken, which have entered the soul through knowledge to the point of demonstration. Now you know that philosophy rejects many of those convictions which are cherished by the common people. For my own part, I can never persuade myself that the soul is of more recent origin than the body. Never would I admit that the world and the parts which make it up must perish. This resurrection, which is an object of common belief, is nothing for me but a sacred and mysterious allegory, and I am far from sharing the views of the vulgar crowd thereon. The philosophic mind, albeit the discerner of truth, admits the employment of falsehood, for light is to truth what the eye is to the mind. Just as the eye would be injured by excess of light, and just as darkness is more helpful to those of weak eyesight, even so do I consider that the false may be beneficial to the populace, and the truth injurious to those not strong enough to gaze steadfastly on the radiance of real being. If the laws of the priesthood that obtain with us permit these views to me, I can take over the holy office on condition that I may prosecute philosophy at home and spread legends abroad, so that if I teach no doctrine, at all events I undo no teaching, and allow men to remain in their already acquired convictions. But if anybody says to me that he must be under this influence, that the bishop must belong to the people in his opinions, I shall betray myself very quickly. What can there be in common between the ordinary man and philosophy? Divine truth should remain hidden, but the vulgar need a different system. I shall never cease repeating that I think the wise man, to the extent that necessity allows, should not force his opinions upon others, nor allow others to force theirs upon him.

No, if I am called to the priesthood, I declare before God and man that I refuse to preach dogmas in which I do not believe. Truth is an attribute of God, and I wish in all things to be blameless before Him. This one thing I will not dissimulate. I feel that I have a good deal of inclination for amusements. Even as a child, I was charged with a mania for arms and horses. I shall be grieved, indeed greatly shall I suffer at seeing my beloved dogs deprived of their hunting, and my bow eaten up by worms. Nevertheless I shall resign myself to this, if it is the will of God. Again, I hate all care; nevertheless, whatever it costs, I will endure lawsuits and quarrels, so long as I can fulfil this mission, heavy though it be, according to God's will; but never will I consent to conceal my beliefs, nor shall my opinions be at war with my tongue. I believe that I am pleasing God in thinking and speaking thus. I do not wish to give any one the opportunity of saying that I, an unknown man, grasped at the appointment. But let the beloved of God, the right reverend Theophilus, knowing the situtation and giving me clear evidence that he understands it, decide on this issue concerning

> me. He will then either leave me by myself to lead my own life, and to philosophize, or he will not leave himself any grounds on which hereafter to sit in judgement over me, and to turn me out of the ranks of the priesthood. In comparison with these truths, every opinion is insignificant, for I know well that Truth is dearest to God. I swear it by your sacred head, nay, better still, I swear by God the guardian of Truth, that I suffer. How can I fail to suffer, when I must, as it were, remove from one life to another? But if after those things have been made clear which I least desire to conceal, if the man who holds this power from Heaven persists in putting me in the hierarchy of bishops, I will submit to the inevitable, and I will accept the token as divine, For I reason thus, that if the emperor or some ill-fated Augustal had given an order, I should have been punished if I disobeyed, but that one must obey God with a willing heart. But even at the expense of God's not admitting me to his service, I must nevertheless place first my love for Truth, the most divine thing of all. And I must not slip into His service through ways most opposed to it—such as falsehood. See then that the scholastici [We would say intellectuals of Alexandria] know well my sentiments, and that they inform Theophilus. (105)

No one who reads that letter could question the honesty of the man. Nor could they doubt that when he became a bishop in 410 he was energetic and outspoken. Although his letters are singularly lacking in quotations from the Scriptures and, as mentioned earlier, the wrangling over theological points did not interest him, he was nevertheless dutiful about prosecuting heretics, for they disturbed the peace of the community (5). Since such dissidents were spawned within the church, it was only proper for the church to sponsor their suppression.

Earlier, Synesius had criticized the soldiers sent to defend the area. Now he found that when able and courageous soldiers were available they were in danger of being demoralized. A letter sent in 411 to Anysius, an officer in the imperial army,[6] speaks of a problem affecting other remote regions as well. The central government does not understand the needs of the local situation.

> Nothing could be more advantageous to Pentapolis than to give honour to the Unnigardae, who are excellent both as men and as soldiers, in preference to all the other troops, not only those who are termed native troops, but also all that have ever come into these districts as auxiliary forces. The truth is that these latter, even when they were much superior to the enemy in numbers, never yet gave battle with courage, but the Unnigardae in two or three engagements, with a handful of forty men, engaged an enemy of over a thousand.[7]
>
> Assisted by God and led by you, they have gained the greatest and most glorious victories. The barbarians had scarcely shown themselves when

some were killed on the spot and others put to flight. They still patrol the heights, ever on the watch to drive back attacks of the enemy, like whelps springing out from the courtyard, that no wild beast may attack the flock. But we blush when we see these brave fellows weeping in the very midst of their strenuous service in our cause. It is not without sadness that I have read a letter which they have sent me, and I think that you also ought not to remain unmoved at their prayer. They make a request of you through me, and of the Emperor through you, which it were only fair that we ourselves should have made, even had they been silent, to wit, that their men should not be enrolled amongst the native units. They would be useless both to themselves and to us if they were deprived of the Emperor's largesses, and if, moreover, they were deprived of their relays of horses and of their equipment, and of the pay which is due to troops on active service. I beg of you who were the bravest amongst these, not to allow your comrades-in-arms to enter an inferior rank, but to let them remain without loss of their honours, in the security of their former position.

This might well be, if our most kind Emperor should learn through your representation how useful they have been to Pentapolis. Make of the Emperor another request on my behalf in your letter, namely, to add one hundred and sixty of these soldiers to the forty that we have already; for who would not admit that two hundred Unnigardae, with the aid of God, like unto these in heart and hand, and no less docile than brave, would suffice, when commanded by you, to bring the Ausurian war to an end for the Emperor? Of what use are many levies and the annual cost of maintaining the troops here? For war we need hands, not a list of names. (78)

Andronicus, the brutal and corrupt governor of Cyrenaica in 411, would have been an affront to any humane and civil man. Synesius describes this official's cruelty in a letter to Anastasius.[8]

I have not been able to do anything for the presbyter Evagrius any more than for any other of the wronged. We have Andronicus of Berenice for ruler, a wicked fellow, whose soul and tongue are equally detestable. It is of no consequence that he holds me in small esteem, but, what is more grave, he appears to me to be ashamed to reverence those things which are divine. In his pride he strikes heaven with his head. I swear by your dear and sacred head that he has wound a web of suffering about Pentapolis. He has invented thumb-screws and instruments of torture for the feet, and other strange machinery for inflicting punishments, which he employs, not against any guilty people, for every one is now free to do evil, but rather against those who pay property-tax, or who owe money in any shape or form. . . . Ever he finds some new evil to add to an old one, whereby torture may be inflicted on whole tribes and peoples. You may be as rich as you please and have plenty of money to pay with; nevertheless you will not escape the lash. Sometimes, while the slave is dispatched to the house to seek his master's ransom, the master is cudgelled, and runs the risk of losing several of his fingers. When Andronicus is without a pretext for making a banquet of cruelty, he falls back upon Maximinus and Clinias, and gratifies his passion upon them. A man so evil as this must, I think, be under the special protection of evil spirits, who pour honours and wealth upon perverted souls whom they use as their tools for the persecution of mankind. . . . When I was away, Andronicus courted my power, for that I twice saved him at Alexandria from prison. When I came back here, however, he showed himself quite another man to me; by your sacred head, I swear it. When I was so unfortunate as to lose the dearest of my children, I might even have rid me of my life, so crushed was I with grief, and grief has always found me too much like a woman, as you know well. If I ended by overcoming my grief, this was not by any effort of my reason. It was Andronicus who changed the whole current of my ideas, and compelled me to think about nothing except public disasters. Troubles have become for me a consolation for troubles, drawing me towards them, and pushing out grief by grief. All the sadness that I felt for the death of my boy has given way to another sort of sadness mingled with wrath. You must know that my death had been predicted to fall upon a certain day of the year. That day turned out to be the one on which I entered on the priesthood. I felt a change in my life, I who up to the moment have held festal assemblies in it, and have enjoyed honour from men, and benevolence such as has been granted to no philosopher before me—no less outwardly than in the state of the soul.

Today I am conscious of the loss of all these things, but the greatest of all my afflictions, and one which makes my life actually one of despair, is that, while accustomed up to this moment to find my prayers listened to, I now know for the first time that I appeal to God in vain. I see my house faring ill. I am compelled to dwell in my native city at a time of distress. I am situated so that all come to me to weep and groan, each for his own troubles. Andronicus has put the finishing touch to my misfortunes; for because of him I never enjoy for a moment the leisure to which I am accustomed. I am unable to be of any assistance to any of those who come to me for help, I am condemned to endure them when they reproach me for my helplessness. I therefore implore and supplicate both of you, but more especially you who are so dear to me, brother Anastasius, and who are said to be a protector of a demented man; if you possess any power, use it, as is only right, in behalf of Synesius rather than of Andronicus, and save Ptolemais from shame, I beg you, that city which appointed me

> its bishop against my own will—as the all-seeing eye of God knoweth. I know not for what misdeeds I am paying so heavy a retribution. If we have incurred aforetimes the envy of any one of the gods, as the saying is, we have made ample expiation. (79)

Although Synesius sounded helpless in that letter, Bregman writes: "It is obvious that such bishops operating in sensitive areas could be useful to the emperors: they could act as a check on members of the imperial administration over whom the emperors had very little control." So, he suggests Synesius was unduly depressed, for "when [he] became bishop, his bold excommunication of the tyrannical provincial governor Andronicus probably checked Andronicus's ambitions and suppressed potential trouble" (p. 175).

Synesius had only a brief tenure as bishop and wrote his last letter to Hypatia from his deathbed in 412 or 413.[9]

> I am dictating this letter to you from my bed, but may you receive it in good health, mother, sister, teacher, and withal benefactress, and whatsoever is honoured in name and deed. For me bodily weakness has followed in the wake of mental suffering. The remembrance of my departed children is consuming my forces, little by little. Only so long should Synesius have lived as he was still without experience of the evils of life. It is as if a torrent long pent up had burst upon me in full volume, and as if the sweetness of life had vanished. May I either cease to live, or cease to think of the tomb of my sons! But may you preserve your health and give my salutations to your happy comrades in turn, beginning with father Theotecnus and brother Athanasius, and so to all! And if any one has been added to these, so long as he is dear to you, I must owe him gratitude because he is dear to you, and to that man give my greetings as to my own dearest friend. If any of my affairs interests you, you do well, and if any of them does not so interest you, neither does it me. (16)

So it was that Synesius died about two years before his beloved teacher was killed by a mob of unruly Christians. It has been believed by some that those who murdered Hypatia were urged on to the deed by Cyril, the bishop of Alexandria, an ardent foe of philosophical speculation.[10] Although there is no agreement about Cyril's role in the event, nobody could doubt that Synesius, who abhorred fanaticism, would have been appalled by what happened.

In the early fifth century, Synesius rose to be bishop in a major province because his strong leadership abilities were needed. Fifty years later, under pressure from a different set of barbarians, the same qualities were needed to defend the province of Gaul. There, too, Sidonius Apollinaris, an aristocrat and an intellectual, became bishop more for his leadership abilities than for his religiosity.

XIV SIDONIUS APOLLINARIS

Champion of a Lost Cause

THE barbarian invasions played a well-known role in the decline and fall of the Roman Empire. Yet in accounts of those dire times, the years, even decades, rush by, and the days seem lost altogether. The 157 letters of Sidonius Apollinaris slow the pace and offer a different perspective. Actually, life did go on rather more normally than might be expected.

Sidonius's lifetime in the fifth century spanned the final years of the western Roman Empire. When he was born in Lyons in 430 or 431, the Vandals were already conquering North Africa, and the Burgundians and Visigoths had begun moving into Spain and Gaul. Shortly after his death, sometime in the 480s, an Ostrogothic king would rule in Italy (technically on behalf of the eastern Roman Empire at Constantinople, but actually on his own). The former imperial provinces of the west, including Gaul, had become barbarian kingdoms. So Sidonius, once a proud and valiant Roman citizen, died a subject of a Visigothic king. Although history texts now make it all very obvious, that fate could not at the time have been foreseen.

Sidonius's ancestors belonged to the old pagan aristocracy in Gaul, his grandfather being the first to be converted to Christianity. They were prominent office holders in the Roman province and very well connected. Sidonius married Papianilla, the daughter of one of the last short-term emperors of Rome. Eparchius Avitus was proclaimed and deposed in the same year, 455, and killed shortly thereafter by the barbarian commander Ricimer. If a distinguished career thus ended in failure, so did his personal hopes for the future of Gaul. Avitus was one member of the Roman-Gallo nobility who favored cooperation with the Visigoths rather than defiant resistance. Indeed, since he was not recognized as emperor by Constantinople, he may have wanted to strengthen his position with the help of the Visigoths. That his bodyguard in Rome was made up of Goths was a telltale sign. His young son-in-law seems to have shared his views. One of his letters, written to his brother-in-law

Agricola about 454[1] after a visit to the Visigothic court in Toulouse, drew a most flattering picture of King Theodoric II, who ruled from 453 to 466.

Although Sidonius was obviously going out of his way to give a good impression of the king, it is still apparent that the roughness of the barbarians, at least at the highest level, was being tempered by association with Roman civility.

> You have often begged a description of Theodoric the Gothic king, whose gentle breeding fame commends to every nation; you want him in his quantity and quality, in his person, and the manner of his existence. I gladly accede, as far as the limits of my page allow, and highly approve so fine and ingenuous a curiosity.
>
> Well, he is a man worth knowing, even by those who cannot enjoy his close acquaintance, so happily have Providence and Nature joined to endow him with the perfect gifts of fortune; his way of life is such that not even the envy which lies in wait for a king can rob him of his proper praise. And first as to his person. He is well set up, in height above the average man, but below the giant. His head is round, with curled hair retreating somewhat from brow to crown. His nervous neck is free from disfiguring knots. The eyebrows are bushy and arched; when the lids droop, the lashes reach almost half-way down the cheeks. The upper ears are buried under overlying locks, after the fashion of his race. The nose is finely aquiline; the lips are thin and not enlarged by undue distention of the mouth. Every day the hair springing from his nostrils is cut back; that on the face springs thick from the hollow of the temples, but the razor has not yet come upon his cheek, and his barber is assiduous in eradicating the rich growth on the lower part of the face. Chin, throat, and neck are full, but not fat, and all of fair complexion; seen close, their colour is fresh as that of youth; they often flush, but from modesty, and not from anger. His shoulders are smooth, the upper- and forearms strong and hard; hands broad, breast prominent; waist receding. The spine dividing the broad expanse of back does not project, and you can see the spring of the ribs; the sides swell with salient muscle, the well-girt flanks are full of vigour. His thighs are like hard horn; the knee-joints firm and masculine; the knees themselves the comeliest and least wrinkled in the world. A full ankle supports the leg, and the foot is small to bear such mighty limbs.
>
> Now for the routine of his public life. Before daybreak he goes with a very small suite to attend the service of his priests.[2] He prays with assiduity, but, if I may speak in confidence, one may suspect more of habit than conviction in this piety. Administrative duties of the kingdom take up the rest of the morning. Armed nobles stand about the royal seat; the mass of guards in their garb of skins are admitted that they may be within call, but kept at the threshold for quiet's sake; only a murmur of them comes

in from their post at the doors, between the curtain and the outer barrier. And now the foreign envoys are introduced. The king hears them out, and says little; if a thing needs more discussion he puts it off, but accelerates matters ripe for dispatch. The second hour arrives; he rises from the throne to inspect his treasure-chamber or stable. If the chase is the order of the day, he joins it, but never carries his bow at his side, considering this derogatory to royal state. When a bird or beast is marked for him, or happens to cross his path, he puts his hand behind his back and takes the bow from a page with the string all hanging loose; for as he deems it a boy's trick to bear it in a quiver, so he holds it effeminate to receive the weapon ready strung. When it is given him, he sometimes holds it in both hands and bends the extremities towards each other; at others he sets it, knot-end downward, against his lifted heel, and runs his finger up the slack and wavering string. After that, he takes his arrows, adjusts, and lets fly. He will ask you beforehand what you would like him to transfix; you choose, and he hits. If there is a miss through either's error, your vision will mostly be at fault, and not the archer's skill.

On ordinary days, his table resembles that of a private person. The board does not groan beneath a mass of dull and unpolished silver set on by panting servitors; the weight lies rather in the conversation than in the plate; there is either sensible talk or none. The hangings[3] and draperies used on these occasions are sometimes of purple silk, sometimes only of linen; art, not costliness, commends the fare, as spotlessness rather than bulk the silver. Toasts are few, and you will oftener see a thirsty guest impatient, than a full one refusing cup or bowl. In short, you will find elegance of Greece, good cheer of Gaul, Italian nimbleness, the state of public banquets with the attentive service of a private table, and everywhere the discipline of a king's house. What need for me to describe the pomp of his feast days? No man is so unknown as not to know of them. But to my theme again. The siesta after dinner is always slight and sometimes intermitted. When inclined for the board-game, he is quick to gather up the dice, examines them with care, shakes the box with expert hand, throws rapidly, humorously apostrophizes them, and patiently waits the issue. Silent at a good throw, he makes merry over a bad, annoyed by neither fortune, and always the philosopher. He is too proud to ask or to refuse a revenge; he disdains to avail himself of one if offered; and if it is opposed will quietly go on playing. You effect recovery of your man without obstruction on his side; he recovers his without collusion upon yours. You see the strategist when he moves the pieces; his one thought is victory. Yet at play he puts off a little of his kingly rigour, inciting all to good fellowship and the freedom of the game: I think he is afraid of being feared. Vexation in the man whom he beats delights him; he will never believe that his opponents have not

> let him win unless their annoyance proves him really victor. You would be surprised how often the pleasure born of these little happenings may favour the march of great affairs. . . . I myself am gladly beaten by him when I have a favor to ask, since the loss of my game may mean the gaining of my cause. About the ninth hour, the burden of government begins again. Back come the importunates, back the ushers to remove them; on all sides buzz the voices of petitioners, a sound which lasts till evening, and does not diminish till interrrupted by the royal repast; even then they disperse to attend their various patrons among the courtiers, and are astir till bedtime. Sometimes, though this is rare, supper is enlivened by sallies of mimes, but no guest is ever exposed to the wound of a biting tongue. Withal there is no noise of hydraulic organ, or choir with its conductor intoning a set piece; you will hear no players of lyre of flute, no master of the music, no girls with cithara or tabor; the king cares for no strains but those which no less charm the mind with virtue than the ear with melody. When he rises to withdraw, the treasury watch begins its vigil; armed sentries stand on guard during the first hours of slumber. But I am wandering from my subject. I never promised a whole chapter on the kingdom, but a few words about the king. I must stay my pen; you asked for nothing more than one or two facts about the person and the tastes of Theodoric; and my own aim was to write a letter, not a history. (I.ii)[4]

That the barbarians were as fond of colorful processions as were the Romans is evident in Sidonius's account of the young Frankish prince Sigismer visiting the palace of his future Burgundian father-in-law. Sidonius's letter to his friend Domicius, written about 470, gives a frequently cited eyewitness account of the manner in which the now very rich barbarians were adorning themselves.

> You take such pleasure in the sight of arms and those who wear them, that I can imagine your delight if you could have seen the young prince Sigismer on his way to the palace of his father-in-law in the guise of a bridegroom or suitor in all the pomp and bravery of the tribal fashion. His own steed with its caparisons, other steeds laden with flashing gems, paced before and after; but the conspicuous interest in the procession centred in the prince himself, as with a charming modesty he went afoot amid his bodyguard and footmen, in flame-red mantle, with much glint of ruddy gold, and gleam of snowy silken tunic, his fair hair, red cheeks and white skin according with the three hues of his equipment. But the chiefs and allies who bore him company were dread of aspect, even thus on peace intent. Their feet were laced in boots of bristly hide reaching to the heels; ankles and legs were exposed. They wore high tight tunics of varied colour hardly descending to their bare knees, the sleeves covering only the upper

arm. Green mantles they had with crimson borders; baldrics supported swords hung from their shoulders, and pressed on sides covered with cloaks of skin secured by brooches. No small part of their adornment consisted of their arms; in their hands they grasped barbed spears and missile axes; their left sides were guarded by shields, which flashed with tawny golden bosses and snowy silver borders, betraying at once their wealth and their good taste. Though the business in hand was wedlock, Mars was no whit less prominent in all this pomp than Venus. Why need I say more? Only your presence was wanting to the full enjoyment of so fine a spectacle. For when I saw that you had missed the things you love to see, I longed to have you with me in all the impatience of your longing soul. (IV.xx)

The anxiousness of many Gallo-Romans to seek an accomodation with the Visigoths and the Burgundians was an advantage which the barbarians could cunningly exploit. It is usually assumed that the barbarians appeared out of a cloud of dust and seized the land. Actually, much of Gaul was given to them as part of an imperial appeasement policy. Turning over land to the less ferocious Burgundians may have kept them at bay, but the aggressive Visigoths kept pressing for more. One of the areas which they attacked was the region of Auvergne where Sidonius possessed an estate, Avitacum, which had belonged to his father-in-law, Avitus. By the time the Visigoths had begun to raid this land every year, he had become the leader of those who were determined to fight back. Thus, by circumstance, did the earlier ideal of cooperation give way to defiance.

In 469, upon the death of the local Bishop of Clermont, Sidonius, being a man of prominence and experience, was, by popular consent, chosen to succeed him. He was expected to be the political and military leader of his diocese as well as its spiritual guide, and he carried out his duties conscientiously, visiting his parishes and exercising a paternal, if patronizing, jurisdiction. Although neither profoundly pious nor well versed in Scripture or theology, Sidonius did recognize and respect those qualities in others. At the time of the following letter, written in 474 to the Bishop Mamertus of Vienne, Auvergne was being threatened by the Visigoths. Sidonius discusses the severity of his problems and his need for divine assistance.

Rumour has it that the Goths have occupied Roman soil; our unhappy Auvergne is always their gateway on every such incursion. It is our fate to furnish fuel to the fire of a peculiar hatred, for, by Christ's aid, we are the sole obstacle to the fulfilment of their ambition to extend their frontiers to the Rhone, and so hold all the country between that river, the Atlantic, and the Loire. Their menacing power has long pressed us hard; it has already swallowed up whole tracts of territory round us, and threatens to swallow more. We mean to resist with spirit, though we know our peril and the risks which we incur. But our trust is not in our poor walls impaired by fire, or in our rotting palisades, or in our ramparts worn by the breasts of the sentries, as they lean on them in continual watch. Our only present help we find in those Rogations[5] which you introduced; and this is the reason why the people of Clermont refuse to recede, though terrors surge about them on every side. By inauguration and institution of these prayers we are already new initiates; and if so far we have effected less than you have, our hearts are affected equally with yours. For it is not unknown to us by what portents and alarms the city entrusted to you by God was laid desolate at the time when first you ordained this form of prayer. Now it was earthquake, shattering the outer palace walls with frequent shocks; now fire, piling mounds of glowing ash upon proud houses fallen in ruin; now, amazing spectacle! wild deer grown ominously tame, making their lairs in the very forum. You saw the city being emptied of its inhabitants, rich and poor taking to flight. But you resorted in our latter day to the example shown of old in Nineveh,[6] that you at least might not discredit the divine warning by the spectacle of your despair. And, indeed, you of all men had been least justified in distrusting the providence of God, after the proof of it vouchsafed to your own virtues. Once, in a sudden conflagration, your faith burned stronger than the flames. In full sight of the trembling crowd, you stood forth all alone to stay them, and lo! the fire leapt back before you, a sinuous beaten fugitive. It was miracle, a formidable thing, unseen before and unexampled; the element which naturally shrinks from nothing, retired in awe at your approach. You therefore first enjoined a fast upon a few members of our sacred order, denouncing gross offences, announcing punishment, promising relief. You made it clear that if the penalty of sin was nigh, so also was the pardon; you proclaimed that by frequent prayer the menace of coming desolation might be removed. You taught that it was by water of tears rather than water of rivers that the obstinate and raging fire could best be extinguished, and by firm faith the threatening shock of earthquake stayed. The multitude of the lowly forthwith followed your counsel, and this influenced persons of higher rank, who had not scrupled to abandon the town, and now were not ashamed to return to it. By this devotion God was appeased, who sees into all hearts; your fervent prayers were counted to you for salvation; they became an example for your fellow citizens, and a defence about you all, for after those days there were neither portents to alarm, nor visitations to bring disaster.

We of Clermont know that all these ills befell your people of Vienne before the Rogations, and have not befallen them since; and therefore it is that we are eager to follow the lead of so holy a guide, beseeching your Beatitude from your own pious lips to give us the advocacy of those prayers now known to us by the examples which you have transmitted. Since the Confessor Ambrose[7] discovered the remains of Gervasius and Protasius, it

> has been granted to you alone in the West to translate the relics of two martyrs—all the holy body of Ferreolus, and the head of our martyr Julian, which once the executioner's gory hand brought to the raging persecutor from the place of testimony. It is only fair, then, in compensation for the loss of this hallowed relic, that some part of your patronage should come to us from Vienne, since a part of our patronal saint has migrated thither. Deign to hold us in remembrance, my Lord Bishop. (VII. i)

That Sidonius fought so bravely to defend Clermont increased his great indignation that it was at last given away by negotiation. Auvergne had looked to Rome for help but received none. Instead a group of four other Gaulish bishops were empowered to enter into talks with the Visigoths, or perhaps they only ratified what had been decided by others. The details are vague, but the result plain; the whole territory of Auvergne was ceded to Euric, the Visigothic king who had murdered his brother Theodoric II and imposed a harsher rule.[8]

All Sidonius could do was write to his friend, the scholarly Graecus of Marseilles, one of the four bishops who handed over the land. The letter that follows tells the story of the fifth century. Here is the bitterness of a patriotic Roman who had been sold out. He is writing, likely in 475, a polite, if frank, letter to a fellow bishop in the Christian faith.

> Here is Amantius, the usual bearer of my trifles; off once more to his Marseilles, to bring home a little profit out of the city, if he is fortunate in his business at the port. I could use the opportunity of his journey to gossip gaily on, if a mind that bears a load of sorrow could at the same time think of cheerful things. For the state of our unhappy region is miserable indeed. Every one declares that things were better in war-time than they are now after peace has been concluded. Our enslavement was made the price of security for a third party; the enslavement, ah! the shame of it! of those Arvernians who by old tradition claimed brotherhood with Latium and descent from the sons of Troy; who in our own time stood forth alone to stay the advance of the common enemy; who even when closely beset so little feared the Goth that they sallied out against his leaguer, and put the fear of their valour into his heart. These are the men whose common soldiers were as good as captains, but who never reaped the benefits of their victories: that was handed over for your consolation, while all the crushing burden of defeat they had to bear themselves. These are the patriots who did not fear to bring to justice the infamous Seronatus, betrayer of imperial provinces to the barbarian, while the State for which they risked so much had hardly the courage on his conviction to carry out the capital sentence. And this is to be our reward for braving destitution, fire, sword, and pestilence, for fleshing our swords in the enemy's blood and

going ourselves starved into battle. This, then, is the famous peace[9] we dreamed of, when we tore the grass from the crannies in the walls to eat; when in our ignorance we often by mistake ate poisonous weeds, indiscriminately plucking them with livid hands of starvation, hardly less green than they. For all these proofs of our devotion, it would seem that we are to be made a sacrifice. If it be so, may you live to blush for a peace without either honour or advantage. For you are the channel through which negotiations are conducted. When the king is absent, you not only see the terms of peace, but new proposals are brought before you. I ask your pardon for telling you hard truths; my distress must take all colour of abuse from what I say. You think too little of the general good; when you meet in council, you are less concerned to relieve public perils than to advance private fortunes. By the long repetition of such acts you begin to be regarded as the last instead of the first among your fellow provincials. But how long are these feats of yours to last? Our ancestors will cease to glory in the name of Rome if they have no longer descendants to bear their memory. Oh, break their memory. Oh, break this infamous peace at any cost; there are pretexts enough to your hand. We are ready, if needs must, to continue the struggle and to undergo more sieges and starvations. But if we are to be betrayed, we whom force failed to conquer, we shall know beyond a doubt that a barbarous and cowardly transaction was inspired by you.

But it little avails to give the rein to passionate sorrow; you must make allowance for us in our affliction, nor too nicely weigh the language of despair. The other conquered regions have only servitude to expect; Auvergne must prepare for punishment. If you can hold out no help in our extremity, seek to obtain of Heaven by your unceasing prayers that though our liberty be doomed, our race at least may live. Provide land for the exile, prepare a ransom for the captive, make provision for the emigrant. If our own walls must offer an open breach to the enemy, let yours be never shut against your friends. Deign to hold me in remembrance, my Lord Bishop. (VII. vii)

While Sidonius considered the treaty an outrageous betrayal of a brave resistance, he was not too hard on Graecus, a man of peace, trying to do his best under the circumstances. There were, after all, townsmen of Clermont itself who would willingly have submitted to Euric rather than endure the horrors of the siege. Worse, some Gallo-Romans became informers for the barbarian kings, reporting on their fellow countrymen. Dealing secretly with the Visigoths was an old story. At an earlier time, in 468, Sidonius wrote to his friend Vincentius about a Roman official, Arvandus, who had been trapped by a letter he had written urging the king of the Goths to divide the Gallic provinces with the Burgundians. Sidonius says the letter was intercepted, and the secretary who had taken the dictation testified against his master. The treasonous Arvandus was condemned to death after his trial in Rome, but may not actually have been executed.

Sidonius's report to Vincentius about these events begins with a passage which says something about himself. He was a constant friend with a good heart even toward a foolish man who had been disgraced.

> The case of Arvandus distresses me, nor do I conceal my distress, for it is our emperor's crowning praise that a condemned prisoner may have friends who need not hide their friendship. I was more intimate with this man than it was safe to be with one so light and so unstable, witness the odium lately kindled against me on his account, the flame of which has scorched me for this lapse from prudence. But since I had given my friendship, honour bound me fast, though he on his side has no steadfastness at all; I say this because it is the truth and not to strike him when he is down. For he despised friendly advice and made himself throughout the sport of fortune; the marvel to me is, not that he fell at last, but that he ever stood so long. (I.vii)

After Auvergne was given to the Goths, Sidonius was sent to prison for having rallied his followers to such a pitch of patriotism and bravery. In the following letter, written after his release, he adds a brief comment about that unhappy experience. He is writing to his friend Leo, who was one of the ministers of Euric and so in a position to have helped him get out of prison, where he had spent about a year. Bowing to circumstances certain of the Gallo-Romans were willing to serve at the Visigothic and Burgundian courts, where, as in Sidonius's case, they did what good they could.

> I send you, at your request, the *Life of Apollonius the Pythagorean*, not in the transcription by Nicomachus the Elder, from Philostratus, but in that from Nicomachus himself by Tascius Victorianus. I was so eager to fulfil your wish, that the result is a makeshift of a copy, obscure and over-hurried, and rough as any version could be. Yet the work took me longer than I expected, and for this you must not blame me, for all the time I was a captive within the walls of Livia,[10] release from which I owe, next to Christ, to you. My mind was sick with care and really unable to fulfil my task even in the most desultory manner; all kinds of hindrances prevented me—various obligations by day, my utter misery at night. When the evening hour brought me at last to my quarters, ready to drop with fatigue, my heavy eyelids knew small repose; there were two old Gothic women established quite close to the window of my chamber, who at once began their chatter—quarrelsome, drunken, and disgusting creatures, whose like will not easily be seen again. As soon as my restoration to my own

home gave me a little leisure, I dispatched the book with all its faults upon it, uncorrected, ill-digested, as you might say, an immature wine; in doing so, I thought more of your anxiety to have it, than of my own responsibilities. Now that your wish is gratified, forsake awhile Apollo's bays and the fount of Hippocrene; forget the measures of which you alone are absolute master, and which, in those who have only your learning without your eloquence, seem not so much to rise from a well-spring as to drip painfully from fevered brows. Stay the renowned stream of an eloquence peculiar to your race and line, which, flowing from your ancestor the great Fronto through successive generations, has now passed in due course into your breast. Lay aside awhile the universally applauded speeches composed for the royal lips,[11] those famed deliverances with which the glorious monarch from his exalted place strikes terror into the hearts of tribes beyond the seas, or binds a treaty on the necks of barbarians trembling by the Waal, [the Franks], or throughout his newly extended realm curbs force.[12] Shake off the burden of your endless cares and steal a little leisure from the affairs and agitations of the court. Not till you surrender yourself wholly to this book, and in imagination voyage with our Tyaneus to Caucasus and Ind, among the Gymnosophists of Ethiopia and the Brahmins of Hindostan, not till then shall you know the story you desired in its right hour and as it should be known. Read, then, the life of a man who, but for his paganism, in many points resembled you, as one who did not pursue riches, but was pursued by the rich; who loved knowledge and did not covet money; who was abstemious among the feasters and went in coarse linen among princes robed in purple; who was grave amid luxurious follies. (VIII.iii)

Either immediately after his imprisonment or a few years later, Sidonius spent some time in Bordeaux, where Euric had his court, seeking satisfaction about land left to him by his mother-in-law, Avitus's widow. The estate was occupied by a Visigoth who had, as usual in such cases, appropriated two-thirds of it. Sidonius was not able even to claim what was left and so wanted a ruling from Euric on the matter. He never got it, and it was obvious to him why. In a letter to his friend Lampridius he says the powerful king was far too busy accepting the obedience of other barbarians. "Here the Burgundian bends his seven feet of stature of suppliant knee, imploring peace" (VIII.ix). Sidonius was now greatly impressed by Euric, even as earlier he had been impressed by Theodoric II. Then, it was because he wanted to be. Now, it was because he had to be. But while his poems might speak of the bravery of the barbarians, in his heart he never learned to like them, and privately he spoke of their "bestial dullness" (IV. i).

For the remainder of his life, with Auvergne now part of the Visigothic kingdom, Sidonius settled into a quiet routine of church duties with his leisure time given to producing a great variety of writings. His theological tracts have disappeared, and his poetry has received at most faint praise, but his letters remain as a major source of news about the fifth century, although, to be sure, that was not his purpose in writing them. O. M. Dalton's two volume work, *The Letters of Sidonius*, from which the letters of this chapter are taken, declares the correspondence to be "in many ways the richest source of information on Roman provincial life during the last years of the Empire in the West" (p. iii). For instance, it is only from Sidonius's letters that anything is known about the Visigothic attack on Auvergne. Sidonius, however, saw the letters in literary terms, not as history, which he steadfastly refused to write though urged to do so.

As Dalton points out, if Sidonius had wanted to seize the opportunity to serve history he would have had much more to say about the unfolding events of his time. His letters say almost nothing about the working classes or about any women of whatever status. Here is a passage which suggests his attitude toward people in general: "We had public prayers of a sort . . . but (be it said without offence to the faithful) they were lukewarm, irregular, perfunctory, and their fervour was destroyed by frequent interruption for refreshment" (V.xiv).

Letter writing was simply a refined cultural exercise that gave Sidonius and his friends a small remaining edge over the powerful barbarians. If in those unhappy times they could find any comfort or continuity, it was in their aristocratic heritage. The landed gentry of Gaul may have lost much of their vast estates to the barbarians, but they nevertheless continued an accustomed style of living and retained a strong sense of class consciousness. The following letter by Sidonius, written about 472 to his relative Avitus, attests to the ties which bound friendships through several generations among aristocratic families.

> From our earliest boyhood and through our youth you and I have been linked by many bonds of mutual affection. To begin with, our mothers were very near relations. Then we were born about the same time and were contemporaries at school; we were together initiated into the study of the arts and employed our leisure in the same amusements; we were promoted by the same imperial favour; we were colleagues in the service of the state. Lastly, in personal likings and antipathies our judgement has always agreed—perhaps a stronger and more efficient factor this, in widening the scope of friendship than all the rest together. The outward resemblance of our careers drew us together by the bond of similar occupation; inwardly we were less alike, for yours was by far the higher and more excellent nature. And now I gladly recognize that yours is the hand to crown the edifice of our long mutual regard by this most timely endowment of the church in our poor town of Clermont, whose unworthy bishop I am. In this estate of Cutiacum, lying almost at its gates, you have indeed made an important addition to its property; to the members of our sacred profession whom

> your generosity has thus enriched, the convenience of access counts for almost as much as the revenue which the place yields. Under your late sister's will, you were only a co-heir, but the example of your piety has already moved your surviving sister to emulate your good works. And heaven has already repaid you as you deserve for your own deed and its effect upon her; God has chosen you out to be exalted by unusual good fortune in inheritances. He did not long delay to reward your devotion a hundredfold, and it is our sure belief that these earthly gifts will be followed by heavenly gifts hereafter. (III.i)

The tone of that letter, with its sense of a special kind of life set apart from the common people, is reminiscent of Pliny the Younger (see Chapter III). The attitude of such men may sound smug, and so it was, but to them naturally so. Pliny's letters were known to earlier authors such as Tertullian, but Sidonius was the first one to quote from them extensively. He, in fact, admitted to using them as models for his own, even to the point of publishing his personal correspondence in the same number of nine books. There are often striking parallels. In a letter, probably written in the 460s, inviting his friend Domitius to visit during the summer, Sidonius gives a detailed description of his country estate and its surroundings. Although written nearly four centuries after Pliny's description of his villa at Laurentium, the letter shows how little life for the well-to-do had changed in that time.

> You may like to know the kind of place to which you are invited. We are at the estate known as Avitacum, a name of sweeter sound in my ears than my own patrimony because it came to me with my wife. Infer the harmony which established between me and mine; it is God's ordinance; but you might be pardoned for fearing it the work of some enchantment.
>
> On the west rises a big hill, pretty steep but not rocky, from which issue two lower spurs, like branches from a double trunk, extending over an area of about four jugera. But while the ground opens out enough to form a broad approach to the front door, the straight slopes on either side lead a valley right to the boundary of the villa, which faces north and south. On the southwest are the baths, which so closely adjoin a wooded eminence that if timber is cut on the hill above, the piles of logs slide down almost by their own weight, and are brought up against the very mouth of the furnace. At this point is the hot bath, which corresponds in size with the adjoining *unguentarium*, except that it has an apse with a semi-circular basin; here the hot water pressing through the sinuous lead pipes that pierce the wall issues with a sobbing sound. The chamber itself is well heated from beneath; it is full of day, and so overflowing with light that very modest bathers seem to themselves something more than naked. Next come the spacious *frigidarium*, which may fairly challenge comparison with those in

public baths. The roof is pyramidal, and the spaces between the converging ridges are covered with imbricated tiles; the architect has inserted two opposite windows about the junction of walls and dome, so that if you look up, you see the fine coffering displayed to the best advantage. The interior walls are unpretentiously covered with plain white stucco, and the apartment is designed by the nicest calculation of space to contain the same number of persons as the semicircular bath holds bathers, while it yet allows the servants to move about without impeding one another. No frescoed scene obtrudes its comely nudities, gracing the art to the disgrace of the artist. You will observe no painted actors in absurd masks, and costumes rivalling Philistio's gear with colours gaudy as the rainbow. You will find no pugilists or wrestlers intertwining their oiled limbs in those grips which, in real bouts, the gymnasiarch's chaste wand unlocks the moment the enlaced limbs look indecent. Enough you will see upon these walls none of those things which it is nicer not to look upon. A few verses there are, harmless lines enough, since no one either regrets perusal or cares to peruse again. If you want to know what marbles are employed, neither Paros nor Carystos, nor Proconnesos, nor Phrygia, nor Numidia, nor Sparta have contributed their diverse inlays. I had no use for stone that simulates a broken surface, with Ethiopic crags and purple precipices stained with genuine murex. Though enriched by no cold splendour of foreign marble, my poor huts and hovels do not lack the coolness to which a plain citizen may aspire. But now I had really better talk about the things I have, than the things I lack. With this hall is connected on the eastern side an annexe, a piscina, or, if you prefer the Greek word, baptistery, with a capacity of about twenty thousand modii. Into this the bathers pass from the hot room by three arched entrances in the dividing wall. The supports are not piers but columns, which your experienced architect calls the glory of buildings. Into this piscina, then, a stream lured from the brow of the hill is conducted in channels curving round the outside of the swimming basin; it issues through six pipes terminating in lion's heads which, to one entering rapidly, seem to present real fangs, authentic fury of eyes, indubitable manes. When the master of the house stands here with his household or his guests about him, people have to shout in each other's ears, or the noise of falling water makes their words inaudible; the interference of this alien sound forces conversations which are quite public to assume an amusing air of secrecy. On leaving this chamber you see in front of you the withdrawing-room; adjoining it is a storeroom, separated only by a movable partition from the place where the maids do our weaving.

On the east side a portico commands the lake, supported by simple wooden pillars instead of pretentious monumental columns. On the side of the front entrance is a long covered space unbroken by interior divisions;

it may be incorrect to call this a hypodrome, but I may fairly award it the name of cryptoporticus. At the end it is curtailed by a section cut off to form a delightfully cool bay, and here when we keep open festival, the whole chattering chorus of nurses and dependents sounds a halt when the family retires for the siesta.

The winter dining-room is entered from this cryptoporticus; a roaring fire on an arched hearth often fills this apartment with smoke and smuts. But that detail I may spare you; a glowing hearth is the last thing I am inviting you to enjoy just now. I pass instead to things which suit the season and your present need. From here one enters a smaller chamber or dining-room, all open to the lake and with almost the whole expanse of lake in its view. This chamber is furnished with a dining-couch and gleaming sideboard upon a raised area or dais to which you mount gradually, and not by abrupt or narrow steps from the portico below. Reclining at this table you can give the idle moments between the courses to the enjoyment of the prospect. . . . From table you may watch the fisherman row his boat out to mid-lake, and spread his seine with cork floats, or suspend his liners at marked intervals to lure the greedy trout on their nightly excursions through the lake with bait of their own flesh and blood: what phrase more proper, since fish is literally caught by fish? The meal over, we pass into a withdrawing-room, which its coolness makes a perfect place in summer. Facing north, it receives all the daylight but no direct sun: a very small intervening chamber accommodates the drowsy servants, large enough to allow them forty winks but not a regular sleep. It is delightful to sit here and listen to the shrill cicala at noon, the croak of frogs in the gloaming, the clangour of swans and geese in the earlier night or the crow of cocks in the dead of it, the ominous voice of rooks saluting the rosy face of Dawn in chorus, or, in the half-light, nightingales fluting in the bushes and swallows twittering under the eaves. . . . Accord me, then, the grace of coming quickly; your return shall be as slow as ever you choose. And forgive me if, in my fear of overlooking anything about our situation here, I have given you facts in excess and beyond the fair limits of a letter. As it is, there are points which I have left untouched for fear of being tedious. But a reader of your judgement and imagination will not exaggerate the size of the descriptive page, but rather that of the house so spaciously depicted. (II.ii)

In another letter, written during the same period, Sidonius, in a charming if jesting way, seeks to entice another friend, Trygetius, to visit him. There is the promise of gourmet feasting. This was before Sidonius became the Bishop of Clermont, but it must be remembered he was chosen for worldly talents and not, as were some other bishops, for the self-discipline of ascetic habits. In fact, the impression seems to be that while not critical, neither was Sidonius fond of his spare-living colleagues in the episcopate.

> A truce to your objections and delays; I could swear that the snail with his house on his back would easily outstrip you. And to think that there is a storeroom at your command crammed with piles of the most exquisite delicacies and only wanting an enterprise to do it justice! Come, then, to be entertained or to entertain; or, best of all, to do both. (VIII.xii)

If life for the well-to-do Romans continued to have its pleasures, there were also some familiar dangers. Sidonius speaks of a man strangled by his slaves in his own house (VIII.xi) even as Pliny had called attention to similar murders in the second century. Interestingly enough, Sidonius's treatment of his own servants is evident because one of them lost some letters. In the fifth century, as true as ever, getting a letter delivered depended on a good carrier. In one letter, written to Simplicius and Apollinaris, possibly his cousins, in about 472, Sidonius speaks of a "blockhead" who delivered his letters but lost the ones written in return.

> The excitable mind of man is like nothing so much as a wrecking sea; it is lashed to confusion by contrary tidings as if it bred its own rough weather. A few days ago, I and the son whom we both regard as ours were together. . . . We were reading, and jesting, and applauding the fine passages—the play charmed him, and he me, we were both equally absorbed—when all of a sudden a household slave appears, pulling a long face. "I have just seen outside," he said, "the reader Constans, back from his errand to the lords Simplicius and Apollinaris. He says that he delivered your letters, but has lost the answers given him to bring back." No sooner did I hear this, than a storm-cloud of annoyance rose upon the clear sky of my enjoyment; the mischance made me so angry that for several days I was inexorable and forbade the blockhead my presence; I meant to make him sorry for himself unless he restored me the letters all and sundry, to say nothing of yours, which as long as I am a reasonable being I shall always want most because they come least often. However, after a time my anger gradually abated; I sent for him and asked whether, besides the letters, he had been entrusted with a verbal message. He was all a-tremble and ready to grovel at my feet; he stammered in conscious guilt, and could not look me in the face, but he managed to answer: "Nothing." The message from which I was to have received so much instruction and delight, had been all consigned to the pages which had been lost. So there is nothing else for it; you must resort to your tablets once more, unfold your parchment, and write it all out anew. I shall bear with such philosophy as I may this unfor-

> tunate obstacle to my desires until the hour when these lines reach you, and you learn that yours have never yet reached me. (IV.xii)

Carriers of course had problems of their own. In the following passage from a letter to his friend Bishop Faustus, written about 477, Sidonius worries about couriers who, if thought to be carrying a message in their heads rather than their hands, were likely to get rough treatment. The cordial tone of the letter is again evidence of Sidonius's way of putting friendship first, for Faustus was one of those four bishops whose negotiations with Euric had meant the loss of Auvergne.

> Your old loyalty to a friend, and your old mastery of diction are both unchanged; I admire equally the heartiness of your letters, and the perfect manner of their expression. But I think, and I am sure that you will concur with me, that at the present juncture, when the roads are no longer secure owing to the movements of the peoples, the only prudent and safe course is to abandon for the present any regular exchange of messages; we must be less assiduous correspondents; we must learn the art of keeping silence. This is a bitter deprivation, and hard to bear when a friendship is as close as ours; it is imposed upon us not by casual circumstance, but by causes at once definite, inevitable, and diverse in their origin.
>
> First among them I must set the examination of all letter-carriers upon the highways. Messengers may run small personal risk, since nothing can be alleged against them; but they have to put up with endless annoyance, while some vigilant official subjects them to an inquisitorial search. At the first sign of faltering in reply to questions, they are suspected of carrying in their heads instructions which cannot be found upon their persons. The sender of a letter is thus placed in an awkward position, and the bearer is liable to rough usage, especially at a time like this, when fresh disputes between rival nationalities have destroyed a treaty of long duration. (IX.iii)

Couriers, by whatever means, were not, of course, always carrying momentous news. In the following letter, for instance, Sidonius is only seeking to help a young man's chances for making a suitable marriage. He wants his friend Sagittarius to know that this suitor belongs to an honorable family. Again, it is the sort of letter Pliny the Younger would have written.

> The honorable Projectus is ardently bent upon your friendship; I trust that you will not repel his advances. He is of noble lineage; the reputation of his father and his uncle, and his grandfather's eminence in the Church unite to lend a lustre to his name; he has indeed all that conduces to distinction; family, wealth, probity, energetic youth; but not till he is assured of your good graces, will he consider himself to have attained the culminating

point of his career. Although he has already asked and obtained from the widow of the late honourable Optantius her daughter's hand—may God speed his hopes—he fears that little will have been gained by all his vows, unless his own solicitude, or my intercession gains him your support as well. For you have taken the place of the girl's dead father; you have succeeded to his share in the responsibility for her upbringing; it is to you that she looks for a father's love, a patron's guidance, a guardian's bounden care. And since it is but natural that your admirable government of your household should attract men of the right stamp even from distant places, reward the modesty of this suppliant wooer by a kindly response. In the usual course of events it would have fallen to you to obtain him the mother's consent; as it is, he saves you this trouble, and you have only to sanction a troth already approved. Your reputation gives you in effect a parental authority in regard to this match; the father himself, if he had lived, could not have claimed a greater. (II. iv)

A man of Sidonius's class received an education in how to speak and write correctly. But neither talent nor imagination, of course, were necessary for what was proper, and Sidonius is not given any palms for his style of writing, which was so obviously contrived to make an impression. Also, frequent references to hallowed poets, especially Virgil, were the way a learned man announced himself. Sidonius was a man trying very hard to maintain standards and painfully aware that others were not trying at all. Listening to noisy barbarians talking in the streets was one thing, but there was also the slovenliness of the speech of the locals to contend with. Sidonius was troubled by what was happening to the language of his ancestors. In this passage to a friend, Hesperius, written about 470, he expresses himself perhaps more politely than do modern critics who air similar complaints.

What I most love in you is your love of letters, and I strive to enhance the generous devotion by the highest praises I can give; your firstfruits please the better for it, and even my own work begins to rise in my esteem. For the richest reward of man's labours is to see promising young men growing up in that discipline of letters for which he in his own day smarted under the cane. The numbers of the indifferent grow at such a rate that unless your little band can save the purity of the Latin tongue from the rust of sorry barbarisms we shall soon have to mourn its abolition and decease. All the fine flowers of diction will lose their splendour through the apathy of our people. (II.x)

Because Sidonius prided himself on his loyalty to traditional standards of style and deplored the obvious decline in literature, he took more than a casual interest in his own letters. They were edited carefully and then published. He even wrote some of them specifically for his collection. Nor did he doubt that they had a future, and, as he assured one of his friends, so did the names of those who received them. Fortunalis, to whom the following letter was written about 480, shared in his own land a common fate with Sidonius. He had watched the Visigoths take over Spain.

> You too shall figure in my pages, dear Fortunalis, column of friendship, bright ornament of your Spanish country. Your own acquaintance with letters is not, after all, so slight as to deprive you of any immortality which they can confer. The glory of your name shall live, yes, it shall survive into after ages. If my writings win any favour or respect, if they command any confidence among men, I will have posterity know that none were more stout of heart then you; that none were goodlier to see or more equitable in judgement, none more patient, none weightier in council, gayer in company, or more charming in conversation. Last, and not least, it shall learn that these praises have been enhanced by your misfortunes. For it is more likely to hold you great, as one proved in the hard day of adversity, than as one who lay hidden in the bosom of kind fortune. (VIII.v)

During the last years of his life, Sidonius was witnessing the Visigoths themselves trying to hold on to their winnings. In a long letter, about 480, to his friend Namatius, now serving as an officer in the Visigothic King Euric's fleet, Sidonius concludes with the following passage about the Saxons who raid by sea as well as by land. His description in this instance conforms to popular notions about the barbarians.

As has been mentioned, the Visigoths, whom Sidonius knew so well, had been converted to Christianity. Regretfully it was the Arian kind, but they did conform to Roman standards of law and order once they had taken over. Now they faced these "ferocious" Saxons.

> Do let me know how things go with you and your household. Just as I was on the point of ending a letter which had rambled on long enough, lo and behold! a courier from Saintonges. I whiled away some time talking with him about you; and he was very positive that you had weighed anchor, and in fulfilment of those half military, half naval duties of yours were coasting the western shores on the look-out for curved ships; the ships of the Saxons, in whose every oarsman you think to detect an arch-pirate. Captains and crews alike, to a man they teach or learn the art of brigandage; therefore let me urgently caution you to be ever on the alert. For the Saxon is the most ferocious of all foes. He comes on you without warning; when you expect his attack he makes away. Resistance only moves him to contempt; a rash opponent is soon down. If he pursues he overtakes; if he flies himself, he is never caught. Shipwrecks to him are no terror, but only so much training. His is no mere acquaintance with the perils of the

sea; he knows them as he knows himself. A storm puts his enemies off their guard, preventing his preparations from being seen; the chance of taking the foe by surprise makes him gladly face every hazard of rough waters and broken rocks.

Moreover, when the Saxons are setting sail from the continent, and are about to drag their firm-holding anchors from an enemy's shore, it is their usage, thus homeward bound, to abandon every tenth captive to the slow agony of a watery end, casting lots with perfect equity among the doomed crowd in execution of this iniquitous sentence of death. This custom is all the more deplorable in that it is prompted by honest superstition. These men are bound by vows which have to be paid in victims, they conceive it a religious act to perpetrate this horrible slaughter, and to take anguish from the prisoner in place of ransom; this polluting sacrilege is in their eyes an absolving sacrifice. I am full of anxiety and apprehension about these dangers, though on the other hand there are factors which encourage me mightily. Firstly, the standards under which you sail are those of an ever-victorious nation. Secondly, men of prudence, among whose number you may fairly be included, are not in the habit of leaving anything to chance. Thirdly, very intimate friends who live far from each other are apt to feel alarm without due cause, because it is natural to be apprehensive of events at once incalculable and occurring very far away. You will perhaps argue that the cause of my uneasiness need not be taken so seriously. That may be true; but it is also true that we are most timid in regard to those whom we love best. So take the first opportunity of relieving the fears which your situation has aroused by a good account of your fortunes. I am incorrigible on this head, and shall always fear the worst for friends abroad until they contradict it themselves, especially those harassed by the watchword or the signal for attack. In accordance with your request, I send you the *Libri Logistorici* of Varro and the Chronology of Eusebius. If these models reach you safely, and you find a little leisure from the watches and the duties of the camp, you will be able, your arms once furbished, to apply another kind of polish to an eloquence which must be getting rusty. (VIII.vi)

Sidonius's later years were apparently not very happy. Declining health may have played a part in this. No doubt, also, his son, Apollinaris, poor in his studies and keeping bad company, had been a disappointment to him. Yet how much comfort Sidonius had taken in family life is hard to say. His letters are not personal the way Cicero's are. He rarely mentioned his wife or even said enough about his daughters to make it certain how many there are. According to tradition, when at last he lay dying in a church, it was his extended family, the congregation, that was at his side.

After Sidonius's death, the devotion of his followers led to his canonization as a saint, but he was better remembered for his manly defense of Clermont rather than for any miracles.

XV
LEO I

Pope Who Faced Attila

ANCIENT Greek philosophers had a well-deserved reputation for the variety of their answers to questions about matters both human and divine. The legacy of such speculations did not bother the worshipers of popular Greek or Roman gods so long as the proper rituals were performed. But in the Roman world of the fourth century that easy arrangement was gradually coming to an end. It may be said to have ended by the mid-fifth century when the strong-willed Leo I ascended to the papacy. He was not a man to countenance variety, and he said so. There was a single truth, and he knew what it was.

Leo was the only pope, besides Gregory I, to be called "the Great," and there can be no doubt that he dealt firmly with many problems. From 440 to 461 it was Leo who stood undaunted by "enemy" religions, fractious councils of bishops, a rival patriarch at Constantinople, the emperors Valentinian III in the west and Theodosius II in the east, and even with the leaders of the Huns and the Vandals.

Leo was most likely a native Tuscan, but Milman, in his venerable *History of Latin Christianity*, made a point of saying that he had the spirit of an Old Roman. Leo was a proud and self-confident man, who, in the manner of a Julius Caesar, readily convinced others of his pre-eminence, having first convinced himself. Here was an upholder of the traditional Roman virtues of *dignitas, gravitas,* and *pietas*. According to Milman: "All that survived of Rome, of her unbounded ambition, her inflexible perseverance, her dignity in defeat, her haughtiness of language, her belief in her own eternity, and in her indefeasible title to universal dominion, her respect for traditionary and written law, and of unchangeable custom, might seem concentrated in him alone."[1] The empire had taken orders from Rome, and the church, too, would be ruled from there. St. Peter had brought the Apostolic authority to the right place.

Leo had no doubts about who he was. He and the bishops of Rome before him had inherited a power from St. Peter that could not be challenged. With conviction, energy, and talent, Leo was equal to the occasion. Nicolas Cheetham, in his *Keepers of the Keys*, writes: "[Leo] described himself as the 'unworthy heir of St. Peter,' meaning that he and all other Popes, while inheriting the Apostle's powers to the fullest degree, did not presume to possess his virtues."[2] This shrewd combination of humility and authority kept alive the old Roman genius for getting things done. While Leo was himself a man of excellent character, an insistence that all future popes should meet Peter's moral standards might have been a threat to continuity.

If the late Augustine had been the architect of a dominant church, Leo was the builder, and by some called the first medieval pope. He was also the first pope whose letters were collected in the fashion of the Roman notables of earlier times, and they have a similar practical frame of mind. Since there are doubts about the genuineness of certain of Leo's letters, a statement that 150 survive might be matched by a claim of 143.

The belief that St. Peter was the founder of the Roman see[3] was often cited during the Middle Ages to legitimize papal authority. According to this view, Peter was directly commissioned by Jesus to watch over the church, and the popes were the direct successors of Peter. A doctrine of apostolic succession was not new even in Leo's day, but Leo was perhaps the first bishop of Rome to make effective use of it. The claim appears several times in his letters. For example, he exercised his authority in a power struggle with the church in Gaul.[4] Bishop Hilary of Arles had, among other things, convened a local synod to depose Bishop Celidonius of Besançon. Leo saw that action as an infringement on Rome's authority to oversee the process used to depose and appoint bishops in the western empire. A strongly worded letter in the summer of 445 to "all the bishops presiding in the province of Vienne," makes it plain that Leo was seeking uniformity of practice, over which he would preside. When speaking directly about Hilary, Leo's indignation was often mixed with sarcasm.

> Our Lord Jesus Christ, Saviour of the human race, desired to have the observance of divine religion shine out through God's grace unto all nations and races. He established it in such a way that truth, previously contained only in proclamations of the Law and the Prophets, might proceed from the Apostles' trumpet for the salvation of all, as it is written: "Their sound has gone forth unto all the earth: and their words unto the ends of the world." Now, the Lord desired that the dispensing of this gift should be shared as a task by all the Apostles, but in such a way that He put the principal charge on the most blessed Peter, the highest of all the Apostles. He wanted His gifts to flow into the entire body from Peter himself, as it were from the head . . . But the man who attempts to infringe on its power by furthering his own desires and not following practices received from antiquity is trying with absolutely blasphemous presumption, to de-

> stroy this most sacred solidity of that rock, established with God as the builder, as we mentioned. For he believes that he is subject to no law, that he is not restrained by any regulations that the Lord ordained. Being intent on novel assumption of power, he departs from what you and we are accustomed to; he presumes to do what is illegal and neglects traditions that he ought to have maintained . . . Your Fraternities should, of course, realize with us that the Apostolic See (out of reverence for it) has countless times been reported to in consultation by bishops even in your province. And through the appeal of various cases to it, decisions already made have been either rescinded or confirmed, as dictated by long-standing custom. As a result, with "unity of spirit in the bond of peace" being preserved, with letters being sent and received, what was done in a holy manner has been conducive to abiding charity. For our solicitude, which seeks not its own interests but those of Christ, does not detract from the dignity given by God to the churches and the bishops of the churches. This was the procedure always well observed and profitably maintained by our predecessors. But Hilary has departed from it, aiming to disturb the status of the churches and harmony among the bishops by his novel usurpations of power. He seeks to subject you to his authority while not allowing himself to be under the jurisdiction of the blessed Apostle Peter. He claims for himself the right to consecrate in all the churches of Gaul and takes as his own the dignity which belongs to the metropolitan bishops. He even lessens the reverence due to the most blessed Peter himself by his quite arrogant statements. And although the power to bind and loose was given to Peter before the others, still, in an even more special way, the pasturing of the sheep was entrusted to him. Anyone who thinks that the primacy should be denied to Peter cannot in any way lessen the Apostle's dignity; inflated with the wind of his own pride, he buries himself in hell . . . .

The letter then describes an inquiry held before Leo and other bishops with both parties and witnesses present. There it was determined that Celidonius had neither married a widow, nor married twice, and was therefore unjustly removed from his bishopric. Next, another case regarding the bishop of Narbonne, Projectus, was considered, for while he was ill, Hilary had transferred his office to someone else.

> What hope of life is left him when he is beset with despair over his bishopric while another is substituted in his place? Just how gentle of heart Hilary is becomes obvious from the fact that he considered his brother's tardiness in dying as an impediment to his presumptious plans. As much as he could, Hilary extinguished the light for Projectus and took away his life, since he added this affliction to prevent his return to health: he put another bishop in his place.

Nor was there any consultation with the people of the congregation as was customary.

> Not being expected, (Hilary) came to the people unawares, and departed without warning, making many trips with great speed, rushing through distant provinces in such a hurry that he seems to have aimed at a reputation for giddy speed rather than for the moderation of a bishop. For this is the way it is worded in the letter sent to us by the citizens: "He left before we knew he had come." This is not to return but to flee, not to dispense the salutary effects of pastoral care but to attack as a robber and a thief, as the Lord says: "He who enters not by the door into the sheepfold, but climbs up another way, is a thief and a robber." Hilary, then, was not so much bent on consecrating a bishop as on killing him who was ill and on deceiving, by an illegal consecration, the man whom he set up as a substitute. But, having taken counsel of all our brothers, we have decided what we believe will please you, as God is our judge: we have ordered that he who was wrongfully consecrated must be removed and that Bishop Projectus is to remain in his bishopric.

Nor was that all.

> As we have learned, a group of soldiers follows Bishop Hilary through the provinces and assists him, relying on the assurance of this armed guard, in the turbulent invasion of the churches that have lost their own bishops. The men to be consecrated are hauled before this tribunal, men unknown to those localities over which they are to preside. Now, just as a well-known and tested man is sought for when there is peace, so when an unknown man is brought in, he must be imposed on the people by force. I beg and entreat you and call upon you with prayers to God, brothers, to prevent such happenings and to remove all cause for dissension from your provinces.
>
> Let individual provinces be content with their own councils, and let Hilary no longer dare to summon synodal meetings and disrupt the decisions of the Lord's bishops by his interference. Let him know that he has been expelled not only from other people's jurisdiction but also from power over the province of Vienne, which he illegally assumed. It is indeed fitting, brothers, that the ancient regulations be restored. For he who claimed the right to consecrate in a province not his own has also at the present time proved himself to be such that, although he frequently sought a sentence of condemnation by his rash and insolent words, he is by our order to retain the bishopric merely in his own diocese. This is granted out of the fatherly concern of the Apostolic See [i.e., Rome]. He is, then, not to be present at any consecration; he is not to consecrate. Realizing what he deserved

> when he was being questioned about the matter, he was of the opinion that he should withdraw by a disgraceful flight, as one not sharing in the bishops' society, of which he did not deserve to be a member. God, in our opinion, brought this about, leading him to our court when we did not expect it and inducing him to withdraw stealthily, while the inquiry was being held, to prevent his sharing in our society. (10)[5]

Leo's skills in diplomacy were part of his success. Years earlier, the Emperor Valentinian III had been so impressed by this intelligent and energetic clergyman that he sent him to Gaul to negotiate problems arising between the military and civil arms of government there, a task reminiscent of Ambrose's diplomatic services under Valentinian II. In time, Leo's powers of persuasion were used on the Emperor himself. So it was that Valentinian III, in 444, legalized Leo's ascendancy over the churches in the western provinces. At the same time, Hunt points out, Leo was far more compromising with those outside the church than in: "Leo the Great was fearless in attacking abuses in the church, but he was surprisingly tolerant of civil rulers. When they summoned councils or made demands, he always tried to comply even against his better judgment" (p. 9).

In asserting the authority of the Roman see, Leo had also to face a growing rivalry with the patriarch of Constantinople.[6] He induced the imperial family in Italy to write to the eastern emperor Theodosius II in support of the Roman claims to supremacy in the church. A series of major church councils in the east were important for both political and doctrinal reasons. Leo's letter to the Council of Chalcedon, the famous *Tome*, was accepted as church doctrine and as the official rejection of the Monophysite[7] heresy based on the views of the priest Eutyches. However, Leo was not pleased over the council's failure to uphold clearly the Roman primacy. He was certainly determined to uphold it himself.

The city of Thessalonica in Greece was one of the major urban centers of the later empire, and support from its bishop was crucial to the Roman see in its rivalry with Constantinople. Leo courted the good will of Bishop Anastasius, adding the district of Illyricum to his sphere of authority. In this letter written in 444, quite friendly in tone, Leo also makes reference to marriage and the requirement that a bishop was to have married only once. Matters that could not be resolved locally were to be sent to Rome for a decision (cf. Trajan's instructions to Pliny in chapter III). Moreover, all were to be informed of this so no one who disobeyed could plead ignorance.

> We urge you by our admonition to allow no carelessness, no negligence, to occur in the governing of the churches situated throughout Illyricum, which we are entrusting to your Charity in our stead, following the example of Siricius of blessed memory. He made this concession for the first time according to a fixed plan to Anysius of holy memory, who preceded

your immediate predecessor and who at that time merited well of the Apostolic See and was praised for his subsequent actions. . . . Throughout the provinces committed to you let only those be consecrated bishops of the Lord who have in their favor meritorious lives and the approval of the clerical order. Do not grant any license to personal favor, to canvassing for votes, to votes that are bought. Let those who are to be consecrated be examined with great care and imbued with ecclesiastical discipline over a long period of their life. Even so, let them be consecrated only if they are in harmony with all that has been preserved from the Fathers and if they have met the requirements set forth for such men (as we read) by the blessed Apostle Paul; that is, a bishop is to have but one wife; and she a virgin when he married her, as the authority of the divine Law warns. We want this observed so carefully as to remove occasion for all excuses. Otherwise, someone who took a wife before he received Christ's grace and then at her death married another after being baptized may believe it is possible for him to become a bishop. That first wife cannot be denied, nor can the first marriage be left out of the count; and he is the father of those children born of the first wife before his baptism as well as of those whom he is known to have had by the second wife after his baptism . . . If any problems arise, they can with the Lord's direction be settled there, so that no dissension may remain, but charity only among the brothers may bind them together. But, if some major problem arises which cannot be settled there under your Fraternity's direction, consult us by sending your report. Thus with the enlightenment of the Lord (through whose mercy we admit we are what we are), we can send back an answer which He himself has inspired in us. In that way, through our inquiry, we may justify our claim to decide [cases] in line with long established tradition and reverence due to the Apostolic See. We want you to exercise authority in our stead, but we reserve to ourself those problems that cannot be decided locally or whenever someone sends an appeal to us.

See to it, then, that this information reaches all the brothers, so that in the observance of these orders of ours no one may hereafter find an opportunity to excuse himself through ignorance. We are also sending our letter to the metropolitans themselves in the individual provinces in order to warn them. This is to let them know that apostolic decisions must be complied with, and that they obey us when they begin to obey your Fraternity as our representative according to our written directives. (6)

Anastasius proved a disappointment. A letter from Rome early in 446 warned him against interfering with matters that rightly belonged to Leo's authority. Leo also criticized Anastasius's harshness to other bishops, particularly the sickly Bishop Atticus of Old Epirus. The letter is a model of a polite disguise of temper and, perhaps, contempt. It is obvious from this letter that Leo thought there was no question about who should be obeying whom, but as time proved, there was.

> As my predecessors did to yours, so I, also, following them as models, delegated to your Charity the task of governing which is mine, so that, while imitating our clemency, you might share in the concern which, by divine ordinance, we above all are bound to show for all the churches, and might in some way take our place in visiting provinces far from us. For it would really be easy for you by regular and timely inspection to find out in all instances what you might settle on your initiative and what you might reserve for our judgment. Now, since you were free to postpone more serious business and more difficult case-solutions until we could pass on them, there was no reason or need for you to err in a matter exceeding the limits set for you. You have at hand plenty of admonitions in writing in which we often instructed you to be moderate in all your actions so as to attract to salutary obedience, through charitable exhortation, the churches of Christ entrusted to you. . . . although men of priestly rank sometimes do things that are reprehensible, kindness toward those to be corrected is more effective than severity, admonition more than anger, charity more than power. But those who "seek their own interests, not those of Jesus Christ," easily depart from this rule. And while they exult more in dominating than in taking counsel for their subjects, honor puffs up pride, and what was counted on to effect harmony tends to do harm. It is from no small anguish of mind that we have to speak thus. I feel that I myself am somehow involved in blame when I realize that you have unduly departed from the instructions given you. If you had small concern for your own reputation, you should at any rate have spared mine, so that what you did only according to your own lights might not seem done through a decision of ours. Your Fraternity should read again what we wrote to you and all the writings which bishops in the Apostolic See sent to your predecessors, and find out whether either I or my predecessors ordained what, we are certain, were merely presumed on your part.
>
> The metropolitan bishop of Old Epirus, our brother Atticus, has come to us, together with bishops of his own province, and with tears complained of the undeserved affliction he has endured. This was done in the presence of your deacons, who by saying nothing to contradict these tearful complaints showed that the report being given us was reliable. . . .
>
> I am much amazed, dearest brother—nay, I am very much grieved—that you could have been so violently and cruelly angry at a man against whom you made no greater charge than that he had delayed coming when summoned and offered his infirmity as an excuse. I am especially grieved since, even if he merited some such treatment, you ought to have waited to see

what answer I would make to the inquiries you sent me. But, as I see it, you correctly estimated my usual dispositions and you quite accurately saw beforehand how gently I would answer in order to preserve harmony among the bishops. Hence, you hastened to pursue without dallying your own inclinations. You knew that, once you had received our moderate answer outlining a different course, you would not be at liberty to do what you did. Was it, perhaps, that you had discovered some illicit act and the burden of the new misdeed was a serious charge against a metropolitan bishop in your area? Even you admit that this supposition does not fit his case at all, since you made no charge against him. But, even if he had committed some serious and insupportable sin, you ought to have waited for our decision; that is, you yourself should not have decided anything until you found out what our pleasure was. We entrusted our office to your Charity, but only in that you were asked to share in our responsibility, not in the fullness of our power. (14).

In a letter dated 22 May 452 to his rival in Constantinople, Bishop Anatolius, Leo accuses him of infringing upon the jurisdiction of the bishops of Alexandria and Antioch and of undermining the rulings of the Council of Nicaea. What bothered him, of course, was, as Cheetham comments, that "Constantinople was accorded the same position in the East that Rome enjoyed in the West" (p. 27).

When your predecessor, Flavian of blessed memory, was rejected for his defense of Catholic truth, there was reason to believe that those who consecrated you had apparently consecrated a man like themselves, contrary to the provisions of the holy canons. But the mercy of God, directing and strengthening you, helped you to make good use of a bad start and to prove that you were promoted by God's kindness, not by the judgment of men. Indeed, this situation is acceptable if only you do not lose this God-given grace by another offense. . . .

Naturally, after such an origin to your being a bishop, one not without fault, after your consecration of the Bishop of Antioch (which you claimed as your right in opposition to canon law), I am grieved that your Charity has also erred in the following matter. You have tried to infringe on the most sacred provisions of the Nicene canons, as though the present time (in which the see of Alexandria has lost the privilege of second place and the church of Antioch its right to third place) gave you an opportunity to substitute your jurisdiction in those places and thus deprive all metropolitan bishops of the honor due to them. . . .

Those holy and venerable Fathers who at Nicaea condemned the sacrilegious Arius with his impiety and established regulations in the canons of the Church that will last to the end of the world, these men are still

> living with us and in the entire world through their canons. And if by resumption anything is anywhere decided contrary to their decisions, it is voided without delay. Thus, the general regulations set up to be useful for all time may not suffer any change, and what was ordained for the common good may not be adapted to suit private interests; and with the preserving of those limits which the Fathers established no one may branch out into a jurisdiction not his own, but each one may spend himself in the fullness of charity, to the extent that he is able, within his own legitimate boundaries. The Bishop of Constantinople can reap the sufficiently rich fruits of this [apostolate] if he exerts himself in the virtue of humility instead of being inflated with the spirit of ambition . . . you can plainly see that I oppose your Charity with a benevolent intention so that by saner counsel you may refrain from disturbing the universal Church. The rights of the provincial bishops are not to be snatched from them, nor are the metropolitan bishops to be robbed of the privileges assigned to them in antiquity. Let the see of Alexandria not lose any of the dignity it earned through St. Mark the Evangelist, the disciple of blessed Peter. And let not the splendor of so great a church be obscured by darkness from other men now that Dioscorus is in disgrace by persisting in his impious heresy. The church of Antioch also should continue in the rank decided on by the Fathers and, having been put in third place, it should never be lowered. It was in that church, where the blessed Apostle Peter preached, that the name "Christian" first began to be used. Now, the sees and those who preside over them are two different things; and each individual's honor is his own integrity. Since this integrity does not lose the glories proper to it in whatever place it may be, how much more glorious it can be when set in the splendor of the city of Constantinople if, through your observance, the canons of the Fathers have a defender and if many priests have an example of right conduct. (106)

In the short time since Augustine's death, the church had greatly expanded its capacity to deal with its enemies. Augustine had himself been an adherent of the Manichaean movement, which in his day flourished openly. In a letter written early in 444, Leo rallied the bishops in Italy to stamp out this "pestilence," which being suppressed in Rome might be spreading to rural areas.

> We call you to a share in our anxiety, that with the diligence of shepherds you may take more careful heed to your flocks entrusted to you that no craft of the devil's be permitted: lest that plague, which by the revealing mercy of the Lord is driven off from our flocks through our care, should spread among your churches before you are forewarned and are still ignorant of what is happening, and should find means of stealthily burrowing

> into your midst, and thus what we are checking in the City should take hidden root among you and grow up. Our search has discovered in the City a great many followers and teachers of the Manichaean impiety, our watchfulness has proclaimed them, and our authority and censure has checked them: those whom we could reform we have corrected and driven to condemn Manichaeus with his preachings and teachings by public confession in church, and by the subscription of their own hand, and thus we have lifted those who have acknowledged their fault from the pit of their iniquity by granting them room for repentance. A good many, however, who had so deeply involved themselves that no remedy could assist them, have been subjected to the laws in accordance with the constitutions of our Christian princes, and lest they should pollute the holy flock by their contagion, have been banished into perpetual exile by public judges. And all the profane and disgraceful things which are found as well in their writings as in their secret traditions, we have disclosed and clearly proved to the eyes of the Christian laity that the people might know what to shrink from or avoid: so that he that was called their bishop was himself tried by us, and betrayed the criminal views which he held in his mystic religion, as the record of our proceedings can show you. For this, too, we have sent you for instruction: and after reading them you will be in a position to understand all the discoveries we have made . . . we cannot otherwise rule those entrusted to us unless we pursue with the zeal of faith in the Lord those who are destroyers and destroyed: and with what severity we can bring to bear, cut them off from intercourse with sound minds, lest this pestilence spread much wider. Wherefore I exhort you, beloved, I beseech and warn you to use such watchful diligence as you ought and can employ in tracking them out, lest they find opportunity of concealment anywhere. For as he will have a due recompense of reward from God, who carries out what conduces to the health of the people committed to him; so before the Lord's judgment-seat no one will be able to excuse himself from a charge of carelessness who has not been willing to guard his people against the propagators of an impious misbelief. Dated 30 January, in the consulship of the illustrious Theodosius Augustus (18th time) and Albinus (444). (7)[8]

Leo persuaded the emperor Valentinian III to expel Manichaeans from the army and from Rome and to revoke their citizenship, which in effect made them outlaws. By doing so he shared Augustine's attitude toward heretics. He was doing them a favor. They should be grateful toward those who brought them to the truth. The Greeks, a thousand years earlier, had found that wherever men were allowed to be free there would be disagreement. Of course, those who cannot abide such problems will sacrifice freedom in favor of peaceful conformity. Leo sought conformity of belief and practice through centralization of power, even as had emperors in the past, because differences of party or opinion so often led to violence.

It is ironic that while Leo worked to bring peace in the eastern half of Christendom, it was precisely the violence and constant theological turmoil there that drew attention to the generally more orderly affairs in the west. There were disputes, to be sure, but Leo could use a relatively calm atmosphere as an argument for unity and obedience under the aegis of Rome's authority.

Leo's letter to five eastern bishops[9] in 457 refers to the murder of the orthodox bishop of Alexandria by supporters of Eutyches, leader of the Monophysite heresy. Don't give in to terror, Leo says as he urges the bishops to uphold the decisions of the Council of Chalcedon against Eutyches. Most of Leo's letters are written about the persistent problem of heresies in the Greek east where bickering over fine points in theology was the current outlet for a tradition in speculation.

> Now that I have learned what was done at Alexandria through the fury of the Eutychians, deeds which I am sure your Fraternities have learned of, I am sending this letter because of the solicitude which I owe to all God's churches. I thought your Charities should be warned by it to resist criminal endeavors with holy constancy, lest the common faith be found to be timid or lukewarm in any of us. . . . After the barbarous crime was perpetrated, they thought that is was possible for them to have the canons of the holy Council of Chalcedon rescinded and a new council of bishops summoned to treat matters in another way. Dearest brother, this is rashly opposed to the Christian faith, and the only purpose in requesting it with so much perversity is to overturn the teaching of the Gospel and the mystery of the Lord's Incarnation. Therefore, I beg your Charities not to unhinge your minds in any way from the decisions of the Council of Chalcedon and not to allow arrangements made with divine inspiration to be infringed on by any novelty. (149–150)[10]

Keeping the peace in the church was more important to Leo than to the average layman, who, with Huns and Vandals on the attack, was more worried about saving his life and property. In 452, Attila had moved his dreaded Huns into Italy, threatening the country with utter ruin. Leo led a three-man delegation sent by Valentinian III to Attila, who, at the time, was camping near Mantua. The Huns withdrew. That decision may have resulted from Leo's diplomacy, or because of bribes to Hunnic leaders, or because of the Huns' own domestic problems, including a shortage of supplies, or because Attila, who died the following year, was, at this point, critically ill.

A scant three years later, Leo reportedly talked to Geiseric, who in turn kept his Vandals from slaughtering the Roman people, at least those who did not resist, while pillaging their possessions. The city was in any event devastated, and it was Leo, to his credit, who took the lead in assuaging the widespread suffering.

Raphael (Raffaello Sanzio, 1483–1520), *Pope Leo Facing Attila.* Courtesy of The Vatican Museum.

Leo's letters make no mention of his direct encounters with Attila and Geiseric. But there is mention of a special problem resulting from their unwelcome invasions. It appears in a letter written in March 458 to Nicetas, the bishop of Aquileia, an important Italian port that had been ravaged by the Huns several years earlier. A number of women, whose husbands had been reported dead, remarried only to have their first husbands return alive some time later. What must the church do in these cases? Leo decreed that the women must return to their first husbands, and if they did, no one was to be judged guilty. Women who preferred to stay with their second husbands were to be excommunicated.

> On his return to us, my son Adeodatus, a deacon of our See, reminded us of your Charity's request that you receive from us the authoritative answer of the Apostolic See about those matters which are apparently quite difficult to decide. We must take care, considering the necessities of the times, that the wounds inflicted by the attacks of the enemy may be healed particularly by the wise action of religion.
>
> You mention that, through the destruction of war and the extremely heavy assaults of the enemy, certain marriages were broken up in this way: When the husbands were carried off into captivity, their wives were left

behind deserted. And because they either thought their husbands were killed or felt that they would never be liberated from slavery, under pressure of loneliness these women married other men. And now that the situation, with the Lord's help, has taken a turn for the better, some of those who were thought dead have returned. Therefore, your Charity is apparently in doubt, and with reason, as to what we ought to ordain about the women who married other husbands. We know that it has been written, "A women is joined to a man by God"; and we have learned still another commandment that "what God has joined together, let no man put asunder." Hence, we believe that the bonds of legitimate marriages should necessarily be restored; now that the evils introducd by the enemy have been removed, each one should get back that which he legally possessed. . . .

Nevertheless, the man who took the place of that husband who was thought to be dead must not be judged guilty,nor considered the usurper of another man's rights. That is, many things belonging to those who were led into captivity could pass into the possession of another; yet it is absolutely just that on their return these men have restored to them what was theirs. If this is the proper procedure in the case of slaves and fields or even for houses and personal property, how much more should it be the practice in the matter of renewing marriages? That is, what was thrown out of order by the duress of war is to be restored by the remedy of peace.

Therefore, if men returning after a long captivity have persevered in the love of their wives to the extent of wanting them to return to union with them, that which was introduced through necessity must be eliminated and judged to be without fault; what fidelity asks for must be restored.

But if some women are so taken with love for their second husbands that they prefer to stay with them rather than return to their lawful unions, they are deservedly to be condemned; that is, they are even to be excommunicated from the Church. For in a situation that is excusable they have chosen to taint themselves with crime, showing that because of their incontinence they were pleased with a condition which a just restitution could rectify. Let them, then, return to their proper status by a voluntary renewal of their marriage; in no way may a condition introduced through compulsion be extended into a source of reproach due to evil desires. For, just as those women who are unwilling to return to their husbands must be condemned, so also those who go back to the love they began with God's approval are rightly to be praised. (159)

By the time of his death in 461, Leo had managed to establish what Milman called "the Western spiritual monarchy of Rome." It was, indeed, strong enough to survive, even under less notable popes and the rule of the Ostrogoths, who, unlike the Huns and Vandals, were not just passing through. Their kings, surprisingly enough, gave Italy an interlude of law and order. Not all the Romans appreciated it, but one of them, Cassiodorus, who wrote letters for the Ostrogothic kings, was happy in his work. These letters are the subject of the next, and last, chapter.

XVI
CASSIODORUS

Writing Letters for the Goths

THE letters in the last five chapters, written by Jerome, Augustine, Synesius, Sidonius, and Leo, although sent from different places in the Roman Empire, had one piece of news in common: nobody was safe anymore. The frontiers had broken down and the local populations were at the mercy of violent newcomers, commonly lumped together as barbarians. If these invaders were more successful than their forefathers had been, it was because the continuing internal struggles for power left the empire in a weakened condition – so weak, in fact, that in the late fourth century barbarian commanders themselves were taking part in the story. Few of those involved were especially memorable. Arbogast, a Frankish general, not able to claim the imperial power for himself, connived at the murder of the young Emperor Valentinian II in 392 and then used the aging usurper, Eugenius, as a proxy. By eliminating all such challengers, Theodosius, a skillful strategist, earned a name to be remembered. He was the last ruler to control alone the entire Roman Empire. He also established Christianity as the only legal religion.

When Theodosius died on 17 January 395 his two very young and, as it turned out, not very able sons were left in charge. Arcadius (383–408) ruled the eastern half of the empire from Constantinople, and Honorius (384–423) pretended to rule in the west. It was, however, Stilicho, a Vandal general recently in the service of Honorius's father Theodosius, who saved Italy from invading armies. Himself in command of mostly German soldiers, Stilicho twice defeated the invading Visigoths, who arrived in 401 fresh from their plunder of Greece. After these defeats, Alaric, the ever resourceful king of the Visigoths, became one of Honorius's provincial governors, just as he had earlier served Arcadius.

In 408, it appears that a jealous Emperor Honorius, or his aides at court, arranged the murder of Stilicho. When Alaric again led his followers into Italy, Honorius took refuge in the secure north Italian city of Ravenna. Alaric, after laying siege to Rome three times beginning in 408, quarreling with his own puppet emperor, Attalus, and then removing him, finally, on 24 August 410, sacked the city for the first time in eight hundred years. The shock was felt everywhere. Jerome retells the horrors he had heard of the event (see Chapter XI). Augustine wrote a book about it (see Chapter XII). Surely Synesius, too, must have heard what happened, but, strange to say, his extant letters do not mention it.

The capture of Rome was, in a sense, a dramatic climax to the clash between a coarse Gothic people and a polite Roman society. In fact, however, Alaric's service under the sons of Theodosius meant he was well acquainted with Roman ways, and he and his followers had become at least nominal Christians.

After Alaric's death, the Visigoths settled in Spain and Gaul under the rule of his brother-in-law Athaulf. By the mid-fifth century, they, as well as the Franks and Burgundians, were well enough established in western Europe to be alarmed by the appearance of the Huns. A joint defense forced Attila and his ungainly horde to turn away from central Europe and invade Italy. There, they faced the indomitable Pope Leo I, whose negotiations with them, mentioned in Chapter XV, may have included bribery. In any event, the Huns withdrew.

A few years later, new invaders arrived by sea from North Africa. The Vandals, however, were not to be turned away with only part of the wealth in Rome, and so the city was taken in July 455 for the second time in fifty years. The Vandals left after three weeks, taking all the art treasures they wanted. That might have been the traditional date for the fall of the western Roman Empire, long since disintegrating, had there not followed a series of title-holders under the auspices of Germanic chieftains. Among them was Sidonius's father-in-law, Avitus, who lasted about a year. The last of these short-term emperors was chosen by a Pannonian, Orestes, who mocked the title by giving it to his six-year-old son, Romulus Augustulus.

In 476, Orestes was killed and the boy deposed by soldiers who hailed their own leader, Odoacer, as king in Italy. Since he acknowledged the supremacy of the eastern emperor in Constantinople, the old western empire did, in fact, disappear. By 489, however, Odoacer was out of favor with Zeno, a new ruler in the eastern capital, who appointed an Ostrogothic king, Theodoric, to replace him. It was not easy. Odoacer, after losing a battle in 490, took refuge in Ravenna, and it was only after a two-and-a-half-year siege that the city was starved into surrender. The question of how civilized Theodoric had become during his time at court in Constantinople is raised by the news that he did not leave the killing of Odoacer to his soldiers, but strangled him himself. Thomas Burns, in *A History of the Ostrogoths*, attributes Theodoric's actions to a bad temper. He writes that "behind the subtlety of his political and cultural programs or his deft handling of the Roman aristocracy lurked a man of ferocious wrath, and all those around him knew it."[1]

If there was brutality, there was also certainly much talent. Although an unlettered man who may never have learned how to write, Theodoric proved to be the ablest notable on the scene since Theodosius. As the letters in this chapter, which

Mausoleum of Theodoric. Ravenna. Photograph courtesy of SEF/Art Resource, New York, N.Y.

were written for him, will show, he was a remarkably enlightened ruler over his Ostrogothic kingdom. The fiction that he served on the Emperor's behalf was supported by the fact that he never dated any documents by the number of years of his own reign. But there was no doubt who was in charge. And Theodoric intended to look the part. In a letter complaining about a delay in the production of purple dye for the king's robes, it was observed that the color "distinguishes the wearer from all others, and makes it impossible for the human race not to know who is the king" (I.2).[2]

From 493 until his death in 526, Theodoric was generally courteous toward the Roman Senate, which still held prestige, if not much real power. He wisely respected Roman law and shrewdly kept experienced Romans busy with civil matters while the army remained firmly in Gothic hands. Merit was rewarded on both sides of this equation, so long as a man was unquestionably loyal.

The classicist Boethius (ca. 480–524) rose to the post of *magister officiorum*, the chief bureaucrat of the civil service, but his talents did not sufficiently offset his snobbish attitude toward his Gothic colleagues. In less than a year he was in prison in Pavia awaiting execution, having been accused of conspiracy. Theodoric, who had been converted to Arian Christianity, was worried about ties between certain of his officials and their orthodox co-religionists at Constantinople. Putting a haughty traditionalist to death would not have bothered many Goths and would certainly have been a warning to other Romans.

Boethius's best known work, *The Consolation of Philosophy*, was written in prison. His texts on arithmetic, geometry, and music, popular in medieval times, have also survived along with philosophical and theological tracts. There are no letters remaining, although we have 297 from one of his correspondents, Magnus Felix Ennodius (ca. 473–521), bishop of Pavia in northern Italy, if to little purpose. Moses Hadas, writes that "they are as empty as those of Symmachus, who was Ennodius's model, and so heavy with rhetorical embellishments as to be frequently unintelligible."[3]

It was Cassiodorus (Magnus Aurelius Cassiodorus Senator),[4] Boethius's successor as *magister officiorum*, who was the last prominent writer of letters in the ancient world. Although a man of an old Roman family and culture, perhaps with Syrian antecedents, he was far more accommodating in his dealings with his Gothic colleagues; and had a long life to prove it. Since Cassiodorus, who was born about 490, lived to about 583, he might also be called the first major author of letters in the Middle Ages. A transitional figure, he spent his early career as a useful civil servant and the last years of his life in a monastery.

Cassiodorus wrote a *History of the Goths*, which gave to a ruling people an agreeably flattering past, but the work remains only in a brief abridgment. The letters he wrote for Theodoric and his successors were included in the twelve books of his official papers which Cassiodorus published in 538. There are also some letters in his own name, along with edicts and other documents. The whole was entitled *Variae* because of the various styles of writing used for different subjects or, possibly, to address the differences in station of those to whom messages were sent. Although only about one-third of the material can be dated, all of it speaks for the rulers of an Ostrogothic kingdom in the sixth century A.D. who, taken all together given the times, look better than might be expected. And that apparently was precisely what Cassiodorus intended. A recent study, *Cassiodorus* by James J. O'Donnell, shows how the papers of the *Variae* were selected and published to put the Ostrogothic period in a positive light. Even the word propaganda is used, if in a friendly way.[5] What Cassiodorus chose to publish of all that he had written was undoubtedly the truth. It was what he left out that allowed for an optimistic picture. He had taken his stand with the Ostrogoths, and when they looked good so did this skillful ghostwriter, who could be proud of his contributions to their success.

There was no record of unpleasantness in the *Variae*. The officials and subjects of the king knew him through the polite and often flattering letters which Cassiodorus wrote. Those who were refused a request were simply unlikely ever to hear about it. Moreover, it was part of the job of Cassiodorus, educated in the traditional Roman way, to provide a lofty moral tone to what he wrote. Conveniently, the letters of this final chapter echo those of Cicero in the first one.

When Cassiodorus decided to publish the official papers stored in the government's archives, he wrote a preface in which he hoped future generations would remember him as a hard-working, uncorrupted, and devoted public servant. Others in the government were expected to follow his example. In a message announcing to provincial officials his principles of good government, he said: "The custom of the ancients was for a new ruler to promulgate a new set of laws to his subjects, but now it is sufficient praise to a conscientious ruler that he adheres to the legislation of antiquity" (XI.8). A letter sent to provincial judges makes it apparent that worrying about collecting taxes, without any cheating along the way, was the same as in Cicero's day.

> It is an excellent thing that the yearly taxes should be regularly paid. What confidence does the consciousness of this give to the taxpayer, who can march boldly through the Forum, feeling that he owes nothing to anybody and need not fear the face of any official! One can only enjoy an estate if one has no fear of the process-server making his appearance upon it.
>
> Therefore, in the Diocese of your Excellency, we desire you and your staff at the beginning of this twelfth Indiction, with all proper gentleness, to impress upon the cultivator of the soil that he must pay his land-tax and end those long arrears, which were introduced not for the assistance of the taxpayer, but for the corrupt profit of the tax-collector. For the officials who in this way professed to relieve the burdens of the people, really imposed upon them a heavier and more hateful weight in the shape of douceurs to themselves.
>
> Let then this hateful swindling be henceforth banished. Let the cultivator pay nothing more than his lawful debt to the Treasury, and let him pay it at the appointed time, thus removing the confusion in which the slowness of collection has involved our accounts.
>
> Make up, therefore, the abstracts of accounts at the stated times, and forward them to the proper bureaux, according to old law and the authority of this present edict; and if you neglect any of these injunctions, know that you do so at your peril. To quicken your diligence we have appointed . . . persons of tried merit in the past, to supervise the proceedings of yourself and your staff, that this double check may prevent the possibility of negligence.
>
> Act then with justice if you wish to receive further promotion. Only those gains are to be sought for which the cultivator gladly offers and

> which the public servant can securely accept. If you take bribes you will be miserable everafter, through fear of discovery; but if you act uprightly, you will have in me a willing spectator and rewarder of your merits. I am most anxious to be your friend; do not force me against my will to become your enemy. (XI.7)

Later, Cassiodorus wrote to the same judges: "Remember that the official staff standing by, is a witness of the acts of every one of you; and so comport yourselves, that both they and all others may see that you in your own conduct obey the laws which you administer" (XI.9). Cicero could have written that. The best was shining through the gloom of these later days. Ostrogothic rule brought a period of peace and order to Italy. O'Donnell speaks of Italy at the time "as a haven of enlightened coexistence between Goths and Romans" (p. 9). Boethius might not have thought so, but Boethius was dead.

Reminiscent of the messages between the Emperor Trajan and Pliny, Cassiodorus's letters show that Theodoric's eye was cast on matters large and small. Getting enough food to the cities was a major problem through all the centuries. To deal with the need, Theodoric was intent on building a navy. He wrote to Abundantius, the praetorian prefect, as follows: "By Divine inspiration we have determined to raise a navy which may both ensure the arrival of the cargoes of public corn and may, if need be, combat the ships of an enemy. For, that Italy, a country abounding in timber, should not have a navy of her own hath often striken us with regret" (V. 16).

What was to be done about crime? The king had a short and simple answer. He addressed it to all those responsible for keeping the peace in the provinces.

> The King's orders must be vigorously executed, that terror may be struck into the hearts of the lawless, and that those who have suffered violence may begin to hope for better days. Often the threat of punishment does more to quiet a country than punishment itself. Therefore, under Divine guidance, we have appointed Fridibad to be your Governor.
>
> He will punish cattle-lifters with due severity, will cut off murderers, condemn thieves, and render you, who are now torn by presumptuous iniquity, safe from the daring attempts of villains. Live like a settled people; live like men who have learned the lessons of morality; let neither nationality nor rank be alleged as an excuse from these duties. If any man gives himself up to wicked courses, he must need to undergo chastisement. (IV 49)

Beginning with Cicero, complaints have been heard about getting a private letter delivered. Theodoric's orders were intent on correcting the problems in the government's internal mailing system. He sent them to a certain Gudisal, who was in charge of the couriers (*sajones*).

If the public post-horses (*veredi*) are not allowed proper intervals of rest they will soon be worn out.

We are informed by our *legati* that these horses are constantly employed by persons who have no right to use them.

You are therefore to reside in Rome, and to put yourself in constant communication with the officers of the *Praefectus Praetorio* and the *Magister Officiorum*, so as not to allow any to leave the City using the horses of the *Cursus Publicus* except the regularly commissioned agents of those two functionaries . . . Our Sajones, when sent with a commission, are to go straight to the mark and return, not to make pleasure-tours at the public expense. . . .

Moreover, the extra horses (*parhippi*) are not to be weighted with a load of more than 100 lbs. For we wish our messengers to travel in light marching order, not to make of their journey a regular domestic migration. (IV. 47)

The gladiatorial spectacles ended with the triumph of Christianity, but horse races continued to be intensely exciting. Theodoric approved of these public amusements (I.20), and one letter records a royal pension for a favorite charioteer:

"Constancy in actors is not a very common virtue, therefore with all the more pleasure do we record the faithful allegiance of Thomas the Charioteer, who came long ago from the East hither, and who, having become champion charioteer, has chosen to attach himself to the seat of our Empire; and we therefore decide that he shall be rewarded by a monthly allowance. He embraced what was then the losing side in the chariot races and carried it to victory—victory which he won so often that envious rivals declared that he conquered by means of witchcraft." (III.51)

Another letter speaks of the recurrent violence between fans of the various teams.

If we are moderating under our laws the character of foreign nations, if the Roman law is supreme over all that is in alliance with Italy, how much more doth it become the Senate of the seat of civilization itself to have a surpassing reverence for law, that by the example of their moderation the beauty of their dignities may shine forth more eminently. For where shall we look for moderation, if violence stains Patricians? The Green party complain that they have been truculently assaulted . . . and that one life has been lost in the fray. . . .

As to their counter-complaints of rudeness against the mob, you must distinguish between deliberate insolence and the license of the theatre. Who expects seriousness of character at the spectacles? It is not exactly a congregation of Catos that comes together at the circus. The place excuses

> some excesses. And besides, it is the *beaten* party which vents its rage in insulting cries. Do not let the Patricians complain of clamour that is really the result of a victory for their own side, which they greatly desired. (I.27)

Among the local problems that came to Theodoric's attention were the hot springs of Aponus (near Padua), which had "many marvellous and beneficial properties, for the sake of which the buildings round it ought to be kept in good repair" (II.39). In Ravenna, the aqueducts were to be cleared of vegetation and made fit for providing "water after using which we shall not require to wash ourselves again" (V. 38).

Turning to a matter of broader importance, the king wanted to speed up the wheels of justice. He wrote to an official named Florianus:

> Lawsuits must not be dragged on forever. There must be some possibility of reaching a quiet haven. Wherefore, if the petitioners have rightly informed us that the controversy as to the farm at Mazenes has been decided in due course of law by Count Annas, and there is not reasonable ground for appeal, let that sentence be held final and irreversible. We must sometimes save a litigious man from himself, as a good doctor will not allow a patient to take that which is injurious to him. (I.5)

Theodoric's enlightened attitude toward religious differences was remarkable in an age of growing intolerance. Writing to the Jews living in Genoa, he granted them permission to rebuild their synagogue as long as they did not enlarge it. The letter contains perhaps the most notable sentence in all the *Variae*: "We cannot order a religion, because no one is forced to believe against his will" (II. 27).

In a letter to the Jews of Milan, Theodoric wondered why they would not "find the rest which is eternal." He nevertheless gave them the shield of his protection:

> For the preservation of *civilitas* the benefits of justice are not to be denied even to those who are recognized as wandering from the right way in matters of faith.
>
> You complain that you are often wantonly attacked, and that the rights pertaining to your synagogue are disregarded. We therefore give you the needed protection of our Mildness, and ordain that no ecclesiastic shall trench on the privileges of your synagogue, nor mix himself up in your affairs. But let the two communities keep apart, as their faiths are different: you on your part not attempting to do anything *incivile* against the rights of the said Church.
>
> The law of thirty years' prescription, which is a worldwide custom, shall ensure for your benefit also.
>
> Buy why, oh Jew, dost thou petition for peace and quietness on earth when thou canst not find that rest which is eternal? (V.37)

A major interest of Theodoric was an ambitious building program. He did not see life in his times as inferior: "I wish my age to match preceding ones in the beauty of its buildings as it does in the happiness of the lives of my subjects" (I.6). To help fulfill that prospect he said he wanted "to build a great basilica of Hercules at Ravenna" with special attention to mosaics.

At Rome, Symmachus the Younger, a descendant of the famed statesman whose letters are the subject of Chapter X, and father-in-law of Boethius, was commended in a letter for his work in restoring public buildings and given a new commission for the rebuilding of the theater of Pompey (IV.51). That was in a happier time. Later, when rumors about the disloyalty of the aristocracy in Rome were circulating among the Gothic officials in Ravenna, Symmachus was put to death, not long after the execution of Boethius. But there was never any hint of those sad events in the letters. That would have cast an incriminating shadow. On the contrary, the inclusion of the pleasant, even beguiling, letters written to Boethius and Symmachus before their downfall gave the impression that nothing had happened. The intention of the *Variae* was to create good feeling among all factions and ceratinly not to open any old wounds.

Theodoric's ties to the Emperor Zeno and his successors in Constantinople were at times tenuous. They did not necessarily have the same friends and enemies. The Ostrogoths pursued an active and independent foreign policy. Frontiers were strongly manned and governors closely supervised (III.23). There were even armed clashes with the eastern emperor's forces. But when the time came to talk peace, Theodoric was able to muster a most friendly, if not totally deferential, tone, as evident in this letter to Anastasius in the early years of the sixth century.

> It behoves us, most clement Emperor, to seek for peace, since there are no causes for anger between us.
>
> Peace by which the nations profit; Peace the fair mother of all liberal arts, the softener of manners, the replenisher of the generations of mankind. Peace ought certainly to be an object of desire to every kingdom.
>
> Therefore, most pious of princes, it accords with your power and your glory that we who have already profited by your affection [personally] should seek concord with your Empire. You are the fairest ornament of all realms; you are the healthful defence of the whole world, to which all other rulers rightfully look up with reverence, because they know that there is in you something which is unlike all others: we above all, who by Divine help learned in your Republic the art of governing Romans with equity. Our royalty is an imitation of yours, modelled on your good purpose, a copy of the only Empire; and in so far as we follow you do we excel all other nations.
>
> Often have you exhorted me to love the Senate to accept cordially the laws of past Emperors, to join together in one all the members of Italy.

> How can you separate from your august alliance one whose character you thus try to make conformable to your own? There is moreover that noble sentiment, love for the City of Rome, from which two princes, both of whom govern in her name, should never be disjoined.
>
> We have thought fit therefore to send . . . ambassadors to your most serene Piety, that Peace, which has been broken, through a variety of causes, may, by the removal of all matters of dispute, be firmly restored between us. For we think you will not suffer that any discord should remain between two Republics, which are declared to have ever formed one body under their ancient princes, and which ought not to be joined by a mere sentiment of love, but actively to aid one another with all their powers. Let there be always one will, one purpose in the Roman Kingdom. Therefore, while greeting you with our respectful salutations, we humbly beg that you will not remove from us the high honour of your Mildness's affection, which we have a right to hope for if it were never granted to any others.
>
> The rest of their commission will be verbally conveyed to your Piety by the bearers of these letters. (I.1)

Whatever strengthened Theodoric's hand in Europe bolstered his standing vis-à-vis Constantinople. To this end, he seems to have rivaled Napoleon in arranging marriage ties. A Visigothic king and a Burgundian king were sons-in-law of his. A Frankish king and a Vandal king were his brothers-in-law. A letter to Alaric II, king of the Visigoths, written probably in 506, shows Theodoric working at keeping the peace among his relatives.

> Surrounded as you are by an innumerable multitude of subjects, and strong in the remembrance of their having turned back Attila, still do not fight with Clovis.[6] War is a terrible thing, and a terrible risk. The long peace may have softened the hearts of your people, and your soldiers from want of practice may have lost the habit of working together on the battlefield. Ere yet blood is shed, draw back if possible. We are sending ambassadors to the King of the Franks to try to prevent this war between our relatives; and the ambassadors whom we are sending to you will go on to Gundibad, King of the Burgundians, to get him to interpose on behalf of peace. Your enemy will be mine also! (III.1)

In a letter to three other kings (of the Heruli, Warni or Guardi, and Thuringians), Theodoric warned that trouble in one place meant trouble for all.

> If Clovis succeeds in his uprovoked aggression on Alaric, none of his neighbours will be safe. I will tell you just what I think: he who inclines to act without law is prepared to shake the kingdoms of all of us.

> Remember how often Alaric' father Euric gave you presents and staved off war from your borders. Repay to the son the kindness of the father. I send you two ambassadors, and I want you to join your representations to mine and Gundibad's, calling on Clovis to desist from his attacks on Alaric and seek redress from the law of nations, or else expect the combined attack of all of us, for this quarrel is really the quarrel of us all. (III.3)

Finally, Theodoric wrote to Clovis, king of the Franks, offering to set up machinery for arbitration.

> The affinities of kings ought to keep their subjects from the plague of war. We are grieved to hear of the paltry causes which are giving rise to rumours of war between you and our son Alaric, rumours which gladden the hearts of the enemies of both of you. Let me say with all frankness, but with all affection, just what I think: "It is the act of a passionate man to get his troops ready for action at the first embassy which he sends." Instead of that refer the matter to our arbitration. It would be a delight to me to choose men capable of mediating between you. What would you yourselves think of me if I could hear unmoved of your murderous intentions towards one another? Away with this conflict, in which one of you will probably be utterly destroyed. Throw away the sword which you wield for *my* humiliation. By what right do I thus threaten you? By the right of a father and a friend. He who shall despise this advice of ours will have to reckon us and our friends as his adversaries.
>
> I send two ambassadors to you, as I have to my son Alaric, and hope that they may be able so to arrange matters that no alien malignity may sow the seeds of dissension between you, and that your nations, which under your fathers have long enjoyed the blessings of peace, may not now be laid waste by sudden collision. You ought to believe him who, as you know, has rejoiced in your prosperity. No true friend is he who launches his associates, unwarned, into the headlong dangers of war. (III.4)

There was an underlying and troublesome religious angle to Theodoric's problems. The Franks in Gaul positioned themselves as the champions of orthodox doctrine against the Visigoths, who had been taught the Arian position, a heresy in the eyes of the eastern emperor. Thus, Theodoric, himself an Arian, was on that issue at odds with the emperor, who backed the Frankish cause.

Technically, Theodoric was succeeded in 526 by his grandson Athalaric. But during an eight-year regency, it was the boy's mother, Theodoric's daughter, Amalasuentha, who gave the orders. The change in command did not interrupt the interest in local problems. The leading citizens of Parma were told: "Cleanse out then the mouths of your sewers, lest otherwise, being checked in its flow by the accumulated filth, it should surge back into your houses, and bring into them the pollution which it was meant to wash away" (VIII.29). A certain Genesius was chosen to direct the project. He was told in a separate letter to "set the citizens of Parma diligently to work at this business, that all ancient channels, whether underground or those which run by the sides of the streets, be diligently repaired, in order that when the longed-for stream flows into your town it be not hindered by any obstacle" (VIII.30).

When a petition was received at court from two men who had lost their property and had been forced into slavery, an inquiry was ordered into the matter. Cunigast, *Vir Illustris*, a civilian of the highest rank, was told:

> Our Serenity has been moved by the grievous petition of Constantius and Venerius, who complain that Tanca [probably a Goth] has wrested from them the farm which is called Fabricula, which belonged to them in their own right, together with the stock upon it, and has compelled them, in order to prevent similar forcible demands upon their property in future, to allow the worst lot of all—the condition of slavery—to be imposed upon them, who are really free.
>
> Let your Greatness therefore summon Tanca to your judgment-seat, and, after hearing all parties, pronounce a just judgment and one accordant to your character. For though it is a serious matter to oust a lord from his right, it is contrary to the feelings of our age to press down free necks under the yoke of slavery.
>
> Let Tanca therefore either establish his right to the slaves and their property, or, if they are proved free, let him give them up, whole and unharmed: in which case we will inflict upon him no further penalty. (VIII.28)

Something had to be done about thieves flourishing at a fair in Lucania on St. Cyprian's Day. A letter about this problem, addressed to a local official, Severus, *Vir Spectabilis*, also shows how pagan traditions were being blended into the Christian calendar of events.

> We hear that the rustics are indulging in disorderly practices, and robbing the market-people who come from all quarters to the chief fair of Lucania on the day of St. Cyprian. This must by all means be suppressed, and your Respectability should quietly collect a sufficient number of the owners and tenants of the adjoining farms to overpower these freebooters and bring them to justice. Any rustic or other person found guilty of disturbing the fair should be at once punished with the stick and then exhibited with some mark of infamy upon him.
>
> This fair, which according to the old superstition was named Leucothea [after the nymph], from the extreme purity of the fountain at which it is held, is the greatest fair in all the surrounding country . . . And this is in

> truth a marvellous fountain, full and fresh, and of such transparent clearness that when you look through it you think you are looking through air alone. Choice fishes swim about in the pool, perfectly tame, because if anyone presumes to capture them he soon feels the Divine vengeance. On the morning which precedes the holy night [of St. Cyprian], as soon as the Priest begins to utter the baptismal prayer, the water begins to rise above its accustomed height. Generally it covers but five steps of the well, but the brute element, as if preparing itself for miracles, begins to swell, and at last covers two steps more, never reached at any other time of the year. Truly a stupendous miracle, that streams of water should thus stand still or increase at the sound of the human voice, as if the fountain itself desired to listen to the sermon.
>
> Thus hath Lucania a river Jordan of her own. Wherefore, both for religion's sake and for the profit of the people, it behoves that good order should be kept among the frequenters of the fair, since in the judgment of all, that man must be deemed a villain who would sully the joys of such happy days. (VIII.33)

In high places in the church, the court heard of simony, the use of money to obtain offices, even to buy the papacy. A letter written in 532 to Pope John II reads as follows:

> The Defensor of the Roman Church hath informed us in his tearful petition that lately, when a President was sought for the Papal chair, so much were the usual largesses to the poor augumented by the promises which had been extorted from the candidate, that, shameful to say, even the sacred vessels were exposed to sale in order to provide the necessary money.
>
> Therefore, let your Holiness know that by this present decree, which relates also to all the Patriarchs and Metropolitan Churches [the five Metropolitan Churches in Rome, and such Sees as Milan, Aquileia, Ravenna], we confirm the wise law passed by the Senate in the time of the most holy Pope Boniface [predecessor of John II]. By it any contract or promise made by any person in order to obtain a Bishopric is declared void.
>
> Anyone refusing to refund money so received is to be declared guilty of sacrilege, and restitution is to be enforced by the Judge. . . .
>
> Anyone professing to obtain for money the suffrage of any one of our servants on behalf of a candidate for Papacy or Patriarchate, shall be forced to refund the money. If it cannot be recovered from him, it may be from his heirs. He himself shall be branded with infamy.
>
> Should the giver of the money have been bound by such oaths, that, without imperilling his soul, he cannot disclose the transaction, anyone else may inform, and or establishing the truth of his accusation, receive a third

part of the money so corruptly paid, the rest to go to the churches themselves, for the repair of the fabric or for the daily ministry. Remember the fate of Simon Magus. We have ordered that this decree be made known to the Senate and people by the Prefect of the City. (IX.15)

It was during Athalaric's regency that Cassiodorus reached the highest civil office in the state. He had left the office of *Magister officiorum* about 527. In 533, no doubt at Amalasuentha's prompting, he was named praetorian prefect and so became, in our terms, the prime minister. A letter in Athalaric's name announced to the Senate Cassiodorus's appointment. It was, of course, Cassiodorus who wrote the letter, and he had some nice things to say about himself.

We have loaded Senator with our benefits, Conscript Fathers, because he abounds in virtue, is rich in excellence of character, and is already full of the highest honors. But, in fact, we are his debtors. How shall we repay that eloquent tongue of his, with which he set forth the deeds of the Prince, till he himself who had wrought them wondered at his story? In praising the reign of the wearer of the purple, he made it acceptable to your nation. For taxes may be paid to a tyrant; praise, such as this, is given only to a good Prince.

Not satisfied with extolling living Kings, from whom he might hope for a reward, he drew forth the Kings of the Goths from the dust of ages, showing that the Amal family had been royal for seventeen generations, and proved that the origin of the Gothic people belonged to Roman history, adorning the whole subject with the flowers of his learning gathered from wide fields of literature.

In the early days of our reign what labour he gave to the settling of our affairs! He was alone sufficient for all. The duty of making public harangues, our own private counsels, required him. He laboured that the Empire might rest.

We found him Magister; but he discharged the duties of Quaestor, and willingly bestowed on us, the heir, the experience which he had gained in the counsels of our grandfather.

And not only so, he helped the beginning of our reign both with his arms and his pen. For when the care of our shores occupied our royal meditation, he suddenly emerged from the seclusion of his cabinet, boldly, like his ancestors, assumed the office of General, and triumphed by his character when there was no enemy to overcome. For he maintained the Gothic warriors at his own charges, so that there should be no robbery of the Provincials on the one hand, no too heavy burden on the exchequer on the other. Thus was the soldier what he ought to be, the true defender, not the ravager of his country. Then when the time for victualling the ships

> was over, and the war was laid aside, he shone as an administrator rather than a warrior, healing, without injury to the litigants, the various suits which arose out of the sudden cessation of the contracts.
>
> Such was the glory of the military command of a Metellus in Asia, of a Cato in Spain—a glory far more durable than any that can be derived from the varying shock of war.
>
> Yet with all these merits, how humble he has been, how modest, how benevolent, how slow to wrath, how generous in the distribution of that which is his own, how slow to covet the property of others. All these virtues have been consolidated by his reading of the Divine Book, the fear of God helping him to triumph over baser, human motives. Thus has he been rendered humble towards all, as one imbued with heavenly teaching.
>
> Him therefore, Conscript Fathers, we make, under God's blessing, Praetorian Praefect from the twelfth Indiction [Sept. 1, 533], that he may repress by his own loyalty the trafficking of knaves, and may use his power for the good of the Republic, bequeathing eternal renown to his posterity. (IX. 25)

It is not surprising that "the flowers of his learning" would be mentioned, for Amalasuentha was herself versed in Roman literature and hoped her son would be, too. His untimely death in 534 when he was about sixteen cut short these better days, and there followed the gradual fading of what has been called an Ostrogothic "afterglow" to the grandeur of Rome.

At first, after the death of her son, Amalasuentha ruled alone as queen. Her decision to accept a partnership with a powerful figure named Theodahad was aimed to ward off the warrior Goths who resented her both because she was a woman and because she was stubborn and not easily influenced. Even so, she only held on a few months until, with the consent of Theodahad, she was murdered. In 534, prior to Athalaric's death, Cassiodorus, unfailingly loyal to whomever held power, had praised Amalasuentha's ability. Writing to the Senate in his own name as praetorian prefect, he spoke of her intelligence and eloquence in both the Latin and the Gothic tongues. Her powerful armies, he said, had cowed the Franks, the Burgundians, and even the Byzantines.

> Happy fortune of our time in which, while the Sovereign himself takes holiday, the love of his mother rules and covers us all with the role of her universal charity. Happy for the young Ruler, who in this difficult position learns first to triumph over his impetuous impulses, and attains in the springtime of his life that self-control which hoary age with difficulty acquires.
>
> As for the Mother [Amalasuentha] whom he so dutifully obeys, her most fittingly do all kingdoms venerate, whom to behold is to adore, to listen to is to witness a miracle. Of what language is she not a perfect mis-

tress? She is skilled in the niceties of Attic eloquence; she shines in the majesty of Roman speech; she glories in the wealth of the language of her fathers. She is equally marvellous in all these, and in each the orator in his own especial tongue feels himself surpassed by her. A great safeguard and great excellence is this in the ruler of so many nationalities. None needs an interpreter with his accomplished mistress. No ambassador need wait, or hear his words slowly filtered through the mind of a go-between. Everyone feels that his own words are listened to, and receives his answer from her lips in the language of his forefathers.

To these accomplishments, as a splendid diadem, is added that priceless knowledge of Literature, by which the treasures of ancient learning are appropriated, and the dignity of the throne is ever enhanced.

Yet, while she rejoices in such perfect mastery of language, on public occasions she is so taciturn that she might be supposed to be indolent. With a few words she unties the knots of entangled litigations, she calmly arranges hot disputes, she silently promotes the public welfare. You do not hear her announce beforehand what will be her course of action in public; but with marvellous skill she attains, by feigning, those points which she knows require to be rapidly gained. . . .

But under this Lady, who can count as many Kings as ancestors in her pedigree, our army by Divine help is a terror to foreign nations. Being kept in a prudent equipoise it is neither worn away by continual fighting nor enervated by unbroken peace. In the very beginnings of the reign, when a new ruler's precarious power is apt to be most assailed, contrary to the wish of the Eastern Emperor she made the Danube a Roman stream. Well known is all that the invaders suffered, of which I therefore omit further mention, that the shame of defeat may not be too closely associated with the thought of the Emperor, our ally. Still, what he thought of your part of the Empire is clear from this, that he conceded to our attack that peace which he has refused to the abject entreaties of others. Add this fact, that though we have rarely sought him he has honoured us with so many embassies, and that thus his unique majesty has bowed down the stately head of the Orient to exalt the lords of Italy. . . .

Happy Princess, whose enemies either fall by the hand of God, or else by your bounty are united with your Empire. Rejoice, Goths and Romans alike, and hail this marvel, a being who unites the excellence of both the sexes. As woman she has given birth to your illustrious King, while with manly fortitude of mind she has maintained the bounds of your Empire.

And now, if leaving the realm of war we enter the inner courts of her moral goodness, a hundred tongues will not suffice to sound forth all her praises. Her justice is as great as her goodwill, but even greater is her kindness than her power. You, Senators, know the heavenly goodness which affliction to a higher state than that from which they had fallen, and exalting to honour those who were still uninjured. . . . (XI. 1)

The statement about Amalasuentha that "with manly fortitude of mind she has maintained the bounds of your Empire" was not written a moment too soon. In the following year, 535, a determined eastern emperor, Justinian, sent his general Belisarius to bring Italy back firmly within his domain. His successes accounted in part for Theodahad and his Queen Gudelina lasting for less than two years after Amalasuentha was killed. Cassiodorus then served for a time under Witigis, the last of the Ostrogothic kings for whom he wrote letters; his public career probably ended in 537, the year before he published the *Variae*. The last letters talk of war and famine, of the defense of cities, and of helping areas that were particularly ravaged. Finally, after eighteen years of warfare, under the last king Teias, the Ostrogothic kingdom disappeared. It was at about the same time, 554, that Cassiodorus was launched on his second career.

The remaining decades of Cassiodorus's long and busy life were devoted largely to religious and scholarly pursuits. Even when occupied with affairs of state in his earlier days, he had been very much the man of culture. He wrote: "All that is good in our minds is the fruit of study, and soon withers if it be separated from reading, which is the parent stem" (XI.preface). A long letter praises "paper which keeps the sweet harvest of the mind and restores it to the reader whenever he chooses to consult it" (XI.38). A salary raise granted to grammarians was very likely the inspiration of Cassiodorus (IX.21).

Subsequent ages would remember Cassiodorus not so much for his statesmanship as for important contributions to Christianity in his later years. A monastery, Vivarium, founded on his family estate in southern Italy, became a famous workshop for monks studying and copying texts. They were among the earliest medieval copyists whose industriousness helped to preserve the ancient writings, including letters, known to us today.

NOTES

I. Cicero

1. The letters in this chapter are from Evelyn S. Shuckburgh, trans., *The Letters of Cicero: The Whole Extant Correspondence in Chronological Order*, (London: G. Bell and Sons, 1912), 4 vols. Used with permission of Unwin Hyman Ltd. All citations are noted in the text as either *Ad Att.* (to Atticus), *Ad Fam.* (to friends), or *Q. Fr.* (to his brother Quintus), followed by book and letter number. Thus *Ad Att.* XVI.5 indicates a letter sent to Atticus and commonly numbered as book XVI, letter 5. Because the Shuckburgh edition rearranges the letters and numbers them in a chronological sequence, it supplies an index of cross reference between the two numbering systems.
2. Polybius, *The Histories*, trans. Evelyn Shuckburgh (Bloomington: Indiana University Press, 1962), IX.10.
3. Later, Sallust (Gaius Sallustius, ca. 86 to 35 B.C.) wrote a monograph, *The War with Catiline*, sharply critical of the *nobiles*, the ruling families in Rome. Scholars have debated for years the authenticity of two letters attributed to Sallust. Sir Ronald Syme, in a lengthy chapter in his much-respected two-volume biography, *Sallust* (Berkeley: University of California Press, 1964), emphatically insists that they are wholly spurious.
4. Caesar liked Cicero the way a man of action might regard a man of words, although it must be remembered that this remarkable general was a superb speaker and author himself.
5. Cicero would then have been a member of Caesar's staff and perhaps in charge of a legion.
6. Such a man was called a nomenclator because he whispered the names of those headed their way.
7. Lentulus was an old friend, having been an aedile during Cicero's consulship in 63. During his own consulship in 57, he had been a prime mover in having Cicero brought home from exile.
8. Placentia and Blandeno were in Cisalpine Gaul, northern Italy.
9. When Cicero was out of town, M. Caelius Rufus, one of his longtime friends, sent him letters with the news from home.
10. *Iudices* were judges or arbiters from the upper classes.
11. Phalaris was an infamous tyrant of Acragas in Sicily during the sixth century B.C., known for his cruelty.
12. Aulus Manlius Torquatus was an old, often helpful, friend.
13. His death?
14. Antony was now married to Sextus Clodius's mother, Fulvia.
15. Decimus Junius Brutus disappointed Cicero by failing in an attempt to thwart Antony's plans and losing his life into the bargain.

II. Seneca

1. Tacitus, *The Annals*, trans. Donald R. Dudley (New York: New America Library, 1966), XIII.11. Further citations will be noted in the text.
2. A *consul suffectus* was a short appointment whereby an emperor could honor distinguished citizens. The year, however, was named after the regular consul, who served a longer term.
3. The letters cannot be precisely dated within the period 63 to 65 except for casual remarks found in them here and there.
4. Letters XCV, LXXIV, LVIII, and LXX are from Richard M. Gummere, trans., *Seneca* (Cambridge, Mass.: Harvard University Press, 1970–71), 3 vols. They are reprinted by permission of the publishers and The Loeb Classical Library. All citations are noted in the text by letter number.
5. Letters LVI, VII, V, and XLVII are from Robin Campbell, trans., *Seneca: Letters from a Stoic* (Baltimore: Penguin Classics, 1969). Copyright © Robin Alexander Campbell, 1969, reproduced by permission of Penguin Books, Ltd. All citations are noted in the text by letter number.
6. Generally speaking, the Stoics did not condemn suicide, and many of them thought that under certain circumstances it was the best answer.
7. Given the circumstances, extreme nervousness was understandable.

III. Pliny the Younger

1. The letters in this chapter are from Betty Radice, trans., *The Letters of the Younger Pliny* (Baltimore: Penguin Classics, 1963). Copyright © Betty Radice, 1963, 1969, reproduced by permission of Penguin Books, Ltd. All citations are noted in the text by book and letter number.
2. A tenth book, published after his death, perhaps by Suetonius, contains 121 of the letters exchanged with the Emperor Trajan while Pliny was on a special assignment.
3. The joyous festival of Saturnus, December 17, when, among other things, gifts were exchanged and slaves were temporarily allowed to behave as if they were free.
4. Edward Gibbon, *The Decline and Fall of the Roman Empire* (New York: Random House, Modern Library Edition, 1932), I:70.
5. According to Eusebius, a letter from Hadrian, Trajan's successor, to Fundanus, governor of the province of Asia, also insisted that Christians be charged by lawful means only and not be persecuted by rash accusations.

IV. Lost Letters

1. The letters in this section, except as noted, are from A. S. Hunt and C. C. Edgar, eds., *Select Papyri*, vol. I (Cambridge, Mass.: Harvard University Press, 1952). Reprinted by permission of the publishers and The Loeb Classical Library. All citations are noted in the text by letter number.
2. The village in the Fayum where his mother lives.
3. I.e., his ship.
4. Victor Tcherikover and Alexander Fuks, *Corpus Papyrorum Iudaicarum* (Jerusalem: Magnus Press, 1960), II: 233–35.
5. Yigael Yadin, *Bar-Kokhba: The Rediscovery of the Legendary Hero of the Second Jewish Revolt against Rome* (New York: Random House, 1971), p. 124.
6. Yigael Yadin, "Expedition to the Judaean Desert," *Israel Exploration Journal* (1961), p. 48. This letter and the two following were translated by Matthew Schwartz.
7. B. Benoit, J. T. Milik, and R. deVaux, *Les Grottes de Murabbaat* (Oxford: Clarendon Press, 1961), p. 162.

8. Alan K. Bowman, *The Roman Writing Tablets from Vindolanda* (London: British Museum Publications, 1983), p. 133.

V. Fronto

1. This letter and the others in this chapter are from C. R. Haines, trans., *The Correspondence of Marcus Cornelius Fronto* (Cambridge, Mass.: Harvard University Press, 1919), 2 vols. Reprinted by permission of the publishers and The Loeb Classical Library. All citations are noted in the text by volume and page.
2. As noted earlier, Seneca had been honored this way in 56.
3. Robinson Ellis, *The Correspondence of Fronto and M. Aurelius* (Oxford: Oxford University Press, 1904), pp. 10–11.

VI. Cyprian

1. Peter Hinchliff, *Cyprian of Carthage and the Unity of the Christian Church* (London: Geoffrey Chapman Publishers, 1974). Further citations will be noted in the text.
2. The confessors were persons known to have heroically defended their faith, or as Hinchliff has it, unlike those who lapsed, they survived because of their courage (p. 52).
3. Letter 14 and the other letters in this chapter, unless otherwise noted, are reprinted from G. W. Clarke, trans., *The Letters of St. Cyprian of Carthage* (Ramsey, N.J.: Newman Press, 1984–86), 4 vols. From the Ancient Christian Writers series. © 1984, 1986, used by permission of Paulist/Newman Press, Mahwah, N.J. All citations are noted in the text by letter number.
4. Clarke, *The Letters of St. Cyprian of Carthage*, I:264.
5. At the time, other bishops besides Cyprian were addressed as *Papatem*, Pope. G. W. Clarke, in *The Letters of St. Cyprian of Carthage*, writes that the first verified use of the term at Rome was for Bishop Marcellinus, 296–304, and did not become exclusive to the bishop of Rome until the eleventh century (p. 207, note 3).
6. Interestingly enough, Novatian, who took such an unbending view on the lapsed, had been a Stoic. The founder of that self-disciplining school of philosophy, Zeno, was also a Phoenician.
7. Letter 76 and the following letter 81 are reprinted from Alexander Roberts and James Donaldson, eds., *The Ante-Nicene Fathers: Translations of the Writings of the Fathers down to A.D. 325*, vol. V (Grand Rapids, Mich.: Wm. B. Eerdmans Co., 1886; reprint, 1951), with the permission of the publisher. All citations are noted in the text by letter number.
8. Naphtali Lewis and Meyer Reinhold, *Roman Civilization* (New York: Columbia University Press, 1955; New York: Harper and Brothers, Torchbooks, 1966), II:466.
9. Forty-four letters of Constantine are preserved, mostly in Eusebius's writings. Although generally described as letters, they are in fact almost all in the nature of public documents dealing with the complex rivalries within the church during Constantine's reign.

VII. Julian

1. There seems to be nothing certain known about Evagrius aside from his having been a rhetorician.
2. Letter 25 and the other letters in this chapter are from W. C. Wright, trans., *The Works of the Emperor Julian*, vol. III (Cambridge, Mass.: Harvard University Press, 1923). Reprinted by permission of the publishers and The Loeb Classical Library. All citations are noted in the text by letter number.

3. Ammianus Marcellinus, *The Surviving Books of the History of Ammianus Marcellinus*, trans. John C. Rolfe (Cambridge, Mass.: Harvard University Press, The Loeb Classical Library, 1963–64), XXV.4.22. This *History*, extant for the years 353 to 378, offers the best available description of the period.
4. Seventy-three are considered to be genuine. There are doubts about other letters which do not sound like Julian and may, in fact, have been forged by enemies.
5. G. W. Bowersock, *Julian the Apostate* (Cambridge, Mass.: Harvard University Press, 1978), p. 4. Further citations will be noted in the text.
6. Robert Browning, *The Emperor Julian* (Berkeley: University of California Press, 1976), p. 58.
7. Thus does Julian call attention to the way in which Constantius was unforgiving towards followers of the Nicene Creed.

VIII. Gregory of Nyssa, Basil, Gregory of Nazianzus

1. Letter XVI and the other letters of Gregory of Nyssa are reprinted from Philip Schaff and Henry Wace, eds., *A Select Library of Nicene and Post-Nicene Fathers of the Christian Church*, vol. V. (Grand Rapids, Mich.: Wm. B. Eerdmans Publishing Co., 1893; reprint, 1954), with the permission of the publisher. All citations are noted in the text by letter number.
2. In Galatia, central Asia Minor.
3. Letter CLXIX and the other letters of Basil are reprinted from Philip Schaff and Henry Wace, eds., *A Select Library of Nicene and Post-Nicene Fathers of the Christian Church*, vol. VIII (Grand Rapids, Mich.: Wm. B. Eerdmans Publishing Co., 1895; reprint, 1954), with the permission of the publisher. All citations are noted in the text by letter number.
4. I.e., to monastic seclusion.
5. Rosemary Radford Ruether, *Gregory of Nazianzus, Rhetor and Philosopher* (Oxford: Oxford University Press, 1969), pp. 32–33. Further citations will be noted in the text.
6. Letter XLVIII and the other letters of Gregory of Nazianzus are reprinted from Philip Schaff and Henry Wace, eds., *A Select Library of Nicene and Post-Nicene Fathers of the Christian Church*, vol. VII (Grand Rapids, Mich.: Wm. B. Eerdmans Publishing Co., 1894; reprint, 1954), with the permission of the publisher. All citations are noted in the text by letter number.

IX. Ausonius and Paulinus

1. Raymond Van Dam, *Leadership and Community in Late Antique Gaul* (Berkeley: University of California Press, 1985), p. 303. Further citations will be noted in the text.
2. Letter XXII and the other letters of Ausonius in this section are from Hugh G. Evelyn White, trans., *Ausonius*, vol. II (Cambridge, Mass.: Harvard University Press, 1921). Reprinted by permission of the publishers and The Loeb Classical Library. All citations are noted in the text by letter number.
3. Not likely the same to whom that earlier letter was written, but rather an offspring of Ausonius's son, Hesperius.
4. Today, sixteen hundred years later, the descendants of immigrants from Nola who settled in Brooklyn, New York, hold a joyful festival every summer in honor of Paulinus.
5. There are extant thirteen letters from Paulinus to Sulpicius Severus (ca. A.D. 360 to ca. 420), another wealthy man who became a monk. Severus is also remembered for his biography of St. Martin of Tours and a *Chronicle* putting events to his own time in a Christian context.
6. Letter 31 and the other letters of Paulinus in this section are from P. G. Walsh, trans., *Letters of St. Paulinus of Nola* (New York: Longmans, Green and Co., 1966), 2 vols. Reprinted with the permission of Random House, Inc. All citations are noted in the text by letter number.

7. Walsh does not include the poems that made up the correspondence between Paulinus and Ausonius among his *Letters*, but in the Loeb edition of *Ausonius*, this poem is included as Epistle XXXI.
8. Malcolm Muggeridge, *Things Past* (New York: William Morrow and Co., 1979), pp. 104–5.

X. Symmachus or Ambrose

1. T. R. Glover, *Life and Letters in the Fourth Century* (1901; reprint, New York: G. E. Stechert and Co., 1924), p. 156.
2. Letter 3 and the other letters of Symmachus in this section are from R. H. Barrow, *Prefect and Emperor: The Relationes of Symmachus, A.D. 384* (Oxford: Oxford University Press, 1973). All citations will be noted in the text by letter number.
3. F. Homes Dudden, *The Life and Times of St. Ambrose* (Oxford: Oxford University Press, 1935), I:39. Further citations will be noted in the text.
4. Barrow, *Prefect and Emperor*, p. 11.
5. Letter 3 and the other letters of Ambrose in this section are reprinted from Sister Mary M. Beyenka, trans., *Saint Ambrose: Letters*, vol. 26 in the Fathers of the Church series (New York: Fathers of the Church, 1954), with the permission of The Catholic University of America Press, Washington D.C. All citations are noted in the text by letter number.
6. As Dudden points out (I:306–7), Ambrose's claim that the skeletons had blood on them has been countered by the suggestion that they were actually prehistoric remains which, according to a widespread custom, had been painted with red ochre.

XI. Jerome

1. A younger sister of Blaesilla.
2. Letter XXXIX and the other letters of Jerome are reprinted from Philip Schaff and Henry Wace, eds., *A Select Library of Nicene and Post-Nicene Fathers of the Christian Church*, vol. VI (Grand Rapids, Mich.: Wm. B. Eerdmans Publishing Co., 1892; reprint, 1954), with the permission of the publisher. All citations are noted in the text by letter number.
3. J. N. D. Kelly, *Jerome: His Life, Writings and Controversies* (New York: Harper & Row, 1975), pp. 100–101. Further citations will be noted in the text.
4. Letters LXXII and the following LXXIII of Augustine are reprinted from Philip Schaff and Henry Wace, eds., *A Select Library of Nicene and Post-Nicene Fathers of the Christian Church*, vol. I (Grand Rapids, Mich.: Wm. B. Eerdmans Publishing Co., 1886; reprint, 1956), with the permission of the publisher.
5. The *Bible* gives only vague references to this subject. Rev. 2.6 reads: "But this thou hast, that thou hatest the deeds of the Nicolaitanes, which I also hate." (cf. Rev. 2.15)
6. Women put to death for adultery.

XII. Augustine

1. Letter XCIII and the other letters of Augustine are reprinted from Philip Schaff and Henry Wace, eds., *A Select Library of the Nicene and Post-Nicene Fathers of the Christian Church*, vol. I (Grand Rapids, Mich.: Wm. B. Eerdmans Publishing Co., 1886; reprint, 1956) with the permission of the publisher. All citations will be noted in the text by letter number.
2. Actually a close friend.
3. There is no salutation.

4. Circumcelliones comes possibly from *cella*, house, or perhaps refers to the tombs of the martyrs whom these people revered. It could come from both sources.
5. Ammianus Marcellinus, *The Surviving Books of the History of Ammianus Marcellinus*, trans. John C. Rolfe (Cambridge, Mass.: Harvard University Press, The Loeb Classical Library, 1963–64), XXII.5.4.
6. Bishop of the Donatists in Hippo.
7. Augustine was now over seventy-five.

XIII. Synesius of Cyrene

1. Before the Romans came, Cyrenaica, the land bordering the Mediterranean Sea immediately to the west of Egypt, was ruled by the Ptolemies, who called it Pentapolis because it included five cities: Cyrene, Arsinoe, Berenice, Ptolemais, and Apollonia. It was willed to the Romans by Ptolemy Apion in 96 and became a province in 74.
2. Letter 54 and the other letters in this chapter are from Augustine FitzGerald, trans., *The Letters of Synesius of Cyrene* (Oxford: Oxford University Press, 1926). All citations will be noted in the text by letter number.
3. The dates of the letters have given rise to much debate, for they are based largely on inferences from the letters themselves.
4. In his introduction to the letters. FitzGerald writes: "[Synesius] returned to Cyrene at about the commencement of the year 404, only to find his native land attacked on every side by the barbarian tribes from the deserts of Libya, whose one purpose was pillage and whose favourite method of war was to overrun the country districts and keep the cities in a chronic state of siege. To add to the difficulties of the situation, a new governor of the province had just arrived in the person of Cerialis, a man without honesty, and with an unbridled passion for lucre . . . [resulting in] a veritable orgy of political corruption. Any one could get exemption from military service if he paid for it, and cities and municipalities were mulcted of revenues for payment of the troops necessary to their protection. In this way disorderly soldiery kept the unfortunate citizens in continual terror of blackmail and they were almost equally terrified of the savage tribes without and of their own protectors within" (p.40).
5. Jay Bregman, *Synesius of Cyrene, Philosopher-Bishop* (Berkeley: University of California Press, 1982), p. 25. Further citations will be noted in the text.
6. For a change, an outstanding Roman commander.
7. Obviously, the tendency to exaggerate in such matters is not uncommon.
8. Anastasius, a close friend of Synesius, was a tutor of the children of the Emperor Arcadius, and so no doubt had some potentially useful influence.
9. FitzGerald concludes: ". . . finally the uneasy soul is lost to us in the mists of an unrecorded death" (p. 69).
10. Cyril's letters, recently published in Lionel R. Wickham, ed. and trans., *Cyril of Alexandria: Select Letters* (Oxford: Oxford University Press, 1983), are of particular importance in the evolution of Christian theology, providing "a cross-section of Cyril's theological work" (p. xi). As for Hypatia, Wickham says that because her murder came early in Cyril's contested bishopric he was unable to prevent it. He concludes that Cyril was not "a fanatical priest, hungry for power, heading a howling mob, but . . . an untried leader attempting, and initially failing, to master popular forces" (p. xvi).

XIV. Sidonius Apollinaris

1. There has been much discussion in the literature about the dates of most of the letters.
2. The Visigoths were Arian Christians and so at odds with the orthodoxy of the Roman church.
3. Couch coverings.
4. This letter and the others in this chapter are reprinted from O. M. Dalton, trans., *The Letters of Sidonius* (Oxford: Oxford University Press, 1915), 2 vols., by permission of Oxford University Press. All citations are noted in the text by book and letter number.
5. Special prayers of supplication.
6. Jon. 3.10: "And God saw their works that they turned from their evil way; and God repented of the evil, that he had said that he would do unto them; and he did it not."
7. Saint Ambrose, whose letters are discussed in Chapter X.
8. For those interested in the argumentation among historians about this treaty, *Sidonius Apollinaris and His Age* by Courtenay E. Stevens (1933; reprint, Westport, Conn.: Greenwood, 1979) is a good place to start.
9. Under the circumstances, such sarcasm had to be excused.
10. A fortress between Carcassonne and Narbonne.
11. Leo, a desendant of the orator Fronto (Chapter V), is a ghostwriter for Euric even as Cassiodorus (Chapter XVI) will be for the Ostrogothic king, Theodoric.
12. Thus does Sidonius concede that the Visigoths respected and enforced Roman laws.

XV. Leo I

1. Henry Hart Milman, *History of Latin Christianity* (New York: A. C. Armstrong and Son, 1883), I:255.
2. Nicolas Cheetham, *Keepers of the Keys* (New York: Charles Scribner's Sons, 1983), p. 26.
3. *See* is from the Latin *sedes* meaning seat and refers to the location of a particular power such as that of a bishop.
4. Here are the seeds of the conflict between the Roman and French churches which surfaced from time to time in the Middle Ages and resulted in the papacy being moved to Avignon in France for much of the fourteenth century.
5. Letter 10 and the other letters in this chapter, unless otherwise noted, are reprinted from Brother Edmund Hunt, trans., *St. Leo the Great: Letters*, vol. 34 in the Fathers of the Church series (New York: Fathers of the Church, 1957), with the permission of The Catholic University of America Press, Washington, D.C. All citations are noted in the text by letter number.
6. Testy relations between the Roman popes and the patriarchs of Constantinople were in the background leading to the Great Schism of 1054 and the ongoing separation of eastern and western Christianity.
7. The Monophysite doctrine held that the human and the divine in Christ constituted only one nature. Leo said that there were two natures united in one person. Another opinion was that of the Nestorians, who believed the two natures to be entirely separate. A prominent anti-Monophysite leader was Theodoret (ca. A.D. 393 to 466), a bishop of Cyrrhus in Syria after 423, whose numerous extant letters are a further source of information about the religious events of his time.
8. Hunt mentions letter 7, but does not include it in his edition of "the principal letters." The translation is reprinted from Philip Schaff and Henry Wace, eds., *A Select Library of Nicene and Post-Nicene Fathers of the Christian Church*, vol. XII (Grand Rapids, Mich.: Wm. B. Eerdmans Publishing Co., 1895; reprint, 1956), with the permission of the publisher.
9. Basil, Juvenal, Euxitheus, Peter, and Luke.
10. So designated because there were minor differences in the copies of this letter, and the one sent to Basil was slightly longer than the others.

XVI. Cassiodorus

1. Thomas Burns, *A History of the Ostrogoths* (Bloomington: Indiana University Press, 1984), p. 79.
2. The letters in this chapter are from Thomas Hodgkin, *The Letters of Cassiodorus* (London: Henry Frowde, 1886). All citations are noted in the text by book and letter number.
3. Moses Hadas, *A History of Latin Literature* (New York: Columbia University Press, 1952), p. 405.
4. Senator was actually part of his name, not a title.
5. James J. O'Donnell, *Cassiodorus* (Berkeley: University of California Press, 1979).
6. Theodoric's good advice went unheeded, and in 507, in a battle near Poitiers, Alaric II was defeated and killed by Clovis.

BIBLIOGRAPHY

Biography

Bailey, D. R. Shackleton. *Cicero*. New York: Charles Scribner's Sons, 1972.

Birley, Anthony. *Marcus Aurelius*. New Haven: Yale University Press, 1987.

Bowersock, G. W. *Julian the Apostate*. Cambridge, Mass.: Harvard University Press, 1978.

Bregman, Jay. *Synesius of Cyrene, Philosopher-Bishop*. Berkeley: University of California Press, 1982.

Brown, Peter. *Augustine of Hippo*. Berkeley: University of California Press, 1967.

Browning, Robert. *The Emperor Julian*. Berkeley: University of California Press, 1976.

Crawford, W. S. *Synesius of Cyrene*. London: Rivingtons, 1901.

Dudden, F. Homes. *The Life and Times of St. Ambrose*. 2 vols. Oxford: Oxford University Press, 1935.

Goggin, T. *The Life and Times of St. Gregory of Nyssa as Reflected in the Letters and the Contra Eunomium*. Washington, D.C.: The Catholic University of American Press, 1947.

Griffin, Miriam D. *Seneca: A Philosopher in Politics*. Oxford: Oxford University Press, 1976.

Hinchliff, Peter. *Cyprian of Carthage and the Unity of the Christian Church*. London: Geoffrey Chapman Publishers, 1974.

Jalland, Trevor. *St. Leo the Great*. New York: Macmillan, 1941.

Kelly, J. N. D. *Jerome: His Life, Writings and Controversies*. New York: Harper & Row, 1975.

O'Donnell, James J. *Cassiodorus*. Berkeley: University of California Press, 1979.

Pando, J. C. *The Life and Times of Synesius of Cyrene as Revealed in His Works*. Washington, D.C.: The Catholic University of America, Patristic Series, LXIII, 1940.

Ruether, Rosemary Radford. *Gregory of Nazianzus, Rhetor and Philosopher*. Oxford: Oxford University Press, 1969.

Stevens, Courtenay E. *Sidonius Apollinaris and His Age*. 1933. Reprint, Westport, Conn.: Greenwood, 1979).

Yadin, Yigael. *Bar-Kokhba: The Rediscovery of the Legendary Hero of the Second Jewish Revolt against Rome. New York: Random House, 1971.*

General Studies

Ammianus Marcellinus. *The Surviving Books of the History of Ammianus Marcellinus*. Trans. John C. Rolfe. 3 vols. Cambridge, Mass.: Harvard University Press, The Loeb Classical Library, 1963–64.

Binns, J. W., ed. *Latin Literature of the Fourth Century*. London: Routledge Kegan Paul, 1974.

Chadwick, Nora. *Poetry and Letters in Early Christian Gaul*. London: Bowes and Bowes, 1955.

Dill, Samuel. *Roman Society in the Last Century of the Western Empire*. 1898. Reprint, New York: The World Publishing Co., Meridian Books, 1958.

Gibbon, Edward. *The Decline and Fall of the Roman Empire*. 2 vols. New York: Random House, Modern Library Edition, 1932.

Glover, T. R. *Life and Letters in the Fourth Century*. 1901. Reprint, New York: G. E. Stechert and Co., 1924.

Hadas, Moses. *A History of Latin Literature*. New York: Columbia University Press, 1952.

Jones, A. H. M. *The Later Roman Empire, A.D. 284–602*. 3 vols. Oxford: Blackwell, 1964. Abridged edition, *The Decline of the Ancient World*. New York: Holt, Rinehart and Winston, 1966.

Jones, Tom B. *In the Twilight of Antiquity*. Minneapolis: University of Minnesota Press, 1980.

Kelly, J. N. D. *The Oxford Dictionary of Popes*. Oxford: Oxford University Press, 1986.

Kramer, Samuel Noah. *History Begins at Sumer*. Garden City, N.Y.: Doubleday & Co., 1959.

Laistner, Max L., and H. H. King. *Thought and Letters in Western Europe, A.D. 500–900*. 2nd ed. Ithaca: Cornell University Press, 1966.

Lewis, Naphtali, and Meyer Reinhold. *Roman Civilization*. 2 vols. New York: Columbia University Press, 1955. New York: Harper and Brothers, Torchbooks, 1966.

Polybius. *The Histories*. Trans. Evelyn S. Shuckburgh. 2 vols. Bloomington: Indiana University Press, 1962.

Quasten, Johannes. *Patrology*. 3 vols. Westminster, Md.: Newman Press, 1950.

Tacitus. *The Annals*. Trans. Donald R. Dudley. New York: New American Library, 1966.

Paganism and Christianity

Brooke, Dorothy. *Private Letters, Pagan and Christian: An Anthology of Greek and Roman Private Letters from the Fifth Century before Christ to the Fifth Century of Our Era*. London: Ernest Benn, 1929.

Brown, Peter. *The Body and Society: Men, Women and Sexual Renunciation in Early Christianity*. New York: Columbia University Press, 1987.

Dodds, E. R. *Pagan and Christian in an Age of Anxiety: Some Aspects of Religious Experience from Marcus Aurelius to Constantine*. Cambridge: Cambridge University Press, 1965.

Fox, Robin Lane. *Pagans and Christians*. New York: Knopf, 1987.

MacMullen, Ramsay. *Christianizing the Roman Empire* (A.D. 100–400). New Haven: Yale University Press, 1984.

———. *Paganism in the Roman Empire*. New Haven: Yale University Press, 1981.

Markus, R. A. *Christianity in the Roman World*. London: Thames and Hudson, 1974.

Milman, Henry Hart. *History of Latin Christianity*. 8 vols. New York: A. C. Armstrong and Son, 1883.

Momigliano, Arnaldo, ed. *The Conflict between Paganism and Christianity in the Fourth Century*. Oxford: Oxford University Press, 1963.

Nock, A. D. *Conversion: The Old and the New in Religion from Alexander the Great to Augustine of Hippo*. Oxford: Oxford University Press, 1933.

Wilken, Robert L. *The Christians as the Romans Saw Them*. New Haven: Yale University Press, 1984.

Special Topics

Avi-Yonah, Michael. *The Jews under Roman and Byzantine Rule: A Political History of Palestine from the Bar-Kokhba War to the Arab Conquest*. New York: Schocken, 1984.

Bell, Rudolph M. *Holy Anorexia*. Chicago: University of Chicago Press, 1985.

Birley, Robin. *On Hadrian's Wall: Vindolanda: Roman Fort and Settlement*. London: Thames and Hudson, 1977.

Brock, Dorothy. *Studies in Fronto and His Age*. Cambridge: Cambridge University Press, 1911.

Burns, Thomas. *A History of the Ostrogoths*. Bloomington: Indiana University Press, 1984.

Cheetham, Nicholas. *Keeper of the Keys: A History of the Popes from St. Peter to John Paul II*. New York: Charles Scribner's Sons, 1983.

Cowell, F. R. *Cicero and the Roman Republic*. New York: Penguin Books, 1948.

Ellis, Robinson. *The Correspondence of Fronto and M. Aurelius*. Oxford: Oxford University Press, 1904.

Evans, G. R. *Augustine on Evil*. Cambridge Cambridge University Press, 1983.

Frend, W. H. *The Donatist Church: A Movement of Protest in Roman North Africa*. Oxford: Oxford University Press, 1985.

Lewis, Naphtali. *Papyrus in Classical Antiquity*. Oxford: Oxford University Press, 1974.

Lienhard, Joseph. *Paulinus of Nola and Early Christian Monasticism*. Cologne: Peter Hanstein Verlag, 1971.

Muggeridge, Malcolm. *Things Past*. New York: William Morrow and Co., 1979.

Van Dam, Raymond. *Leadership and Community in Late Antique Gaul*. Berkeley: University of California Press, 1985.

Warmington, Brian H. *The North African Provinces from Diocletian to the Vandal Conquest*. 1954. Reprint, Westport, Conn.: Greenwood, 1971.

White, K. D. *Country Life in Classical Times*. Ithaca: Cornell University Press, 1977.

Wiesen, David S. *St. Jerome as a Satirist: A Study in Christian Latin Thought and Letters*. Ithaca: Cornell University Press, 1964.

The Letters

Barrow, R. H. *Prefect and Emperor: The Relationes of Symmachus, A.D. 384*. Oxford: Oxford University Press, 1973.

Bell, H. I. *The Abinnaeus Archive*. Oxford: Oxford University Press, 1962.

Benoit, P., J. T. Milik, and R. deVaux. *Les Grottes de Murabbaat*. Oxford: Clarendon Press, 1961.

Beyenka, Sister Mary M., trans. *Saint Ambrose: Letters*. New York: Fathers of the Church, 1954.

Bowman, Alan K. *The Roman Writing Tablets from Vindolanda*. London: British Museum Publications, 1983.

Campbell, Robin, trans. *Seneca: Letters from a Stoic*. Baltimore: Penguin Classics, 1969.

Clarke, G. W., trans. *The Letters of St. Cyprian of Carthage*. 4 vols. Ancient Christian Writers Series, ed. Johannes Quasten, Walter J. Burghhardt, and Thomas Comerford Lawler. Ramsey, N.J.: The Newman Press, 1984–86.

Dalton, O. M., trans. *The Letters of Sidonius*. 2 vols. Oxford: Oxford University Press, 1915.

FitzGerald, Augustine, trans. *The Letters of Synesius of Cyrene*. Oxford: Oxford University Press, 1926.

Gummere, Richard M., trans. *Seneca*. 3 vols. Cambridge, Mass.: Harvard University Press, The Loeb Classical Library, 1970–71.

Haines, C. R., trans. *The Correspondence of Marcus Cornelius Fronto*. 2 vols. Cambridge, Mass.: Harvard University Press, The Loeb Classical Library, 1919–20.

Hodgkin, Thomas. *The Letters of Cassiodorus*. London: Henry Frowde, 1886.

Hunt, A. S., and C. C. Edgar, eds. *Select Papyri*. Vol I (of 5 vols.). Cambridge, Mass.: Harvard University Press, The Loeb Classical Library, 1952.

Hunt, Brother Edmund, trans. *St. Leo the Great: Letters*. New York: Fathers of the Church, 1957.

Radice, Betty, trans. *The Letters of the Younger Pliny*. Baltimore: Penguin Classics, 1963.

Roberts, Alexander, and James Donaldson, eds. *The Ante-Nicene Fathers: Translations of the Writings of the Fathers down to A.D. 325*. Vol. V, Cyprian. Grand Rapids, Mich.: Wm. B. Eerdmans Publishing Co., 1886. Reprint, 1951.

Schaff, Philip, and Henry Wace, eds. *A Select Library of Nicene and Post-Nicene Fathers of the Christian Church*. Vol. I, *Augustine*; vol. V, *Gregory of Nyssa*; vol. VI, *Jerome*; vol. VII, *Gregory of Nazianzus*; vol. VIII *Basil*; vol. XII, *Leo the Great*. Grand Rapids, Mich.: Wm. B. Eerdmans Publishing Co., 1893–95. Reprints, 1954–60.

Shuckburgh, Evelyn S., trans. *The Letters of Cicero: The Whole Extant Correspondence in Chronological Order*. 4 vols. London: G. Bell and Sons, 1912.

Tcherikover, Victor, and Alexander Fuks. *Corpus Papyrorum Iudaicarum*. 2 vols. Jerusalem: Magnus Press, 1960.

Walsh, P. G., trans. *Letters of St. Paulinus of Nola*. 2 vols. Westminster, Md.: Newman Press, 1966–67.

White, Hugh G. Evelyn, trans. *Ausonius*. 2 vols. Cambridge, Mass.: Harvard University Press, The Loeb Classical Library, 1919–21.

Wickham, Lionel R., ed. and trans. *Cyril of Alexandria: Select Letters*. Oxford: Oxford University Press, 1983.

Wright, W. C., trans. *The Works of the Emperor Julian*. 3 vols. Cambridge, Mass.: Harvard University Press, The Loeb Classical Library, 1923.

INDEX